By the same author

ELOHIM—Masters & Minions (Winston Trilogy Book II)
WINSTON'S KINGDOM (Winston Trilogy Book III)
ALEC (Alexander Trilogy, Book I)
ALEXANDER (Alexander Trilogy, Book II)
SACHA—The Way Back (Alexander Trilogy, Book III)
YESHUA—Personal Memoir of the Missing Years of Jesus
PETER AND PAUL (An intuitive sequel to Yeshûa)
THE AVATAR SYNDROME (Prequel to Headless World)
HEADLESS WORLD—The Vatican Incident (Sequel to Avatar Syndrome)
MARVIN CLARK—In Search of Freedom
THE GATE—Things My Mother Told Me
NOW—Being and Becoming
THE PRINCESS
GIFT OF GAMMAN
ENIGMA of the Second Coming
WALL—Love, Sex, and Immortality (Aquarius Trilogy Book I)
PLUTO EFECT (Aquarius Trilogy Book II)
OLYMPUS—Of Gods and Men (Aquarius Trilogy Book III)

Short stories

THE JEWEL & OTHER STORIES
CATS AND DOGS
Sci-Fi Series 1
Sci-Fi Series 2

Non-fiction eBooks by Stanislaw Kapuscinski

VISUALIZATION—Creating Your Own Universe
KEY TO IMMORTALITY
[Commentary on the Gospel of Thomas]
BEYOND RELIGION: Volumes I, II and III
[Collections of essays on perception of Reality]
DICTIONARY OF BIBLICAL SYMBOLISM
DELUSIONS—Pragmatic Realism

Poetry in Polish
[with illustrations by Bozena Happach]
KILKA SŁÓW I TROCHĘ GLINY
WIĘCEJ SŁÓW I WIĘCEJ GLINY

INHOUSEPRESS, MONTREAL, CANADA
http://inhousepress.ca

One Just Man

PREQUEL TO

ΣℒΟℋℐℳ
Masters and Minions

A Novel by

Stan I.S. Law

INHOUSEPRESS, MONTREAL, CANADA

Published in Canada in 2008 by
INHOUSEPRESS
http://www.inhousepress.ca

Design and layout
Bozena Happach

Cover design after a sculpture by
Bozena Happach

This book is a work of fiction.
Names, characters, titles, places and incidents are
either the products of the author's imagination or are used fictitiously.

Library and Archives Canada Cataloguing in Publication

Law, Stan I. S.
One Just Man: prequel to Elohim:: Masters and Minions:
a novel / by Stan I.S. Law – 2nd ed.

ISBN 978-0-9780267-6-9

I. Title.

PS8623.A92053 2008   C813'.6   C2008-905065-7

Printed and bound in the USA

The unexamined life
is not worth living for man

Socrates
as reported by Plato
[Apology, 38a]

Contents

Autumn
1   The Interview   11
2   The Ball   27
3   Second Interview   41
4   A Fellow   55
5   Worse than a Cure   67
6   End of an Era   81

Winter
7   The Search   97
8   Good-bye   110
9   Nomad   124
10   A Working Man   136
11   A Flashback   148
12   Winston Smith   160

Spring
13   Escape   173
14   Cathy   187
15   A Day in Town   201
16    $E = mc^2$ 215
17   As below so above   227
18   Lazarus   242

Summer
19   The Present   259
20   The Prophet   272
21   The Mountain   285
22   The Note   300
23   Gdansk   314
24   Rome   329

Acknowledgments

Autumn

*. . .for he maketh his sun to rise on
the evil and on the good,
and sendeth rain on the just and
on the unjust.*

Matthew 5:45

1

The Interview

The time is six o'clock in the morning. It is quite normal for Dr. Peter Thornton to arrive at the Montreal General Hospital well before the appointed time. Today is no exception. Dr. Thornton does not expect a mere five hours of sleep to have an adverse effect on his performance. *Performance.* That's how he thinks of the Rounds. The dreary morning tour of the Wards with the usual contingent of residents and interns. An ignorant lot.

"Good morning, Dr. Thornton." The tone is coquettish. Halfway between a greeting and a giggle. Dr. Thornton turns his head.

A regular set of white teeth smiles at him. The grin seems incongruously awake below the still sleepy eyelids. A spotless white tunic accentuates the girl's hourglass figure while a crisp white cap is fighting a losing battle in an attempt to regiment the nurse's abundant blond hair. Dr. Thornton tries not to show that he finds the greeting a mite annoying. People shouldn't smile this early in the morning. Not even student nurses. Then he remembers the pixie face. Actually, not so much her face as the soft, resilient body in a darkened linen closet. Last week? Possibly.

Dr. Thornton manages a thin smile. Could it have been last Tuesday? There are so many nurses... Thank God they are all certified STD free. As he is, of course.

"Morning, Nurse."

Dr. Thornton quickens his pace. He missed the nurse's name on her lapel nameplate. Dinah or Donna or something. Peter Thornton enjoys a photographic memory for facts. Scientific facts. They do not include his sex life. Anyway, there are just too many nurses. He smiles again. This time at his own thoughts.

He enters a tiny office. As a final-year resident in Internal Medicine, Dr. Thornton rates his own private office. He takes off his trench coat and flips on the computer terminal on his desk. He scans the moving data at a rate that would leave most people gaping. Each single glance covers the whole screen littered with meticulously tabulated information. At five to seven, a white coat dangling over his shirt sleeves, a perfunctory stethoscope swinging from his neck, Dr. Thornton steps out again into the lacklustre corridor.

It is a good five-minute walk to Ward A-12. Today he must cover three wards in two hours. Hopefully not too many patients will require his personal assistance. Actually, the patients seldom do. It is the inferior, the inept, the inexperienced residents and interns who tax his time and patience. At no time had he been as ignorant as they all seem to be. Never. Not even during his own internship. Dr. Thornton walks quickly, his mind mulling over the patients' medical histories he had just scanned in his office.

There once was a time when, crossing these same passageways, Peter Thornton could sense, almost see, the sauntering shadows of those unfortunates who had come here looking for help. Their empty carcasses were already dispatched to Pathology in the basement, but their unrequited demands, hopes, emotions still persisted, wandering the corridors, unsated. There was a time when Peter could almost hear the disembodied echoes of their pleas, see their silent screams frozen in the horrified eyes gradually submitting to the inevitable. Why had those people been so afraid of dying? Had they had a foreknowledge of some unspoken horror lying ahead, or were they merely ignorant immortals still unaware of their ultimate destiny? There was a time... once...

Now the corridors are empty.

Peter's feet is absorbed by the polymeric carpet. He is the only shadow in the shadowless labyrinth. The nurses rested in at their stations. This was no-man's space at no-man's time.

When Dr. Thornton reaches Ward A-12, the interns and residents are already waiting. There is a murmur of recognition accompanied by a nodding of heads: Peter, George, Brenda, Joan, Fred... whatever. He nods back, reciting his colleagues' names in return. Then he stops dead in his tracks.

"Dr. Brent?" Peter nods his head a little lower.

As Chief of Medicine, Dr. John B. Brent is the senior member of the teaching staff. He rarely attends the Rounds. Dr. Brent is available as a consultant for difficult, unorthodox cases only. Peter clears his throat to hide an amused smirk as he shakes Dr. Brent's bony hand. This is a Godsend. Peter Thornton never bothers to show off his knowledge in front of the interns and junior residents. This is different. He might score points for his career.

For the next two hours they greet, smile over, prod, push and pull, examine, discuss, pamper, disturb, annoy, soothe and prescribe for some three dozen patients. Three minutes per patient. By nine the Rounds are over. The patients are fed, again drained of fluids and faeces. They have already been washed, scrubbed clean since dawn, in readiness for the Rounds. After all, hospitals are not built for patients to be sick in, only for doctors to cure them.

"A spot of lunch, Peter?" Dr. Brent asks, in an offhanded manner.

"I would be honoured, Sir." Peter smiles, then adds, "I must check with the office first, though..."

"Of course. I'll see you in my office around noon."

Peter bites his tongue, but it's too late. He realizes he has overdone the zeal. One does not treat the Chief of Medicine's invitations conditionally, nor does one imply one's own indispensability. Peter swears under his breath. Lately he'd been making mistakes. He hates his own slips even more than those of his subordinates.

At twelve sharp, Dr. Thornton knocks on the Chief's door. A middle-aged secretary waves him on. He knocks again and enters Dr. Brent's office. He stops at the door, looking down at a mop of

At twelve sharp, Dr. Thornton knocks on the Chief's door.
A middle-aged secretary waves him on. He knocks again and
enters Dr. Brent's office. He stops at the door, looking down at a
mop of gray hair bent over a desk cluttered with stacks of paper.
Whatever happened to computers, Peter wonders? The old man
doesn't move.

"Sit down, Peter."

The Chief doesn't raise his head. The office is ten times
bigger than Peter's. One wall is lined with Dr. Brent's private
library, the other with case histories. Against the third wall is a
settee wide enough for a nap. Peter chooses one of the two
moulded chairs opposite the large desk. Dr. Brent pushes a
button on his intercom.

"Mary? The usual. For two." He releases the button and
continues working. A minute or two later Dr. Brent looks up and
seems to notice Peter for the first time.

"Glad you could make it. Wanted a word with you."

Dr. Brent's voice sounds cordial enough, but Peter detects a
certain hesitation in the Chief's voice. Is the man ill at ease?
Why? Why am I here? Peter is more interested than worried that
he may have perpetrated some medical misdemeanour. He
decides to wait.

Mary comes in with two plates of raw vegetables, two large
glasses of vegetable juice and a basket of rehydrated bread. She
places them on the few empty spots she can find on the desk and
smiles at the old physician.

"Would you like anything else, Sir?" Her warm smile
reflects genuine affection for the doctor. Peter finds himself
wondering what makes an attractive, blithe woman show
fondness for a man known as a driving workhorse. Dr. Brent
looks at his guest.

"Dr. Thornton?"

"That will be just fine, Sir."

Peter grins at his passing thoughts: 'When I was wishing to
be a rabbit, I was referring to its sex life, not to its dietary
preference.' Chief of Medicine and Mary take Peter's grin as
grateful acquiescence.

For a few minutes they eat in silence. The vegetables are crisp and obviously fresh. Rather a step up from the subsidized cafeteria on the fifth floor. Halfway through his plate of salad, Dr. Brent leans back and lights a cigarette. Peter had heard about the Chief's smoking habit, but had never actually seen it. Dr. Brent never indulged his weakness in public.

"This morning I asked you for three diagnoses and three proposed treatments," said Dr. Brent, speaking through a cloud of smoke. Peter waits, though suddenly he feels a little uneasy. "All three of your diagnoses were correct."

Dr. Brent again draws on his cigarette, then stubs it out and returns to his salad. Peter is becoming nervous. He chews his *assiette de crudités* slowly as though having difficulty with swallowing. What the devil is the old warlock driving at?

At last his plate is empty. They finish almost simultaneously and both lean back.

"Cigarette?" Dr. Brent extends his old-fashioned cigarette case.

"I don't..."

"Of course!"

The old man again leans back in his high-backed armchair. He joins his palms together, his gaunt, long fingertips touching in silent prayer while pointing his long-stemmed cigarette at Peter like an Amazonian blowpipe. A thin line of smoke rises from its tip in a perfectly straight line, then wavers as though uncertain of its future. A little later, the host's bushy white eyebrows draw together as though arriving at a decision. As Peter stirs expectantly, Dr. Brent, incongruously, blows a perfect smoke ring. Peter wills the Chief to come to the point. He can't imagine what the devil he is doing here other than exposing himself to the noxious fumes of a filthy habit. Peter hates being nervous.

"The proposed treatments were also correct." Dr. Brent continues as if he had never stopped talking. John lets out an inaudible sigh. "What I cannot understand is, why did you recommend the biopsies in Mr. Clayton's case?"

"Ah, Mr. Clayton...?"

For a briefest instant Dr. Brent's eyes turn hard. Then he puffs another smoke ring. Peter knew of his mistake before the smoke left the Chief's lips.

"Yes, Peter, Mr. Clayton's. The third case we examined this morning."

The Chief looks at Peter over his half-moon spectacles. His tone is kind, his gaze once more fatherly. Peter thinks he must have imagined the hardness in the old man's eyes.

"Yes, of course, Sir."

"There were three other treatments you could have recommended... Could you comment on that? Rather more, shall we say, standard treatments?"

"Yes, Sir. I believe that any other preventive measure would have only delayed the operation. The symptoms were characteristic of the three cases which you had treated..." (Peter knows that he just made his third mistake) "...which I had treated this morning exactly as per your diagnoses of three, four and six years ago. Quite rare cases. Very rare indeed."

Dr. Brent seems preoccupied with a speck on a blank sheet of paper. Then, almost absentmindedly, he reaches for another cigarette. "Why have you been looking up my past medical histories?" The Chief looks the young man straight in the eye.

Peter swallows hard. He cannot, he should not try to fool the Chief. It would never work. No bloody way.

"I have made a study of the most unusual cases of all the teaching staff in this hospital," Peter answers bluntly, returning the Chief's steady gaze. He then crosses his legs. He does his best not to show his irritation.

"Why? Why specifically at the General?"

"It is the best hospital." Peter's voice carries all the confidence he can muster.

Dr. Brent lowers his penetrating eyes to his watch. He draws the last puff and puts out his cigarette.

"I'm afraid I must go. Thank you for having lunch with me."

Dr. Brent rises to his feet and puts on his jacket. They leave the office together. Peter looks small next to Dr. Brent's six-foot frame. The old man is pushing seventy and seems to have twice

Peter's energy. And twice his memory. At least of his patients' names.

Peter goes back to his office. He cannot understand the reason for the Chief's interrogation. It wasn't a lunch, it was more like a lynching. But why? Why was it necessary for the Chief of Medicine to know why Peter had made the *right* diagnoses?

At 18:00 Peter is free.

He always walks to and from the General, though he prefers early morning or late night for negotiating *Côte des Neiges'* intersection with Pine Avenue during the rush hour. The heavy traffic with its attendant pollution does little to improve his spirits. During the day Peter was much too busy, but now his thoughts return to the interview with Dr. Brent. It left him unhinged. Being unsettled is a luxury Peter cannot afford. Not with the Royal College of Physicians Fellowship exams coming up later next month.

This would be the second time in his life when, in a way, he would be making a final commitment. The first had been a failure. A fruit of inexperience. Of the irresponsibility of youth. The first time he had run away. He cannot afford another failure. Not now. This could be the reason why lately his thoughts drift to distant images, perhaps better left alone. Yet he remembers them so well. As though it all had happened yesterday.

Peter shrugs. *I was no more than an adolescent...*

Perhaps. Perhaps all boys dream, at one time or another, of becoming a priest. They do if they have been brought up by good, practising Catholics. The old, traditional variety. The type who do not question authority.

Peter questioned authority, but it wasn't even that.

He had gone through a period in his young life, apparently inherent in most boys' lives, when they think they are ready to give up all, give up life itself, for a cause. A passing phase. But not for Peter. He had gone a stage further. He had entered a seminary. The Seminary of St. Francis of Assisi. He had spent years strengthening his faith, his resolve. Anything less than perfection, than obeisant sainthood, was not good enough. As with most things he did, Peter had tried too hard. Or his expectations had been too great. He'd never know. Not now.

Peter had been too honest to aspire to sanctity, to that exalted state which his role models had achieved throughout history. Why? He had questions. Questions which one does not ask in a seminary. He did not mind the rough cloth, the binding girdle or the sandals, but his head could not be contained within the brown, drooping cowl. It limited his vision. His inner vision.

Or maybe he just lacked the necessary humility.

On the day before Ordination he had left the heavy metal gates of his temporal prison. His confessor had given him absolution. The old priest had understood him, or else had been very wise. Or a fool?

"Come back to us when you are ready."

"Yes, Father. I will."

Peter has had no opportunity to keep his promise, as yet. He doubts he ever will.

There followed a long period of guilt. Peter could not even pass by a church, let alone enter one, without feeling guilty. He tried to sublimate his self-condemnation by giving large sums of money, as large as he possibly could, to the Saint Francis Seminary. For years there had been no money left for anything extra. Anything over and above the bare necessities of life. Then, one day, the guilt was gone. He was a second-year student of medicine by then. His inherent hunger for immortality had taken a strange turn. Rather than peruse the intangible, Peter Thornton applied his powerful faith to the physical body.

Later, much later, came the nurses. By today's standards, Peter was a throwback. At the age of 24, Peter was still a virgin. A male virgin. By choice. A nurse his own age, but with ten years' experience, took advantage of his innocence. Or had it been just plain ignorance? Since that day nurses had become Dr. Thornton's hobby—the various linen closets at the General his private if transient seraglios. Peter did his level best to make up for his early shortcomings.

Today, however, was not a day for frivolity.

This afternoon one intern and two nurses suffered the consequences of his mounting tension. He had practically bitten their heads off. Peter Thornton hates anyone witnessing his weaknesses. Not that he indulges himself in many. His driving ambition leaves little room for complacency. He sees himself as a man on the cutting edge of modern medicine. Being brilliant carries its own responsibilities. *Noblesse oblige.* He intends to break new professional ground. He is going to prove that the human body, when properly maintained, can last forever. Virtually for ever. It's only logical.

But the damage was done.

Still, a few well-placed words and they'll forget. They always do. He could spin the junior staff around his little finger. A smile widens Peter's narrow mouth. They call it charisma. He can turn it on and off when necessary. Ask any nurse. Any pretty nurse.

On occasion, Peter loved to give an impression of a phlegmatic country squire. Reserved, polite, elegant, detached. Affable when necessary. An *arbiter elegantiarum.* He is none of these. No time right now. First, the exams. And his five-foot-six stature does not carry an air of commanding detachment. He is too short, his hair neither dark nor truly blond; his eyes, once a fine blue, now seem faded, blurred from incessant reading, staring at the screen of his computer. Peter runs his palm over his inch-long crew cut. At least his hairstyle gives him an extra inch.

The bloody exams.

Finally Peter leaves the winding *Chemin de la Côte-des-Neiges* and enters the serenity of Upper Westmount. After his brother Andrew died, Ruth, his sister-in-law, had asked him to stay at her opulent residence. She had asked him right then, at the funeral. She seemed awfully broken up. People did not take kindly to the death of their loved ones. They didn't give a hoot about others dropping off like flies.

"The children need a role-model. Someone to balance my..."

"Surely you don't think of me as a father image!?" He remembers having spoken too loudly next to the open grave. Ruth's request had come as a shock.

"Peter, please help me."

There had been enough pain in Ruth's voice to convert him into any image she liked.

Ruth had really broken down. Even his shoulder seemed inadequate. Physically. Ruth was taller than he was. He had promised he would come and stay with her as long as she needed him. He had surprised himself. It had not been in his nature to make concessions for human weaknesses. Not even his own. But what could he have done? Ruth and Andrew had adopted the two kids some years ago. The kids had lost a father for the second time. Now there was Smith, of course. But, Peter had reasoned, it was not the same. Blood is stronger than water. Or is it?

Peter inhales deeply. Even the air is different in Upper Westmount.

What a magnificent difference! Whenever Peter walks through the upper reaches, he thanks his lucky star for being among the chosen. The superb, mature elms join their crowns into a continuous gothic arch. The living cloister fosters a sense of peace. A sense of protection from the foibles of this uncertain world. The manicured lawns, the meticulously maintained front gardens create an air of well-being, of being apart, above and beyond the masses swarming on the other side of the tracks. Upper Westmount always had ruled, and continues to rule, Montreal, Quebec and a good part of Canada. And that only twelve years after Quebec had rejoined the fold. The New Canada. Sixteen provinces with two more State applications still pending.

Dr. Thornton loves Westmount. The bastion of the mighty.

As he reaches for his key, Winston opens the door. He nearly always does. The man is psychic. And, at three in the morning, scary.

"Good evening, Sir. May I take your coat?"

Winston Smith speaks in as deep and smooth a voice as Peter has ever heard. The butler could probably sing Boris Goudonov at the Met. He could also fly a kite. Literally. He often does, with the kids. He is also the best *major-domo* and general *factotum* Ruth could ever hope to find.

"Hi, Smith."

Peter drops his coat on Smith's extended arm and continues to his upstairs room without losing stride.

"Thanks..." He throws over his shoulder, waving his arm in an offhanded greeting.

Peter is the only member of the family who addresses Smith as Smith. He insists that this is the proper form of address to a servant of Smith's stature. Particularly towards a stature exported from England. Of course, the English don't have butlers anymore. Can't afford them. Not since the Solidarity. All the same, Winston Smith is an enigma.

Two days after Andrew's funeral (heart attacks are on the increase in Westmount), Winston Smith had appeared at the door of the Thornton residence. As Ruth opened the door, the tall, gaunt man handed her a sealed envelope. It had been hand-addressed to Mrs. Ruth Thornton. The writing was familiar. Then Ruth recognized the writing and broke down. Some weeks after the event, Ruth confessed to Peter that she had actually fainted. Later, she said, she had found herself lying on the settee, two pillows under her head, a glass of water at her elbow and Andrew's unread letter on her lap. Winston Smith was standing at the door quite motionless.

"I came to," Ruth continued her confession, "and before I even noticed Winston at the door, I again saw the envelope. It was definitely Andrew's writing. I have no idea why I had fainted. It must have been the shock of seeing a communication from beyond the grave. That's how it looked at the time. Or maybe it was the strain of the funeral, the poor children... Oh, I don't know. Perhaps I am just a weak woman."

Ruth always had a well-modulated, mezzo-contralto voice.

"Anyway, I tore open the envelope and read the letter. A note really. Andrew said simply that should anything ever happen to him, unexpectedly, I should consider making use of Winston Smith's service. 'You can trust him, darling,' the note said. I broke down again, but I didn't faint anymore..."

At the time Peter wondered if Andrew had suffered from a premonition.

"I asked Winston how he met Andrew. He gave me a roundabout answer that he had occasion to be of service to him during a mission in China when Andrew was building a number of dams across the Ch'and Chiang, or the Yangtze river. I recall Andrew had had a serious mishap there of some nature and apparently Winston had helped him out. That was about all he would say. Winston, not Andrew, of course."

For some strange reason, as Peter passes the living room, he visualizes the scene of Ruth lying in a fainting spell on the settee. He shrugs and continues up to his room. He needs all the time he can spare for his studies. Thank heaven the kids are out at the Centre. Normally he would have to dodge them or be caught in a tumble for at least fifteen minutes. The little brats have absolutely no idea of the importance of time.

"Dinner will be at seven, Sir."

Peter ignores the ponderous announcement as he closes the door to his room.

Smith isn't a bad chap. A bit stiff, speaks in a stilted accent, is about three feet too tall, but he certainly has a way with the children. This last trait invariably left Peter baffled. Neither Jonathan nor Moira ever minded doing anything the black-draped beanstalk told them. There were never any long-winded arguments, as there would be with him or their mother, at bedtime. Never a pouting look or an attempt at an emotional blackmail the kids seem otherwise so good at:

"You never play with us anymore...

"Just five more minutes, pleeease...

"I'll do it first thing tomorrow...

"Oh, pleeease, mommy, I already read that book for hooours (meaning ten minutes) today, I'll read for two hours tomorrow... if you let me stay a little longer..."

Whenever Winston appeared on the scene, Jo and Mo would get up, kiss their mother, sometimes his own cheek and, if so instructed, leave in a fray of joyful obedience. Smith accomplished this feat without ever raising his voice, let alone a punitive hand. In fact, the children seemed to like him. A lot.

Peter glances at his watch. With dinner at seven it's hardly worthwhile to do any cramming. Nevertheless, he clicks on the computer and sprawls on his padded armchair with his feet on the side table. His right hand toys inconsequentially with the mouse, opening a dozen windows on the computer screen, then closing them again. His mind drifts to the midday interview.

What the devil was the old goat after?

Whatever it was, it couldn't have had anything whatever to do with matters they discussed. Of that Peter was certain. He may have been weighed for a possible future addition to the permanent staff. But there are better ways of doing that. And anyway, with the workload Dr. Brent has, he would have waited till after the Fellowship exams. After all, less than 35% of the residents taking them manage to pass at the first sitting. The knowledge required is just too great. And now, with the computer simulations, those desirous of keeping down the numbers of the Illustrious Fellowship are free to make up pathological syndromes virtually *ad infinitum*. Often, there are no right or wrong answers.

Peter's twisted smile reflects his onerous thoughts. It occurs to him that medicine, in an attempt to stimulate life, succeeds only in deferring death. Marginally.

It just ain't good enough!

Peter closes his eyes. He recalls quite vividly the first years of his Medical School at McGill. Then he had felt that the scope, the range of knowledge was so overwhelming that no sane man could or should possibly aspire to it all. This feeling had never left him. It grew. Sometimes, in moments of great stress, perhaps of excessive fatigue, he tried to imagine that the information, the knowingness, was already within him; that it could manifest itself even without his conscious participation. I am a healer, he repeated often. The life force of nature works through me. Regardless of my subjective limitations.

What limitations?

After a rare good night's sleep, Peter did not recognise limitations. Not for himself. He was however becoming more and more aware of the limitations of medicine. His reading extended well beyond the standard curriculum stipulated by his chosen profession. Peter felt compelled, urged on in his studies, almost as if he were running out of time. Yet, the more knowledge he absorbed, the more he became aware of the underlying chaos which seemed to saturate the universe around him. Peter was becoming convinced that the laws of thermodynamics were bent on restoring a state of primordial chaos. From this all-pervading random, disorderly turmoil of matter and energy, life, the Force of Life, wrenches a small degree of harmony. At times It fights a losing battle. Occasionally, only occasionally, science provided some answers as to how, where or even when this bedlam of confusion came under a semblance of order.

It never explained *why* ?

Peter discovered that life is not a natural arrangement of atoms and molecules, but that it strives to sustain an unstable, indeed, an unnatural condition. Nature seemed to defy itself as it formed random alliances from chance encounters between the countless particles of the universe. Life not only created but maintained a precarious balance between a temporary suspension of chaos and the ever demanding, debilitating, waiting in the aisles—death. Over the years, Peter had become convinced that to be a physician one could not take man out of the context of nature. Man was the first product of the Life Force that asked *why*. For that alone the phenomenon of man should be cherished in its totality. Yet the medicine practised at the General Hospital was oriented towards the symptomatic, the resultant, not the causative stimuli.

"And the General is the best!" Peter says out loud, a perverse sneer on his lips.

Yesterday he left the General at midnight. The stars were out, amused, mocking, winking at his ineptness, his primitive ineptitude. Five hours later he was up and ready to repeat the crazy cycle. The morning Rounds, two hours with the illustrious Chief of Medicine, an illustrious watchdog bent on trying to catch him on some symptomatic technicality. For crying out loud... They are all bloody ignorant!

"And so am I..." The sneer relaxes into a sardonic grin.

In all he had ever read, in all the books, tapes, disks, memory banks he had scanned, in all the information he had once treated with respect fed by his insatiable hunger for knowledge, in all the lectures he had attended, in all the countless laboratory tests, in the medical journals flaunting the purportedly greatest brains of the medical profession, in all that, Peter Thornton had never, never found *any* scientific reason why people had to live or... die.

Peter switches off the computer and leans his head against the back of the tall padded armchair. He stares into the ceiling, trying to empty his mind of despondency. He fails. Dejection, almost agony, contorts his normally relaxed features. There had been moments in his young life when he wanted to throw in the towel, when he thought he could give it all up and join Ruth at the United Nations in some capacity which carried prestige, with the attendant financial rewards. The Thorntons have all the right contacts, and this means a bright future in politics. Why not? Does he not share a sufficiently low opinion of humanity?

Peter is vaguely aware of a knock on the door. He ignores it. Probably some nurse or a moronic intern. The second knocking is louder.

"Yes, Smith, I'm coming," Peter calls out without moving.

He glances at his watch. It is 7:05.

"Uncle Peter?" A squeaky voice precedes a pair of wide-open eyes peeping through a crack in the door.

"Hi, Jonathan. Come in."

Jonathan's neck seems to stretch, allowing the blond, curly head to peek farther into his uncle's room. The place is out of bounds. This fact alone makes it fascinating. There is no tension or fear as little Jo's eyes wander over the room. No hunger. Just curiosity.

Is that what it is? Curiosity? Is that all that motivates me?

Peter takes Jonathan's hand and they go down together. When they reach the bottom of the stairs, Moira runs up and jumps astride just above Peter's knees. Her eyes are filled with the wonder of youth.

"Gochya, Uncle Pether!" Last week Moira had left her two front teeth under her pillow for the tooth fairy.

Perhaps that's enough. Perhaps the search is all that matters... Somehow the answer doesn't satisfy him. The hunger remains.

Peter catches Mo and carries her to her chair at the table. Jonathan sits down opposite his sister. There is just a touch of jealousy in Jo's eyes. Of course, at seven he is too old to jump on Uncle Peter's lap. Except when they are alone.

"There are moments, Sir, when hunger seems difficult to satisfy?"

The sonorous voice comes from the direction of the butler. Winston Smith is standing behind Peter's chair, ready to push it in once Peter sits down. The table is set for three. With Ruth in New York on UN business, Peter takes the head of the table. He's hungry.

"You might well have a point there, Smith. All the same, we shall try."

A delicate aroma of home-made soup reaches Peter's nose from the tureen waiting on the dining-room sideboard. As Peter sits down, a quizzical smile parts his lips almost against his will. He stares into his plate, unable to look up.

Suddenly he is quite certain that Winston Smith was not talking about dinner.

* * *

2

The Ball

After six hours of continuous study, the tiny lines of concentration release their tight hold at the edges of Peter's eyes. Peter blinks, rubs his eyes with the back of his hand, takes a deep breath and clicks off the screen. His joints are stiff from long immobility. Some moments later he walks over to the dormer window overlooking the front lawn and the street. There he sits down again, sideways, on the deep sill and peers outside. His tired smile turns into a lopsided grin of masochistic satisfaction.

It is that time of year.

The weather looks as bleak as he feels. From the first day of the fortnight he had taken off from the hospital, the dull, listless drizzle enveloped Montreal with ubiquitous persistence. There was nothing outside to tempt him, nothing to dissuade him from his resolve to recap all the data he believed pertinent to the Fellowship exams. A mammoth task. For eighteen hours a day, with devotion bordering on fanaticism, Peter stared at the luminous screen. Occasionally his arm moved his fingers, dialling some numbers on the modem. New texts would appear, new voluminous compilations that might not help him in his professional career but were apt to assist him in impressing his mentors.

Peter is glad the fortnight is over.

He feels near the end of his physical and mental resilience. He had awoken this morning with a headache. He had been dreaming. He had dreamt that he was attending the usual morning Rounds and couldn't remember any of the patients' names. Dr. Brent, wearing a long white robe with oversized sleeves, was persistently whispering into his ear that he, Peter, was much too clever, that he should try to be original in his approach. The Chief suggested he should try a little black magic. Peter, who in his dream was much taller than Dr. Brent, told his superior to go fly a kite. Dr. Brent immediately spread his arms wide, flapped them a few times and flew off towards the quickly receding ceiling. At the very last moment Peter tugged on the string, but Dr. Brent was not attached to it any more. Peter felt guilty about allowing Dr. Brent to get away.

Now the headache is gone; the memory of a kite-like Dr. Brent, flying, remains.

Peter shrugs. He had never paid much attention to any of his dreams. He isn't even certain that the Chief will be one of his examiners. Either way it didn't matter a damn. Not now, anyway.

Peter continues to stare through the streaky window.

In spite of the rain, the view is beautiful. Melancholy, but beautiful. The pavement is almost hidden under a glistening carpet of red and gold. The rich embroidery slopes gently to the south, thick in places, elsewhere opening up to allow tiny rivulets to find their way between clumps pushed to one side by a gust of wind or a passing car. Here and there tiny rills disappear under larger heaps only to emerge on the lower side, ever descending, down and down, towards Sherbrooke, then lower, ever lower, through St-Henri, to the broad river of the St. Lawrence. Then lower still until this falling haze, these tears after the departed summer, this persistent drizzle would be swallowed, drop by drop, with equal persistency, by the ocean from whence it had once risen towards the sky.

The cycle of life.

"Divinity is like water, it always finds its lowest level..." Peter murmurs now, looking at the ever-changing pattern of lines on the wet windowpane.

He had read this sentence somewhere. Sometime. When he was still attending church on Sundays. Before, like Beethoven, he had shaken his fist at the thunder. Now it is his job to decide on the fate of those living and dying. He no longer has time to wait for the capricious gods to make their trite decisions for him. Some of his patients would live. Some would die. Up to heaven or down to hell. Thank God there is no metaphysical platitude for lateral orientation.

Peter feels tired. Very tired. Mentally and physically. He even feels drained emotionally. The sheer volume of knowledge is dwarfing. Smothering. Oppressive. Perhaps 'I am taking all this too seriously?' he ponders. Perhaps medicine, power over life, should not be left to the lesser gods. Perhaps we should all accept the dictates of Mother Nature. Eat or be eaten. Succulent morsels of human flesh. There would be no shortage of food in the world. Selection of the fittest. The tastiest.

"I must get some sleep!"

Peter looks at his watch. It is nearly four. He must take a nap to survive tonight's ball. The annual Ball of the Montreal General Hospital. At the Ritz-Xentung. A posh affair. All the capital bores will attend. Capital takes great interest in medicine these days. People seem very preoccupied with remaining healthy. Or at least alive. At any cost. Transplants galore. Get your spare parts at the General! Tuesdays and Fridays two kidneys for the price of one. The rich can afford them. Those with influence and connections. Anyway, he had promised Ruth he would escort her. Just this once. Frankly, he could do with some good contacts after having acted like a hermit since his first year at McGill.

Hope to God she'll not be too argumentative, he grimaces.

The last time Ruth was in town, they had argued all during dinner about the merits of orthodox religions. Peter never realized how strongly Ruth felt about the Pope's infallibility. Strange. She is such a practical woman.

Peter stretches on the bed and closes his eyes. He pictures Ruth with red cheeks, excited, spoiling for a good fight.

"Only in matters of faith, of course," she confides.

"And pray tell me, sister, just what are those matters of faith?"

"All things dealing with your soul. And heaven," she adds.

"Then after you define my soul, you might care to give me a quick tour of your heaven?"

That was a week ago. Ruth had neither looked nor sounded amused. Since she lost Andrew, she seemed to be searching for something to lean upon. Some dogma, some broad shoulder she could take with her when she went to her office. More so when she went out of town.

Peter wonders if his sister-in-law would ever remarry. At 42 she is young enough. Slim but not skinny––certainly a 'handsome woman'. In high heels, a little taller than Peter. Her liquid brown eyes can look demure and intelligent at the same time. And she certainly keeps her copious dark hair pinned up in the latest fashion. Even in the morning she manages to look as though she had only just left the best hairdresser. Peter smiles at his thoughts. His only means of comparison are the nurses, and two women staff doctors. Not much competition there, he muses.

As the chief representative of the Canadian Confederation at the United Nations, Ruth has brains, too.

"You must have faith, Peter!" she commanded.

"Fine, but in what!?"

Peter recalls he was becoming exasperated himself. He seemed to live in a permanent state of exhaustion.

"But in what?" He had repeated, having received no answer.

"In that which is beyond our understanding!" Ruth had lowered her voice slightly.

"And just what good would that do for my patients?" He recalls having asked.

"Who are we to know...?" There had been a plea in her voice.

Peter feels like a heel. Ruth had needed help and he had managed to upset her. To weaken what tiny straws she still grasped at. Being a single mother of two can't be a picnic. Thank God for Andrew's insurance. At least she would never have to face financial problems. Not that she couldn't take care of herself. Her own income vastly exceeds Peter's. For the present. Soon, very soon, this will change... The day after the exams he'll start looking around. At last. At long last!

Peter slept for three hours. Like a log. Like a new-born babe.

Like a resident before a Fellowship examination.

"Peter?"

Sleep. Perchance to dream...

"Peter!?"

No peace for the guilty. "Yes, Ruth?"

"I'll be ready in one hour."

A threat? A warning? A reminder.

"The dinner is set for nine. We shouldn't be late."

The dinner at the Ritz-Xentung. To hell with Xentung. Let them get their own Ritz. Then Peter smiles. They did. He shrugs.

"I'll be ready!"

One hour later, showered, his crewcut at a perfunctory right angle to his scalp, sporting the latest black-tie garb (he refuses to wear tails), Peter finds Ruth already downstairs. She looks stunning. Peter thinks of his brother. You must have been crazy, old man. If I'd been you, I would have taken her with me.

"Is something wrong?" Ruth asks as Peter continues to stare at his sister-in-law.

"Only that I may be accused of having bumped off my brother just to take you to the Ritz!" His voice is quite serious.

"Peter, that's not in the best of taste."

"Well, you're worth it. And no, it isn't. A sherry?" He counters.

Only then does he notice that Ruth already has one.

"Sorry. Where are the kids?"

"Jo is playing with Winston, and Mo went next door to a pajama party."

There is a short silence.

"Peter?"

"Yes, Ruth?"

"Thank you. Maybe I needed reassurance." Her smile is radiant. "It's been quite a while, hasn't it?"

"You are working too hard," Peter says.

He means it. Ruth seems to be filling the vacuum Andrew left with work. She had asked him to escort her to the Ritz because she is the official representative of the UN. The World Health Organization, the WHO, had asked her to say a few words on their behalf. Asking for money, of course. Everyone wants money.

From the moment the doorman opens the taxi door, they step into a different world. Not a world to which Peter is accustomed. He offers his arm to Ruth as they cross the vestibule into the plush atrium.

The Ritz remembers far better days. The canopy over the main entrance is shaped like an over-decorated, gilt-edged, jewel-encrusted pagoda. The new, three-story atrium is more reminiscent of a building flanking Red Square than the quiet elegance of the old Ritz-Carlton. The Chinese ownership is unmistakable. It proclaims its control with vulgar ostentation. No one seems to object. After all, it was Hong Kong money that cut unemployment in Montreal from sixteen to six percent. Since the Queen of the Orient reverted to China, the expatriates owned Montreal. After buying out the controlling interest in the most prestigious locations in the Western provinces, there was still money left over. Montreal was an obvious choice on the East Coast. The Japanese already owned New York.

Peter finds the glitter of the interior distracting. Almost annoying. He has neither time nor inclination for frivolity. He is a little sorry he agreed to escort Ruth. Then he looks at his sister-in-law and smiles.

"Is this the modern version of Babylon?"

"Quiet," she admonishes him in a half whisper. "Smile to the people. That's what we are here for."

A uniformed man appears at their elbow to escort them to the head table. As they cross the ballroom threshold, a resplendent general in full livery announces them in a stentorian voice. To Peter, the man looks like a lugubrious town crier or an unemployed president of a banana republic.

"Doctor and Mrs. Thornton!"

Peter wonders if anyone is listening.

"Do you think they think that we are hitched up?" Peter asks innocently.

"Shut up, Peter!"

Ruth smiles left and right with the grace of a princess. Peter begins to understand why at the UN they insist that Ruth be their spokeswoman at every social gathering they can think of.

Three men rise as Ruth approaches. All three are dressed in tails with wide silk sashes across their underdeveloped chests and overdeveloped paunches. The sashes display a number of stars, medals and other pieces of glittering metal.

The tallest of the three performs the introductions at the head table. Peter and Ruth shake hands with the nearest diners, nod and bow to those further away. People stare at Ruth. Peter never realized how beautiful she really is. Familiarity breads contempt, he muses. Or at least lack of appreciation.

Finally the pleasantries are over and they sit down. Peter is three chairs away from Ruth. A gray-haired woman on his right has already announced that she is hard-of-hearing in her left ear. This leaves Peter with a petite woman on his left.

Brunette, well put together. A severe dress, *à la chinoise,* flowing down from a diamond-studded collar at the neck, clinging to every curve, every nuance of her body. Judging by her facial bones, the girl is only half-Chinese. The other half could be Spanish or some other Latin extraction. Or Irish after the Spanish Armada. Peter ignores her until she raises her long eyelashes. Two superb, polished jades filled with intelligence. No face with such eyes could be ugly. The intelligence is almost overpowering.

Peter leans over to check again her name on the placement tag. Dr. Catherine Mondellay. Surely, not another MD. Enough is enough. Yet the eyes are too intelligent to ignore. They radiate magnetic power.

"Dr. Mondellay?" Peter raises his glass. "We seem to have a common interest."

"Cathy."

"I beg your pardon?

"My name is Cathy. We can't spend these next hours sitting next to each other throwing titles around."

So much for breaking the ice.

"Peter. Dr. Peter Thornton. Delighted."

"I know. I read your name tag. Are you?"

Peter has slept for a few hours but this is a little too fast for him. He retreats into a defensive posture, sips the dry champagne, and plays for time.

"And I am not a Doctor. I am a Ph.D. They always get that wrong," Catherine Mondellay assures him.

"A Ph. D. in...?"

"Physics. Nuclear. Subatomic." Then she looks again at Peter with those amazing eyes. "Very tiny." She says without smiling.

"Ph.D. is a Doctor," Peter counters.

"Is this what we are going to discuss tonight?" This time there is a suggestion of a smile at the corners of her very red lips.

"Politics, religion or sex?" Peter offers.

"Sex."

Peter takes another sip from his oversized flute. He is saved by a waiter serving the entree. Scampi Cantonese. What else? Suddenly he feels as though he hasn't eaten for a month. He remembers he hasn't had lunch. He helps himself to roll and butter and downs it with the abandon of a man within an inch of dying from starvation.

"Would you care for my Scampi?"

"Oh, Miss Catherine..."

"Cathy. And yes. I am a Miss."

Peter swallows hard. This is going to be a very peculiar evening.

"I haven't had time for lunch."

"Patient?"

"Computer. Cramming. The Fellowship."

Cathy's eyebrow rises and stays up.

"I got my licence five years ago, but wasn't sure of my choice of specialization. Took time off to get my Master's in biochemistry. Wanted some information."

Partially true. Peter did his Master's concurrently with his medical studies. He didn't feel like telling Dr. Mondellay about his bout with St. Francis.

Her arched eyebrow comes down and her smile broadens.

"Do you normally get a Master's when you need some information?"

They laugh. Her teeth are perfect.

"What do you do?" Peter asks.

"I continue the work of my father."

Then a little red light flashes hazard signals in Peter's head. God, what a fool I am! Dr. Bartholomew Mondellay put the first Chinese man on Mars. After returning to Montreal, he started the Mondellay Institute. Twenty years ago he had been instrumental in producing the world's first fusion reactor. He had achieved it on a relatively small scale. So small that within ten years each town, each village in Quebec had their own source of power. Now individual houses can own one. Hydro Quebec has gone bankrupt. Energy became clean and cheap. Its sheer abundance and availability opened up the North of North America. Within fifteen years—Peter was only ten then—the population of Canada had swelled to 85,000,000. And that's not counting the northern states of the old USA which had joined the Confederation. Dr. Mondellay is a multimillionaire. Perhaps billionaire. And a genius.

"Dr. Bartholomew Mondellay." It wasn't a question. Just an affirmation.

"Daddy doesn't work anymore."

Not surprising. The old man must be well over a hundred.

"I never realized...?" Peter doesn't know what to say. He is in awe.

"Do you mind?"

Only now Peter puts down the fork and leans back.

"Dr. Mondell... Cathy. You are the first woman in my life who appears to be constantly two steps ahead of me. Yes, I do mind. I find it embarrassing. Please slow down sufficiently for me to catch up with you."

"Would you like my Scampi?" Cathy repeats innocently.

"Yes!" They swap plates. "Thank you!" At least he doesn't have to talk while he's eating. It sort of keeps his feet out of his mouth.

The soup is green. The main course—stuffed pheasant. The dessert—Peach Melba. Then comes the music. Peter asks Cathy to dance.

"We haven't talked about sex yet," she reminds him, nestling comfortably in his arms.

"I could ask them to play a tango?"

"Would that help?"

"I heard somewhere that tango is a vertical expression of a horizontal desire."

"Ask them."

They dance together perfectly. Peter is not an experienced dancer. His five-foot-six plus heels does not encourage him to indulge in this particular form of foreplay. But Cathy is two inches shorter. She's a perfect fit. Each time Peter takes a wrong step she does it with him. It looks and feels like a new figure. A new *pas-de-deux*. Halfway through the third dance, Peter realizes that he hasn't thought about medicine since he looked into Cathy's eyes. He also forgot, completely, about Ruth. At that very moment he sees Ruth a few paces away in the arms of a distinguished-looking gentleman. She winks to him lasciviously. This is not like Ruth. Then he realizes her wink is a tacit comment on him and Cathy. Not on the gray-haired partner guiding her around the floor.

His thoughts return to Cathy. They don't talk much. Her body feels like no body had ever felt before. Talk would spoil it. The rhythms change, their proximity doesn't. Then, in the middle of a foxtrot, Cathy takes him by the hand.

"Follow me. Stay a few steps behind me."

Peter is lost. He has no idea what is going on. Cathy makes her way between the dancing couples and turns left towards the lobby. Peter follows a discreet distance behind her. She is

waiting for him at the bank of elevators. When he catches up
with her, she shows him her back.

"This place is too ostentatious already," she murmurs over
her shoulder.

Four more people enter the ornate cab with them, then leave
on various floors on the way up. The elevator takes them to the
top floor. Cathy leaves and walks three paces in front of Peter.
He can't believe what is going on. Dr. Mondellay? Cathy and
he?

Ridiculous!

She pushes a piece of plastic into the door slot. She steps
inside without waiting for Peter. Peter follows slowly, his knees
feeling weak. He had gone through the motions of this sort at
the hospital with a dozen—with dozens of nurses. The Ritz is
different from a linen cupboard. Very different. Or maybe
Cathy is different. She isn't a nurse.

Peter pushes the door shut with his back and leans against it.
Cathy is standing in the middle of the room, quite motionless.
She is still facing away from him, balanced on her toes, as
though pressing against an invisible barrier. Then her hands
reach behind her neck and the silk dress peals, unfolds down to
the floor in a ridiculously slow motion. She steps out of it and
turns to face Peter. For a moment they both keep very still. They
make love with their eyes. Then Peter moves forward. He tries
pretending she is just another nurse.

She should have been. Her bedside manner is exemplary.

Peter feels mesmerized. The woman is simply beautiful.
Intelligent, sexy, gorgeous. Beautiful. A thought passes through
his mind: why me?

They leave the light full on. Cathy insists.

"I don't want to miss any of this."

She doesn't.

The music weaves strange sequences Peter has never heard
before. He knows the tunes, but now they sound strangely
romantic. He had never listened to the lyrics before. Everything
is different. Normally after a tumble in the hay Peter feels
relaxed, rejuvenated. Today he feels embarrassed. He has no

idea why. After they return to the table, he takes a long time sipping coffee and green bitter-sweet liqueur. Cathy looks perfectly relaxed. She acts as though nothing has happened. She is even more beautiful than before. Her slightly oriental complexion is enhanced by beautiful shades of rosy colour high up on her cheeks.

"We could talk politics now, if you like?" She gazes sideways at Peter, who is busy sipping green Chartreuse. She looks vaguely amused.

Peter raises his glass again. The fiery liquid complements the colour of her eyes.

"Don't have much time for it. Never did." He admits.

"Religion?"

He doesn't answer. Peter has never felt so inexplicably silly in his life. He always, always was in full control of any and every situation. He held the reins. He made the decisions. Tonight he feels like a sixteen-year-old on his first date with an older woman. He feels way over his head.

Cathy's chest heaves in a deep, exaggerated sigh.

"That leaves only sex, I suppose." She looks demurely at Peter over the edge of her fluted crystal. She doesn't like liqueur. The green jade of her eyes sparkles with more bubbles than the champagne. "I don't suppose you want to go upstairs again?"

Peter starts coughing. He feels caught in a spasm, somewhere between a sudden constriction and acute dryness at the back of his throat. He pretends something got stuck in his larynx. She is totally impossible. God, those eyes! He could take her to the dance floor but he is afraid to hold her in his arms. He is afraid of her.

"Tell me about neutrinos," he says at last.

"Then come and dance with me."

They get up. Peter tries to keep himself at arm's length. He has no idea why. It doesn't work. She snuggles closer and closer. Then the band starts playing an Argentine tango. La Cumparsita. There are too many people on the floor to move freely. All he can do is sway with the erotic rhythm.

"Shall I ever see you again?" Peter manages when he regains his breath. He had been holding it for the last hour.

"Do you want to?"

"Rather a silly question."

"You mean you are used to loose women?"

And then Peter realizes what was wrong with Cathy. She felt different. She acted differently. She was willing, almost driving, yet reticent. Suddenly Peter feels faint. No. It can't be!

"You were a virg...?" He asks before he can stop himself.

"You couldn't tell?" She looks proud of herself.

"Why? Why me??"

"I am twenty-nine. I thought it was time."

"But... but...?"

"Was I... all right?" There is sudden concern in her eyes.

Peter decides not to ask any more questions. He has always found women relatively easy to read. As a doctor he is well conversant with their anatomies, has professional training in female psychology. Women have an established place in his life. A relation of mutual respect and understanding and convenience. Until now.

"You were wonderful," he tells Cathy in a very serious voice.

"I bet you say that to..."

"No. I never lie," he lies. Until now.

And then they don't talk anymore. They just dance.

About two in the morning Peter sees Ruth waving to him over her partner's shoulder. When they get closer, she tells him not to look for her. The ambassador of Mexico has offered to take her home. He is the distinguished gentleman she danced with before. And most of the time. Peter thanks her. He wants to stay a little longer. About a million years.

Cathy and Ruth had been introduced before dinner. They wave each other good-bye. As Ruth dances away, she smiles and again winks at Peter. Peter looks away in exasperation. Do women know things? Again he is embarrassed. For a moment he is angry. With himself. Then he is conscious only of Cathy's body gently melting into his own.

It seems like only a few minutes have passed.

He and Cathy are the only people on the dance floor. The only people in the ballroom. The headwaiter is trying hard to stifle a yawn. The other waiters are surreptitiously gazing at their watches. The band leader leans against the piano with a resigned smile of understanding. There is always that last, last couple...

It is morning.

* * *

3

The Second Interview

"*The phenotype is a mixed hyperlipoproteinemia...* and the same to you!"

Peter throws a copy of *The Medical Clinics of North America* into the out-of-date basket. He has now reached the state of a zombie-like stupor. He goes through the functions, carries out all his duties without thinking of the consequences of his decisions. He is too tired to worry. The exams are scheduled for next week. He has reached the point of no return. If he doesn't collapse from exhaustion, then he will pass them. If not, they can bury him together with his modem and his computer. A worthy company. Peter presses his fists into his eyelids, hard, rotates the tension out of his shoulders and stretches out on his bed. The instant he closes his eyes, his beeper cuts the silence. Peter is on call till eleven at night, then free till tomorrow. Till the second interview.

"Thornton?" Peter had a private line installed in his room.

"This is Jarvis, Dr. Thornton. It's about Mrs. Denton." The intern on the other end of the line sounds embarrassed.

"Get to the point, Jarvis!" Peter snaps into the mouthpiece.

Felix Jarvis is a perfectly good intern. He knows as much as an intern can be expected to know. But he can't win.

The point is that Mrs. Denton is under the personal care of Dr. Peter Thornton. The intern knows that if he doesn't call the senior resident, he will get a rude dressing down in the morning. He will also get one if he calls Dr. Thornton at home. A Catch-22. At least that latter alternative would take place on the telephone and not in front of other interns, residents and nurses. Dr. Thornton is not known for being the most tolerant senior resident at the General.

Peter listens to the problem without further interruption, gives his instruction and hangs up. He stares at the black receiver with disgust.

Yesterday Peter barked at the same intern. He has no idea what makes him rude to people. Lately. It can't be just his cramming, or lack of sleep. He did that all his life. Can't blame it on Cathy, either. Since the ball last week, she hasn't called even once. He told her he was boning up for the Fellowship, of course. It must be something else. He didn't use to be like that. At least, he doesn't think he was.

Peter is also a little nervous. Tomorrow he is to have another interview with the Chief of Medicine. What a waste of time! Surely Dr. Brent has better things to do. The old goat knows about Peter's upcoming Fellowship. Maybe he's going over the edge? Both, the old goat and myself, he muses.

The other half of his brain tells Peter that there is a reason. He just can't put his finger on it. Not right now. Maybe that is what makes him snap at people. The unknown? Too many unknowns.

And Dr. Brent isn't the only enigma that has barged into his life. There is Cathy, of course. Will she wait for him to get past his exams? Does she want to? Why should she... At least with the nurses he has a mutual understanding. They satisfied each other's urges on an equal footing. A doctor and a nurse. A man and a woman. But Cathy? A man and a goddess? Nuts. A Ph.D. with jade eyes. That's all.

Like hell!

And there is also Smith, the butler. A strange kind of a fish. Peter can't deny that Winston Smith is damn good at his job. Over the last two years, Peter discovered that the perambulating mummy also has an impressive knowledge of Latin, ancient Greek and, to Peter's utter amazement, a working knowledge of Sanskrit. His English is impeccable, if you can ignore the Oxonian overtones of his accent. His French is correct if stilted, his Mandarin sufficient to cope with the Chinese influences in

Montreal. In addition, the man gives veiled evidence that he can hold his own with any group of people, on virtually any subject.

Peter is at a loss to understand how a man of such wide interests can be content to spend his life playing with juveniles, do the shopping, keep the house in an overall good order and, when required, mix a first-class Martini. This latter ability had been predicated repeatedly by Ruth's friends. Peter is almost prepared to take up drinking—just to verify Smith's dexterity.

Last week, just for the hell of it, Peter had given Smith a series of argumentatively contradictory instructions. Peter wanted to find out if the butler could get mad, or at least if he would lose some of his dumbfounded stoicism. Not only did Smith not break under Peter's puerile onslaught, but the walking enigma managed to carry out the instructions quickly, to the letter, avoiding the apparent contradictions. On top of that, Smith managed to complete his tasks without looking superior!

Smith had acted as though the orders given to him were perfectly reasonable. In no way did the old scarecrow show that he was aware that Peter was acting like a spoiled, obnoxious brat.

"And here am I, snapping at poor, nervous interns for doing their job the best way they know how!" Peter mutters under his nose as he drifts off to sleep, fully dressed, half sitting, half reclining on his bed.

There are moments when Peter finds himself a trifle annoying.

On the following day, Friday, Peter presents himself at Dr. Brent's office.

A fair night's rest converted his misgivings into reasonably high expectations. Whatever the Chief wants, Peter wants it resolved. He has no time to play around the bush for whatever reason. Contrary to the previous interview, today Peter knows that he could not have committed any errors of judgment; not even an innocuous *faux pas*. At least not recently. Since their last meeting, Dr. Brent had not attended any more Rounds. Nor had they met since the last time the illustrious Chief had called him into his presence. Unless... being rather short with the junior staff rated as a misdemeanour. Peter very much doubts that. And whatever his personal shortcomings, he knows that his medical knowledge is well respected. By all. Including the junior physicians.

Peter knocks on the door, enters and smiles at the Chief's secretary.

"Good morning, Dr. Thornton," she responds, looking up from her computer terminal. The woman's eyes seem to study him with an air of quiet disbelief.

"Something wrong?" He smiles again.

"Why, no, Dr. Thornton. Nothing is wrong. Nothing at all." Yet her eyes continue to linger over his face a lot longer than on his first visit. She can hardly tell him that she has never seen Dr. Thornton smiling. "Dr. Brent is expecting you. Please go right in."

She half rises to open the door for him.

"Do not trouble, milady." Peter tries to imitate Winston's voice. Suddenly, for no reason, he finds himself in a good mood. Or perhaps he is just past caring. Too tired? "Thank you just the same," he adds in his normal voice.

As usual, Dr. Brent is hiding behind stacks of papers. Peter wonders what makes a perfectly good, perhaps even a brilliant physician choose to spend most of his time shifting scraps of paper instead of getting on with the business of curing people.

"Come in, Peter!" The Chief sounds relaxed and friendly. He points to a chair in front of his desk. "Be with you in a moment."

Peter takes the chair that he had occupied only a few weeks ago. He sits down and regards the elderly doctor with quiet interest. Dr. Brent has indeed a splendid record. He not only runs the biggest Department of Medicine at the largest Montreal hospital, but in addition he finds time to teach, to act as a consultant to the Federal Ministry of Health, to be available to his staff—often at a moment's notice. He also, Peter recalls, makes an annual tour of the North American continent, delivering lectures on the concept of holistic medicine. Not bad for a man who must be way past his seventieth birthday.

Dr. Brent sits up, makes some cryptic annotations on an official-looking printout, and picks up a new folder from his cluttered desk. He checks a note in the margin and hands the file to Peter.

"Would you look this over? You might find it interesting."

Neither his tone nor facial expression gives Peter any indication of what to expect. Having given Peter something to do, the Chief reverts to his work as if there had been no interruption at all.

Peter leans back and opens the folder. He scans the mass of figures and numbers with detachment. He fails to see why he, of all people, should find anything interesting about the numbers of patients who come in and out of the hospital. Surely Dr. Brent is not looking for an executive assistant to dive into the swamp of bureaucracy at the expense of medicine.

The statistics, for that is all that the computer printouts are, cover all the departments of Internal Medicine at the General over the last four years. Almost. They start on the day Peter started his residency. The last entry is dated October 15th, the day Peter returned to his duties after taking the two weeks off for study. He scans the figures looking for some, for any significance. He finds none. During his stay at the General, Peter had been rotated through all the wards, one way or another; he had been deeply involved with most if not all of the departments. The same was true for his briefer stints at the Victoria and the Veterans' hospitals. The rotations were part of his training.

Internal Medicine is a very broad subject. So broad that most physicians opt for a narrower field by the time they get to their third year of residency. The spectrum covers a number of sub-specializations such as immunology, neurology, cardiovascular disorders, bronchial and pulmonary diseases, rheumatoidal derivatives, and many, many sub-sub-disciplines dealing with complex syndromes. Somehow, Peter had found it difficult to narrow his field at the expense of general knowledge. He was slowly but surely becoming the most all-round physician that the modern teaching methods can produce. Peter's general knowledge had already made him sufficiently unique to have him rotated through more departments than he cares to remember. In the past, the residents also had to rotate through different teaching hospitals. Now this method proved no longer practical, yet Peter managed to put in time at two other hospitals in addition to the General. In a way, Dr. Peter Thornton is a throwback to the old teaching methods.

This must be it! Peter sits back with satisfaction. The Chief's personal interest in holistic medicine must have precipitated this interview. But... it still doesn't say why now?

"Well, Peter? Anything of interest?" Dr. Brent looks up from his papers.

"I'm afraid, Sir, I am not quite sure what I am looking for?" That was an understatement. Peter has no idea at all.

"Look at this folder." Dr. Brent hands him a photocopy of the same documents. This time Peter notices little red marks next to some of the numbers. There is no pattern that he can detect. He returns the folder to Dr. Brent and says as much.

The old man leans back in his armchair and lights a cigarette. He regards Peter through a cloud of smoke. Once again Peter cannot reconcile in his mind how a man of Dr. Brent's stature and convictions can indulge in such an unhygienic habit. He keeps his thoughts to himself.

"Haven't you noticed that on some wards the turnover of patients is faster than on others?" The Chief fixes Peter with a penetrating stare.

Peter reexamines the statistical printouts. The red marks in the right-hand column do indeed represent the fluctuations in the patient-per-bed ratio. Peter sees nothing unusual about them. Such fluctuations are to be expected. He looks up at the Chief, expecting more explanations. He still has no idea why he was called in to see the old man. Dr. Brent says nothing but seems to be studying Peter with detached interest.

"The fluctuations are up to 23% above random chance..." Dr. Brent allows the sentence to drift with the smoke from his cigarette. He then holds up another printout he was studying just after Peter walked in.

"This is a letter from the Ministry of Health. They advise me that there must be some inefficiency on the other wards, rather than offering congratulations on selective successes..." The Chief takes another puff without taking his eyes from

Peter's face. A vague, crooked smile touches his deeply lined features. Dr. Brent seems strangely amused.

"How does all this affect me, Sir? Surely you do not think that my work could have adversely affected..." Peter stops when the Chief raises his hand.

"Now look at the last two weeks on the report. Note that none of the wards indicate the random chance of increased efficiency to correspond with the previous months." Dr. Brent stubs out his cigarette and immediately lights another one.

Peter again scans the printout. Indeed, the figures do support the Chief's statement. Then a triumphant idea dawns on Peter like a protracted flash of lightning.

"But, Dr. Brent! I wasn't even here, the last two weeks!"

Peter knows that he could not have made any errors. The Chief's own data vindicate his innocence. Following a few minutes of mounting tension, he relaxes visibly.

Dr. Brent remains silent. He keeps regarding Peter with an air of speculative disbelief. He continues to puff on his cigarette with absentminded deliberation. He appears to be weighing something in his mind. Then the Chief leans forward in his chair.

"Peter, do you remember having lunch with me a few weeks ago?"

Peter nods. "Of course, Sir. Right here, in your office."

"I asked you then some pointed questions about your methods of treatment. Remember?" Dr. Brent stubs out his cigarette and leans forward over his cluttered desk. "I was trying to find out from you whether you employed any diagnostic, therapeutic or post-operative techniques which differ substantially from my own methods. Did you tell me the truth?"

"Are you implying...?!"

"Peter, please. Bear with me and answer the question. Your answer will remain between these four walls." The old man's voice carries paternal reassurance.

"Well, of course, Sir!" Peter's voice sounds only partially mollified.

"You mean that you told me the precise truth, is that right?"

"Yes, Sir. The precise truth." Peter shrugs in an exaggerated resignation. He is still annoyed at having his integrity questioned. What the hell is going on here, anyway?

Dr. Brent seems to collapse deeper into his chair. His hand reaches for a box of cigarettes but stops short. Instead, he looks up again at Peter. There is determination in the old man's eyes. Determination or... pleading? Peter is not quite sure. Once more the Chief changes his mind, and his long, gaunt fingers reach out for the offensive weed. His worn features give an impression of being either nervous or a little angry. Peter wishes he knew Dr. Brent well enough to judge his facial expressions. For his part, Peter is intrigued by his own speculations as to what caused those strange fluctuations in the Chief's behaviour. He arms himself with patience and keeps quiet. At last Dr. Brent appears ready to speak. He finds it necessary to clear his throat, as though still uncertain of his words.

"I had these figures checked three times. There is no room for error." Dr. Brent speaks with a slow, measured voice. "The statistical data cover a wide range of diseases, syndromes or what have you. However, in every single case when the recuperation period of any patient was substantially, and I might add inexplicably, reduced, you, Dr. Thornton, you were the attending physician."

Dr. Brent leans back in his chair. Peter has no idea what the old man is trying to tell him. He waits for the Chief to continue. After a moment or two, Peter breaks the uneasy silence.

"Are you trying to tell me, Sir, that my patients recover sooner than other patients?" Peter grins broadly as he asks the inane question. Dr. Brent does not share his humour.

"Yes, Peter. Your patients consistently recover substantially faster than those in the care of any other members of my staff," the Chief replies gravely.

"But... how? Why??" Peter looks and sounds totally perplexed. He still doesn't treat Dr. Brent's data as a matter requiring any particular attention. "Coincidence?" he asks. "Pure coincidence," he repeats, nodding vigorously.

"Twenty-three percent above the norm?" Dr. Brent fixes him with a stern gaze.

"Then how...?" Peter waves his arms in sheer exasperation.

"This, my dear boy, is what we are here trying to find out!"

By seven o'clock Peter is on his way home. As usual he is walking. It is already quite dark. The street lamps flood the street with a cold, impersonal light. No longer do they wash the underside of the branches spanning the sidewalks. The leaves are gone. Most of them. There is a wet chill in the air, the type that penetrates through your clothing and skin right down into your bones. Peter raises his collar against the shifting breeze. Even his favourite Westmount avenues seem uninviting. He shrugs. It all looks so different when you're tired. He quickens his pace.

Peter tries to reevaluate the peculiar interview that he had had this morning. Right now, none of it makes any sense. Dr. Brent had finished the meeting by insisting that Peter take the weekend off.

"You need a bit of a rest, my boy," he had said. "Want to see you here bright and early on Monday. I arranged for my colleagues from the Victoria to join us for your Fellowship... a formality, you know, but mustn't be accused of favouritism."

Peter grins at the recollection. The smile had changed the Chief's stern features into an image of paternal concern.

"Thank you, Sir. I dare say, I could do with a few hours off." He had thanked the old man. Not such a bad egg, the Chief, after all, Peter thought.

Peter is glad he will be examined by the staff from the Royal Victoria Hospital. He regards their specialists as topnotch in all matters related to neurologically based disorders.

Dr. Brent had offered Peter a firm handshake. Reassuring.

"Good luck on Monday," he had said. And then he had added: "And don't worry about your patients. I'll stand in for you myself."

Peter was flabbergasted. The Chief had practically accused him of dealing in black magic. Then, a minute later, the man who was manifestly the most overworked member of the staff took on extra duties to give Peter a respite. The old warhorse does have a heart hidden somewhere under those stacks of papers.

The Chief had little to add to their discussion. He didn't belabour the points. He allowed the facts to speak for themselves. Perhaps he intended only to plant the seed and let time, or time and Peter's subconscious mind, come up with an answer. There and then Peter decided to do likewise. To dismiss the interview from his mind. The so-called facts didn't make sense, anyway. Still don't. Statistics can be turned and twisted in a thousand different ways. Time enough after the exams. For the next two days, Peter doesn't even want to think about medicine, let alone bureaucratic statistics. He quickens his step again to put more distance between the hospital and himself.

At the front door he is greeted by Ruth. She was supposed to have left this morning for New York.

"You're just in time for supper," she says.

"What happened?"

"I've been grounded."

Peter hangs up his coat, turns towards Ruth and raises an eyebrow.

"Solidarity," Ruth explains. "They closed all the airports. It's a first, down here."

Peter takes Ruth by the arm and leads her to the dining room. Jo and Mo are already seated. They are ready to rush up to greet Uncle Peter, but he restrains them by raising both arms.

"Whoa... Sit!"

Jo and Mo remain seated, looking like offended puppies.

They eat together very seldom. Peter's hours are unpredictable. Ruth often leaves on a moment's notice. Peter walks around the table, ruffles Mo's hair, then shakes Jo's hand.

"Do not get up, Sir," Peter tells little Jo with a straight face, then turns again to Ruth. "I'll be with you presently. Need a quick wash."

Peter leaves the room to return five minutes later. By the time he gets back, an extra setting is already laid, and his soup is waiting on his plate. Winston, framed by the kitchen doorway, bows to him with superb dignity. Peter acknowledges the major-domo with a wave of his hand.

"Good to see you, Smith!" he adds, seeing his steaming plate.

For a while they all eat in silence. Generally, during the meals, children are not allowed to speak unless addressed by Ruth or Peter. Or Winston, of course. He looks after them more than anyone. An old-fashioned custom but eminently practical.

"So what's all this Solidarity business?" he asks Ruth.

"Solidarity International," she corrects. "To my knowledge this is the first time they managed to cross the ocean. On such a scale."

Peter has no idea what Ruth is talking about. His commitments of the last few months—correction, years—had left no time at all for newsprint or television. None at all.

"Go on?" he encourages.

"Well, in Europe they seem very powerful. They are not exactly a union, a trade union I mean, but they are an organization which has managed to infiltrate the key positions in the Common Market countries, particularly as regarding communications. This seems to include all the media as well as the railways and, of course, the airports. They say that when they place a demand in any of these industries, such demands are carried out without an argument."

"What demands?"

"Well, we don't know as much about them as we would like." Ruth hesitates. "They are very cagey people. Not at all like the old-fashioned unions. It seems that their initial demands were directed at the salaries of management. They stated that no administrative officer of any industry should earn more than six times the national average. Later, I understand, they reduced the coefficient to five and extended the demand to cover all salaries. The idea was so popular that masses of employees joined the Movement, demanding that its ideas be put into practice."

"That's all? Doesn't sound too unreasonable."

"No, it doesn't, does it? Considering that the company presidents, television anchors and suchlike had been earning, say, three or more millions of Euros as compared to the average being little over forty thousand. That's a spread of eighty-and-up to one."

"You mean that the bosses had been taking home over eighty times the European average?"

"And more. But don't look so surprised. We are no better," Ruth admits.

"No wonder the idea became popular. I suppose just about everyone joined? People don't like being exploited. No matter what colour their collar."

"Right. The response to the Solidarity manifesto had been very far-reaching. But all the same, out there things are getting a little out-of-hand. They had started with the communications, and gradually took over all the major industries. The upper crust, if you want to call them that, had been forced to give in. Apparently the key personnel in the Solidarity International are extremely well organized. They have just begun flexing their muscles over here... I really don't know what is going to happen."

"It is easy to see what makes them so popular, but what is their seat of power?"

"From what I understand, they have a very broad base. Anyone can afford a biannual $10 donation. Multiply that by about 800,000,000 people and you have a tidy operating budget. They are all over Europe, Northern Africa, the Middle East and a good chunk of Asia. We are next. The UN estimates that their numbers grow at the rate of a million people a day. They don't do much as long as they have things their own way. It not..."

Ruth is doodling with her fork and a couple of peas. Mo and Jo look at each other and start a game of their own. Soon a dozen peas are rolling along the table. Peter gives them a stern look. The game stops with a restrained giggle.

"You seem to take them rather seriously. I hardly heard anything of them at the General." Peter doesn't seem worried. It all has nothing to do with medicine nor with his Fellowship exams.

"You hardly had time to hear about anything much at the General. And that goes for most people. Since Solidarity International does not make much noise, one doesn't hear about them until suddenly all the airplanes are grounded across the Eastern Seaboard."

For a while they eat in silence. Ruth remonstrates gently with Jo to finish everything on his plate. Then, having finished herself, she sits back and looks at her brother-in-law. There is just a touch of jealousy in her eyes. She knows that he is well insulated from world affairs. She isn't. The United Nations represents the *status quo*. Solidarity seems very much the wave of the future.

"From what I've heard in New York," she resumes, "their executive power lies in communications. Apparently they are in a constant, worldwide computer link. Not just across Europe, but now apparently over here. They hire the very best pollsters, get them to find out what are the most widespread pet hates of the *populus* at large, and then base their demands on their research."

"A *vox populi*. Brilliant! No wonder their popularity is growing. I have a few pet hates of my own."

Peter finishes his Chicken *à la* King. For the hundredth time he wonders where Smith learned to cook with such an Epicurean proficiency. Surely not in England. No one ever accused the English of being extraordinary cooks.

"So now what?" he muses aloud.

"Now we wait. They want the top salaries of all the executives, in all the main airlines, to be reduced immediately to five times the national average."

"That's all?"

"Yes, Peter. That's all!"

"Doesn't seem like all that much?"

"They never ask for all that much. But they always get what they want. Apparently they have an executive cadre-in-waiting all ready, in case the present executives simply resign. By the way, the Chairman and the CEO are both making over two million dollars; nobody seems to know exactly why..."

"Two million annually...?" Peter lets out a low whistle.

Mo and Jo look up. They purse their lips. Ruth wags her finger. Peter is thinking of the money that he will start raking in the moment he passes his Fellowship of the Royal College.

"Do you know, Ruth! After all the years of my slaving away in medicine, I never expected to make more than five times national average."

"I know. This is what makes the Solidarity so powerful. Do you know, until recently, in England, 90% of the wealth was held by no more than 5% of the population? Even most of the established professionals feel like joining the Solidarity to get the few moguls off their back. There is a certain sensual pleasure in being a participator in getting the multi-million dollar salaries down to where they belong."

"And that is their true seat of power." Peter nods to his own thoughts.

"I wonder if they know where they are going..." Ruth's eyes drift to her children.

There is a prolonged silence.

And then Mo and Jo finish their dessert and there is silence no more. Not until bedtime. That is the deal. Ruth always keeps her part of the bargain.

* * *

4

A Fellow

"**L**adies and gentlemen. I present to you Dr. Peter Thornton. May he live long and strengthen our ranks."

The President of the Royal College of Physicians raises a fluted glass and drinks a bubbly ginger ale as he recites the age-honoured toast to Peter's health; a toast dating back to the time when the 'Royal' affiliation actually meant something. Dr. Peter Thornton, FRCP, will henceforth be known as a Fellow. As one of 'Us'. Dr. George Tsan, the President, is taking part in the *impromptu* initiation at the personal invitation of Dr. Brent. The President and the Chief go way back.

"For he is a jolly good Fellow, for he is a jolly good Fellow, for he's..."

The couplet is as apt as any song can be at the investiture to the ranks of the select few. Relatively few. Over the years, the ranks had been kept down to maintain the exclusivity of the club. Is it a club? In a way. It is treated as such particularly by those who have ambitions to bring home more than five times the national average. Not all Fellows are as magnanimous as Dr. Brent. Nor as able.

For Peter the end of the exams means being able to devote more of his time to the patients, and have some time left over for an occasional game of golf. And to be able to buy Ruth as nice a present as she had bought him last Christmas. And to spoil Jo and Mo. Just a little. A Senior Resident doesn't make that much money. Less than a senior nurse!

And to see Cathy.

"Thank you, ladies and gentlemen, my Fellow Canadians," Peter quips, acknowledging the good wishes. "I trust I shall prove worthy of your faith in me."

That's all. Peter does not specialize in long speeches. Anyway, this isn't the real, pompous, officious Investiture. That would come later. This is unofficial. This get-together was organized by Dr. Brent, in his office, after submitting Peter to five days of the most exhaustive cross-examination Peter had ever endured in his life. Just the four examining Fellows, five of the General staff members and Dr. Tsan. A few Fellows proud of swelling their ranks. Peter is not an average physician. Not by a long shot.

Dr. Brent pulls Peter to one side.

"I don't suppose you had a chance to give our last meeting much thought?"

Peter is in too good a mood to get angry. These last few days he had other things on his mind than some stupid statistics.

"What, this last week?" He grins broadly. "I have been trying to survive, Sir!"

"Thought as much. I've given a copy of the printouts to George. George Tsan," the Chief explains when Peter looks up. "I wonder if he can make head or tail of all those ah... coincidences."

Now Peter pays a little more attention. The President can still raise objections to his official investiture next month. Peter is a trifle annoyed.

"You really thought that necessary, Sir? I would have thought Dr. Tsan has more interesting..."

" ...I find all enigmas interesting. George is a personal friend of mine. He might have heard of similar cases elsewhere." The Chief takes a sip of the ginger ale. "Surely, you don't mind, do you?"

"I just didn't think..."

"Peter, you seem on the defensive. Relax, my boy. No one is accusing you of anything. We would simply like to know..."

"We?"

"We." Dr. Brent smiles, waving his arm. "I, Mary, George, the computer statisticians, the Ministry of Health..."

"Oh, my God!"

Peter's pale face loses the remainder of its scant colour. He no longer finds the stupid affair amusing. For crying out loud! The old goat is making a mountain out of a mole hill.

"We'll let that go, for now, shall we?" Dr. Brent pats Peter on the shoulder. "This is your day of celebration. Mustn't get you muffed, my boy..."

"No, Sir. I'm sorry. I had other things on my mind," Peter murmurs.

"Of course you did." Dr. Brent looks at his watch. "Fellow travellers. It is time for take off. Enough of this revelry. We all have our work to do, and our new colleague," here he raises his glass again towards Peter, "has earned a good rest."

"Peter Thornton!"

"Peter Thornton!" "Thornton!" The Fellows echo the final toast.

The glasses are raised again, accompanied by hearty handshakes. Peter's adrenaline keeps him going. He smiles his thanks and tries hard to address the staff members by their first names. After years of tradition he doesn't find it easy. He and the staff doctors are the first to leave. The four examining physicians stay behind.

Peter feels that there was something missing. Something he had expected. He is too tired to think. He walks down the corridor to his office. He wants to shed his white smock in his office, pick up his trench coat and make for home. Sleep. Sleep till springtime. Perhaps a little longer.

Then Cathy, he muses vaguely.

As Peter leaves his office, he hears two women arguing with a nurse. In French. One woman sounds very insistent, the nurse equally unbending. The nurse is trying hard to restrain the older woman from going down the corridor towards his office. To get to the elevators, Peter has to pass by the bellicose trio. He feels he ought to help the nurse, whatever her problem. But surely, not today. Not...

"Doctor Thornton!" One of the women sees him and shouts his name on the top of her voice. She has a strong French accent. His name sounds like Tonton. The *h* is gone and the *on*'s are pronounced the French way.

"Tssss!" The nurse does her best to quiet her down. One does not shout in hospital corridors. Not unless one is in pain.

"Docteur Tonton, please..." The shout is converted into a screaming whisper.

"Madame Ouellette. Ce n'est pas un couloir public. On ne peut pas entrer ici. Je vous prie, Madame. Venez avec moi." When the woman doesn't move, she raises her own voice and adds: *"Maintenant, Madame Ouellette!"*

By this time Peter is within ten steps of the arguing women. He is desperately trying to think of a way to avoid them. How to pass by without getting involved. Just then the older woman starts sobbing. The halting, gasping kind of sobs which seem to take the air into one's lungs with none coming out. It sounds painful.

"What can I do for you, ah, Mrs. Ouellette?" Peter stops. The woman seems at the end of her tether. I must be nuts, he thinks. That's how I feel.

The woman looks at him, her sobs making it impossible for her to speak. The other woman, about ten years younger, takes a step forward.

"I am sorry, Dr. Thornton. I told them..." The nurse looks worried.

Peter raises his hand. He addresses the younger woman.

"And you are...?"

"I am Lucille's sister, Sir. My name is Janinne."

Janinne looks about Peter's age. A little younger. She looks familiar. Pretty in a common sort of way. Both women have blond hair, but that is where the similarity ends. Lucille looks about forty, perhaps more. A tired forty. Peter thinks that their light coats are quite inadequate for this weather.

"So what seems to be your problem?" He asks against his better judgment.

"Madame Ouellette's son has just been brought into the emergency," the nurse answers instead. "I told Madame Ouellette that he is in good hands."

"Henri is my only son, *docteur*." More sobs shake her whole body. "*Mon petit Henri....*"

"There, there, Madame Ouellette. *Ne vous en faite pas.* Your son, ah, Henri is well looked after."

Peter strokes the older woman's thin shoulder. Her sobs are gradually coming under control. Suddenly she lunges at Peter, falls to her knees and kisses his hand. Peter jumps as if bitten by an animal. A reaction aggravated by his own wrought nerves and exhaustion.

"What...?"

"Please, *docteur*. If you could just touch him. Just touch him."

"Madame Ouellette. Please believe me. Your son is in the best of hands. The best possible. There's nothing I could possibly do that is not already being done."

Peter is embarrassed at his nervous reaction when the woman grabbed his hand. He should have better control of himself. As he talks, he edges towards the elevators. Then the elevator doors open. Two chunky orderlies join them in the corridor. The nurse must have pressed her emergency beeper.

"Hold that door!" Peter shouts to the orderlies.

One of the men keeps the elevator door open, the other takes three steps forward and takes hold of the older woman's arms from behind. He is gentle but firm. Lucille Ouellette does not offer any resistance. She seems to have lost the battle. Her sister stands to one side, her hands hanging loosely at her sides. (Peter is sure he had seen her before. He tends to forget names, never faces.) For Lucille, it all happened too quickly. She seems lost. Bewildered. As Peter steps into the elevator, he smiles at Madame Ouellette. Her eyes hold a desperate plea.

"Just touch him... just..." The woman utters as she collapses against the burly man behind her.

Peter presses the button. The elevator stops at the emergency floor. What the hell? Peter could have sworn he had pressed the button for a different floor. Damn! I must get some rest, he mutters to himself. Nevertheless, he steps out of the elevator.

Immediately to his right are the double doors through which the orderlies wheel in stretchers from the Emergency Department to take them upstairs to the various wards. Or to the Emergency Operating Rooms. Sometimes, to Pathology. The latter is a one-way trip. Peter hesitates, then turns on his heel and pushes the double doors. It's been a while since he held duty in the Emergency. The Specialists are normally called in only to the wards.

The light inside the Emergency is twice as bright as behind the doors he just crossed. The silence is gone, also. Here people are working at a different pace, a different attitude permeates the sterile walls. The only words spoken are short, a sort of controlled rapid-fire exchange between the doctors and the nurses. The patients do not talk much. They groan mostly. Or whimper. This is the Friday evening traffic emergency.

Peter walks to the nearest nurse.

"Who's in charge?" he asks.

"Dr. Cunningham, Sir. He's in room nine."

Peter walks on and waits in front of room 9 for Dr. Cunningham to emerge from behind the curtain. They are not rooms, really, but cubicles with no front wall. The staff on duty refer to them as cages. Only the patients who can't be left outside are kept here. Some are wheeled directly into the ICUs. Others... the worse cases, those with little hope, are in the cubicles. One must determine what to do with them. The less injured are in the outer main waiting area—those who are able to sit or walk and talk.

"Dr. Cunningham?"

Peter addresses the young man who emerges from behind the curtain. He is tall and gaunt. His green tunic hardly reaches halfway down his thighs. Peter had met him once or twice but does not remember his face too well.

"Dr. Thornton! It's a pleasure to see you, Sir. I believe congratulations are in order?" Dr. Cunningham is all smiles.

For a moment Peter is lost, then he remembers his Fellowship. News travels fast. Too fast for his liking. No matter.

"Thank you." He nods to the younger man. The resident can't be more than twenty-three or -four years old. Peter remembers going through the same tortuous training. Night duties in the Emergency on Fridays and Saturdays had been the worst. People drink more.

"You have Henri Ouellette here?"

"Cage three. They brought him in about an hour ago. Some drunk smashed into their car. The mother and her sister are O.K. Funny. He's the only one hurt. Punctured spleen and kidney, hemorrhage all over the abdominal cavity. Lost too much blood. His spine is twisted... Can't do miracles. Put him on morphine. I give him a couple of hours. At the most." Dr. Cunningham keeps smiling. He has to. He would go crazy otherwise.

"Thanks. I won't keep you." Peter dismisses the younger man.

Dr. Cunningham nods and walks away. Peter is not really impolite. The resident is in charge of the whole Emergency ward. He can call a senior resident, and even a senior staff member, if he is over his head. He tries not to. It is his job to cope as best he can.

Peter hesitates, then walks over to cage 3. He pulls the curtain to one side and walks into the cubicle. A boy, perhaps twelve or so, is lying on the emergency stretcher. He doesn't move. He seems at peace. Obviously Cunningham gave him enough morphine to kill the pain. Peter stares at the boy without moving. He feels anger stirring inside him. The boy is twelve. His mother forty. He's her only son. She's probably too old to have another child. And they weren't drinking. There was no alcohol on his mother's breath. None at all. And her boy is dying. Shit. SHIT! It's all wrong.

Peter's fists are clenched in anger, pressed against his thighs. He takes a deep slow breath. It helps. He takes another. Slowly his fingers loosen. "Just touch him..." Henri's mother's request crosses his mind. "Just touch him..."

Poor woman. Superstitious. A mother will try anything.

Peter walks to the stretcher. He bends over. The boy's breath is hardly discernible. His eyes are closed. His chest doesn't rise at all. Just touch him. Peter's anger is gone. In its place a great feeling of tiredness. He knows he can do nothing. Even if he could, he is too tired. *Just touch him.* Yes, Mrs. Ouellette. Yes, mother. Just as you say. A good-bye. A farewell to youth. To life. To immortality.

Peter leans over further and embraces the boy's slight body. There is no response. He holds him close. Peace. Just peace. No more pain. No more hurt. No more...

He straightens up and walks through the curtain. He feels awkward. He touched briefly thousands of patients; he never before embraced one. Peter quickens his pace through the Emergency Ward to the Emergency Exit. As he walks through the outside door, the orderlies bring Madame Ouellette and her sister to cage number three. The mother leans against the stretcher and closes her eyes. She doesn't weep any more. She has no tears left.

The wind hits Peter in the face like a tight fist of ice. He raises his collar. From his coat pocket he pulls out a woollen hat and pulls it down over his ears. He walks quickly to keep warm. Having left the hospital by the lower entrance he must walk uphill, then left to get to Westmount. It will take him about twelve minutes. He presses his hands deep into his trench coat pockets. He doesn't feel tired any more. Just numb. As though he had drunk too much alcohol. He wonders what it must be like to drink too much. So much as to kill a small boy. An only son.

Winston Smith opens the door for him. It is past supper.

"Good evening, Sir. May I prepare you something to eat?" Winston asks.

"Yes, Smith. Two fried eggs on bacon, a dozen rolls, lots of butter and a few gallons of coffee. Around nine, tomorrow."

"Very good, Sir." Winston Smith bows, taking Peter's coat. He still looks superior.

"Madam sends her congratulations, Sir. May I add my own?"

"How did she know that I passed?" Peter asks.

"She telephoned and I told her, Sir."

"Oh. Thank you, Smith. Good night."

Peter assumes the children are already in their beds. He unbuttons his shirt as he walks upstairs. He drops his trousers at the door of his room. He collapses on the bed with a protracted sigh. Then the corners of his lips edge upwards in a contented smile. He suddenly remembers what had been missing at his unofficial investiture. It was the smoke. Dr. Brent hadn't been smoking.

After that he remembers nothing at all.

Breakfast is exactly as he had requested. Perhaps the numbers or quantities of certain items differ, but the essence is there. Peter is free till Monday morning. Two free weekends in a row. It feels like being a member of the Staff. He feels great.

So this is what it's like to be a Fellow?

"Will there be anything else, Sir?"

Winston steps out of the woodwork with a grave smile. He is the only man Peter has ever met who can arrange his features in such a way. A grave smile. Sometimes Peter thinks that Smith is deliberately enigmatic. That he enjoys being mysterious. Sometimes, on the other hand, he seems to be pulling my leg, Peter muses. Hard.

"No, thanks, Smith." Then he remembers. "Where are the kids?"

"At the *Conservatoire de Musique*, Sir. They are attending a dress rehearsal of the Youth Symphony Orchestra."

"At nine in the morning?"

"It is now 10:27, Sir," Winston answers without looking at his watch.

Peter raises his hand and stares at his watch. The time is 10:28. He must have spent close to an hour in the bathtub reading the *Saturday Gazette*. It is the first time since his student days at McGill that he has taken a morning bath. He never had time before. He always was a strictly shower-and-run man.

"So this is what it feels like to be a Fellow?" he mutters, again under his breath.

Then he remembers something Winston had said last night.

"You told me last night that you advised Mrs. Thornton that I had passed my Fellowship exams. How did you know?"

"I never doubted it for a moment. Did you, Sir?" Winston takes a step backwards towards the hall.

"Why, no. As a matter of fact, deep down I didn't."

"Nor did I, Sir."

With that assurance Winston Smith takes another step backwards, and suddenly Peter finds himself all alone. It is a strange feeling. Not to be alone. He had spent innumerable hours cramming data into his head with no one but his shimmering computer screen for company. No. It is a strange feeling to sit here, in the dining room, without having to either rush to the hospital or upstairs to his computer. Peter begins feeling almost ill at ease. He is not used to leisure.

Once more he glances at his watch. The green face stares back at him, mocking his discomfort. It is now 10:31. Ten-thirty-one and twelve seconds. Thirteen, fourteen...

"God, how time flies when you're having fun!" he says aloud.

There is no one to hear him. Winston has melted into the innards of the house, the kids are out, Ruth in New York, nurses in hospitals, patients... Poor Madame...? Peter can't remember her name. Poor mother... The patient in the morgue.

He gets up and walks to the window. The leaves are all gone. Not only from the wide elms and maples, but even from the pavement. The giant vacuum cleaners had sucked them all up. They are now in the process of being converted into compost. Like people after the Pathology department gets through with them.

He shrugs.

"Must call Cathy." He looks at his watch. "Damn!"

The time is 10:35. Too early. One doesn't telephone young ladies so early on Saturday mornings. He sets his jaw. He crosses over to the living room, sits down in an armchair next to the telephone table and remembers that he doesn't remember Cathy's number. He's got it somewhere upstairs. He sits back and tries to remember Cathy. Catherine Mondellay, Ph.D. A nuclear physicist. Daughter of a billionaire. A woman he had made love to the first time he met her. Even with nurses that would be a coup.

With Cathy...?

With Cathy it was a miracle. She had said she thought it was time. There is a time for everything. A time to live and a time to die. Poor mother.

Cathy wasn't at home. A squeaky-voiced housekeeper asked him to call later. Around twelve. How can anyone hire a squeaky-voiced housekeeper? Now Smith...

He had over an hour to kill. God, it's good to have time to relax! Maybe I could go for a walk? Without going anywhere. Just a walk. Or I could take a drive around the Summit Circle. Peter remembers that the view from the top of Westmount is fantastic. It is years since he stood there, at the lookout. Nowadays you had to be on the top of a mountain to look over the slums into the distant hills. There is Westmount, and there are the distant hills. In between—the 'have-nots'. Montreal has six million of them. Six million people living on government assistance. Enough to keep body and soul together, not enough to live. To Live.

Now he had time to *live*. Only Cathy wasn't there. Not yet.

What idiot invented time? Science had already proven that time is a figment of our imagination. At the velocity of light, time stands still. To an outside observer, of course. Inside the impossible spaceship it ticks on as usual. Only clocks don't tick anymore. They just spit new numbers at you. Silently.

Isn't it quiet on Saturday mornings?

At the velocity of light, time stands still; but your mass gets to be infinite. That covers a lot of space. Infinite? In a manner of speaking, a circle is infinite. So is going in circles. Round and round. Forever. What's the point? You always get back to the same spot and don't even know it. Round and round.

"Is Miss Mondellay there, please? This is Doctor Thornton." Dr. Thornton, FRCP.

"Peter?"

A room with dimmed light, a single button at her neck. She presses that button and the green silk slithers down slowly...

"Cathy?" Of course it's Cathy. "Yes, it is I. How are you?" What an inane question. After all this time.

"Congratulations." On the telephone her voice is like liquid honey with a touch of oriental aroma.

"Oh?"

"On your Fellowship!" she adds unnecessarily.

"I didn't know there had been an official press release."

"When shall I see you?"

"Lunch?"

"One o'clock at the Jinhua."

"Where is that?"

"I'll pick you up."

"Thanks. I'll be waiting."

She hangs up. Why must she always be in charge? The time, the place, the mode of transportation. A strange woman. Yet at the Ritz, she was pliant. Giving. Forgiving. Malleable. Strangely submissive.

It is 12:14. Must get ready. What does one wear on a Saturday to a restaurant patronized by a billionaire's daughter? A Chinese restaurant? Ruth had said the best restaurants in Montreal are all Chinese. Mostly named after Chinese towns or cities. They are by far the best cooks, she had said. In a crude world they are subtle. Refined.

Peter runs upstairs two at a time. Energy is bursting out of his veins. He feels he could fly if he had to. Suddenly he is short of time again. He is active. He is going to see Cathy. He sneers at the silent computer. The sneer becomes an indulgent grin of contrived superiority.

Peter pulls on a freshly pressed pair of slacks and ties an Ascot around his neck. He presses a matching handkerchief into the pocket of his Harris Tweed jacket. He examines himself in the full-length mirror on the bathroom door. Last time he studied his image, he thought himself about six inches too short. Right now he feels ten feet tall.

From under his crewcut, a pair of eyes are smiling back at him.

"Wonder what she looks like in daylight?"

* * *

5

Worse than a cure?

"Very well, Sir. Gin or Vodka?"

Winston's voice reaches Peter from somewhere just below the ceiling. When you are addressed by a minaret almost two meters high while you are sunk in a deep armchair, the sound that reaches you seems filled with an illustrious propensity. Particularly if the voice reaching you appears to emanate from a great depth (presumably from the vicinity of your interlocutor's toes), whence it is swept up by a divine current to prohibitive heights only to float down in sublime magnanimity to your miserable, mundane level. In the process, the voice seems to develop an echo. It also develops certain forbidding authority that you feel you should not question. Perhaps that is why the children always respond to all Smith's commands without question.

"Whatever you think best, Smith. Thank you."

What could he say? He has never had a Martini in his life.

Peter feels distinctly discombobulated. His weary bones are impregnated with a sort of neither-here-nor-there feeling. He had settled into his favourite armchair to perform the inevitable autopsy of his lunch with Cathy. He diagnoses it, the lunch, somewhere between peculiar and just short of the what-am-I-doing-here category. Peter surmises that at the Jinhua he simply felt out of place. Yet it wasn't the ambience. The atmosphere was pleasant enough. The decor was Manchurian, the porcelain

Ming, the crowd cosmopolitan. But it was none of these that had given Peter an out-of-place feeling. He doesn't believe he belongs in a restaurant where people spend more on hors d'oeuvres than a fourth-year resident makes in a week. Almost. Even then, it also wasn't just the money. Since during the last few years he had had little opportunity, or time, to spend any of his income, he could well afford a dip into this Epicurean debauchery. Money was definitely not the problem. It was Cathy.

She wasn't the same. Better? Perhaps... but different. Too different.

She seemed bent on overwhelming him with facets of her personality that piled one on top of the other at break-neck speed. Whatever mask she had worn at the Ritz Ball, well—that woman didn't exist anymore. At least, not today.

The new Cathy was more of a Catherine. Perhaps even a Ph.D. An intellectual. She scrutinized the world from behind a set of enormous spectacles. Extra large, perfectly round lenses. Peter found it difficult to say whether she needed them or if they were part of the mask with which she had decided to present him on this particular occasion. Once or twice she had removed them. Peter had not noticed any difference in her ability to read the menu or recognise and acknowledge perfunctory bows and smiles from the elite delicately gorging themselves on the minuscule morsels at astronomical prices.

"Do you really need those?" Peter had asked, pointing to her glasses.

"Don't you like them?" she had countered.

"I don't know."

"Then why do you ask?"

It wasn't that she was imposing her logic on him. Nor was she contrary on purpose. She just seemed to need a purpose for whatever she did. Or said. Maybe even what she felt or thought. Peter admits to himself that he had met her to get away from work, from thinking, from responsibility. He was looking forward to a frivolous lunch in a fashionable den—just for a change. To be different. To get away...

"Would you care for anything with it, Sir?"

Winston places a Martini at Peter's left elbow, then hoists his head again to the upper reaches. Peter switches off his thoughts of Cathy and looks up at the shape looming above him. Smith must be somewhere between 40 and a 100 years old, he muses. When he wants to, he moves like a genetically bred basketball player. On other occasions he seems to exude the wisdom of the ages.

"What does one have with it, ah, normally?" Peter has no idea.

"Nuts."

"What?"

"Nuts, Sir. Salted or baked. Mixed or of singular persuasion."

"You are pulling my leg."

"If you say so, Sir. Though, if I may, Sir, I am attempting to titillate the sensual receptors at the opposite end of your lower extremities." Winston actually said this with a straight face.

"Half and half, then. Or whatever."

Peter hadn't asked for a Martini to study the merits of the ancillary tidbit attendant to the art of drinking. He wanted to try one because Cathy had one at the Jinhua and he had refused. She survived the concoction, therefore he decided to find out what it's like in the privacy of his home. Peter would never admit to anyone that he was shy. Men who are five-foot-six seldom do. Peter sighs. One-hundred-sixty-seven-point-five centimetres does sound a little better. But not in Westmount. In Westmount you are born and you die on an Imperial scale. For ever.

As Winston withdraws to get the nuts, Peter raises the glass to his nose. No smell to speak of. It must be Vodka. He takes a cautious sip. It is cool...and smooth; just a hint of tartness. An aftertaste of a dry lemon. He takes another sip. It's even better. It's definitely smoother. Very, very cool.

"I am told you are good at this sort of thing?" Peter asks when Winston returns with the nuts. "Why don't you have one?"

"Thank you, Sir."

Winston doubles up his body and takes a single nut from the crystal bowl he has just placed on the table next to Peter's Martini. Peter starts laughing. This peregrinate mummy is just too perfect.

"Do you ever relax, Smith?" he asks Winston, still laughing.

"Yes, Sir. Most of the time."

"Are you trying to tell me that you are relaxed right now? I mean really relaxed?" Peter probes deeper since Winston remains in a position of rigid attention.

"Not so as to fall down, Sir. But sufficiently not to take life too seriously."

Peter stares up at Winston in an amused amazement. He finds it difficult to accept that during the last two years the inveterate butler had never taken a wrong step. On any account. Peter had read somewhere that perfection consists of doing ordinary things extraordinarily well. By such a definition, Smith is perfect.

"Don't you ever drink yourself?" Peter probes further.

"Frequently. Though I avoid beverages which tend to cut down on the oxygen in my brain."

"Like booze?"

"I take a little wine, occasionally."

"Why?" Peter thinks he has found Smith's Achilles heel.

"It gives me pleasure, Sir." Winston replies, with his usual straight face.

"That is the only reason?"

"I find it an adequate stimulation for most of my actions."

"So you won't have a drink with me?"

"I would rather decline, if I may. Unless my refusal would adversely affect your good humour, Sir?"

Peter laughs again. He leans back, tilts his head even further and downs the Martini to the last drop.

"What is it like to be perfect, Smith?"

Throughout this conversation, Winston has appeared frozen at rapt attention. Now, at this very moment, his voice changes. It loses its usual detached quality. It becomes quietly commanding, impregnating.

"It is a question of balance, Sir. It is all a question of balance."

Peter knows that Smith is not talking about nuts, Martinis or perfection. Not in the normal sense of the word. How? He just knows. What is the beanstalk talking about then? Peter feels as if his memory cells have been etched with the single word *BALANCE*. In the same moment Winston, without waiting for dismissal, withdraws. One instant he was towering over Peter, the next he is not there. Not even the slightest sound of a footstep accompanies his disappearance. Peter looks at his empty Martini glass. Suddenly he understands. Smith didn't want me to have another one. So he just disappeared. He does that sometimes. He had done it before. Then Peter realizes that Smith had replied to his inane question with a straight face. For a moment Peter is convinced that Smith had responded to a different question, a question he hadn't asked. Then the moment is gone. He knows Smith to be too intelligent to take himself seriously. So how come a straight answer? Peter reaches out for his glass. It is quite empty. And Smith is gone. He could call after him...

Somehow he doesn't.

She had been wearing a high-cut white blouse, a pair of tweed slacks and a loose shawl draped over her left shoulder. Most women wore something like that, but Cathy looked as though all others were just copying her style. She had a quiet, demure air of owning the space she occupied. Perhaps she does. Peter wonders if she or her father did in fact own it. The waiters seemed to have ignored their assigned tables to rush at the slightest wave of her hand.

To start with, they had chatted about nothing much. Peter refused to admit it to himself, but he was hoping that Cathy would take his mind off the events that had taken place in the Emergency Ward last night. Peter thought he was already immune to death. He had to be. His job is to do the best he can and ignore the consequences. He thinks he does that. But yesterday? What had he done? Yesterday he had carried out the last wishes of a boy's mother. A fat lot of good that would do.

Peter listened to Cathy expounding snippets of gossip circulating about the *crème de la crème* of Montreal's society. Peter found it boring, inconsequential. Quite brutally he told her so. She smiled.

"I was waiting for you to interrupt me."

Suddenly Cathy's smile had something of the Ritz-Xentung. Open, inviting, enigmatic. All at once. She then pulled down her absurd spectacles and asked from under her curved eyelashes: "Politics, religion or sex?"

Peter grins at the recollection. He then asked about her work. He cannot remember a single thing she had said about gossip, but the rest of the conversation he remembers practically *verbatim*.

"Mostly neutrinos, lately." She said. "Not much to look at."

"Why?"

"Too tiny. That is why I have to wear these glasses."

Peter recalls rewarding her with a polite chuckle.

"You know, Peter, my work is very similar to yours. We both deal with life, only you limit yourself to a tiny fraction of it."

When she looked up, Peter felt drawn into those mysterious, polished jade jewels. Then her eyes changed into the Dr. Catherine Mondellay mode. If intelligence can propagate radiation, then her eyes were shimmering with dancing points of light. With green fireflies.

She must have noticed. For the first time since Peter saw her this day, his own face registered interest. Real interest. "Perhaps I have a one-track mind," he remembers chiding himself. "Perhaps life is all that ever did interest me." Perhaps it is.

"Well... It all depends how you look at life," Cathy said. "You may define life in terms of a biochemical construct functioning within predetermined limits of energy transference. You put in food at one end, add a little oxygen, and expel it at another. In between the energy produces certain effects which, if conforming to a majority, we define as normal."

"Others define it as the presence of spirit residing in various portions of our anatomy—depending on religious bias or cultural preference," Peter put in. "Since I have little influence on this premise, I prefer to concentrate on the biochemical construct."

"I thought so. But physicists deal with the macro and the micro universes. We do not have such a privileged choice." Cathy's smile became mysteriously wanton, though it had nothing to do with sex. It expressed a lascivious desire for knowledge.

"Go on...?"

"My predecessors had it easy. Matter was matter, and energy was set apart. Then came Einstein and mixed the two together. He said that the two were one. But that is not all he did. He introduced the concept of a field. Electromagnetic, gravitational... he got rid of the duality of energy and matter, but brought in the duality of field and matter in its place. Yet he wasn't satisfied with it. He died in a state of frustration. Although he recognized that a field is also energy, and energy has mass, and therefore a field is no more than a very diluted form of matter, he could never eliminate the duality of the concept."

"Duality of the concept?" In spite of himself Peter felt beguiled into Cathy's world.

"Yes. He worked all his remaining life to modify the laws governing a field in such a way as to have them stand up in areas where energy is extremely concentrated."

"And that has something to do with your concept of life?" Peter asked.

"To me it does."

Peter thought he saw sadness in Cathy's eyes. "Tell me about it," he urged.

At that moment Cathy's eyes seemed as much to drift towards the distant stars as to recede into the inner realms of her soul. The macro and the micro universes seemed to meet, merge into a single state of consciousness. Peter thought it must be his imagination, but at that moment she was as beautiful as when she had stood naked in his arms. A second later he was embarrassed by his own carnality.

"A stone is alive," she said slowly. "Its life is limited by the period it takes for its atoms, its body, to disintegrate by radiation. It may span millions upon millions of years; it may be little more than a life span of a human being."

Cathy's eyes shone with a life of their own.

Peter sits back as he stares into the images fused into his memory. Is the life in her eyes also limited by the radiation she sends out into the world around her? What is the half-life of jade? Longer than plutonium, he hopes. Then Peter closes his eyes and stares again into the memory of her face.

"A plant goes beyond this," she had said. "Here we evidence a magnetic field. Electromagnetic. Not as strong as in animals, a field nevertheless. This very same field becomes much more powerful in our own species. People call it an aura, an emanation, whatever... A Russian named Kirlian photographed it way back in 1939. Science chose to ignore him, yet all he did was to prove the existence of a field emanating from or surrounding our physical body. Which is our real self? Is this field our soul? A physical soul? Is it our essence?"

"Our soul?" Peter had found it hard to believe that a physicist dealing with pure science would resort to metaphysical concepts.

"Why not? Perhaps our physical soul. A soul that can be measured. You can be sure of one thing. A dead body quickly loses its aura. Check it. Find out for yourself. Perhaps you, Peter, should not be attempting to cure the body but rather repair the damage in the electromagnetic field. The field of life?"

Peter's eyes rest on his empty Martini glass. For a brief moment he wonders why people drink. An escape? From what? From life? Then his thoughts return to Cathy. She has a magnificent ability to breathe life into scientific concepts. Her ideas don't end with a human being.

"Look at our earth," she had said. "There is an electromagnetic field surrounding our whole planet. Do you think if some force were to sweep this field away the earth would die?"

"Sweep the Earth Soul into oblivion?" Peter remembers adding.

"Oblivion? I don't believe there is such a state. Such a force could, perhaps, absorb our field. Absorb it into a Greater Whole..." She had accented the words 'greater' and 'whole' as if to capitalize them. Her tone had given them a mythical quality.

"And solar systems..."

"....and the galaxies. Universes throughout realities... all wrapped in souls, life, pulsating, emitting waves, influencing all that ever came in contact with them..."

"Like people?"

"Like giants.... Like gods of the continuum..."

Peter tries to dismiss the images of the lunch. He wonders what happened to Smith. When the children are away, the house is as dead as a mausoleum. Ruth took them to the country cottage at Mount Burton. About ninety kilometres straight North of Montreal. The last chance before the snow would close the access road for the winter. One could still get there later. Her cottage has its own generator, which maintains an ambient temperature the year round. But the only access would be by a skidoo. They should be back soon. It's already getting dark and they only went for the day.

As if in response to his thoughts the doorbell cuts through the uncanny silence. Forgotten her key? That's unlikely. Peter dallies. By the time he is ready to get up he hears Smith's voice from the hall.

"Very well, thank you, madam. I shall be sure to tell him. *Au revoir, Madame.*"

Next follows the sound of the door closing. So it isn't Ruth yet. Must be some door-to-door peddler. There are so many of them these days. Everyone wants to make a living. It is no longer easy. Too much automation.

"These are for you, sir. Would you like me to put them in water?" The question is presumably academic.

Winston Smith holds an enormous bunch of purplish, white, blue and pink asters. They are partially wrapped in a soggy newspaper. For some reason Winston allows them to drip on the carpet. The flowers look as though someone had collected them

at random, perhaps surreptitiously, and hid them in a newspaper
to conceal detection. Winston manages to hold this large chunk
of someone's front garden in one hand, stretched outwards, as
though maintaining a good distance between himself and the
impromptu bouquet.

Peter is equally as amazed as he is amused by the image
before him.

"Has someone died?" His question is followed by a
prolonged chuckle. "I assure you, Smith, it's not me!"

"Apparently, Sir, nor did anyone else. The lady who
presented these flowers asked me to thank you for saving her
son's life."

Peter's smile remains poised on his face, but there is no
longer any mirth in it. It is a frozen grimace, a remnant of a
smile. His eyes narrow in an effort to understand what Winston is
saying. He refuses to accept the words at their face value.

"The woman said her name is Lucille. Said you would
know who she is."

Throughout all this exchange, Winston's hand has remained
outstretched in front of his equally immobile body. The bouquet
seems to be growing out of his palm. If Peter were in full
command of his senses, he would notice that there are strange
fires smouldering in Winston's eyes; but at this moment Peter is
not at his sharpest. He leans farther back against the armchair as
if retreating in search of support.

"...Lucille?" The name sounds like a question. Then,
haltingly, seemingly gasping for air, he enunciates a single word:
"Mother."

Peter doesn't seem to notice that Winston has withdrawn. He
is alone in the sitting room, in the world. Alone with his thoughts
and the smell of wet newspaper. Do asters have a smell, he
wonders incongruously? Does autumn smell of asters? Mother...
Just touch him.

"Winston!!!"

Peter jumps up from his chair and rushes to the front door.
He flings it open and runs out into the biting drizzle driven by
gusty wind. There is no one there. He runs out onto the street. It
is empty as only a late-autumn street wrapped in ubiquitous rain

can be. Street lamps shimmer, highlighting the descending droplets. Peter seems oblivious to the penetrating cold as he continues to scan the street. His teeth are set, lips drawn back—he seems ready to scream, to call out... Then his arms drop down in resignation. He turns reluctantly. Only now he notices the rain. He quickens his pace. Winston is silhouetted by the light of the open doorway.

"May I be of any service, Sir?" Winston closes the door as Peter enters.

"What...?" Peter seems in a daze.

"You called me, Sir."

"Yes. I did, didn't I..." It doesn't sound like a question.

Peter drags himself to the living room. His feet feel unbearably heavy. His shirt is drenched. He stands facing the dark, cold fireplace, seemingly staring at nothing in particular. Winston passes by him and puts a match to the laid-out fireplace. In seconds the flames dance in the cavernous interior of the old-fashioned hearth. The next moment Winston disappears only to return with a dry shirt and a flannel dressing gown.

"You'd better put these on, Sir," he says quietly.

Peter ignores him. Winston steps forward and holds the shirt in front of Peter's face.

"Put this on now, Sir!"

Winston's voice is of the quality he normally uses only when addressing Jonathan or Moira. Peter obeys without a word. He then takes off his trousers and puts his arms into the dressing gown held out for him by Winston. He continues to stand in front of the fire. Behind him, on a low central table, is an enormous bouquet of multihued asters. There must be hundreds of them.

Peter turns towards the butler.

"Thank you, Winston. You are very kind." He then seems to notice the flowers for the first time. He catches his breath. He always thought of asters as flowers of death, of autumn. Flowers for the graveyard. Are these a celebration of life? They seem to hold the freshness of springtime daisies. Of joy.

"Then why am I so depressed?" Peter asks no one in particular. He is alone.

He is very alone. There is something wrong. An omen of death in spite of the flowers. If it isn't Lucille's son, then what is it? What is dying with an irrevocable certainty of an incurable disease?

"I made you a plate of hot soup."

Peter is completely oblivious to Winston's comings and goings. The butler places the tray with the steaming plate on the low table previously occupied by the Martini. Peter looks at it and shivers. Suddenly he feels very cold. He has no idea how long he had been outside in the rain. There are wet stains all over the carpet. They will dry, he assures himself. They will disappear. Like Winston. Like all things. In time. Only death seems permanent. Eternal.

"Winston?" Peter stares into the fire.

"Yes, Sir?"

"What is life? What is immortality?"

"Immortality is a state of consciousness, Sir. If it were otherwise, we would all live forever."

Peter hardly listens to Winston's answer. His own thoughts are much too pressing. Too vital. Surely the body is immortal. IMMORTAL. All cells can regenerate themselves. Always. *Ad infinitum.*

"Yes, Sir. But the mind is programmed to kill it in due course. Don't you agree?"

"You mean we all commit suicide?" Peter sounds as though he's thinking aloud.

"In a manner of speaking. In a protracted sort of way. When we no longer need our bodies, we discard them. Will there be anything else, Sir?"

Peter looks at Winston as though he sees him for the first time. Then Peter's features contort in an effort to find something missing. Something which happened only a minute or two ago.

"No, thank you. And it's good of you to bring me the soup. It seems I needed it."

Winston again melts into the background.

Peter sits down and tastes the warming puree. His mind is jumping from one thought to another; like a butterfly unable to make up its mind which aster to sit on. He shakes his head in an attempt to clear it.

Lucille. Mother. Henri. And Winston.

And Winston. Something has happened. And then he knows. He had addressed Smith by his first name. He had called him Winston. Peter wonders why. It had seemed appropriate. At least at the time.

But there was something else. He can't put his finger on it.

As Peter swallows the last spoon of the life-giving soup, the front door opens and the sound and Mo and Jo fill the house to overflowing. With life. Ruth is back.

"I wish we had a covered link between the garage and the house. I must have it done before winter," she announces for the hundredth time. She makes this commitment each time it rains. "Mo, Jo, take off your shoes before you step on the carpet!"

They already did. Winston is putting the wet galoshes away. Mo and Jo rush over and jump simultaneously on Peter's lap.

"Hello, Uncle Peter!"

They shout their greeting on the top of their penetrating voices. In fact, they always talk like that. They are extremely alive. Mo and Jo plant wet kisses on both of Peter's cheeks. For a moment he seems stunned. They are so different from all that happened today. Is this what life is?

"We saw a bear! He was so close and so big," Jo announces. The first 'so' is tiny, the second as wide as his arms allow. "As big as..."

"I saw him first!" Mo insists.

"No, you didn't!"

"Yes, I did! And he was much bigger than that." Mo is pointing at the ceiling.

Peter smiles. It all depends on the point of view.

"And he was so close!" she affirms, giving Uncle Peter another hug.

"Dinner is served, Madam." Winston announces from the dining room door.

"I'm coming!" Ruth calls from upstairs. "Children, wash your hands!"

Mo and Jo climb down from Peter's lap, reluctantly, then chase each other to the powder room in the hall. A moment later they emerge and hold out their still damp hands for Peter's inspection. He dries their tiny palms with the flap of his dressing gown and then directs the children to the dining table.

As Peter follows them, he watches Winston putting finishing touches to the table. He is acting as though nothing of any importance had ever happened in his life. Perhaps nothing did. Not to his life. But... And then, as though through an obscure veil, Peter remembers a different place, a different time. Just before the children barged in, he had asked Winston a question. The man had answered. And then something happened. What the devil was it? It was something the butler said or didn't say. Or was it the way he said it...?

"There, now." Ruth's entrance interrupts Peter's thoughts. "Hello, Peter. Had a good day?"

"Thanks, Ruth. Stimulating."

"I noticed the flowers in the living room. They look gorgeous. A secret admirer?" she asks, tasting the soup.

Peter already had his earlier. He sits back, watching his sister's cheeks rosy enough to rival her children's.

"Yes. Sort of."

And then a strange thought crosses his mind. A powerful image converted into an unspoken symbol. He almost says: "They were sent for my funeral."

He almost says it aloud.

* * *

6

The End of an Era

"Can I take it then, Peter, that you accept our offer?" Dr. Brent has a habit of phrasing the obvious in a hypothetical manner.

"I consider it an honour, Sir."

"The position will be retroactive to the first of this month. Welcome to the faculty, Dr. Thornton. It is a pleasure to make official that which had been a reality for the last few years anyway."

The last statement did reflect the truth. In all but name, Peter had been a member of the teaching staff for at least two years. He just hadn't been officially recognized as such, nor had he benefited from the attendant perks. Overnight, in fact as of the first of December, his income will be quadrupled. He would no longer have to perform any night duties. He would still be on call, periodically, but from the comfort of his own home. Heretofore, he had been the nearest approximation to slave labour our political system allows.

Peter knows that he cannot blame the Chief for this apparently flagrant oversight. The government has full control over the finances of all facets of Medicare, including the hospital budget. To elevate Peter to the Teaching Staff, Dr. Brent would have had to dismiss someone to make room for him, and probably suffer punitive litigation. For his part, Peter could have left the General and practised general medicine elsewhere. He was empowered to do so since he had passed the Provincial License Examinations. This he had done over three years ago.

The Fellowship was not necessary for the practice of the profession, though it was recommended for positions of influence and prestige. There was a time when such had been very important to Peter. That was before he became a Fellow.

Peter had dedicated the last four years almost exclusively to the procurement of the position that had just been offered him. But now, hardly a few minutes later, his back pressed against Dr. Brent's office doors, from the outside, it feels like a great let-down. All the titles, the professional recognition and the attendant creature comforts exemplified by much greater income for much less work seemed like an anticlimax.

"Your new duties will be assigned shortly," Dr. Brent had said.

He could have added: "...as well as the allocation of hospital beds (reserved for our boys), the number of rotating interns and residents, the qualified doctors, all of whom will work round the clock while you reap the financial benefits from their labours—they will all be also assigned to you." This is the system. The time-worn, proven method of exploitation. In the name of tradition. A system of fleas feeding upon fleas, sucking their blood for the benefit of maintaining the almighty *status quo*.

"I had to go through this, my boy..." a senior staff member had once told him. "Your time will come to play golf during the afternoons, my boy... Your time will come!"

My time has come.

"I don't want the stupid position, Dr. Brent!" he could have said.

But he didn't. He couldn't have. Dr. Brent didn't invent the system. He doesn't even practice it. He alone continues to work round the clock while his colleagues practice their medicine on the green fairways or in the plush offices of investment brokers. After all, was this not precisely Peter's plan? His intention? Is this not why he had spent the last ten years slaving day and night, giving up personal life, personal pleasure, holidays, even the thought of a family? All to gain recognition?

No bloody way!

Peter glances over his shoulder to make sure no one overheard him speaking to himself. Lately, he's been looking over his shoulder quite often. He's been living in a state of agitation, of inner turmoil. During the last month he'd discharged his hospital duties in a strange atmosphere of an emotional vacuum. Could it be that he'd lost more than physical contact with his patients? He is afraid to touch them. He tells the nurses, the interns, the residents to do the actual examinations while he limits his participation to diagnoses, once the facts are presented to him.

He has to. Since the Henri incident, he is afraid to touch anyone. He is not about to jeopardize his life's work because some hysterical woman indulges in some voodoo manipulations to save her son's life. Peter has direct evidence of the power of such women, but he refuses to have anything to do with them. Lucille had a tan complexion, probably some Creole blood. He is a doctor, a damn good one. Not some mumbo-jumbo healer. He had worked too hard to lose it all now. Harder than anyone he has ever met.

Lucille Ouellette. As common a name as you can think of in Quebec. Yet a name indelibly imprinted on Peter's mind. A simple-looking woman, but what an actress! Why was she bent on destroying him? And her sister! The stupid girl is actually a trainee nurse right here, at the General. What bloody luck!

And she talked. She even practically convinced Dr. Cunningham that the X-rays didn't really get mixed up. What damn nonsense... Peter took time to examine the boy's plates in Radiology. Rearranging the records wasn't easy, but not harder than passing the Fellowship exams. By the time Peter finished, there was no sign of a twisted spine or of the internal abrasions Cunningham had spoken about. Not that Peter blamed Cunningham. With over fifty stretchers brought in on a weekend evening, it's a wonder that more data didn't get screwed up. Peter remembers being on duty in the Emergency. God Almighty! So many years... The art was to stay awake, let alone carry all the cases constantly in one's head. Seventy-two hours on duty. Continuously. Sleeping propped up against the wall, falling off the toilet seat... It's a crazy system. Tradition!

Nuts!!!

It wasn't easy. Whatever the reality, Peter couldn't afford another misunderstanding. Another miracle. Imagine being a physician and avoiding touching your patient.

I am a physician. Please, God. Let me stay that way!

Only now, a month later, the junior staff and particularly the nurses are beginning to treat Dr. Thornton as a normal human being. For a while they gave him surreptitious looks as if expecting him to wave a magic wand. But he was too smart for them. This trick of not touching the patients really worked.

"I got them where I want them!" Peter awards himself a congratulatory smile.

"Then why do I feel like a cheat and a liar?" he muses a second later.

Ruth is delighted with Peter's appointment to the teaching staff. In Upper Westmount one is expected to reach the top. That's what it's all about. People who envy those on the higher slopes seldom realize what effort goes into reaching the upper reaches. The days when Papa's or even Mama's college connections translated into instant success are long over. True, they don't hurt, but they would do you no good at all unless you worked your butt off on top of that. Except in politics, of course. There, connections are *all* that matters. Some things never change.

"Does this mean that we shall see more of you, Peter?" Ruth asks as Peter tells her about Dr. Brent's offer.

"I haven't exactly accepted the position. I just told him I consider it an honour...."

Ruth looks up, her eyes half as large again as usually.

"Peter! Have you been drinking?"

"Well, Brent said that I have been a teaching Fellow for the last two years, anyway. So why change things?" Peter deliberately speaks in an offhanded manner.

It works. Ruth's face shows a deep concern.

"You need a holiday. I shall call Judy. She will let you use her Palm Beach condo for a week or two." She speaks to Peter's back. "Peter? Peter! You need a rest."

Peter had to turn his back on his sister-in-law to hide his grin. He needs humour to release the tension that seems to build up each day in the hospital. In the past he felt tired. Often very tired. Now he only feels an overwhelming stress. It builds up slowly during the day, then gradually diminishes at home. A cycle.

"Surely you don't want me to take the position just for the money?" he says over his shoulder. His grin is becoming broader.

"And may I ask what is wrong with money?"

Ruth's face is perfectly serious. God knows she works hard enough to maintain her standard of living, Andrew's life insurance policy notwithstanding.

Peter manages to control his features sufficiently to wipe away his supercilious smirk. At this particular moment he feels superior to the world around him. He feels free, unfettered. He turns round and hands Ruth a flat suede box. It has the gold insignia of Montreal's best jewellers.

"Nothing that I can think of. Unless one spends it on trinkets. By the way, these are for your last Christmas."

Last year Peter had spent the whole of Christmas at the General. Some of his colleagues were already married. He took on their duty to allow them to spend their holidays at home with their families. Peter did not regard his action as magnanimous or sacrificial. He preferred spending his time at the hospital. Medicine was his life. Under the circumstances, Christmas became so meaningless to him that he had also forgotten to buy Ruth a present. Later on, he had made it up to the kids, Winston got the usual cheque, but Ruth? Well, somehow later on it seemed too late.

Today, on his way back from the General, Peter suddenly realized how totally meaningless money was to him. He realized that whatever his motivation in the pursuit of excellence in his profession, it wasn't and never could have been money. Once he may have thought otherwise. But it wasn't so. Not in his heart. The desire for financial success was never any more than a conditioned reflex, a platitude fed by the environment in which he functioned. Peter neither had nor has any objection to money. It is just that he had no desire whatever to assign even the smallest effort towards its acquisition. Money is necessary for the performance of certain tasks. Once such are taken care of, money loses its *raison d'être*.

When Peter was no more than a hundred yards from home, he hailed a taxi and told the driver to take him to the best jewellers in town. The drivers servicing Upper Westmount are used to unorthodox requests. The man drove Peter to Pillington's, waited until Peter did what he had to, and returned him to the Westmount address. Peter's action was an intuitive, spur-of-the-moment caprice, perhaps motivated by fear that his new position on the Teaching Staff of the General might swell his bank account to unprecedented if not ignominious heights. Peter spent more money on the ruby earrings and necklace than he had spent during his last two years of residency on keeping his body and soul together.

Ruth's eyes again widen perceptibly. She seems to regard the insignia on the elegant box with a strange fascination. She knows the name, of course, she has just not had the occasion to open one of their boxes before.

"Oh... oh, my God!" It would have been an exclamation if it weren't for the fact that her utterance is hardly audible. "Wha-a-at... what are these?"

"Oriental rubies. Supposed to be the best. Andrew once told me that your skin and hair colouring were specially designed for rubies."

Although Ruth's mouth remains open, no further questions follow in the succeeding seconds. Peter is really enjoying himself. This is the first time in months that he feels the taste of freedom. I am broke, he tells himself, and I like it.

"Got them on sale. Bit of luck, really."

For a moment Peter is afraid Ruth will refuse to accept the belated present. He need not have worried. Ruth is too stunned to make any intelligent statements.

"Andrew....?" she whispers at last.

"Right. He told me to get them for you."

"For me?" Her voice is almost normal.

"Didn't have much time before."

Ruth gets up, walks to the hall mirror and slowly puts on the necklace, then the earrings. Peter looks over her shoulder. He thinks that Andrew was right. The rubies were made for her. Ruth studies herself in the mirror, then turns around and faces Peter.

"I have no idea how much these cost. But I know a liar when I see one. Why did you do it, Peter?"

"I thought you would like them."

"Don't be stupid. There is no woman alive who wouldn't love them. Why did you do it?"

"A Fellow's folly?"

Ruth doesn't buy that either.

Peter looks at the fiery droplets of blood around Ruth's slim neck. He smiles at the filigree perfection of the necklace, at the way it enhances and complements Ruth's own natural beauty. Andrew was crazy to die at forty-seven.

"I guess I had to," Peter shrugs. "I needed to be free..."

Ruth continues to stare at Peter's face. He looks triumphant yet haggard. A contradiction. A living paradox. Her face reflects her concern.

"Is there anything I can do?" she asks.

She knew nothing about Peter's encounters with black magic. Or with the stupid statistics. Obviously, if Winston suspected anything, he kept it to himself. Just as well.

"I don't know, Ruth, but thank you for asking."

There is a silence punctuated by the sound of Jo and Mo having a lively argument in the playroom. Then, suddenly, there is a strained silence. Winston must have said something after all.

"I don't need these, but I shall look after them for you for as long as you want. You are very sweet, brother dear." Ruth walks up to Peter and gives him a warm if sisterly kiss on both cheeks. Then she pulls back, holds him at arm's length and looks him straight in the eye. "And you are quite a good liar, as well."

"Thank you, sister dear. I try!"

Peter is happy. For the first time in his life he is broke. Truly broke. He might have a few dollars in his pocket, but he couldn't take Cathy to a restaurant. It is a strange feeling. He knows, of course, that come the end of the month, he will receive a fat cheque from the government. The elegant salary of a Teaching Fellow.

Still, for now he is free.

For now he has covered his tracks. Dr. Brent said not a word about the statistics. Not a word. He couldn't have heard about Henri. The stupid nurse, Lucille's sister, had spread all sorts of gossip, but the facts had contradicted her. The blood samples, the X-ray, the diagnostic notes. It wasn't as though Henri had been dying and didn't. It was as though he was never in danger of losing his life. Cunningham was the most difficult one to convince. Finally he, too, had credited it to fatigue.

"It never happened to me before, Dr. Thornton," he insisted when Peter told him that we all make mistakes. "I just don't see how...?"

"Just forget it, Cunningham. You are the best we have. Don't let it get to you!"

That worked. Dr. Thornton was not known to throw compliments around loosely. Let sleeping dogs lie, Cunningham told himself. Anyway, there were new patients requiring his attention. A great many during the last month. And Peter hadn't physically touched a patient since. Not once. He couldn't. He was too scared.

I shouldn't let it get to me, either, he kept repeating in the solitude of his office. The problem was that Peter knew that Cunningham hadn't made any mistakes.

"Here comes Megabyte!"
"Beware of the Prancing Paragon!"
"Look out, the QQ's on the prowl!"

The nurses and interns have many names for Dr. Thornton. Behind his back. Peter is not particularly concerned about the opinion junior staff hold of him. The first moniker refers to his incredible, computer-like memory. The second to his habit of appearing where least expected, with full knowledge of the medical problem in hand. But the last is neither deserved nor fair. It stands for Quintessential Quack. Peter knows his job and is damn good at it. Sometimes he even surprises himself. Lately he found he could quote whole paragraphs from the medical journals. *Verbatim*. He is perfectly aware that the younger physicians are in awe of his knowledge. This is exactly as it should be. Once, it seems like ages ago, he also had been in awe of his Teaching Fellows.

But there were other, more insidious problems.

Peter seems quite unaware that he was becoming stilted, emotionally disjointed. He seems equally unaware that he was treating people like objects under a microscope. Evidently he cannot help himself. He had to create a barrier between himself and the patient. He must keep his distance. *His* distance. They, the residents, do not seem to have noticed that he doesn't touch patients anymore. Not that he believes in voodoo or any other bloody nonsense. Given time, things will get back to normal. He is sure of it. Most of the time.

Surely, the charade cannot last forever. Sooner or later he will have to demonstrate to some medical upstart a correct procedure which will involve physical contact with a patient. Peter is half convinced that nothing will happen. Nothing peculiar, that is.

He is half convinced. He is also half scared out of his wits.

The next evening Ruth has a splitting migraine. She has been suffering for hours. She hadn't said a word, but Peter can see the pain in her eyes. Peter loves Ruth as though she were his own sister. She is his only family. Peter goes up to his bedroom and brings back a single pink pill wrapped in a tissue. It is a placebo. He gives it to Ruth and tells her to suck on it. He says it is an experimental sample. Not yet available on the market. Very confidential. He then walks behind her and holds her head gently between his palms. The migraine disappears. Instantly.

Peter goes straight up to his room. His hands shake for an hour.

Today, Peter must touch a patient. A number of patients. He is to demonstrate a new diagnostic procedure to the Teaching Staff and senior residents. He had spent three days last week at the Victoria Hospital to learn it. He had been instructed by Dr. George Tsan himself. For at least a generation, Dr. Tsan had pioneered all aspects of oriental healing methods. The Nobel Prize had given him world recognition. Acupuncture, acupressure and later electro-pressure techniques had become an important part of general medicine. Particularly in combination with computer technology. There is very little nowadays that one can accomplish without electronics. Now it is Peter's turn to pass on the manoeuvre he had learned from the great man. He has no choice.

Dr. Brent will be present.

They all meet at 1400 hours in the Demonstration Theatre. The residents are waiting at the door. Peter enters with Dr. Brent on his heels. Three other members of the teaching staff are already in the theatre. The overhead scanners are ready. Peter will manipulate the patient under the scanners, which will record his every movement from all possible angles. Obviously, it must be done by hand. Both hands. His hands must come in direct, prolonged contact with the patient. The manoeuvre relies on judgment and experience. Peter is good on judgment, poor on experience.

"Gentlemen." Peter feels hot in the $18°$ C temperature. This is the first time he will be teaching the Teachers. He is nervous as hell. "As you know, I have spent three days at the Victoria to learn the Ganzhou manoeuvre. We shall all try it on each other without engaging the Neurotrone. Once we feel easy in its application, nurse Prim will wheel in the patients whom we shall treat using milliampere doses from the Neurotrone. When we are confident of our technique, we shall commence the full treatment."

The silence seems filled with reverence. This is the Tsan-Gauzhou manoeuvre. It is a privilege to witness its first application. Yet no one volunteers to be the guinea pig. They are all familiar with Neurotrone procedures, but only with the standard electro-pressure techniques. They know that the technique is akin to homeopathy. In small doses it saves lives. Used in excess it can kill.

Dr. Brent steps forward.

"Would you care to try it on me, Dr. Thornton?"

The younger physicians feel and look embarrassed. It's too late.

"Thank you, Dr. Brent. Please remove your shirt and vest. Then lie down, please."

Dr. Brent does as he is told. Peter goes through the complex preparation, sets up the Neurotrone for neutral, then demonstrates the manoeuvre. They all take turns in examining Dr. Brent. Then each other. They work quickly, with professional efficiency. Soon they have all had more than one turn. As they get dressed, there are murmurs of appreciation. Peter has scored a hit.

"Bring in the first patient," Peter commands.

The nurse leaves the theatre and returns with a man on a wheeled stretcher. The patient is about sixty years old, looking older. He is already stripped to the waist. His skin is a sickly yellow. One of the symptoms. Peter takes over.

"Watch carefully. Remember: the object is to minimize the voltage by paying equal attention to the scanner and to the patient's reactions. The synaptic response to the Neurotrone..."

At this point Dr. Thornton's language becomes very technical. In the last few years medicine had passed the point of no return. Over fifty percent of procedures had been relegated (or raised) to computer technology. The residual half remains in human hands. A delicate balance between the old and the new. With a good dose of Oriental influence. Computer-assisted surgical procedures have become the order of the day. For much of the diagnostic work, the physicians also rely on the computer's probing capability. Yet with all this progress, the human hand still remains the most sensitive instrument for certain manoeuvres.

Peter works with poise, control and confidence. The patient is the sole object of his concentration. Whatever may have churned at the back of his mind these last few months is of absolutely no consequence. Dr. Peter Thornton is a physician solving a medical problem. That is all. That is all he has ever wanted to do.

To guide man towards inherent immortality.

The patient's breathing becomes deeper, more regular. An instant effect. The manoeuvre works. It must have been administered magnificently. The other doctors applaud. More patients are wheeled in. All the staff take turns. More often than not, Peter has to intervene. With his hands. There are instant results. The Teaching Staff is spellbound. They do their best to emulate Peter's exact movements. They are all experienced physicians. Some with years of similar manoeuvres behind them. True, not identical but similar. Yet none can begin to match Peter's incredible dexterity. The patients seem to improve at the very touch of his fingers. Only Peter is too involved to notice. Peter is a doctor. A total physician practising his craft. First time in a month.

God, it feels good!

All in all, eleven patients are treated. Six of them benefit from Peter's direct or partial participation in the application of the manoeuvre. Four respond well to the treatment administered by other physicians. They are doing quite well. One woman virtually recovers while Peter demonstrates the technique before he has time to apply the Neurotrone. The patient improves sufficiently to be wheeled back to her ward.

Such things happen. Occasionally.

Don't they?

Peter slept very well. For the first time in a long while he feels at peace with himself. He takes a long bath and comes downstairs feeling on top of the world. He greets Winston with a broad grin. Winston serves him orange juice, coffee, scrambled eggs, toast and marmalade. A big breakfast. Like on holidays.

At 8:05 the telephone rings.

"Dr. Brent, for you, Sir." Winston hands Peter the telephone.

"Thornton, Dr. Brent. Good morning to you!" Peter's voice is practically joyful.

"I must see you at once, Peter."

"And how are things at the General?"

"In my office. Now!" The Chief doesn't actually raise his voice, but his tone is commanding.

"Have they all recovered?"

"Only the six you treated or manipulated yourself. I checked the scanners."

The Tsan-Gauzhou manoeuvre should bear results in three to four weeks. After initial improvement the patient basically reverts to the previous condition. Only repeated application, over a period of time, is expected to lead to complete recovery.

"And the others?" Peter's voice is conversational.

"The others responded quite well, but..."

"But they haven't recovered completely..." It wasn't a question.

There is a prolonged silence. Neither man seems anxious to resume the conversation. Neither man knows exactly what to say.

"Well, Dr. Brent. I am grateful for your call."

"Peter, I spoke to Dr. Tsan this morning. It just isn't possible..."

"Yes?"

There is silence. Dr. Brent seems to have difficulty breathing. Peter is perfectly relaxed. Almost gay.

"I'll see you, Dr. Brent. Sometime. When I recover..."

Peter replaces the receiver in its holder. There is little more to say. Both men know it. The General is a temple of medicine. That is all one can practice there. Medicine.

Peter thanks Winston for breakfast and goes upstairs. Winston's eyes follow him with a strange satisfaction. Under the circumstances it doesn't make any sense. Peter stays in his room for about an hour. He puts his things in order. Then he goes to see the children. He plays with them. He touches them. He is very tactile in all the little games. At long last he says good-bye to them.

"Going to the hospital, Uncle Peter?" Jo asks when Peter puts him down on the floor. He then lifts Mo up, swirls her in the air, kisses her cheeks before answering.

"Not exactly, little fellah. But I shall be back. In the meantime, look after your Mom for me."

Ruth isn't there. She left last night for New York.

"Are you going away, Uncle Peter?" Mo seems too perceptive for her years.

"No, Moira. I am not going away. I am not sure where I am going. I only know that I must go. Somewhere. Now be good, you two. Until I come back. Promise?"

"Yes, Uncle Peter. I promise!" The two speak in unison.

Peter leaves the room and goes to the front hall. Winston is waiting for him with his coat. He has gotten the winter coat out. A coat Peter hardly ever used in town.

"You'd better take this one, Sir. It's quite nippy this morning."

Peter doesn't argue. He seldom does with Winston.

"Thanks, Winston."

Then Peter looks up into the steady eyes a full head higher than his own. Winston's eyes are dark, sober, reliable. There is also something else in them. Something Peter hadn't had much time for lately. Or for the last ten years or so. Deep in those dark eyes there is a great serenity. A sort of timeless peace. And something else...

"Thanks again, Winston," Peter repeats. He seems a little mesmerized.

The two men shake hands. Peter has never shaken hands with a butler before. He wonders why. He pushes the door open and steps outside. He walks towards the sidewalk. Winston was right. The air is crisp. Later on there will be snow. It is that kind of a day. For a little while, Peter stands still and looks in the direction of the General Hospital. Then he smiles. The smile stays on his lips as he turns and takes the opposite direction. Down the hill. Towards the river.

* * *

Winter

"Shall mortal man be
more just than
God?"

Job 4:17

7

A Search

Time matters little. A lazy morning. An empty afternoon. An end of an era. A challenge? A new beginning. Down, down, south, ever down, towards the rising haze, towards the breathing, misty river. Peter's synthetic soles make little sound on the descending sidewalk. His feet follow their own predetermined course. An escape towards freedom.

Cowardice?

Down, down, ever lower, lower, away from life. From fame. From money, recognition. From Ruth and the children, from Winston. From Cathy. From Catherine. What would she say? Would her jade eyes laugh or sneer? Would she perhaps cry? A scientific mind giving up without a fight. Fight what? I don't even have windmills. Peter de la Mancha. Nor have I a Sancho Panza to lean on.

A self-inflicted funeral of dreams.

Peter stops and looks back. Only yesterday, it seemed verdant and golden and crimson in its beauty. A mountain of glory. A status symbol. Upper Westmount. Now it seems cold and somber. Peter regards the sloping streets with a strange indifference yet also with a certain detached curiosity. It's been ten years since he took a walk without a definite destination. Without hurrying, without being preoccupied about something important. Like a matter of life or death. Literally.

And now? Freedom. A persistent sense of unfettered freedom. Freedom of one who escapes, alive, from a battlefield. From the field of glory.

"What else can I do?"

Two people stare at Peter as he voices the question. He was addressing no one. Perhaps only the mountain.

He refuses to feel guilty. I owe nothing to no one, he avers his own thoughts. Should I die, this very moment, my slate would be clean. No man or beast could lay claim to my burden. I have none. None at all.

Or have I?

That's stupid! Everyone is indebted. If for nothing else than for the air he breathes. For the blue sky, even if it is turning opaque... Peter turns up his collar. The wind is northerly, bending his overlong crewcut forward. A progenitor of snow. Then once again he looks up at the mountain.

On his right is Upper, on his left the almost-as-good Middle Westmount. He walks, looking at the trees stripped down to millions of twigs reaching in mute supplication towards heaven. They needn't bother. God's face is hidden behind the heavy, impenetrable clouds. Trees! Trees! There is nothing there to answer your prayers, Peter feels like shouting. You might as well wait for springtime.

Will there still be a springtime?

Peter's feet thread an up-and-down zigzag towards the West. Like Cinderella's, his shoes, imbued with power of their own, refuse to leave the conclave of iconoclastic barbarians who took away his claim to fame. The Upper crust of Upper Westmount. You do not practice quackery in the Upper Reaches. Not among those who rose high by the use of mind power. The higher realm leaves no room for charlatans, quacks or mountebanks.

Peter's feet turn sharp left.

Perhaps the Middle ground will offer some solace. Perhaps people here will be less demanding. Peter glances at some men, women, then peers into their faces, searching for eye contact. So many people. Busy, contented, just leaving the restaurants after their three-Martini luncheons. Is there no one here who would like to be cured? Of anything?

A taxi divests itself of the body of an overindulged woman.

An army of minks crawl up her back, then come down her front in orderly, regimented fashion. She seems content to carry their burden on her overstuffed torso. She seems content—behind a mask of powder. Below, a red smear of a smile gone astray. Perhaps she gnawed the minks with her own teeth in order to wear them?

I, too, have shed blood once, Peter muses, a dry, sardonic smile distorting his own mouth. In the operating theatre.

It is time to turn down, southward. There are no people here. No people who need me. Just mannequins.

The sky seems to get darker with each step Peter directs down towards the river. The streets now are hardly sloping. The universe is becoming flatter, fairer. More honest. And then, down the last slope, ahead are the tracks—the great divider between the haves and the have-nots.

Where are the trees?

Peter peers left and right. Why are there no trees below Lower Westmount? No maples, no oaks, no sedate elms to cast their protective shade even on a summer eve. No rest for the weary. For anyone. Perhaps there are no people down here, either. The streets are deserted.

Peter looks at his watch. It is only 3:30. Have I been wandering for hours? Strange. Getting so dark so early. Peter had never noticed the exact changes in the natural daylight. Never had time. The General kept artificial lights on at all times. Why not? Energy was no longer a problem. Perhaps the only problems were the people. Or lack of them.

His feet reach the tracks, two hard lines of rust on either side of the sidewalk. But... where are the people? Peter is quite alone now. Alone and strangely lonely. He senses that if he were to meet someone, he might have to approach him with the stealth of a hunter. He is entering a desert. A hostile, forgotten, bereft of trees jungle.

His feet step onto the tracks. It is quite flat now.

The old CP rails are no more than an old, discarded, once mighty symbol of national unity. From ocean to ocean... Peter looks left and right and he thinks of Cathy. Of Dr. Catherine Mondellay and her relativistic physics. Five sets of rusty rails bear witness to the Einsteinian postulates. Parallel lines really are receding into the darkness seemingly to meet, to unite, to join somewhere. Perhaps in infinity, though it seems—a lot sooner. At least they did once. Now most of them are torn up for scrap metal. No more railways. Not even monorails. Those few who still wish to watch the sun set over the Pacific must fly. Most prefer to see it on their 3D projectors. Perhaps there is too much comfort in the world. Perhaps there should be more than 70% of the population working.

Peter wonders why some streets are wrapped in great, mature trees and other streets, like down here, stretch like a barren wasteland framed by hard walls of masonry. Prison walls behind which people vegetate, seemingly resigned, hoping for a better day? Peter had met some of them at the General. Mostly accident victims. Ex-workers, ex-labourers, ex-members of the human race. Yet, once stripped of the pungent rags, scrubbed, rinsed and wrapped in a hospital tunic, they all looked the same. Almost human. Except for their eyes. Those glassy windows-to-the-soul seemed empty, devoid even of hunger. They stare at you in abject apathy. With the indifference of December. Of an approaching winter. Like today.

The St-Henri syndrome, they called it.

Peter remembers seeing photographs in which St-Henri had been semi-fashionable, especially on either side of the Lachine Canal. The bohemian gypsies, who had once wandered as far east as *rue St-Denis*, then hovered for a spell among the limestone façades of Old Montreal, had moved southwest to the Lachine Canal. Then. Way-back-when...

There the artists dwelled longer than expected. Like a last fling. Last chance.

They were gone now.

Yet then there were trees on the sides of the Canal. Trees casting quivering images on the narrow, still water. Like Monet, or Sisley. Later the trees had been cut down, mostly for firewood. It was during the third Long Depression. The Permanent One, they called it.

Why is it that when a city expands beyond its natural borders, only the urban Westmounts retain their limits? What expands are the slums. Only now they call them the suburbs. By the time Montreal had reached a population of nine million, the slums extended from St-Henri to the foot of St. Bruno. Another mountain. Even as the crow flies, kilometres away. Or miles, as they still said in Westmount. Those who had been successful either remained on the tight slopes of Westmount or moved out with their modems, their communication paraphernalia, to the still distant lakes of the far-reaching Laurentians. Fuel, once again, is cheap. Practically all business could be conducted by means of electronics. Yet the vast masses preferred to remain in a hovel—in the ever-expanding, inexorably advancing, yet stagnant, unemployed suburbia. They run like lemmings only to drown, to fall prey to the magnetic attraction of a Metropolis. Perhaps like ants—only seldom working.

There is no hunger here. At least no physical hunger. All people are granted quite adequate subsistence. For nothing. Abundant energy drives armies of robots, which result in an era of growing abundance. An era of a common denominator, the lowest possible but adequate. An extra reward for breeding fewer children. Finally.

Some still work—part time. The few are getting fewer. It is too easy to do nothing. Just vote for Solidarity. Too easy to bring others to your own comfortable level.

Peter has no idea for how long he's been walking.

Away from the glaring street lamps, the spaces between the buildings are filled with darkness. Even here, cheap energy converts the pavement into daytime. The lamps provide a mixture of ultraviolet and infrared radiation. The sporadic snowflakes which gyrate downward from behind Peter's back melt as soon as they touch the concrete. Only on the sides, along the narrow setbacks, their white presence shimmers in the fast-approaching darkness.

A wilderness of illuminated concrete.

Peter seems oblivious to the wind, the snow. His mind is luxuriating in a silent void. He refuses to think, to analyze his actions. His drooping head directs his eyes downwards, towards the cold pavement. Now and again he peers ahead, then to his left, his right, then reassured down again towards his feet. A million lumens cascade with the snow onto the empty sidewalk. Perhaps there are no people here, either. Not even behind the blind squares of the windows. Only the light-washed pavement. Perhaps someone had switched on the street lights and left them on in silent homage to those who once lived here—a cemetery of the long departed.

Suddenly Peter sees a furtive figure cut a dark shadow across the street. Almost as soon as he sees it, a hole opens in the stucco wall and the figure is swallowed up within a feebly glowing interior. Peter crosses the street. He was right. It is a shop front. The sign says: TAVERN. Underneath, in tiny letters: *Gaston Brown, proprieteur.*

A diner?

Peter pushes the door open and enters. It is darker inside than out. A lot darker. It must be the people. Perhaps they do not like daylight. The semidarkness, the heavy air, the background to an incongruous lightness of a *valse musette,* stops Peter at the door until his eyes readjust to the murky interior. Why do these cave dwellers prefer darkness to light?

Eight tables with red and white chequered cloth are shoved against the even darker walls panelled up to waist level with dark-stained wood dado. A lone man sits at one table, another stands at the counter talking to the owner. The trio look up as Peter walks in.

"A *soup d'onion*?" Peter asks the man behind the counter.

The man doesn't answer. He continues to stare at Peter from behind a row of glasses hanging upside down over the service counter.

"*Bouillabaisse?*" he asks at last.

Peter assumes that *soup d'onion* written in large letters over the headboard as *spécialité de la maison* is not on today. He smiles to himself.

"*Ça va,*" he replies.

The man lifts a flap in the counter, goes over to a table and smacks the chequered tablecloth with the rag attached to his belt. Even in the relative darkness of the tavern, Peter sees a cloud of dust rewarding the owner's hospitality. The man straightens the tablecloth and points Peter towards the table.

"*Ça va?*"

"Yes, thank you."

Peter wonders if the man speaks any English. He can't tell by looking. The place looks pseudo-French, the music is definitely not English. By the time Peter takes off his coat and throws it on the empty chair opposite, the steaming bowl of soup arrives. It is the largest bowl of soup Peter has ever seen. The man also places on the tablecloth of dubious cleanliness a large chunk of fresh, crusty bread.

"Anything else, Sir?" he asks in English with hardly a trace of an accent.

"Not for now, thank you."

Peter needs this soup. Until he came in, he had no idea how cold he was. His hands are now too stiff to hold the spoon. He rubs them together to restore life into them.

The fish soup is as tasty as any he has ever eaten. Of course, he's so hungry that anything resembling food would taste good. He tries to eat slowly, to let the warmth percolate from his stomach to the rest of his body. It does. As he thaws out, Peter begins to study the small tavern. The owner, his guest at the counter, as well as the only other customer at the window table, are all sipping draft beer.

A cold night for a beer, Peter thinks.

A cold night for a walk through the cemetery, he also acknowledges. The soup has done him good. He begins to feel human. Peter vaguely wonders what made him walk all the way down to this part of Montreal. He hadn't planned it. He merely wanted to walk so as to clear his head. To do some thinking. In fact he hadn't thought very much at all. Then Peter remembers saying good-bye to the children. Is this where I belong, he muses? What am I searching for?

"Do you have any rooms?" Peter asks the man at the counter.

The man again regards Peter without answering. Why would anyone want to stay here? But the sign over the counter also says CHAMBRES. Perhaps they are for people who wish to sleep off the beer they downed at the owner's counter.

"Ten dollars in advance," the man replies eventually.
"Eight for two nights, thirty-five for a week."

His voice trails off. He doesn't expect Peter to stay for more
than a night.

"I'll take one. May I use your telephone?"

The publican points with his chin to the receiver on his right
on the counter. Peter nods, finishes his soup. He has no idea why
he asked the man for a room. He knows only that he cannot
negotiate a walk back to Upper Westmount. Not just the getting
there—theoretically he could dial for a taxi. No. It is the being
there that he cannot quite face yet. He gets up and walks to the
telephone. The earpiece is greasy. He dials his home number.
Winston answers.

"I shan't be home tonight," he says.

"Very good, Sir."

Peter hangs up.

"How much for the soup?"

"*Deux piastres.*"

The man changes to French. As cheap as the cafeteria at the
General, Peter feels like saying, only tastier, if you don't get
poisoned. He pulls out $15 from his wallet and puts the notes on
the counter.

"One night," he says.

The publican gives him back $3. Does one tip here, Peter
wonders?

"If you wait at the table, I'll get your room ready."

The publican presses a button on the counter. A woman
with a cigarette hanging from the corner of her mouth appears
from the darkness behind him. Why is it so dark here? The
people seem to shun light on purpose. It can't be the money.
Electricity is practically free.

"Number three, upstairs." He points to Peter at the table.
"One night."

The woman goes away without saying a word. Ten minutes
later she is back. She nods to the man, presumably her husband,
and waits in silence.

"Your room is ready, mister," the publican announces. Is
there pride in his voice?

Peter looks at his watch. It is 6:30 p.m. He wants to linger, to watch people. Not much to look at here. He gets up and picks up his coat. The woman is still waiting for him at the counter. She looks tired. Or, maybe, just bored. As they climb the stairs, Peter tries to hold his breath. There is a distinct smell of a dog having urinated on the carpet. Lots of dogs. Or cats. Or anybody. An old smell. The woman leads him up two flights of stairs and leaves him at an open door. Before she leaves she gives him an old-fashioned key. It looks like a museum piece. Cast iron with a decorative ring at one end. One could see such a key only in books on history. In Westmount, that is.

Peter closes the door and looks around. The room is small, clean, but the air is stale and overheated. Cheap energy. A coloured print of the Immaculate Heart of Jesus is tacked to the white-painted wall at the head of the bed. Peter wonders if the picture gave comfort to the previous occupier of the bed. Then he looks around and sniffs cautiously. At least the smell of urine did not percolate from the staircase. Peter walks to the single window. A vertical sliding sash from the previous century.

I bet they still have iron counterweights hiding in the stiles, he murmurs to himself.

He tries to lift the window. It doesn't budge. He hangs his weight on the upper frame. It opens a crack and stays there. Better than nothing, he shrugs.

The window is facing the street. Peter leans against the frame and watches the flakes hover over the sidewalk and then disappear as though they had never existed. A short life. Not like humans. We are immortal. He grins in spite of himself. He wonders why we are immortal.

From his present vantage point he sees more people than he had noticed when he walked down from Westmount. Perhaps I wasn't really looking, he muses. Perhaps my search for human beings wasn't in earnest. Maybe I don't really want to find people. They might well be better off without me.

Maybe I died and this is hell.

The street is a lot lighter than his room. The inhabitants of St-Henri seem to live in hiding. When they walk down the street they walk fast, as fast as they can, and then they disappear into the darker doorways. In fact, people don't seem to walk here. They dart through the uncomfortable glare of street lamps from one house to another, or to a tavern, or a shop. Whatever. There are a lot more of them now. Perhaps they only leave their lairs after dark. Peter sees at least five men and two women enter the tavern downstairs. They must be gravitating towards beer. And company. I should be down there, with them—Peter breathes on the window pane, clouding it over. The mist clears quickly. Even here they use double glazing. Peter continues to stare out onto the street. In half an hour he counts thirty-seven people and eleven cars. How come the street was so empty before? Perhaps it was me. Perhaps people knew I was coming.

There is no mirth in Peter's smile.

A bang and a shout wake him from an uneven, tossing sleep. He glances at his watch. A quarter of midnight. More noise downstairs. Peter pulls on his trousers and walks up to the window. It is a lot colder now. He shouldn't have left the window open. He tries to close it. It's jammed. He puts on his shirt to keep warm.

Down below a car is parked diagonally on the sidewalk, and five or six men are talking with their hands. Large, staccato gestures of anger. Peter can't really hear what they are saying; there is too much wind humming through the open slot. He is also two floors up from the illuminated sidewalk.

As the men move back, Peter sees two bodies lying on the sidewalk. He puts on his jacket, slips on his shoes and goes downstairs. There are still some people in the tavern drinking as if nothing has happened. He goes past them to the front door.

"Close the door fast, will yah!" one man shouts after him.

The temperature outside must have dropped by fifteen degrees. Part of his mind tells him he's an idiot not to have put on his coat. He pushes past two men arguing the right-of-way of a driver. A woman lying on the sidewalk is bleeding. She looks up at Peter. With chattering teeth she whispers: "...c-cold-d..." The man beside her doesn't move at all. Peter studies both bodies, trying to determine, just by looking, if their spines might be hurt. It is impossible to tell; but if the two stay here any longer, they will die of hypothermia, pneumonia or other complications. It's funny working without a diagnostic computer.

"Take them inside."

Peter speaks in a normal voice, but somehow the men stop arguing. The one behind the others pushes forward.

"We called for the cops, they'll be over pronto!"

"Aye, when they finish their donuts, ha ha!" adds a tall man laughing. The others join him.

"Take them inside," Peter repeats. "Now!"

The tall man scratches his neck under his cap. "Guess it's a bit nippy out here at that... OK, Joe, give's an 'and."

Two men take the woman and carry her inside the tavern. The publican opens the doors for them. It might be good for business. You never can tell. The other men do nothing. With the bodies being carried away, they seem to lose interest in further argument. The two men who carried the woman return to pick up the older man. His hair is wet from the falling snow. No one thought of putting something under his gray head.

"'e don't look so good, guv," the smaller man says.

"Take him inside," Peter repeats.

The original self-appointed porters carry the man inside. As Peter follows them, the rest of the men finish their argument and also go inside. They seem annoyed at Peter for having spoiled a bit of good fun on a dull evening. They go directly to the bar and order another beer.

The two victims of the accident are both placed in a room to the left of the main drinking area. It is a room designed for private receptions. Both bodies are put on the tables pushed together to form provisional beds. The men who carried the bodies stand to one side, their hands dangling loosely on each side. They seem lost now that they have carried out Peter's instruction.

"Stand at the door and don't let anyone in," Peter commands.

"Not even the cops, Sir? I don't want no trouble with the law." The younger man looks uncomfortable. The tall man seems happy to have something to do.

"You may let the police in. When they arrive."

The man looks placated. They both move to the door. Somehow Peter is sure that nobody but the police are going to interrupt his efforts.

"Here goes nothing..." Peter murmurs to himself.

He walks round the table and opens the man's coat. There doesn't seem to be any blood, but even in the darkish room the man looks pale. Peter puts his ear to the man's mouth. The man's breathing is hardly discernible. He carefully runs his hands over the man's body searching for broken bones. There don't seem to be any. Then Peter remembers Henri. Little Henri Ouellette. He leans over the table and covers the man's body with his own. Nothing happens. Nothing at all. A loud salvo of laughter is heard from the tavern. People are having fun in St-Henri.

Peter leaves the old man and turns to the other table. The woman is quietly moaning. Her left arm is covered with blood. It is also bent at an awkward angle. For a moment Peter holds his palm over the women's forehead and then sets her arm at an angle resembling normal position. He runs his hand up and down the rest of her body. There is surprise in her eyes. Almost a suggestion of a smile. Then, as before, Peter leans over the table and covers the woman's body with his own. He stays like that for a few seconds and straightens up.

"You'll be all right, now," he tells her.

She doesn't look all right. She looks pale and tired and frightened.

"How is my father?" she asks.

"He'll be all right, too," Peter assures her.

It doesn't cost him anything to do so. And she needs to relax and rest. In addition to her arm, the young woman is suffering from shock. Only now Peter notices that the woman is hardly more than a girl. Her long hair is mottled with slush from the sidewalk, her lipstick is smeared yet she still looks pretty. Pale but pretty. And scared.

"Thank you, Sir, I am sure."

The girl tries hard to smile. It doesn't quite work. She grimaces instead. Her arm must hurt like the devil, Peter thinks. It's broken in at least three places.

"Don't you worry now, you hear me?"

Peter is vaguely surprised at his own words. He seems to regard the young woman not as a patient but as a person. As a human being. He smiles reassurance and quickly walks to the door. There is nothing he can do here. He doesn't have any backup.

"They won't get any worse before the police get here," he mutters to himself. Then he asks the shorter of the two, who seems to have more initiative, "You sure they're coming?"

"I called them myself, mister. Must be a half hour ago," the tall guy answers instead.

"All right, then. Keep the others out. These people need peace and quiet."

With this Peter walks past them and through the door. The room inside is full of people. The accident must have brought extra customers. He pushes his way through the crowd to the staircase. The odour of urine is still there, but now it is mixed with the pungent tobacco smoke. He climbs quickly and closes the door of his room, cutting off the downstairs noise.

The room is cold but quiet. Peter walks to the window and pushes the upper sash upwards. It closes easily. He takes off his jacket, shirt and trousers and just in his underwear climbs under the single blanket. He shouldn't have left the window open for so long.

He feels tired. He is not used to long walks. He is grateful that the noise from the tavern is no more than a distant echo. He closes his eyes. Suddenly he remembers. He remembers what it was that he had seen in Winston's eyes when they shook hands this morning. It was friendship. No, it was more than that. It was love.

It was compassion.

* * *

8

Good-bye

" **W** ho may I say is calling?"
The apron-clad woman stands her ground. She is
taller than Peter. Her smile in no way detracts
from her apparent resolve to guard the gates of her castle. For it
is equally as apparent that it is her castle she is guarding. The
woman's hair, rolled in a severe, tight bun, is as gray as Dr.
Brent's. Peter had never met her, yet the woman's face seems
familiar. She reminds him of the Chief of Medicine at the
General. The same hair, the same penetrating eyes. The same
inviting smile belying her staid position. Peter thinks she looks
more like Dr. Brent's sister than his wife. Perhaps she is.

"Who is it, dear?" Dr. Brent's voice reaches Peter from
inside the house.

"My name is Thornton. Peter Thornton."

"He says his name is..."

"Peter! Thank God you're all right."

Dr. Brent takes Peter in his arms and hugs him like a long-
lost child. Peter seems to disappear within the tall man's
embrace.

"Come in. Come in. Dear, this is Peter Thornton.
Doctor..."

"How do you do, Mrs. Brent."

"My name is Lucy. I'm so glad to meet you."

Thank God there is no 'I've heard so much about you' platitude. Peter extricates himself from the tall man's embrace sufficiently to be able to shake hands with Dr. Brent's wife. Her firm handshake is accompanied by a slightly concerned expression. She knows, Peter concludes. Her face shows more than she is willing to admit. Peter's own smile is artificial; taut lines continue to surround his probing eyes.

Dr. Brent takes Peter's coat, throws in on a chair, and all three walk through a wide archway to a spacious room to the right of the hall. The room is furnished for comfort. It is the antithesis of Dr. Brent's office at the General. The crackling fireplace, the warm light washing the walls adorned with a number of old-fashioned oils of landscapes, the deep, soft furniture all combine to create a cozy atmosphere conducive to rest and relaxation. The room has an air of a den more so than a living room. There are no visible signs of anything to do with medicine. This place must have been created by a woman who knows how to recharge her husband's batteries. It goes a long way to explain Dr. Brent's seemingly inexhaustible resources of energy.

"Come, this way." Dr. Brent takes Peter's elbow and leads him through the length of the room towards the fireplace. "There. Now sit down and tell me all about it."

"Yes, doctor. Well, it only hurts when I laugh..."

Both men chuckle, then laugh. Perhaps Dr. Brent is unaware that he had addressed Peter as though Peter were a patient; perhaps he had worded his phrase on purpose. Whatever the truth, it helped to discharge any rigidity that might have remained in the room.

"May I offer you a drink or a coffee?" Dr. Brent asks again.

"Nonsense. It's almost seven. Dr. Thornton will have supper with us."

Peter's denials are to no avail. Mrs. Brent disappears into the hall, and soon the men hear additional plates being set at the table in the dining room across the hall. Peter is surprised to see that the Brents do not seem to have domestic servants. Mrs. Brent is as old-fashioned a wife as the decor she must have selected for their home. For his part, Dr. Brent leaves Peter alone by the fire only to return a minute later with a bottle of Chablis and three glasses on a small crystal tray.

"Lucy won't mind if we start without her," he assures Peter.

Peter had waited for close to an hour outside Dr. Brent's door. First he hadn't thought the Chief had already returned from the hospital. Later, when he saw the doctor's car pull into the driveway, Peter had no idea how to justify his assault on Dr. Brent's privacy. For many years the Chief had represented, in Peter's eyes, a pinnacle of medical achievement. Now, theoretically, Peter had achieved academic parity; but old habits die a slow death. There still remained an aura of the great man looking down from his Olympian altar. When Peter finally did press the entrance bell, the last thing he expected was to see an elderly woman opening the door. He was put off his stride. Now, he was just beginning to recover.

"Chin, chin." Dr. Brent raises his glass.

"Your very best health, Dr. Brent..."

"It might be easier if you address me by my first name. If you don't, Lucy will give me hell. She already thinks that I am a pompous ass," Dr. Brent says in a hushed, conspiratorial voice. Peter takes a sip of Chablis before replying.

"It might not be easy, Dr. Brent. John?" Peter finds it difficult. Apart from anything else, there must be over forty years' difference between them.

"Sorry, lad. It's either John or I'll address you as Dr. Thornton."

Suddenly Peter's face clouds over.

"That might be a considerable misnomer," he says darkly.

There is a moment's silence. A somber cloud seems to return and hover over Peter's mind. Only the fireplace refuses to submit to the recurring tension.

"We must talk about that, Peter. As friends." John Brent sips his wine before adding: "This had nothing to do with medicine, you know, don't you?"

"Just voodoo?"

Momentarily Dr. Brent's smile disappears.

"It would make things a lot easier if you stopped feeling sorry for yourself, young man." His voice is steady but there is just a thin edge of steel in it.

"What do you expect me to do? Rejoice?"

"You could do worse."

Peter gets up and starts pacing. John Brent doesn't interrupt his thoughts. He knows that a battle is raging in Peter's mind. It will be easier to find a common ground when the adversary gets a little tired. Or at least, when he understands that there is no adversary outside his own thoughts.

"Ten years!" Peter says at last. "Ten years...." he repeats in a resigned tone.

Mrs. Brent appears in the archway, but John Brent waves her away.

"Why now? Why not ten years ago?"

"Would you rather it happened ten years from now?" John Brent asks quietly.

Peter spins on his heel as if only now realizing that he is not alone.

"I'm sorry, Dr. Brent. I guess I'm a bit tired..."

"You have a perfect right to be, Peter. And don't call me Dr. Brent."

Again Peter smiles. To his surprise, he regards the old man with affection. Peter hardly knew his own father; John Brent has been more of a father figure for him than anyone else. Only Peter had never realized that before. Yet this is the very first time that they've met outside the hospital grounds.

"Look, boys," Mrs. Brent is again framed by the archway. "I know you want to talk, but my salmon will be ruined if you..."

"I am sorry, dear. Come on, Peter. Good food is the best invention known for sating hunger."

Dr. Brent picks up the tray with the bottle and the glasses and follows his wife into the dining room. A low-shaded lamp over the table leaves the rest of the dining room in a warm if mysterious semidarkness. Again the room is cozy, intimate. Peter feels the warmth emanating from his hostess. Incongruously, he

wonders if the Brents have any children. He had never heard of
any. He is surprised how little he knows of John Brent's private
life.

The food is simple but tasty. The knives and forks tap the
plates in a random pattern, as though trying to fill an uneasy
silence. But the silence weighs heavily. Even Mrs. Brent, who
usually provides the necessary good humour her husband had
learned to rely on, today seems preoccupied, even worried.
Whatever the reason for Peter's visit, it casts a shadow over her
usual casual serenity.

"She knows, Peter," John murmurs, confirming Peter's
earlier suspicions. "She told me she would give half her life to
have such a gift as..."

"A gift!?" Peter spits out in hardly controlled anger. The
word 'gift' sounds like a curse.

"Those were her very words. A wondrous, magnificent
gift." John Brent continues to speak very softly. He isn't trying
to convince Peter. It could be that the Chief is trying to convince
himself.

"A gift...?"

Peter whispers the word like a personal anathema. His voice
wavers in abject incredulity. He turns his head and glares at Lucy
Brent as though she had cast at him a sentence of
excommunication. Up to this moment, both men were acting as
though she weren't even there. It wasn't difficult. Mrs. Brent
possesses that rare quality of being able to withdraw her
personality until she has something constructive to contribute.

"There are three thousand three hundred and forty-eight
physicians in Greater Montreal." Dr. Brent enunciates the
numbers with scanning precision. "3348 Doctors of Medicine!"
He repeats as if to further stress the number and the titles. "Not
one of them has the power..."

"Please, spare me the details of your statistics." Peter tries
hard to control his rising anger.

"...not one of them has the power to return an only son to
his aging mother."

"You knew?" Peter is taken aback. He felt sure he had
managed to camouflage the incident rather well.

"I knew the day it happened." Dr. Brent smiles almost sadly. "In a way, I think I knew before it happened."

This time the silence seems to drag even longer. All three only half finish their plates. This is not an occasion for festive dining. Peter stares into his plate. He appears to be studying the elaborate pattern on its edge as if searching for an elusive answer. Mrs. Brent rises and quietly removes the plates from the table. In a few moments she returns with an urn of coffee. She hesitates, then goes to the sideboard and takes out three cognac snifters and a bottle of Remi Martin. Throughout all this, the men remain silent. John Brent taps his pockets as though looking for something; Peter's eyes wander over darkened walls. He seems to be attempting to decipher the secrets hidden in the arabesque patterns of the old-fashioned wallpaper. Secrets jealously guarded by the receding penumbra.

"But I am a doctor of..." He sighs deeply. " I am a doctor..."

"No, Peter. You are a healer. You alone are that which the rest of us aspire to be. And fail. All of us."

Again a moment of poignant silence. Mrs. Brent pours the coffee. She places the glasses in front of each cup and pushes the bottle towards her husband. He takes the bottle and puts it down again.

"My husband was a healer once." Lucy Brent speaks for the first time. Unwittingly both men turn towards her. She smiles wistfully. "Oh, yes, he was. Really," she repeats as though both men needed reassurance.

"You mean...?"

"Oh, no. No. He used more traditional methods. He used to practice medicine."

"Used to.... Mrs. Brent?" Peter regards Lucy Brent with doubt in his eyes.

"Yes, Peter, used to. And please, call me Lucy?"

In spite of himself Peter smiles. "Thank you, Mrs., I mean Lucy. You said..."

"I said that John used to be a healer. And a damn good one. He abdicated his calling when he became Chief of Medicine at the General." There was acceptance in her words, there was also a shade of sorrow.

John Brent pours a few drops of cognac into his wife's glass, then places the bottle in front of Peter. Peter ignores him.

"Mrs. Brent. Lucy. Your husband is a most respected authority on Internal Medicine, on Preventive Medicine, on Holistic Medicine, on..."

"I know, Peter. But he is not a healer."

"Mrs., Lucy! Really!" Peter throws up his hands.

"He is not a healer."

Lucy's tone is so quiet that Peter has to strain to hear her words. As before, there is acceptance in them, but this time there is also longing pain. Peter fills his glass with the cognac, then lifts it and pours the content down his throat. He puts the snifter down hard on the table.

"I don't think, dear, we should burden our guest with our troubles."

By now, there is a gentle smile on Lucy's face. The sorrow is gone, displaced by memories of a better, kinder past.

"Did you know, Peter, that Dr. Brent married a nurse?"

Peter's head moves from side to side. For a moment he seems absorbed in Lucy's story. For the first time in weeks he is involved in someone else's troubles. Troubles? Well, we all think we have problems, he muses and immediately dismisses the thought. In spite of himself he senses that he must hear the rest of the story.

"Oh, there is very little to add. I was a nurse and... I got pregnant. You know how it is. A young, handsome, promising doctor, a shy nurse looking up to her god in a white tunic. I was pretty, you know? Sharing night duties, sickness, suffering, dying. Tension. Stress. The usual appurtenances which a healer must suffer."

Peter remembers well. Years. Years of stress, of tension.

And then Lucy looks up at Peter with the serenity which he had intuitively detected when he first met her an hour or so ago. She seems her old self again.

"A healer, Peter, not a doctor of medicine," she says simply.

Immediately Peter is again on guard. He feels he must defend his right to suffer.

"But, but..." Suddenly he doesn't seem to have much to say.

Lucy's face is a picture of detached serenity. Again she looks into Peter's eyes.

"We lost that baby, Peter. John was good, very good, but..."

But not good enough.

"We tried twice more. There must have been something wrong with me. Perhaps too much tension. Too much daily stress. That was when John decided to veer towards more administrative posts. He did it for me, you know. Funny. It was too late by then. And at the time, we didn't know a great healer."

She turns toward her husband. Her eyes are filled with gratitude. The words, 'he did it for me', are churning in Peter's mind. What have I ever done for anybody? A string of pearls? A ruby necklace... Bah! But a life? To give up one's profession...

Peter reaches for the Remi Martin and pours himself a little of the golden cognac. He is lost in his thoughts. It all seems to look or sound different somehow. He feels strangely embarrassed. He tries his best to smile.

"I didn't know, Mrs. Brent. I am so sorry, Lucy," he utters, uncertain of his words. They seem so very inadequate.

"If only we had known you then, Peter..."

Good God! They do envy me!

It is a long walk back to St-Henri. Peter is only three blocks below his own home, but somehow he cannot return to the elegant surroundings of Upper Westmount. He feels that somehow he doesn't belong there. Not yet, anyhow.

Peter had gone to see Dr. Brent to say good-bye. He felt he ought to. Whatever his future, it is abundantly clear that he cannot practice medicine in an institution where each time he touched a patient he would break the established procedures. He can hardly spend his days walking the wards, hugging hundreds of prostrate bodies. Anyway, there are no guarantees. Are there?

Peter quickens his pace. Just like yesterday, the street is a deserted strip of daylight cutting across a forbidding darkness. The night is cold. For the next four months, all nights will be like that. Thank heaven for cheap energy. Thank heaven? What has heaven ever done for me? It's all right for the Brents to dream in hindsight. John Brent is still a doctor. A Fellow of the Royal College. He enjoys respect, position, prestige, even fame. And a comfortable income.

I have a gift.

A gift I neither want nor understand. A gift I have no control over. A gift which destroyed all I had ever worked for. God, had I worked for it...

Thank heaven for nothing!

NOTHING!

God, it's cold!

At last the Tavern. The insipid lights leaking through the unadorned windows seem like home. A place of warmth in the middle of a Canadian winter. As Peter comes closer, he hears a commotion coming from the half-open entrance. Then the doors open wide and a man is propelled outwards. He practically cartwheels over the narrow sidewalk into the gutter. He gets up, shakes his head and storms the door.

A tavern brawl.

Peter hides into a recessed doorway on the opposite side of the street and waits for the hiatus to subside. His fingers are stiff with cold. His legs and arms are shivering. Peter has never walked such a long distance on a December night. Except for yesterday. And yesterday it wasn't so cold.

It was only yesterday...

Another man gets thrown out. This customer picks himself up, spits at the tavern door and walks away along the bright sidewalk. The man has a problem keeping a straight line. Peter doubts he is injured. At least not externally. The drunk is not wearing a coat—must live locally, Peter muses. The man's arms are pressed into his sides, his knees together, his gait that of a beginner skater. Three steps forward, one backward. A sort of subarctic fandango. To know what precipitated the man's grotesque condition—you don't have to be a doctor.

Or a healer.

The commotion seems to be running out of steam. Men leave the tavern in groups of twos and threes. Some have women hanging onto their arms. They are all noisy, laughing, belching loud enough to be heard from across the street. One man only makes it to the street gutter before he spills most of the beer he'd absorbed during hours of drinking. Must have been long hours. The street is so well lit that Peter can see a number of men sporting bright red bruises, angry blotches on their faces. One man displays a lot of blood on the collar of his coat. All the same, he seems happy.

Peter crosses the street.

There are half a dozen men left in the tavern. They seem quiet enough. The publican is missing. His wife looks nervous as she takes Peter's $10 and gives him the key.

"I made up your room," she says, the ever-present cigarette dangling from her over-painted mouth. "I thought you might be coming back."

"Now why would you think that, madam?" Peter asks, amused at the woman's presumption.

"I really meant hoped, Sir." The woman's voice is on the defensive. "I meant no harm. We don't get many gents from up there," she nods her head towards the mountain.

Peter picks up his key and turns towards the staircase. He has to cross the stench before entering his room. My room? Good God, do I really belong here?

"Your husband took a night off?" Peter asks over his shoulder. He hates the pungent staircase.

"Oh, naw, Sir. He got a bit clobbered in the scuffle, that's all?" the woman replies, tilting the last syllable into a question. Peter detects worry in her voice.

"I'd better take a look at him, Mrs. Brown." Peter remembers the name of the owner under the outdoor sign.

"What, you a doctor?"

She remembers Peter giving commands last night, but it wasn't as if he examined anyone. Not really. He didn't have any of that fangle-dangle equipment the paramedics have when they pick up anybody. The police called an ambulance, and they took the two away. She hasn't heard any more about them.

"Sort of..." Peter says softly.

"Aw, all right then. Come this way."

She nods to one of the customers to look after the till and takes Peter through a dark corridor to a room at the back of the house. Peter is amazed at how these people seem to despise light. After all, it is just about the only thing they can really afford. Perhaps it's no longer a status symbol. Finally the woman spits out her cigarette, rubs it into the floor with her foot and pushes a door open.

The room is filled with twice as much furniture as the space can comfortably accommodate. On a double bed lies a man. It is too dark to recognize him as the publican.

"I'll need a little more light," Peter says. Almost simultaneously he wonders: For what?

Peter wonders why he volunteered to look at the publican. He wonders how long it will take him to stop reacting as a physician. A clobbered man who had to lie down presumably requires medical attention. Yet is it any of his business?

Peter also wonders for how long he will continue to question not only the rationality of his own actions, but the rationality behind all the years of study of medicine. His head feels more and more like a container of disjointed facts, useful for feeding a computer but of little intrinsic knowledge or usefulness in the art of healing people.

"Will that be enough, Sir?"

Two dim naked bulbs expose the cobwebs at the junction of the walls and ceiling. Perhaps that is why people don't light their interiors. It saves on cleaning.

"Yes, thank you, Mrs. Brown. You may wait outside."

The woman hesitates for a moment, then shrugs and leaves the room. Peter looks down at the publican. He is either asleep or unconscious. In the hard light of the exposed bulbs the man looks so pale he could be dead—except for his chest moving up and down in a regular motion. Nothing wrong with his pulmonary system. Peter takes Mr. Brown's pulse as he sits down on the edge of the bed, looking at his foolhardy patient.

What of the art of healing? Only those who know little about medicine raise it to the dubious distinction of calling it a science. The few who are more concerned with curing, rather than lessening the apparent symptoms and the attendant discomforts of a patient, cannot but regard it as an art.

Fewer still realize that the supreme creative art is life itself.

It is the enhancement of this art which is, and must be, the prime responsibility of a physician. The restoration of the harmony, the fine-tuning of the instruments within the symphonic structure of our mind, our body, perhaps our spirit—we should demand from our physicians. Instead, the countless books, the thousands upon thousands of pages, are filled to overflowing with gory dissertations on pathological conditions of our anatomy. On many occasions Peter's brain was so filled with the abnormal, the pathological aspects of man that there was little room left among his tired neurons to recognize that which a man should be. Which a man is.

A miracle of a creative act.

Peter touches the man's forehead. Cool, a little too cool. If he lost any blood, there is no evidence of it.

Peter pushes his hand behind the man's head. He feels sticky, warm wetness. Mrs. Brown was right. Her husband had been clobbered by one of his customers on the proverbial noggin. Peter feels a stinging in his finger. Glass?

Mr. Brown is a large specimen of *Homo sapiens*. At least large on the Homo. The seat of his sapience may have sustained an injury.

"Mrs. Brown?"

No answer. Peter wipes his hand on the pillow and leaves the room. He finds Mrs. Brown behind the counter.

"I need a bowl of water, some towels, any sterilizing solution you may have and a clean pillow. And a bandage, if you have any."

"Is he all right, Sir?" Mrs. Brown looks really worried.

"How come you didn't call an ambulance?"

"Aw, Gawd, he is not going to die, is he...?"

"No, Mrs. Brown. He is not going to die. But he might bleed to death if you don't hurry up and get me what I asked you."

Peter walks back to the room at the back. It would take a lot more than a bottle smashed on the back of Gaston Brown's head to kill him. But he will probably wake up with a king-size headache.

A half hour later Mr. Brown's head is washed, the wound cleaned and bandaged with a towel torn into long strips. Unfortunately, while Peter washed the wound, the water revived the injured man. Fortunately, the pain was evidently so great that Mr. Brown grimaced, winked, sighed and closed his eyes, apparently reverting to a semiconscious state. He was too weak to raise any objections to Peter's ministrations. Then, almost as an afterthought, Peter placed both his hands on Mr. Brown's head and just held it for a few seconds. He did it almost as a test. If he did have some voodoo powers, then he must learn about them. Preferably quickly. Before he went mad and really started believing in them.

Back in the tavern Peter is still curious. It is evident that Mrs. Brown attempted to sublimate the worry for her husband's welfare with a few shots of 'something stronger'.

"Mrs. Brown," he asks, "you haven't told me why you didn't call an ambulance for your husband. He must have been unconscious for quite a time."

"Last time I did, Sir. He gave me such a dressing down I wasn't about to take the risk. I learned my lesson."

Peter can only imagine what the dressing down entailed. Obviously it had been sufficient for the woman to risk her husband's life. However innocuous Mr. Brown looks at present, his long drooping macho mustachio does suggest a man who likes to have things his own way. Also, his heavy-set, around 90-kilo physique certainly commands a pinch of cautious respect. In spite of all this, the big man's eyes seem to blend an instinctive slyness with, paradoxically, an intrinsic kindness. Peter feels sure that whatever scars Mrs. Brown may have sustained must have been inflicted principally to her ego rather than to her comfortable though still curvaceous body.

The art of survival is practised a bit differently on the other side of the tracks.

Up in his room, Peter tries to analyze some of what Dr. Brent and his wife, Lucy, had told him. He tries to remember their discussion. His usually excellent memory does not serve him well tonight. He lies on his back and stares into his eyelids. All he remembers is a pair of dark eyes peering into his own. Peter smiles at his own thoughts. They don't make any sense.

The dark, deep-set eyes look exactly like Winston's.

* * *

9

Nomad

The second knock on Peter's door is a little louder.

"Who is it?"

No answer. Peter pulls on his trousers, tucks the shirt inside and steps into his shoes. He doesn't bother about the socks. He wonders who it might be. Then he remembers Mr. Brown. Surely, he's all right, isn't he?

"Come in!" Peter calls out, pulling the loose cover over his bed.

A woman looking about thirty coming on forty puts her head through a crack in the door. Her eyes scan the room suspiciously before turning toward Peter. The eyes are old, pale, lacklustre. Too much living in too short a time?

"Can you help my baby?" Her voice is hoarse and brittle.

By now six little imps push their way into the room. Judging by what Peter can see of them, they all look under ten years of age. They all seem to be wrapped up in thick padded windbreakers, hats, mitts and equally padded plastic boots. They look like a bunch of fat fairies. Peter wonders which of the kids requires his help. Anyway, what help?

"I have no money..." he starts.

It is true. Today is the last day he can spend in St-Henri. Last night he had spent his last $10 bill. There may be something left in his bank account, but he doesn't have his chequebook with him and he doesn't carry the account number in his head. He always refused to use plastic. He didn't need to. At the General all his needs had been provided free of charge, and at home he gave a monthly check for his room and board directly to Winston. The beanstalk did the grocery and suchlike while Ruth looked after all the major expenses. The first time he checked the solvency of his bank account was when he bought Ruth the rubies. Peter smiles at the memory. God, it felt good—at the time. He recalls an almost euphoric sense of freedom. And now? Now he is enslaved again—by a gift.

By a bloody GIFT!

"Money?" The woman looks surprised. Only now the equally overfed, rotund woman comes into the room. She looks about as fat as she is tall. "What money?"

"I'm sorry. I thought... no matter. What can I do for your baby?"

"He vomits."

"And which 'he' are you referring to?"

The woman unbuttons her loose, padded cape and from beneath two more layers of oversized sweaters she pulls out an infant. After she completes the peeling process, she no longer looks fat. Peter can't believe his eyes. The fat woman suddenly looks emaciated.

"This little cadger, Sir. He vomits somethin' awful."

To prove her point she leans the baby face down, presses on its stomach and a little stream of saliva mixed with remnants of baby food spills on the threadbare carpet. Peter steps forward and takes the infant from her yellow, nicotine-stained hands. It's a baby boy about six months old. His skin is yellowish. The large blue eyes are trying hard not to follow the emptiness lurking in the eyes of his mother.

"Leave the baby and wait outside," Peter tells the woman.

As the delinquent, if not prolific, mother comes closer to hand over her latest asset, Peter catches a whiff of gin on her breath. His watch insists that it is only 7:37 a.m. Peter's jaws harden. She starts early, he muses. Before breakfast. Or maybe gin was her breakfast. The woman doesn't say a word but grabs

the nearest four of her children by various parts of their clothing
and files them outside. The other two follow.

"He's a good boy, sleeps a lot. And vomits," she throws
over her shoulder.

"He's drunk, you stupid..." Peter hisses under his breath
as mother waves her contribution to humanity through the door.

Peter waits until they all clear out of the room, then places
the infant on his bed. He removes the baby's overalls. The tot
looks as healthy as can be. He could take him to the hospital and
conduct a few dozen tests. With Medicare, everyone can afford
them. Instead he dresses the boy again, lifts him to his chest and
holds him close for a little while. Almost instantly the baby
responds with the international gurgle talk. The lad sounds
happy and healthy. There is no reason for him to vomit if the
mother stops feeding him laced toddies for breakfast. Or any
other time. He puts the baby on his lap. The lad rewards him
with a glorious smile. The eyes look better already. An instant
response... to what?

"And what is your name, little one?"

"It's Andrew. Andrew Mactavish, Sir."

The voice is muted by the door but clearly recognizable.
Peter makes a mental note not to talk to himself when alone in
this room. Somehow he is not even angry. It is not possible to
show anger in the presence of innocence.

"Come in, Mrs. MacTavish."

The six kids file in, followed by their mother. Peter ignores
her and turns to the six fairies. They must be sweating like hogs
under all this clothing.

"You kids go and wait outside. Stay on the sidewalk and
wait for your mother." Peter looks them over. "Which is the
oldest?" he asks, looking as stern as he can. It is not easy. This is
the most amusing bunch of goblins he's seen in a long time.

The mother is about to speak, but Peter silences her by
raising his hand. After a short hesitation a girl steps a little
forward.

"I am thirteen and three months, Sir." She looks half-
proud and half-frightened.

"Then you are in charge. You must make sure that nobody steps off the sidewalk."

The girl looks pleased as punch. In her family the boys were always in charge.

"I'll be watching you all from this window. Now go!"

There is a quiet ramble on the staircase followed by a stampede through the tavern. Peter closes the doors after them and faces the mother.

"Sit down, Mrs. MacTavish."

The woman seems spellbound. She takes the only chair in the room by the small table. She is about to speak, but Peter silences her again. He puts the baby back on his bed and faces the woman.

"Mrs. MacTavish." Peter remains standing, doing his best to tower over the sitting woman. "If you do not stop breast-feeding the baby, I shall report you to the police. You are to come here, tomorrow, and show me your membership card from the AA. That's Alcoholics Anonymous, Mrs. MacTavish. After all your children reach the age of eighteen, you may drink as much as you want. That will be in about seventeen and a half years. Do I make myself clear?"

"I never touch a drop..."

"Do you know what the penalty is for poisoning infants?"

The woman's pale face turns even paler. She stands up, raises her hands, and drops them again to her sides. Then she sits down again. She looks beaten, dejected. A loser.

"I wouldn't hurt the little blighter for the world, Sir. I really wouldn't..."

"Your boy is cured, Mrs. MacTavish. It wasn't easy!"

"Oh, I thank you, Sir, I am sure." She tries to lunge forward and kiss Peter's hand.

"Now stop that and take your children home. When you get there, look up the telephone number of the AA, and call them. Immediately! If you have no one to leave the children with, they will send someone over. Do you understand?"

"Yes, Sir."

"Good-bye, Mrs. MacTavish."

"Good-bye, Sir. And thank you ever so much."

Was there gratitude in her eyes? Yes, probably. Contrition? No. Peter shrugs. There is only so much a physician can do. A few seconds after Mrs. MacTavish leaves the room, Peter quietly creeps to the door and opens it a crack. The mother, looking fat again with the baby wrapped close to her body, is already down at the first landing. She bends down to see if anyone is coming up the other flight of stairs. Then, from the folds of her many layers she pulls out a small, flat bottle. She puts it to her lips, tilts her head back and empties it into her gullet. She probably stayed sober this morning to see him. Peter sighs deeply. He closes the doors quietly and stretches out on his bed.

There is only so much a healer can do.

Peter reaches out for his jacket and pulls out his wallet. He counts out three bills amounting to $9.00. Just enough for a taxi up the hill. It is time to go home. He might as well go. He doesn't expect the mother of seven to come and see him tomorrow. You can't really make people do things. He closes his eyes and tries not to think about people who have problems. After all, he had come here to get away from his own dilemma. He has not succeeded, but... perhaps he was useful. To someone. Perhaps...

And then there is another knock on his door. And another.

And another.

The news was out.

The couple involved in the accident came late last night to find Peter and thank him for whatever he had done to them. At the hospital, the Montreal General, they were told that the wounds they had sustained should have taken weeks to heal, particularly the elderly man's internal abrasions, and instead, next morning the evidence contradicted all the diagnoses and even the X-rays. But that wasn't all. The elderly gentleman, the father of the girl, now felt, moved and looked a good ten years younger than before the accident.

Ten years!

They had wanted to see Peter earlier, but had waited even longer than Peter had for the brawl to fizzle out. By the time they came in, Peter had finished with Gaston Brown and was sleeping in his bed upstairs. Mrs. Brown refused to let them disturb Peter in his room. So, the couple talked. And talked. People listened. There was not much going on in their lives that was out of the ordinary. And then the couple repeated what they had heard at the hospital. "There were some funny stories," they had said. Some very funny stories.

Apparently Peter's exploits at the General spread like wildfire. The daughter with the broken arm had also heard that there are people camping in the front garden of his home.

"In this cold, imagine?!"

But Dr. Thornton has disappeared, she said. Just disappeared. No one knows what happened to him. These were good beer-side stories. They bought her another pint. On the house.

"Dr. Thornton is rather short, they told me, and he wears a funny-looking crewcut. Just like the gent who set my arm in that room last night," the girl said. She waved her arm again. "Broken in three places!" she repeated for the tenth time.

People nodded their heads.

"To be sure. I carried you into that room myself," said a shortish young man knowledgeably.

"Aye, so did I," jumped in a tall, skinny man.

The two tavern regulars became instant celebrities. Overnight. Peter had escaped just in time.

By ten in the evening Peter had seen fourteen more women, eleven men and twelve children. At least that is what Gaston Brown told him later. Mr. Brown himself supervised people cueing along the dingy staircase. His wife was busy serving the new customers with food and drink. Peter didn't leave his bedroom all day. As the door kept opening and shutting, there was no way to keep the pungent, acrid stench of urine out of his room. By evening the smell was mixed with the stale sweat of bodies protected by too many layers from the Canadian winter. The window was still stuck. It was a long day.

A few minutes after ten, Peter sighs with relief. Five minutes and no knocks.

There are no more patients. Visitors. It is drinking time. A drunk man doesn't need a doctor. And if he does, he is not aware of it. Cheers!

At ten-thirty Peter washes his face in the corner sink, wipes it on a towel he used to wipe blood and dirt from five or six peoples' injuries, puts on his coat and goes downstairs. He tells Gaston that he does not have enough money to stay the night. Could Gaston please call him a taxi?

"I can't rightly say that I would accept any money from you, Mister...?" The publican leaves the sentence unfinished with a question mark.

"My name is Nomad." Peter says without hesitation. "Simon Nomad."

"Well, Mister, ah, Nomad, I can't rightly say that I could accept any money from you considering what you did for me last night. No. Can't say that I would, Mr. Nomad." The man pronounces the name Nomad with a bawdy wink in his eye.

Peter is tired. He completely forgot about the publican's own mishap with the wrong end of the bottle. The stout man looks all right, though.

"How do you feel, Mr. Brown?"

"Everyone calls me Gaston, Mr. Nomad. And I would be pleased if you would stay in my inn for as long as *you* please."

"Why?"

"Well, Sir. Can't say that it is bad for business, 'cause it ain't. I can only imagine that it would get better. If you would stay, Sir, that is."

The man is brutally honest. In a strange way, Peter admires that. He used to practice medicine that way. Sometime. Somewhere. And he had heard just too many lies today already.

"I can't even pay for my food..."

"Elsie always cooks too much, anyway. I wouldn't worry about it, Sir."

Mrs. Elsie Brown looks up from behind the counter with a challenging look. She seems ready to question her husband's accusation.

"Elsie, my love, give Mr. Nomad 'ere a bowl of soup and the day's special." His voice softens when he speaks to his wife.

Peter reckons Gaston Brown feels guilty about yesterday's exploits. He must have taken an active part.

"You just sit down and Elsie'll serve you our *soup du jour*. It's good to take in a hot plate on a day like today. Then she'll make up your room."

Before Peter can answer, two men get up from their table and make room for Peter to have a table all to himself close to the bar. It must be some sort of prestigious table because there are other chequered squares unoccupied. Peter remembers the odd duo vaguely. A skinny tall fellow and a youngster about Peter's own size. Then it clicks. They are the chaps who carried the old man and a girl into the reception room adjacent to the tavern proper. About a hundred years ago. Peter wonders what happened to the injured people. The two men smile and wave to Peter as if acknowledging recognition.

"This is our best table," Gaston assures him without explaining the propriety of the distinction. "Joe and Tom kept it for you in case you wanted to eat something."

Joe and Tom. The overnight celebrities.

Peter looks at his watch. It's a bit unfair to have Winston prepare a meal for him at eleven at night. And the soup he had the night before last was very good. Mrs. Brown might be a chain smoker but it did not seem to interfere with her culinary talents.

"That is very kind of you, Mr. Brown. Gaston. I think I'll take advantage of your offer. But could I ask you just one favour? The window in my bedroom is stuck. Could you loosen it for me? The room needs a bit of air..."

"Not another word, Mr. Nomad. You just enjoy your soup!" Gaston points to the bowl with the attendant crust already waiting for Peter at his table. The publican beckons the odd duo who made room for Peter, whispers something in their collective ears and the two disappear up the stairs.

Peter sits down. Suddenly, unexpectedly, surprisingly he feels very relaxed. Dog-tired but completely relaxed. He feels none of tension that terminated each and every working day at the General. He doesn't have a penny to his name, nor does he have the job he had longed for all his life, yet he has a roof over his head, people are feeding him for free, and he helped, at least he thinks he helped, more people in a single day than in twice the time at his old job.

No paperwork, Peter smirks to himself.

He also appears to be surrounded by a bunch of people who practically read his thoughts in their, albeit often feeble, attempts to please him. It's a strange world I live in, he tells himself, savouring again the excellent *bouillabaisse*. The same soup he had enjoyed just two nights ago.

Two nights...?

Peter wonders about the meaning of truth. At the General he used an array of electronic gadgets to prepare his diagnoses of the various ailments. But were those instruments really necessary? All they showed were the deviations from the norm, the excesses or deficiencies of whatever chemical or physiological conditions were recognized as normal. But, what is normal? Today his delinquent patients often lied to protect their fragile egos. They lied about the probable causes of their diseases, their lack of ease about themselves which translated into physical ailments. Is that it?

What is truth, anyway?

Whatever the vanguards protecting the secrets of life, Peter is determined to find the answers on his own terms or, at the very least, within his own terms of reference.

His mind drifts back to the last few weeks before his Fellowship exams. He wonders how the other residents fared, the residents who presumably had not enjoyed the benefits of his scanning techniques, of his photographic memory, of his near perfect recall. They must have filled their minds with masses of disjointed bits of information, masses of data about what is or can be wrong with the human body. A pathological fiesta. But is it really the body that we must cure in order to restore the patient's health?

Why am I asking such questions?

Peter acknowledges the necessity for specialization. If one is to be concerned not with health but with the disease, then at least one should know more about less. One should become a proficient mechanic, a skilled repairman of kidneys, lungs or livers. Surely there is no art to handing out prescriptions. And if one talks about science, then, surely, this branch of human endeavour belongs to the industrial giants, drawing billions upon billions of dollars from their pharmaceutical cauldrons.

And to Cathy and her billions upon billions of atoms. And stars. And galaxies.

God, she was beautiful!

Peter can identify with his colleagues who opted for surgical disciplines. At least the removal of a defective part or the insertion of a new and improved substitute offers some hope for a lasting remedy. It does little or nothing for the patient if the cause requiring a surgical procedure was not resultant from an external abrasion but from an organic or physiological origin. Oh, one could still improve a posture, enhance one's sight or hearing or freedom of movement, but what of the reason for the pathological conditions which precipitated the impairments? What incentive does a patient have to avoid the errors that brought about the malady to start with? The more proficient my profession (my ex-profession), the greater advances in the techniques of relieving the symptoms, the less care people will take to avoid their causes.

A stupid vicious circle.

"Would you like some more soup before I bring you our special?" Elsie smiles, screwing her eyes to avoid the smoke from entering her eyes.

"No, thank you, Mrs. Brown. I would like to taste your *special du jour*," Peter assures her gravely. He seriously doubts that there is anything on the menu that is not identified as special.

Frankly, Peter never ate very much. He already feels almost sated. And he had neither breakfast nor lunch, although three of his patients had brought him apples, pears, and some chocolate. He washed the chocolate down with water from the tap. The water tasted better than in Westmount. Or he was just more thirsty.

Elsie Brown takes the empty soup bowl and soon brings him an enormous plate of spaghetti with tomato sauce and meatballs. Peter tries hard not to look disgusted by the sheer size of the serving. For a moment he considers asking her for a half bottle of Chianti. He thinks better of it. After all, this special is on the house. He thanks Elsie and digs into the yellow worms crawling in red, bloody puree.

He decides not to think about the spaghetti.

Peter smiles, remembering his last semester of residency. What great plans he had had for conquering the world! To see the other interns, residents, even staff doctors impressed with his knowledge gave him, then, just reward for his years of round-the-clock study. Now, having acquired all this knowledge, he would gladly settle for being in a position of facing a single man, woman or child and stating from this great pool of acquired wisdom, firmly, with conviction, that there is no reason for sickness or even for dying. He would tell them of the wondrous way that man is constructed. He would tell them that the whole body is in a constant process of renewing itself, cell by cell, in cycles, that the magic of immunological defences assures us of survival against all the foes of nature. He would tell them that the only virus that threatens our survival is our gaunt refusal to reject our atavistic belief in our limitations.

I shall stand on a street corner and shout: YE ARE GODS!

But who will listen? Am I a doctor? A pillar of an ancient and noble profession to indulge in such sophistry? Or am I a healer who by my very actions denies the veracity of my postulates. I am a healer. A man with a gift. A gift over which I have no control. No control at all.

Physician, heal thyself.

"Would you now like some coffee?"

Would you like to be healed? This cigarette is killing you. You are committing suicide, woman. And you are immortal.

"No, thank you. I think I shall just go upstairs and get some rest."

"Did you enjoy it, Sir?"

"What?" Peter looks down at his plate. It is empty. Quite empty. He cannot believe his own eyes. "Why, yes, I guess I must have?"

"Thank you, Sir." Elsie is pleased as punch. "Now if you want anything you just call. Any time. I'll be up in a jiffy."

Elsie's pulchritude jiggles up and down as she giggles her appreciation.

"No, Elsie. It is I who thank *you!*" Peter insists.

Elsie giggles all the way back to the kitchen. She's a good soul. I might cure her after all. Even in spite of herself.

At this moment Peter has a strange insight. He suddenly feels quite sure that he is not allowed to volunteer his gift. Also, he can't refuse it. But people who want him to help them must, *must* come and ask for it. This is the Law, a voice says inside him.

Not a voice but a sudden, powerful conviction. The type you don't argue with.

Upstairs the air is as bad as before he went down for supper. Peter walks to the window, slides the latch and leans on the sash. It comes down with a bang. Luckily the glass didn't break. So they fixed it but didn't bother to air the room. Perhaps they felt no need for it.

Peter closes the top half of the window and opens the bottom part as far as it can go. He then goes to the closet and puts on his coat. He sits on the table next to the open sash, watching people dart along the sidewalks: occasional couples but mostly single men and some single women. Their hands tucked deeply into their pockets, fur hats pulled over their ears, they all look straight ahead as if in a hurry to escape the offensive brightness of the excessive street lighting. The offensive light invading their dark, sombre lives.

I wonder why?

Peter inhales deeply. It is an almost forgotten smell. It is the same smell he used to inhale on his way back from the General in the middle of the night. After a good day's work.

* * *

10

A Working Man

Peter dreamt last night. He doesn't sleep much, but whenever he awakens at night his head is filled with dreams. It seems that he must dream almost continuously, but only some of them remain anchored in his memory until the morning. This one does.

He was sitting on a throne. He had the power to decide who would live and who would die. As he waved his wand, people either rose up or collapsed at his feet. It was so easy, so effortless. But even as he performed his tricks, his patients' symptoms were transferred into his own body. He began to ache all over. As he regarded his own arms, his own legs, his torso, from the top of the throne they all seemed to elongate themselves. He became very tall. Skinny, like a scarecrow. He suddenly realized that he was looking at the body of Winston Smith. Peter woke up laughing.

He was also aching all over.

Simon Nomad starts his working day around six a.m. It depends on the people. He sleeps until the first knock on his door. Some people spend the night in the tavern to be his first patient. Otherwise their wait could be even longer.

Peter no longer sleeps upstairs. Gaston has moved him to a small room off the reception room, downstairs. The room is quiet, facing the back of the house. The only contact with the outside world is a small square window and a glazed panel in a door opening onto the backyard enclosed by a two-meter fence. The room is dark during the day, very dark at night. Not at all like the street-side where he could read a book in his bed with light borrowed from the street lamps. Only he didn't have any books. In his new room, Peter can actually see the stars when he looks out just before collapsing on his bed. The room has a sink and Peter can use the bathroom adjacent to the kitchen. The reception room is used as a waiting hall as well as an extended service area. Elsie never stops brewing her favourite *bouillabaisse*, sometimes alternating it with a thick pea soup laced generously with juicy chunks of bacon. Both soups are warming. They have to be. The winter is particularly severe this year.

All in all, Peter's new room is better than the one he slept in upstairs. The walls and ceiling are freshly painted, white, the small window actually works, both up and down, the carpet looks clean. Initially the carpet fooled him. When Peter first moved downstairs, he was pleased because he had left behind the smell of the staircase. It was a welcome relief. Then the snow which people brought in on their boots and galoshes melted on his new carpet. The moisture brought out the aroma. Apparently this is where the Browns had once permitted the dog they kept in the backyard to hide during the rain. This had been after they had moved the dog to the yard to save the stair carpet. It had proven too late for the stair carpet, too early for the one in the back room. Usually the air was all right until summer, when the humidity brought out the latent rancidness. Or until the snow melted off people's shoes.

Anyway, it's all right now. Not only do people wait in the reception room long enough to lose all the snow from their footwear, but Gaston makes them remove their galoshes, boots and outer clothing before they enter Peter's room. After two weeks, the smell in the room has reverted to normal. St-Henri normal. Except for the perspiration. When people are nervous they perspire. It doesn't help when the whole inn is overheated. Whatever electricity the Browns save on lighting, they more than spend on converting their whole building into a hermetically sealed hothouse. Except for the front door, of course. Regardless of the sub-zero temperatures outside, Peter sleeps with his window permanently ajar.

The days grow monotonous.

No two people have the same complaint, but the causes don't change much. While the symptoms vary, the reasons behind them remain invariably the same. People abuse their bodies. They overeat, overdrink, oversmoke, are overly nervous, worry too much, want too much. They rejoice too little, love too little. Give of themselves too little. Are intolerant of each other. They are ordinary people. Nice people.

A simple folk.

Not all Peter's cures are permanent. Nothing is. Some 'treatments' suppress the symptoms only for a period of time. Peter had asked Gaston to keep a provisional record of what happens to his patients. Gaston had delegated the duties to Joe and Tom who, for some time now, also keep order in the reception room. In addition, Joe helps out in the kitchen, Tom deals with the garbage and general clean-up. Both men are now regular employees. Their first jobs in over four years.

Peter remembers the day he moved downstairs, some two months ago. Gaston had approached him during his usual late supper.

"We can't get rid of the smell on the stairs, Sir. No matter what we do," Gaston said. He tried to look exasperated.

"And what did you do?" Peter asked innocently.

"Well, we can't do that much with all the people cueing up there, now can we?"

The man's logic was exemplary. Peter did not pursue the subject. He continued eating his pea soup. His temperamental window still worked and the aroma that lingered upstairs, well, Peter was beginning to get used to it.

In five minutes Gaston was back at Peter's dining table.

"We have just freshly painted a room we have behind the reception area. There's no smell there at all," he said. Peter continued eating. "You would have the bathroom next to the kitchen for yourself."

"You don't need it anymore?" Peter asked between mouthfuls.

Peter always seemed hungry nowadays but continued to eat only once a night. Except for an occasional apple or a bar of chocolate during the day. His visitors still thought they needed to reciprocate with some sort of a gift. Most were left with the Browns, c/o Tom and Joe. Peter gave the tokens away, later, to those who had less than others. He did not feel free to keep the donations, mostly because he did not believe he had earned them. He merely passed on his own 'gift'. For the same reason Peter refused to take money.

"So where are you and Elsie going to wash?"

"Except for me and Elsie. But we don't use the bathroom much."

Peter could attest to that. Gaston had been horrified when Peter told him that he likes to take a shower twice a day. "Is that healthy, Sir?" Gaston had asked at the time.

"Are you trying to tell me something, Gaston?"

"Me and my missus, Elsie, well, we thought you might be more comfortable down 'ere, at the back. It's quiet."

"It's quiet upstairs, thank you," Peter replied.

It is always quiet in the tavern during the day. Quiet but for the occasional cries of joy. Or a nervous, then surprised, happy laughter. People in St-Henri seem to drink booze only at night.

"But the smell..."

"I am sort of getting used to it."

"Know what you mean." Gaston's eyes lit up in sudden understanding. "It's gettin' so I can't smell it no more."

"I didn't say I couldn't smell it."

"Ah, yes. That you didn't. And that's what got me to paint the room downstairs. We thought, my missus and me, that is, that you might be much better off downstairs."

Peter continued eating. Gaston, usually towering behind the counter, on that evening had taken over, from Elsie, the duties of bringing Peter his food. The moment the soup was finished, Gaston was back with pork sausages. This time he looked around, assured himself that there was no one within easy earshot, and pulled a chair to Peter's reserved table.

"I can use the reception room as a waiting area, and Elsie can serve them her soup all day long. When people come in from outside, they are real cold, you know."

"And you can't serve them so well on the stairs," Peter replied in an equally conspiratorial tone of voice.

"Bull's eye in one!" Gaston was halfway to slapping Peter on the shoulder but thought better of it.

"And just how much extra do you expect to make on my visitors?"

"Oh, between... hey, what do you mean?"

Peter continued to look the big man in the eye.

"We reckon.... it could go up to an extra grand a week."

Essentially, Gaston is an honest men. He was providing a service and he believed it was his right to be rewarded for it. He held Peter's steady gaze.

"As much as that, eh?" The pork sausages and mashed potatoes had never tasted so good.

Gaston scratched his head.

"The liquor would be extra."

Peter remembers putting down his knife and fork. He had leaned back and regarded the publican for a while. When he spoke, it was in a very even voice.

"Gaston. I don't care what you do with all your customers in your own time. I don't care how often they get drunk on your premises during your tavern's normal opening hours. But if I smell alcohol on a single one of my patients' breath, that same day I am moving out of here. Do I make myself clear?" Peter may have been half the publican's size, but his voice carried all the authority of a sergeant major.

The big man sat silent for a minute. He seemed to have shrunk just a little. His great chest heaved a deep sigh, and then it seemed to collapse into a deep void.

"If you say so, Sir," he said at last.

"I do say so."

"Will you be moving down then?" When Peter didn't answer, Gaston added: "My missus will be wanting to know." Apparently Gaston gave Elsie dressing-downs only when he had one drink too many. The rest of the time she wore the trousers around here.

"I shall be glad to move down, Gaston."

The man's eyes lit up in obvious pleasure. He beamed from ear to ear. As he turned to deliver the good news to Elsie, he hesitated, took another step towards the kitchen, then stopped to face Peter again.

"What if they already left you. I mean, after you cured them?"

"What about them?" Peter was already back masticating his pork sausages.

"Well, can they have a drink then?"

That had been two months ago.

Gaston's profits exceeded his wildest expectations. As winter progressed, the cold spell held on well into the beginning of February. No soup in St-Henri had ever been held in greater demand. Although there were virtually no return customers—to Peter, that is—most came back to express their thanks, to leave gifts, and to enjoy the by now famous *bouillabaisse*. In addition there were the curious, those who offered to renegotiate people's insurance premiums, now that they had become healthy. There were also those who offered to treat Peter. They firmly believed that Peter used devil's power and they, they alone, could free him from being an instrument of Satan.

Peter ignored them.

But there had been some he couldn't ignore. They were those whom Peter refused to treat, to cure, until they took steps to straighten out certain aspects of their lives themselves. He refused to cure a man suffering from chronic bronchitis until the patient stopped smoking for at least a week.

He once told one wreck of a woman, who came at the instigation of her elderly mother, to spend twenty minutes a day, for two weeks, lying down and imagining herself in her very favourite spot in the whole world. The woman was a typical manic-depressive, at least partially caused by the accumulation of unfortunate events in her life. She didn't know that her negativity was the principal cause of those unfortunate events.

The woman, no more than twenty-five, had multiple scars on her body from attempted suicides. She had failed in those even as she had failed in most other endeavours. Two weeks after she first saw Peter, Mr. Nomad, the woman returned, with her elderly mother, to thank Peter for his advice. The woman wasn't cured, but for twenty minutes a day she did relax in her private version of heaven. Her whole day rotated around those twenty minutes. Only then did Peter hug her, as tears of happiness poured out of her so very recently sad eyes. Peter's embrace may have influenced the chemical imbalance, which could have contributed initially to her sickness.

Once Peter refused to set a broken bone in a man's arm.

The man, albeit unwillingly, confessed that he had broken the lower bone in his forearm while fighting with his wife. Apparently his pride had delayed him from going to a hospital. In time the bone had set itself. Badly. When the intrepid pugilist finally visited an orthopaedic surgeon, the doctor had to perform osteoclasis to reset the bone correctly. In the process there had been some damage to the ulnar nerve. Peter suspected that the latter injury may have been responsible for the ulnar tissue failing to fuse. The arm remained broken. Peter insisted that the man pay him a return visit together with his wife. To do so, the man and his wife would have to reconcile a feud, which apparently had been going on for some time. The constant tension, in Peter's opinion, aggravated the efficacy of the man's self-healing mechanisms.

The man became furious.

"Not you, mister, nor anybody else will tell me what I have or have not got to do with my wife!"

No doubt, his temper had a lot to do with the original mishap. The fuming patient shook his good arm at Peter, demanding that the gift he had left with Joe and Tom be returned to him. The gift was been returned, but the man never had came back. Neither alone nor with his wife. He had sustained a much greater injury than his arm. His pride had been injured.

There had been odd cases enough to fill a book.

Sometimes Peter asked his visitors why they had come to see him rather than go to what they called a regular doctor. Their answers varied. Some simply mistrusted any function taking place in a building taller than three or four stories. Some refused to have anything to do with "a business run by the bureaucrats."

"You can't trust them to treat you like a human being!" they would say. "They are all the same, them doctors. They stick their fangle-dangle la-dee-das all over your body, but they only look at their watch—to make sure they don't miss their Tee-off time."

"Well, what about the winter then?" Peter tried to humour some of the more dejected patients. He had never played golf himself.

"Aw, that's even worse. You can catch a death of cold just waiting to be seen. Them corridors are real draughty, what with all them doctors running after them pretty nurses. Anyways, when you ask them to see you in the winter, they make an appointment for you for late spring. And by then, it's the old Tee-off time again!"

Christmas had been difficult.

On December 24th, Peter had left the tavern about four in the afternoon to walk home to Westmount. He had telephoned up ahead to say he would be coming. Winston answered the phone. His voice hadn't changed. The sonorous, polite, trifle distant English aristocrat. Do all butlers sound like that, Peter wondered?

It had been snowing.

It should snow at Christmas. Peter always welcomed the snow. Nothing looks so good as the myriad tiny red and blue and yellow lights suspended on invisible wires on spruces and pines and firs all along the front gardens. If Jesus had had another chance, he would have been born in a northern climate. Just to see those sparkling, tingling, oscillating points of light. They gladdened the eye.

Originally, Peter had left home without his overshoes. On Christmas day, by the time he reached Lower Westmount, his socks were wet. By Middle Westmount, his feet produced a quiet slurping sound. Finally he got there. He stood on the opposite side of the street, his feet freezing, his head in a vice of ice. He also wore no hat. Pretty stupid. At the time of going for a walk, Peter had had no idea he was going to be away for more than a...

He didn't know for how long.

There was a group of people standing at the door of his house, talking. They didn't look familiar. One carried a large, professional-looking camera. They stamped their feet to keep warm.

Peter leaned against a tall elm about a hundred feet from his front door. He stood for a good ten minutes. Maybe longer. He tried to catch a glimpse of Ruth, or Mo or Jo, or Winston through the drawn drapes. He couldn't. Once or twice he caught a shadow fleeting by like a lost memory in a deserted ghost house. It hurt to stand there. Things were coming back. Memory things. A sparkling fireplace. A beautifully furnished, tasteful, elegant interior. A clean carpet. A room with a door on which no one knocked every few minutes. A light catching the living blood in Ruth's necklace. The concern in her eyes. Jo and Mo jumping simultaneously on his lap.

"Hello, Uncle Peter. I love you very much!"

"No, you don't. I love you very much more!"

I love you both.

And Winston. There was something about Winston that didn't add up. He would have to look into it later. After he had a good night's sleep. Sometime.

God, it's cold.

Maybe Jesus was right. It's a lot warmer down there, in Bethlehem. Even if you had to be put up in a stable. Who needs coloured trinkets when you are King of the whole world? Good night, kids. Good night, Ruth.

Good night, Winston.

Merry Christmas.

After that it all looked easy. Saying good-bye to people who had been part of your life only to drift away, disappear, melt into a haze of memory. Memories are no more than frozen yesterdays. Frozen in a Canadian winter. Some forever, some would melt with the first thaw. Peter never realized how many people needed help. They came to him to be cured. Not just of physical abrasion, a physiological disorder. Many had been hurt by life itself. Those people never discovered that life itself is the greatest gift of all. That is what Peter had been trying so hard to restore.

Life. The art of living.

And broken bones. Ulcers. Pernicious anaemia. Diminishing eyesight. Approaching deafness. Cancer. Cancer. A lot of cancer. Also old age. Depression—an absence of joy.

Joy ever since Christmas.

And a compendium of syndromes for which Peter would only be able to attach names if he had an array of diagnostic equipment at his disposal. He didn't. He called them "diseases". Syndromes which interfered with people's ease. With their state of mind. Even if the sicknesses had been of viral origin. The last time Peter dealt with some of these syndromes, they had been recognized as deadly. Bloody nonsense, he told people.

Ye are Gods, he whispered, embracing their divinity.

Peter had learned to shrug without lifting his shoulders. People had a million and one excuses, reasons, for being unhappy. Regardless of their family ties, of their financial standing, even of the state of their health. They liked being unhappy. It was their way of invoking solace from others. Or trying to. Instead of giving.

It doesn't work, he told them. It doesn't work that way.

By the end of February the sixteen-hour-a-day routine does not bother him at all. He is used to long hours. Peter has forgotten if he ever lived in any other way. If he did, it does not matter. He is a healer. A physician with a gift. John and Lucy had been right. They had to be. And he is learning. He is beginning to formulate certain theories about his healing power. About the healing power which flows through him. For definitely it is a power. Enormous validity. It has nothing to do with his will, but it cannot operate without his acquiescence. Without his concordance in its application.

Well, yes and no.

Mostly no.

He cannot stop it from flowing through his hands, through his whole body. But he can refuse to use his hands. He can keep the gates closed. But should he ever withdraw his gift? Should a mortal man be more just than God? He is but a working man. Keeping a roof over his head, his belly full, his soul and body together. Is that not what man is supposed to do?

Jo and Mo are riding a rainbow like Alice in Wonderland. Winston is standing on the very top and waves to Peter to join them. Peter approaches the rainbow, then tries hard to climb the arch—but his feet are slipping. Also the rainbow looks so much higher from up close. He cannot understand how come the children find climbing the arch so easy. So effortless.

"Come on, Uncle Peter."

"Come on, Uncle Peter," Moira echoes Jonathan's invitation.

Another Winston is standing at the other end of the rainbow, way out in the distance. He catches them in his arms as they slide down, waving their arms with glee in their eyes. The kids climb right up again. So fast. So easy.

"Look, Uncle Peter. Look, it's so easy!"

"You just pretend and it just happens! Look, Uncle Peter!"

"Please, Uncle Peter. Please, Uncle..."

"...please join us on the rainbow..."

Peter sleeps even less lately. There is no time. Sometimes people come in the middle of the night. They seem afraid of daylight. Joe and Tom take turns to rest. They have a bed just outside the door to Peter's room. They have put a few shelves up for the records. And to give them a bit of privacy. They are good lads. They don't ask for much. But the people are sapping Peter's strength. He doesn't seem to know it. Elsie told him to take it easy. To take some time off.

"They will still be here tomorrow, Sir. No need for you to hurry."

Elsie doesn't smoke anymore.

Peter doesn't even listen to his own inner voice that warns him to relax. To step up on the rainbow and play. Relax. To let people be.

By the middle of March the days grow longer. Peter's stay the same. Peter looks like a shadow of his former self. The crewcut has grown quite long, down to his shoulders. It gets in his way. He is thinking of shaving his head. He has also grown a beard. It is scrubby and irregular. He once wondered what Cathy would say if she saw him. The next day he borrowed Gaston's razor and took the beard off. As he did before going home for Christmas.

Almost home. Almost Christmas.

People don't have to be sick. They are perfect creations. Perfect.

They are immortal.

He must do his duty. After all, it is a gift. A unique gift. Dr. Brent had said so himself. He must... God, I am tired. I'm so tired. After I cure them, they go right back to their old ways. A gift of futility.

By the end of March Peter looks like a miniature Winston. A beanstalk with a crop of hair on top. His face even looks a bit green. It must be the light. He has lost over forty pounds. That's twenty kilos, outside Westmount. In St-Henri.

I'm so tired.

* * *

11

A Flashback

"**C**ome!"

The knock sounds like any other knock. Tentative, perhaps with just a little more authority. Peter doesn't analyze the intensity that a trembling hand imparts to the door of hope. Not any more. And never after continuous fourteen hours of patients.

The time is 8:00 p.m. Almost exactly.

"And what can I do for you, my friend?"

Peter asks automatically, his eyes closed, itching from lack of sleep. Two more hours, a supper, a brisk walk around the backyard, and sleep. Once the weather had turned a bit warmer, Peter had started taking brief but vigorous walks. He thought his body needed exercise. A lone ghost in a deserted prison courtyard. A ghost in solitary confinement. He and the stars. So many stars. So many... Why is nature so irresponsibly prolific? Like an experiment gone mad.

The walks have become less brisk, lately.

"Yes?" he asks again, having heard no answer. Then he opens his eyes.

For a while he doesn't move. My eyes must be playing tricks on me. Perhaps I should take it a bit easier. Why am I so tired?

"Is that you, Peter?" The tone of voice is disbelieving.

Peter doesn't move. He has learned how to conserve his energy. Never move unless you have to. Except for the night walk. But... the voice sounds familiar. Something from the past. He must have treated this woman and it didn't quite work. Peter rubs his eyes with his knuckles, blinks and smiles before opening his eyes. As he does so, he realizes that the female voice addressed him by his real name. His mouth opens to say: My name is Nomad. Simon Nomad. But nothing happens. No voice leaves his throat.

"Peter... my God, Peter..."

A slim girl. Her coat, green, tight-fitting, a narrow delicate trim of white fur, fluffy, like the first morning snow on the hem and cuffs. A matching hat like a winter's crown on her lustrous black hair.

"Cathy," he manages finally.

A smile remains on his mouth. By now, it is an automatic reflex. All his patients need reassurance. They need to be put at ease. Most people are either afraid or embarrassed to see him. It offends their rationality. But mostly afraid of mumbo-jumbo. Of faith healing, or whatever. He still doesn't know what it is exactly that he does. All he knows is that it's very tiring. Particularly lately. It is as if the tiredness were cumulative. Progressive.

He tries to get up from his wooden armchair.

"No, no. Don't move, Peter. Please don't..."

Cathy takes three steps forward across the tiny room and squats, half kneeling at Peter's feet. In her eyes undisguised horror seems to override her concern at the apparition before her. It is not easy to recognize the Dr. Thornton she had once known. It isn't just the hair hanging loosely at his collar, nor the two-week old beard. It is the whole spectre smiling at her.

A wiry neck seems too weak to support even the skin stretched tightly over the angular bones of Peter's face. The high forehead seems cut with a rough hand from a yellow, greenish stone. The nose protrudes like a beak of a bird of prey. Bloodless thin lips stretch unnaturally from incongruously white teeth, too large for the smiling mouth. The skin is too thin to soften the contours of his cranium, his nose, his jaw. But the worst are the eyes. Dark, smouldering with turbulent fires, they peer at Cathy from deep, unnaturally sunken sockets as though retreating from the horrors which they must witness.

"Peter, oh Peter. What in God's name has happened to you?"

Cathy's voice is hardly more than a whisper. She is desperately trying to recover from the first shock. She lowers her eyes slowly, down to Peter's feet. Two sticks protrude from the oversized trousers. The feet are loose in the dirty, water- and salt-stained shoes.

"I'm just fine, Cathy. My, you look good!"

Peter gets up and, by an inhuman power hidden somewhere in the vestiges of his desecrated body, he lifts Cathy to her feet. "There now. You sit here." He offers her his own armchair. He retreats a step and seats himself on the bed. The armchair, the bed and a small table, and the small sink are all the room can accommodate. Anyway, Peter doesn't need anything more. He told Gaston that himself.

Suddenly a shadow passes across Peter's face.

"You're not sick, are you?"

"Oh, no. Not at all. But you, Peter, are you sure you're all right?"

Cathy's tone, her head moving from side to side, precludes the acceptance of a positive answer. Peter is some four months away from being all right.

"Why did you come to see me?" Peter asks. His eyes descend to his hands resting on his lap. He usually allows no more than fifteen minutes per patient. Many, many people need his help. His gift.

"Never mind that. She will keep." Cathy gets up from the armchair and again squats at Peter's feet. "Peter, let me take you away from here. You need a rest."

"She?"

Cathy shrugs. "My mother."

"Is she ambulatory?"

"Why, yes...?"

"And she is unwell?"

"They say she is dying."

"Of what?"

"Old age, I think. They call it Alzheimer's syndrome."

Ye are Gods. Ye are immortal.

"Is she in command of her senses?"

"Most of the time."

"Then why didn't she come to see me if she needs my help?"

Cathy, who answered Peter's questions with her eyes hovering around Peter's shoes, suddenly looks up.

"Mother here?!" Her voice is filled with surprise.

There is silence. If Peter were on the lookout for such things, he would have noticed that Cathy blushed. Her lips move as if searching for words. None come. She sinks to the floor, her elbow against the edge of the bed. Suddenly her chest heaves haltingly, and from her constricted throat Peter hears convulsive, uncontrollable sobbing.

"Oh, Peter... I've waited so long."

For the second time Peter performs the impossible. He lifts her again to her feet. This time, though, he puts his arms around her and holds her for a brief moment. As though by magic, her sobs quiet down. Her tense body relaxes in Peter's gaunt arms. He takes her to the door. She seems in full command of herself.

"I shall be glad to see your mother. If she wants to come."

Peter opens the door. Cathy looks into his eyes.

"Shall I ever see you again?" she asks.

"You can bet on that, Cathy. We have lots of time. After all, we are immortal."

Peter smiles reassurance. Cathy cannot tell if his eyes are also smiling. They have already sunk too deep. Perhaps past the point of no return. Even as Peter stares at Cathy's face, her features become hazy. A fleeting memory. Cathy doesn't belong here. Not in his room. Not in the tavern. Not in St-Henri. She is from a very different world. Where she comes from, people don't think that the world owes them a living. A world of quiet elegance. A flashback.

Peter closes the door quietly. He takes a few deep breaths. After hardly a moment there is a knock.

"Come!"

Peter glances at his watch. It is 8:15. One hour and forty-five minutes to go.

Peter has been eating in his room for some time now. It seems easier, quieter. Out there, in the tavern, he caught too many whispers, side glances. Some people actually stared at him as if dissecting his thoughts. He found it unsettling.

He likes his room. He knows every spot on the walls. Every intricate cobweb over his bed. The spiders like overheated places. Provided there is humidity. And he has plenty, from the kitchen next door. Humidity and the aromas. Peter can tell, in advance, what will be the day's special. Actually, it is not difficult. The menu doesn't change that much. Nor does his routine. The faces change, the bodies are similar. Abused. Poisoned. The people inside them suffer. Souls imprisoned in constraints of lesser gods.

His mind drifts away occasionally.

Peter listens to people's complaints, he embraces their heads, their arms, legs, their torsos, while his mind wanders to Westmount, to Mo and Jo sliding down the opalescent rainbow, to Winston. He thinks more and more about Winston. He thinks about him and then has no idea why. Perhaps because Winston seems to invade his dreams lately. Quite often, in fact.

It is 9:45. One more. I wonder if I have to eat tonight. I don't seem hungry. After all, I didn't do much. Just embraced some people. Mothers do that with their children all the time. Some fathers do, too. Don't they?

"Come."

The last knock on the door is the best knock. It sounds like music. How come they don't play *valse musette* any more?

Peter recognizes the man. A surly-looking individual. His lungs are in the final stages of cancer. A black, pungent carrion. How come I know that? Peter had heard his wheezing through the closed door.

"Sit down, George." Peter points to his bed.

The man remains standing.

A month ago, Peter saw him quite often. George occupied the room which Peter had used upstairs. He paid only $5, so

Elsie had made him move upstairs. The man resented having to climb another flight of stairs, what with his lungs hurting. He coughed half the night between puffs at butts he collected on the sidewalk and dried on the old window sill heater. Peter often counted the man's coughing rather than sheep, waiting to fall asleep.

"I'm glad you came," Peter says.

He smiles as usual. Someone once told him that he didn't smile much. Who was it? Must have been a very long time ago.

The man looks like a total wreck. Aren't we all? We must learn the secret of life. The secret of perfect living.

"How come you waited so long before coming?" Peter asks. He is gathering his strength to get up and cure that errant smoker. It is no good to give him any conditions. The man is past it. Oh, he could live a healthy life all right. If only he changed his ways.

Now I sound like a television preacher.

"Can't get up the stairs no more," the man replies.

He is still sour about having had to move upstairs. Or maybe he's always sour. Peter gets up, walks behind the man and puts his arms in front of the man's meager chest. Gradually he draws the man closer to himself until their bodies touch. The smell is ghastly. The man smells like rotting flesh. Acrid. Nauseating.

Peter closes his eyes and tells the man that he is healthy. He tells the man that he is a miracle of nature. Unto the image and likeness. Only Peter doesn't speak. He tells the man without speaking. Does that make any sense?

After ten minutes the man grows impatient. He starts fidgeting. Then he tries to disengage himself from Peter's embrace. He sees no reason for it. He feels just fine.

"I ain't got no money," the man says, still surly.

"I ain't got any either, George," Peter replies.

The man is not cured. He is better, though. Much better. Under an extended anaesthetic. His smell is gone, also.

"So how do I pay you?"

"Don't smoke." Peter replies.

"That's it?"

"Yes."

The time is 10:00. The day is over.

Elsie comes in with a tray. *Spécial du jour*. The best. She puts the tray on the table, smiles in an embarrassed sort of way, and leaves. She used to say a few words. She used to be of good cheer. Now she has grown afraid of Peter. Or perhaps afraid for him. Each time she comes in, she's not sure Peter will still be alive.

Peter plays with the food. He is not so hungry lately. He eats because it is the right thing to do. How can I help others if I don't do as I should myself? He swallows a few spoonfuls, nibbles on the sausages and pushes himself away from the table. Must take a little nap, then I'll finish, he tells himself. And after that I'll take a walk. A walk under the stars. So many stars. Like in Cathy's universe. Cathy...? I remember seeing her. It was quite recent. She looked quite beautiful.

Peter moves three steps to his bed. He lies down. Just for a moment or two. She was quite beautiful. All those stars... Like atoms in the heart of a universe.

My God, she is beautiful...

The knocking is persistent.

It must be morning. The ceiling light is still on. It is 12:30.. Must have overslept. No. The square of the window is dark. It must still be night. Ah, yes. Must finish my supper. Peter drags his feet from the bed.

Another knock.

I don't see people after ten. That was our agreement. Agreement? That's right. With Gaston. It would interfere with the tavern drinking time. Or was it closing?

"Come in?"

It is Gaston. Behind him Joe and Tom and Elsie.

"I am real sorry, Mr. Nomad. Real sorry. But the police..."

"...have I murdered somebody?" Peter smiles in spite of himself.

"No, Sir. But it seems as if George has."

"George?"

"Yes, Sir. George from upstairs."

There is a prolonged silence. Peter remembers. George from upstairs. The man with the rotting lungs. Peter rubs his eyes with his knuckles. They are itching more and more lately. Funny. My lungs hurt, too.

"What happened?" he says at last.

"It seems that George had been celebrating. He said he hadn't felt so good in years. He said..."

"Yes, I know. I saw him a few hours ago."

"Aye, that's just what Joe here tells me."

"Well? What happened."

"As I was saying, Sir. It seems that George had in mind to celebrate, feeling so good as he was. He invited a girl upstairs with him for a night-cap. She felt sort of sorry for old George, so they took a couple of beers with them and went upstairs. Only it seems George wanted more than a slap an' a tickle, if you get my meaning. A lot more. When Mavis didn't want to play—he sort of forced her. I reckon she went upstairs with him because she thought she was much stronger than George. Only she wasn't, see? He held her down with one hand on her throat. Only he held her down a bit too long..."

"He had newly found strength..." Peter whispers to himself. Then he looks up. "You sure the girl is dead?"

"Oh, yes, Sir. Quite dead. You might say extremely. Had been for hours. George went up just after he left you. Looks like he got frisky the moment they got upstairs. We heard some shouting, but we thought they're just having a bit of fun. Later, around twelve, I sent Elsie upstairs to find out if Mavis's alright. Only she wasn't, see. Not by then."

Not by then. How long does it take before people can no longer be resuscitated? Not in a hospital, but by my hands? By the gift.

"You sure she went upstairs willingly?" Peter remembers the man's smell. He forgets it was gone, later.

"He gave Mavis all his cigarettes, provided she went up to his room. Looks like she was short on reefers."

"He gave her his cigarettes," Peter repeats. He paid my fee.

"Yes, Mr. Nomad, Sir. And he had said he had something stronger up in his room. I think he meant a bottle of gin. They found an empty one under the bed. He said he used it for medicinal purposes," Gaston explains.

There is a commotion behind the group at Peter's door. A uniformed policeman peeks over little Joe's head and clears his throat.

"I'm told you're a doctor, Sir?"

The officer peers into Peter's room. When he sees Peter's face up close, he catches his breath.

"I say, you all right, Sir?" His eyes screw up in disbelief.

Peter is fully clothed, still sitting on the edge of his bed. He does the usual. He smiles. He also squints. There is a lot more light in the waiting room than usual. It hurts his eyes.

"Yes, officer. I am a..." He hesitates. He almost said a healer. A healer of murderers. "I am a doctor."

"Yea, well. There's been an accident. Could you look at the victim. I mean you being a doctor..." There is a mounting doubt in the policeman's voice.

Peter lowers his feet to the floor and squares his shoulders. It looks almost grotesque, at least comical, only no one laughs. He reaches for the jacket hanging on the door, but it drops out of his hand onto the floor. He ignores it and walks on. Gaston, Elsie, Joe and Tom all make way for him. There is a strange deference in their stepping aside.

The girl, Mavis, has just been carried down to the tavern. George, his hands handcuffed behind his back, is standing against the wall, looking at the floor. Two sturdy-looking uniformed men flank him on each side. They look relaxed but ready to pounce. Like alley tomcats—sure of their prey but wanting to savour the kill. One policeman keeps his right hand on the holster. Peter walks forward, the others follow him in silence.

"This is the victim," another policemen tells Peter. How many policemen does it take to overpower George?

Peter walks up to where they had put the girl on the floor. He kneels down and puts his finger against her jugular vein. He then presses his ear to her chest. He then lifts her eyelids, one at

a time, and peers into the void of indifference. He doesn't have
to do any of this. He knows she is dead. She is dead because he
had given George the strength to kill her. George could never do
it without his help. Next, Peter examines the girl's neck. The
blue marks correspond to the fingers of George's left hand.
Someone's left hand.

God, if only it hadn't been George.

The girl is a woman in her mid-forties. She looks quite
peaceful. Somehow, after she died, her features must have
relaxed. She could be sleeping. Except for the blue marks on
her neck. Perhaps death is not that bad, after all. Even for the
immortals.

"Do you want me to sign some kind of document?" Peter
used to do such things.

"Naw. I reckon we can get her to the morgue all right. Our
medic will do the paperwork. It's just routine," the original
policeman tells him.

Peter is grateful. He wants to go back to his room. Right
now. He wants to be alone with his thoughts. And the ghosts. He
nods to the policeman and turns towards the reception area. Just
then he hears a voice.

"Hi, doc!" It is George. He has a wide grin on his face.

Peter turns slowly and takes a few steps towards George. He
finds the smell of gin nauseating, repugnant. The smell precedes
George by a few feet.

Peter wants to ask: Why? But he doesn't. Instead he is
thinking about the cigarettes George had given to Mavis. The
whole pack. Why couldn't she have said yes to George? Just
then one of the policemen guarding George takes him by the
arm.

"Let's go, lover boy. It's time for a ride." The man pulls
him roughly towards the front door.

"Seeyah!"

George's head is lolling to and fro on his narrow shoulders.
He is grinning from ear to ear, displaying brown and cracked
teeth. But he is no longer surly. He is happy. And drunk.

"Seeyah, doc!" he repeats, covering Peter in a cloud of gin
vapour.

In hell! Peter smiles his usual smile.

They are all good folk. Only weak.

Gaston walks Peter to his room. The publican's eyebrows are drawn; he looks as if he wants to say something. Whatever it is, it is churning heavily on his mind. He must be worried about the reputation of his tavern. It could hurt business. It would be a shame. Business has been very good lately. Very good, indeed!

Peter looks at his tray. He has hardly touched the food. He has hardly slept. And he has taken no walk in the courtyard. Peter asks Gaston to take the tray away.

"Would you like Elsie to warm it all up for you?"

He is a good man, Gaston is.

"No, thank you. I am not very hungry."

"All right, Sir. Only you gotta eat. I'll have Elsie make some scrambled eggs for you for breakfast. In a couple of hours." Gaston grins.

"Did you want to speak to me about something?" Peter asks.

The publican opens his mouth to speak, but instead he shrugs. "It'll keep, Sir," he mutters.

Peter smiles his thanks. Gaston leaves the tiny room. Finally.

Alone.

We are all alone.

So many of us—like the stars. Yet we are all alone. We all live in our own tiny universes. We all guard them jealously from invaders.

Peter picks up the jacket lying on the floor. He puts it on. He switches off the light and opens the door to the backyard. The cold air makes him catch his breath. March nights can be either warm or chilly. Depending on your luck. Tonight it is chilly.

It is a moonless night. In spite of the street lighting on the other side of the inn, the sky is fairly dark. Less pollution since Cathy's father gave us clean energy. The air is good. Chilly but good. One could live forever. The sky is darker particularly towards the south, away from downtown. Away from Westmount. From Cathy.

Is her mother all right? Are any of us?

Without a conscious thought Peter starts walking around the courtyard. Twenty paces to the right, twenty straight forward, then back again. A square circle. We all live in a circle. At least we walk in circles. Winston once called it the Wheel of Awagawan. Great, enormous circles. From birth to death. Only we are immortal. Except for Mavis. But that was an accident. That's right. An accident. She could as easily have said yes to George. After all, his breath didn't smell any more. At least, not as bad as before.

And he had given up his cigarettes. Some people don't have much to give up.

Peter looks up again. There are so many stars. Each one different. Like us. We all provide the light in our private universes. Without us there would be no light. We are the channels through which light flows. Through my hands. My body.

It is not so cold anymore.

Might as well sit down. Must take a rest. Gaston told me to. So did Elsie.

And Cathy. Didn't she?

I wonder why she came...

Thank God George doesn't smoke any more.

It is so nice here.

So quiet.

Good night, Mavis.

And it's warm.

* * *

12

Winston Smith

A shimmering point of light. One of so many. Cold,
brittle... It detaches itself from the firmament, hovers in
one place, then accelerates, swells, becomes an enormous
living orb of fire. A hurling star... It flashes by with an explosion
of a thousand volcanoes, then, as quickly, disappears into
oblivion. Peter instinctively ducks his head. Then he grins. It was
a good trick!

Let's do it again? His thoughts formulate a question. A
request.

The spaceship seems to remain in one spot while the
universe is dancing to the rhythm of the vibrations of light and
sound. Actually there is only darkness, but the space is not
empty. The void is a syndrome. A compendium of fields
invisible to the human eye. Only Peter can see them. Some of
them. The others he can only feel.

And there is no spaceship, either. Is there?

"You are the spaceship."

That's nice.

The fields are like harmonics superimposed on one another.
Peter knows what they are: the gravitational fields of planets and
stars and galaxies. And vast areas of rarefied gaseous forms,
spanning thousands of light-years, which are not yet. Which are
not yet... The stars of the future.

Duck!

A star just shot past in an instant of near eternity. The next
moment, a point of light appears at the very perimeter of his
vision. What...? The light expands at an incredible rate. It now

covers half the space ahead of Peter. It seems to accelerate still faster. Then it is here. All space is light. A brightness which obliterates darkness into nonexistence. Ubiquitous Light...

Then it is gone. An afterglow lingers, diffused, hesitant, then—darkness again. And the points of light. Dancing.

"A supernova."

A supernova?

"Yes. The birthplace of new planetary systems."

A series of whirlwinds persist after the supernova's passage. What's that?

"The magnetic fields are upset by the supernova's passage. They will settle down. They are very unstable in a free state."

Magnetic fields like in a magnet?

"Well, no. More like in a planet. Or like in your body."

Ha! Ha! I don't have a body!

"Yes, you do. Only it is too fluid for you to encompass it with your consciousness. You must rely on your attention."

How come?

"Your consciousness has been quickened. Think of it as travelling at near the velocity of light."

But we are not going anywhere.

"That is because you are not. It is your consciousness which was accelerated. Rather like increasing the vibrations of your body."

So what happened?

"It cannot quite be explained in words. Words are symbols for phenomena that occur in the physical universe. When applied to concepts at different levels of perception, they lose a lot of meaning."

Try me!

"All right. Think of yourself travelling at near the velocity of light. When this happens, the atoms in your body enlarge their mass close to infinity. Actually, you can never quite reach the velocity of light with any physical object, but if you could, the mass of each atom would be infinite. Time would stop. And the magnetic field of your body would also be infinite."

You're kidding!

"So you would be, so to speak, infinite, eternal and the field of your influence would transverse the universes."

Sounds like God.

God, it hurts. My whole body must have gone to sleep.

Peter feels countless needles pricking his arms, legs, back, neck, even the back of his head. He remembers vaguely walking the courtyard until he got tired. He recalls deciding to take a quiet nap. Just before closing his eyes, he thinks he looked up at the stars. There were a great many of them. He remembers feeling their warmth.

How come I can't see anything? What happened to the stars, anyway?

Then Peter remembers the dream. What a funny dream! Something about stars and magnetic fields. It must have been Cathy talking. She loves her stars... How come I can't see anything?

The pins and needles subside a bit. Peter tries to raise his arm to his face.

"Don't try to move yet."

Who the devil is this? And why shouldn't I move? Peter never considered taking orders as a good way to cross new horizons. He raises himself to one elbow and immediately a wave of nausea rocks his head. Very carefully he lies down again. His mind winces with pain racking his whole body. For a fleeting moment a foreign thought crosses his mind. It sounds like: Physician, heal thyself.

What for? Am I not immor... Who said that?

"You need some more rest."

A deep, sonorous voice tells him. A familiar voice.

Winston?

"Relax now. Give it another couple of hours."

Winston. What am I doing here?

"I brought you back. It seemed like you needed a rest."

Back? A mass of tiny fragments of memory flood Peter's disjointed mind simultaneously. A courtyard. The tavern. Gaston. St-Henri. This place doesn't smell like St-Henri. Its smell is familiar, though.

"I am in my room."

"Yes, Sir."

The night is too bright. It is those lights in the waiting area. There are too many of them. They hurt my eyes. And too many people. I don't see people after ten! There is Gaston, Elsie, Joe and Tom... and someone in blue. A policeman.

George. Mavis.

"Seeyah, doc!"

Oh God. So I am mortal? Winston has taken me to hell. I always thought he was peculiar. It's so dark in here and everything hurts. Why does it hurt so much?

"You are healing yourself too quickly. Your organism cannot absorb the metabolic changes at such a quick rate."

But I have no control...

"But I have no control over it. Whatever it is."

"Yes, you do. Think of your magnetic field and relax."

Relax the field?

"Try to steady it."

Peter tries to steady his magnetic field. He tries to ignore the pain and relaxes as best he can, placing all his attention on what he considers his aura. There is an oscillating angry colour vibrating all around him. There are deep reds and crimsons, and browns all mixed up. He tries harder to relax. Nothing happens. It hurts badly. He gives up. The angry colours steady just a little. There are segments of green, bright green, insinuating themselves into the mass of tangled colour. Like in a rainbow.

Come on, Uncle Peter, join us!

When did I hear that?

God, it hurts... HELP ME!

A golden light forms around Peter's aura. Around his magnetic field. The golden light doesn't touch him, nor his aura, it just seems to hover all around him. A calm, steady golden light. The vibrations of his own magnetic field respond immediately. Peter watches in amazement as small, tentative fingers of light reach out from his own body as if prodding the cocoon of the perfectly steady golden aura. Strange, a thought crosses his mind, the golden light doesn't seem to vibrate at all. It just is.

"Am I dead?"

"No. Not quite."

Then I think I'll take a nap.

The stars are quite steady now. They are not moving. It is very peaceful. There is no noise except for a steady hum. A melodious hum. A little like the transformer outside the upstairs room's window at the tavern. Only it is not annoying. Or unnerving. It just is. Like the golden light he saw just before...?

Before I got here.

The stars are receding against the approaching grayness. It must be daylight. The background is becoming lighter and brighter until he can't see the stars anymore. Just light. It is more peaceful than Peter could ever imagine. There is no space, no up or down, no measurable distance, no point of reference, no time... Just light.

"Where am I?"

The stars are back again. Tiny pinpoints of light.

"You are always here."

"Where is here?"

"Wherever you are."

Thank you for nothing.

"Don't mention it."

Wherever I am, or have been, there is a sense of humour. That's good. It would be horrible to be somewhere where there isn't any. Even if it was just light.

"The light is not a place."

Kidding is all right, but I've been there. I'm not stupid. Or blind.

Well, no answer? No quick repartee?

"The light is you. And you are the light."

Then how come I am here now?

"You always were. Only for a moment you were just yourself. Then you started thinking. You started formulating symbols in your consciousness. Your consciousness responded by placing you in an environment where thoughts or symbols have their existence. The universe."

You mean I have been outside the universe?

"No, I don't mean that at all. You are always here."

So where am I? Ah, all right. I am wherever I am. So to speak.

"I told you it isn't easy."

The stars are no longer fixed points of light. They are all moving away from Peter. Faster and faster. For an instant he is afraid to be left alone. In the centre of the universe with no one there for company. Not even the stars. Just impenetrable void. An infinite nothing. Peter panics. With an enormous effort he reaches out for the stars. They keep receding. He reaches out harder. Still nothing.

HELP!

The stars continue to recede, but they seem to slow down. Right! They are no longer travelling away at the same rate.

What happened just now?

"You expanded your consciousness."

I did?

"You did. Instead of bringing the stars closer to you, you just got closer to them."

There really is a sense of humour around here. Wherever here is. I know, I know, wherever I am. Very funny.

But that would make me enormous...

"As many light years across as you choose to be."

You're kidding.

He is not kidding. He doesn't seem to kid that much. How come he knows all the answers?

How come you know...

"I don't. I am a student. Just like you."

Ha! Ha!

"Suit yourself, but it's true."

You are Winston, aren't you.

"Am I?"

The world is a jigsaw puzzle. And you're not helping much.

"Sorry. I told you I am just a student, like you."

Like me and a billion billion others. Like the stars. I wonder if anyone ever tried to count them. I suppose there would be little point. Some go supernova, some shrink into neutron stars or even black holes, some new ones are born every day. Like babies. Only babies have someone to look after them.

Who looks after the stars?

"God."

What is God?

"God it that which looks after the stars."

Thank you for no...

"You're welcome."

Ouch.

I must have slept for hours. How come it's still dark? I don't seem to hurt quite so much. If I don't try to move, that is. Thank God the pain is subsiding. Funny thing, pain. It is a natural defence mechanism which nature provided us with, in order to help us on our journey towards immortality. Only I am not going anywhere and it still hurts. I suppose I could be doing something wrong.

Peter tries hard to tell himself that it doesn't hurt any more. It doesn't work. He tries a few more times, and again nothing happens. The same dull, throbbing pain throughout his body. Like being in a decompression chamber and the air was sucked out too quickly. Or pushed in too quickly. Whichever. Peter had never been in a decompression chamber. It also feels as though his blood is boiling.

Peter tries to remember what happened. He carefully avoids the images of the last hour or two at the inn. He remembers peculiar dreams and a lot of discussions with Winston. Where is Winston, anyway? I thought he took it upon himself to look after me.

Hey! I thought I was looking after other people.

A knock on the door. Oh, my God! It's starting again. It must be six already.

"Peter?" A whisper.

Peter hears the door opening very slowly, quietly and someone coming in. They are supposed to wait until I call them in. Ah, to hell with it.

"Come," he says belatedly.

"Are you awake?" A bit louder.

Of course I am awake. How do you think I can help you unless I am awake. He tries to get up. A racking pain shoots across his whole body, terminating at the back of his head. A moan escapes from his parched lips.

"Don't move. It's me, Ruth."

"Ruth? What are you doing here? Are you sick?" Peter tries to move again. Again he gives up.

"Lie still, dear. Winston said I am to give you a sip of this liquid. You are quite dehydrated." Ruth sits down on a chair next to Peter's bed.

"Ruth?" Peter asks again. Then his head clears a little. "Where am I?"

I know. I am wherever I am.

"You are at home. Now take a sip. Only slowly."

Ruth places a curved straw in Peter's mouth. He sips obediently. He is trained that those lying down on beds obey those who are standing up. The liquid is tepid and sweet. Probably glucose with some minerals and vitamins, he thinks. It tastes good.

"Slowly..."

He slows down. He had not realized how thirsty he was. I should give myself an intravenous...

"That's enough for now. You will get more in two hours."

Good. A smaller dose but often. Every two hours. Peter approves.

"Could you draw the curtain, please?" he asks. His throat doesn't hurt as much.

"They are drawn. Winston bandaged your eyes with a compress. He has some herbs which he said will help ease the itching."

Winston Smith. A strange fellah. How did he know my eyes had been itching?

"How did I get here?"

"You sure you are well enough to talk?"

"I am not well enough not to talk." A weak smile. Too many things have happened. How did I get here? How long have I been here? Why am I here? Who is Winston Smith?

"Winston brought you."

Of course. Winston brought you. Who else? If he can bring
me back from the centre of the universe, he can equally as well
bring me here from St-Henri. At the memory of the tavern
Peter's thin lips tighten. Who is looking after my patients?

"How long have I been lying here like this?"

"Today is the third day."

That's between 150 and 200 patients. Women, men and
children. What will happen to them? Then a clear question
formulates in Peter's head. As clear as if someone actually said it
for him: What did they do before you went there?

"Miss Mondellay called and told Winston about you. He
waited until dark, to elude the reporters. One or two are still
hovering around in case you turn up."

Cathy! Well, at least Winston didn't teleportate, or whatever
it's called, to see that I needed help.

"He found you in a courtyard at the back of the house. A
fellow called Gaston didn't want to let you go, but Winston has a
way with people. He sort of does whatever he sets his heart on."

"Do they know where I am?"

"No one knows. Except for myself and Winston. The
children are on a skiing week at Mont Tremblant. They say
spring skiing is great this year."

"Alone?"

"With the Social Integration Centre."

Of course. Stupid question. With the children studying at
home they have to attend Social Integration once a month.

"So how come you're not with them?"

"I was. Winston called me..."

Does the man make all the decisions around here?

"I just don't know what I would do without him. After you
left..."

Good God! I didn't say good-bye, did I?

"I am very sorry, Ruth." Winston is right. Words are very
inadequate means of communication. Only fit for this big ball of
dirt.

"You did what you had to do."

"You knew?"

"Winston told me. I also spoke to John and Lucy Brent. They all said that I must leave you alone. That you must..."

".....learn in my own way." On my own mistakes.

"That sort of thing."

"Will my eyesight be all right?" Nuts! A doctor of medicine, a Fellow of the Royal College of Physicians asking his sister-in-law to consult with her butler. And don't forget the gift.

"Oh, yes. He was quite sure of that. Only you must help."

Physician, heal thyself.

"How?"

"He said he would tell you himself."

"I think he already did."

"Oh? He spent the first two days and nights at your side. But he didn't say you had come to."

"You mean I've been unconscious?"

"Well, more like in a coma."

"And you didn't call a... ah, doctor?" Why did the word sound like a dirty word?

"Winston said it wasn't necessary. He said that you are not an ordinary man."

No. More like a freak.

"You should sleep now. That is when your recovery progresses at its fastest."

No doubt Winston said so.

"At least Winston said so." Ruth smiles, but there is tremendous concern in her eyes.

"Really?"

Ruth gets up slowly, gently touches Peter's forehead, then bends down and kisses his cheek. Peter feels strange. It is the first time he recalls being touched by someone, instead of the other way round, for a number of months. Or was it years?

"Ruth?"

"Yes, Peter?"

The dryness has returned to Peter's throat. A hard, constricting dullness. He tries to swallow and he can't. His throat is too dry. Ruth comes back from the door and gives him another drink from the bottle by the bedside. She does not let Peter take more than a few sips.

"Thanks, Ruth."
"You wanted to tell me something?"
"Yes. I wanted to thank you."
"Oh... Well, good night now."
"Good night, Ruth."

The stars haven't moved. They seem to have waited for
Peter to return. Only now they are brighter. A little more
sparkling, more joyful. Stars are like that sometimes. They look
joyful or lonely, depending on your mood.
        "It's your universe. It's your decision."
        Thanks for waiting for me.
        "No problem. I like it here."
        I see what you mean. It's a beautiful universe, if you only
open your eyes.
        "It also has a lot to do with attitude."
        Like with being immortal?
        "That's the sort of thing."
        Winston, are we immortal?
        Peter waits in silence, but there is no answer. All he can hear
is the wind. Only there is no wind. He turns his eyes in all
directions simultaneously. He finds he can see through immense
distances. Through the centres of stars, through the central cores
of gigantic galaxies. But he cannot see Winston.
        He is quite alone. Again.

* * *

Spring

. . .there shall be resurrection of
the dead, both the just and
the unjust.

Acts 24:15

13

Escape

"Good morning, Winston."

While Peter feels as weak as a newborn infant, he does not feel any pain. It doesn't even hurt to smile. It is good to be alive.

As Winston draws the curtains, the room is flooded with the crisp March sunshine. Peter had slept, on and off, for six days. He vaguely remembers Winston carrying him to the bathroom and later laying him down again with the ease of a mother returning her child to the crib. The inscrutable butler may be slim, perhaps skinny, but he does not lack in strength. Not that much muscle power was required. Peter weighs no more than a pair of undernourished lambs—though he's nearly as hairy.

"Good morning, Sir. The bath is drawn and I took the liberty to lay out my own shaving equipment for you."

Peter reaches up and tugs on his beard. His electric shaver would fight a losing battle with this jungle.

"You mean my vacation is over?"

Winston continues to adjust the perfectly laid out clothes, which evidently Peter is to don after the very necessary ablutions.

"I shall be there to assist you, Sir."

"Not in a million years, my friend!"

Peter throws away the sheet and blankets. He sits up, swings his feet out to the floor, takes two steps forward and is caught just in time by the quick-handed butler. Winston puts Peter back on the bed and steps back to give him time to recover.

"What have you been feeding me—90% alcohol?"

Winston doesn't answer. Peter knows his vertigo was to be expected. He'd been a doctor once. A physician. Before the gift came into his life. The black spots before his eyes give way to a coolness in his forehead, then gradually returning warmth. He looks around. His room is exactly as he had left it during the last ice age. The computer's cyclopean eye stares blindly into space. It looks dormant, almost dead. There is a thin layer of static dust on its screen.

There is not that much more that could have changed. A bed is a bed, the desk is not as cluttered as it once had been; the books, files and magazines are arranged in neat piles. Winston? Must have been. Who else would restore sanity to his private domain?

"I think we can now proceed to the bathroom, Sir."

"What? Ah yes. Of course we can."

Peter grins at the Nightingalean 'we'. Nevertheless, he puts on his dressing gown to cross the corridor. A force of habit.

This time there are no problems with his sense of balance. What blood remained in his emaciated body seems equally distributed in all the requisite compartments. All the same, Peter is glad that the bathroom is so much closer than at the tavern. And the carpet is so much softer. And there is no smell. It is almost sterile. Not like in a hospital, but sterile all the same. There are no distinct smells lingering around. No *spécial du jour*.

Peter hangs his dressing gown on the door hook and removes his pajamas. For a moment he remains motionless. This is the first time he sees himself, naked, in a full-size mirror. All his body parts are still there. What's left of them. All the same, to anyone in his own condition Peter would recommend an extended holiday. Away. Far away from whatever caused this horrifying result. The last time he had seen such contours on a human frame, they had been attached to a victim of a Nazi concentration camp. The documentary dated back to the middle of the last century.

He forces himself to close his eyes, then to turn his head away. A full-length mirror can be very unnerving. Especially to inept faith healers.

Am I? Is that what I am? A faith healer?

Not in this condition. Peter leans against the cool, tiled wall for support.

The bath is like a warm massage. His first bath in months. A luxurious celebration of my physical humanity, he muses. The caress of an impersonal lover. The sweet smell of the balmy ocean, the sun...

"Dr. Thornton?"

The sun becomes an infrared light in the ceiling, the balmy ocean is disturbed by Peter's own feet. The magic, the serenity is gone.

"Yes, Winston?"

"I believe that fifteen minutes are enough for the first time. A warm bath is relaxing, but it might also sap your returning strength."

"Five more minutes?"

"I think not, Sir."

(Those reclining obey those standing up.) Peter pushes himself up, out of the warm embrace. Halfway up, Winston's strong arm steadies Peter's matchstick legs.

Again he must face the impertinent mirror. Must it scream the truth so blatantly? Winston takes the blade from Peter's unsteady hands. The edge is much too sharp for an inept surgeon, let alone a specialist in internal medicine—a distant memory. Winston performs the tonsorial improvements himself.

His beard gone, the fresh scent of cologne, a clean shirt on his back, a pair of freshly pressed slacks, a fluffy pair of socks comforting his feet, soft slippers... is this what heaven is like? Ask and it shall be given. One just had to know whom to ask.

"Winston?"

"Yes, Sir?"

"Where is Mrs. Thornton?"

"Milady is downstairs waiting for you, Sir. She suggested a brunch at eleven."

"You mean I shall partake of real food?"

"You have since the day before yesterday. In small doses."

I was dead the day before yesterday. I was buried and the key to my sarcophagus had been thrown away. You and Ruth brought me back to life.

"May I offer you my arm, Sir?"

Peter finds it difficult to resist the temptation of turning down the offer. Tomorrow, he muses. Tomorrow I shall fly solo. He nods and Winston takes hold of his left elbow. Peter's right hand grabs the handrail almost convulsively. God, we're so high up... The living room is a great distance below them, way down there, way down... It can make your head spin. For a moment it does.

As they come down the stairs, Ruth watches them from the dining room archway. She doesn't say anything. She looks rested, relaxed. There is nothing to indicate that during the last four days she has spent most of her time at Peter's bedside. Winston had told her that it wasn't really necessary, but she would have none of it.

"What if he wakes up and needs something?"

Even Winston had no answer to this innocuous question. It was based on emotion, not on intellectual judgment.

Finally Peter and Winston reach the bottom rung. Step, only it feels like a rung. Peter looks up and sees Ruth. For no reason he can understand, her eyes are filled with tears. She is unable to speak. Peter smiles.

"I think I know what Lazarus felt like."

Peter attempts a broader grin and winces. His skin is still tightly stretched on his bones. He imagined it would be otherwise. He imagined it would be hanging in loose folds at the bottom of his face, ready to offer reserve flaccidity for facial grimaces. He was wrong. His skin had shrunk with the rest of him.

Ruth approaches, takes Peter's other arm and leads him to the table. Winston withdraws to the kitchen. Before sitting down, Ruth takes Peter into her arms. She holds him close, as a mother would hold an errant child, a prodigal son. Then she wipes away her tears.

"Welcome back, Peter," she manages finally. Her eyes are still misty.

"It's good to be back, sister dear." Peter regards Ruth with genuine affection. "Something tells me that I have sapped your strength a little, these last few days."

There should be so much to say, yet they eat in silence. Perhaps there is too much to be said. Each has too many questions, too many enigmas to resolve. They finish eating and move to the living room. Slowly, Peter again on Ruth's arm, but this time keeping his own balance rather well. They settle down in front of the fireplace. It is almost warm enough to stop heating, but Ruth had laid it out herself for Peter's homecoming.

"What do they say about me?" Peter asks after a while.

"They?"

"People. Neighbours. Whoever."

Ruth wiggles uncomfortably.

"The *Gazette* had a few articles about the purported miracle cures at the General. The last about the middle of January, mostly speculating on what had happened to you. The TV interviewed a girl whose nephew had reportedly been brought back to life. They also cornered a young doctor, apparently on duty that night in the Emergency, but he denied everything. I forget what he said, exactly, but..."

"No, Ruth. Not the press. Not television. People." Ruth still looks uncomfortable. Peter tries to explain. "I am trying to discover who or what I am . Do you understand?"

"The neighbours complained to the police about the people camping in our front garden. I could have had them removed, but I didn't have the heart. Some of them looked and sounded sincere."

"What did they say?"

"They said, as near as I can remember, that you are a..." Ruth looks and sounds uncomfortable, "...a faith healer. That you have been blessed with a gift of God."

Winston serves them an extra coffee.

"What do you say I am, Winston?"

"You are what you believe you are, Sir. Who do you believe you are?"

"Who or what?"

Silence. Winston leaves the jug with extra coffee on the low table and directs his steps towards the kitchen. Quietly, impersonally. As usual.

"Would you mind awfully spending a few minutes with us, Winston."

The butler stops, then slowly turns round.

"Will there be anything else, Sir?"

"Yes. I want you to tell me about the expansion of consciousness."

Without the slightest effort Peter recalls the dreams he had, when Winston had first placed him in his bed upstairs.

"What is it that you would like to know, Sir?"

"Is it all true what you told me a week ago?"

"I do not recall discussing the matter with you, Sir."

It doesn't work. Peter racks his brains to know how to make the enigmatic butler drop his guard. He tries another tack.

"What is a faith healer?"

"It is a person who heals by an act of faith." Winston replies in a tone most people reserve for discussing the weather.

"Am I a faith healer?"

"No, Sir."

A sharp crack precedes an array of sparks from a log in the fireplace. The kernels of light smash against the black metal screen and split into still tinier particles which shed their luminosity, their life, before reaching the hearth. An exploding atom. A nova. Ruth shrinks away as if to avoid the flare-up, although no ember could possibly reach her. Peter seems fascinated.

"Could you elaborate on what is a faith healer?" Peter refuses to let go.

"A faith healer is a person who relies on the faith of the prospective recipient to alter his or her own magnetic field in such a manner as to precipitate a change in the metabolism of the biological host."

"Winston! A healing is an act of God!" Ruth cuts in and immediately displays a subdued redolence on her cheeks.

"Yes, Madam. It is."

"Then...?"

Winston waits until he is sure that milady is no longer talking.

"I dare say, Madam, it depends on our definition of the divine."

Peter ignores this exchange. His mind is still digesting Winston's last statement.

"Then healing is basically an alteration in a person's aura?"

"Yes, Sir."

Another silence.

"Will that be all, Sir?"

Winston is again ready to withdraw. Throughout the discussion he remained a consummate butler.

"Just one other thing. You said that I am not a faith healer. Why?"

"Because you rely on your own inner convictions, not those of your patient."

"There is a difference?"

"It is a question of semantics. There are occasions when the so-called non-believers are the recipients of healing when exposed to certain electromagnetic fields. But basically, their subconscious mind is already prepared for the event to occur."

Peter scratches his head. His face looks gaunt, but his eyes are already regaining their old inquisitive hunger.

"So faith healing is not a spiritual but... a physical process?"

"I would prefer to call it mental, Sir. But it all depends on your definition of the word faith, Sir."

"That which one firmly believes in?"

"That which is firmly anchored in one's subconscious."

"So to cure the body one must first cure the subconscious conditioning of the prospective patient..."

"Most of the time, Sir."

"Aha! So it is not always so!"

"Very few things ever are, Sir."

Peter feels tired. This is the first day he actually got dressed and came downstairs. He has eaten a more or less regular breakfast. Brunch. And now Winston was filling his head with more ideas to chew on than he could manage on the spur of the moment.

"How do you know all this, Winston?"

"I really couldn't say, Sir." Winston's face remains supremely impassive. "Will there be anything else, Sir?"

Peter smiles. He is ready to take an oath on everything that's holy that Winston can say a great deal more. He only 'couldn't' say it *right now*. I probably wouldn't understand it just yet.

"Milady?" Winston turns deferentially to Ruth.

"Thank you, Winston. The brunch was excellent."

It should be. With Winston looking after Peter upstairs, Ruth helped to prepare the light meal herself. For many years Ruth had been coping in the kitchen quite well on her own.

"Thank you, Madam."

Peter takes a nap on the sofa alongside the fireplace. Ruth spends the next hours doing whatever women do when they are not working. This consists of a thousand and one things that convert a house into a home. Convert and maintain. And Ruth makes sure that her children grow up in a home filled with love and beauty and warmth. Unbeknownst to her, she, herself, is the best example of all three.

About three o'clock Peter awakens. His head is full of fresh ideas. His body a little less depleted. It takes time to recover from three months of self-inflicted punishment. He wonders what is new in the outer world. The world at large, outside the confines of his own little universe. He gets up and takes a stroll around the house. He walks cautiously, keeping close to the walls or supporting furniture. The carpet feels like a massage to his feet. He leaves his slippers behind and walks on in his socks. It gives him a sensual pleasure.

Passing next to the children's playroom, Peter hears muted voices. Surely the children are away? As his hand reaches out for the door handle, he hesitates. It is months since he heard people talk about anything other than their ailments, or the quality of the *menu du jour*. He rests his back against the wall and slowly lowers himself to the carpet. Right next to the door. The muted voices sound louder.

"...already lost most of his faith. Don't you realize he once attended a seminary? He was within a day of being ordained a priest. How can you destroy what little remains?"

"I do not volunteer information, Madam. I only answer the questions posed."

"But you are still responsible, aren't you?"

"I most certainly am, Madam."

There is a short silence.

Peter wants to know about the UN, about Solidarity International, about the great big world out there but, for the moment, he seems riveted to the carpet. He feels a mite guilty about his eavesdropping but cannot help himself. There is something about Winston talking that commands attention. No matter what he says.

"Do you believe in God?" Ruth's voice is very quiet.

"Yes, Madam."

"Do you practice any religion?" Ruth had never seen Winston going to any church or asking for time off to visit one.

"In a way, Madam, all of them."

Peter cocks his ear. Another one of Winston's enigmatic answers. The amazing thing is that if anyone else said it, it would sound stupid. Coming from Winston...

"Please be serious, Winston. I am Jonathan's and Moira's mother. I am responsible for their moral upbringing. Their code of ethics. You seem to have a great influence on their outlook."

"I am always serious in matters concerning children's souls, Madam."

"I know you are. Only, well, you seem so..."

"...unorthodox, Madam? Yes. I suppose I am. I am also very ordinary."

"Please explain what you mean?"

Peter can picture Winston standing erect, relaxed, in perfect command of the air he displaces with his body. A truly dramatic presence. The man would make a fortune on the stage.

"Any religion is a dangerous concept, Madam. It fosters an elitist ideology. It is divisive. It creates and upholds the concept of *us* and *them*. *Us* being the good guys, if I may use the term, Madam. Religions, in general, are an unnatural concept. They interpose themselves between an individual and his or her highest potential. Furthermore, they require an organizational super-structure. The organizations, normally referred to as churches, require elitist cabals: the priests, high and low, men of power, of prestige, influence, position, title. Mercifully, history has shrouded most of their misanthropic transgressions against humanity into oblivion. And whose deeds have survived in racial memory? The non-conformists'. The rebels'. The troublemakers'. And who were these opponents of the establishment? The Prophets, the Seers, the Teachers who disdained religion. Not God, Madam, only religion."

Winston's voice is measured, relaxed, monotonous—almost reticent. He does not sound as though he is trying to convince Ruth of anything. He merely shares his knowledge. All the same, his words have an air of immutability.

"The present-day church leaders claim those few *were* the religion, but not so. They who dared to defy the *status quo* of their day were killed. Tortured, exiled, crucified. And who are the rebels of today? Certainly not those who wield power, civil or ecclesiastic. They will soon join their predecessors in the cauldron of oblivion."

"Not all Christians are bad." Ruth's voice sounds muted. Her mind wanders among the ghosts of those tortured, exiled. Those crucified.

"Nor were all the men they murdered. This is not my point. My point is that we must distinguish between the Rebels, the Prophets, the Saviours and their purported followers who usurped their teaching to gain power. To create religions. Each and every religion has been, was, is and always will be little more than a method of controlling masses of people, essentially by exploiting their emotional weaknesses."

"There are honest men in all churches." Ruth's tone is depressed. Her voice is almost pleading.

"Of course there are. Churches have produced great saints. But I might suggest, Madam, that those giants of all the religions have become giants not because of their allegiances but in spite of them."

"So there is no hope for any of the churches?"

Peter shuffles even closer to the door. He holds his breath.

"It is not a question of hope. All the hundreds of churches, cults, social systems serve a purpose, often in spite of their leaders. People learn by both: good and bad example. They learn by observing the opposites. And ultimately, what matters is not a church, nor an organization, but the individual consciousness."

"So you feel that one should not attend a church?"

"Not at all, Madam. Every soul is on an individual journey. Each serves a unique purpose in the realm of God. There are those who will advance greatly by being active members of an established religion. Others will be retarded. Those others should seek a more personal journey. Ultimately only those are truly feebleminded who do nothing. Who are indifferent."

"The lackadaisical majority?"

"I sometimes think so, Madam."

"Is there no hope for them?"

"We are immortal, Madam. There is no hurry."

I knew it! Peter almost falls against the door. His wan cheeks take on a delicate hue at the thought of being discovered at the door. He tries to distance himself from the compromising position. As he crawls on all fours away from the children's playroom, he can just hear Winston's and Ruth's final exchange. The question is not surprising. The answer is.

"Winston?"

"Yes, Madam?"

"Just before going to the Centre, Jo asked me a strange question. He asked me if I remembered what I did in my previous life. Are you teaching my children about reincarnation?"

"Not really, Madam. I am teaching them how to avoid it."

After that Peter finds himself too far away to hear what is being said. He had hoped to hear something that would help him in his own dilemma. He heard Winston's statement about immortality; but, on second thought, the man may have been talking about soul. From Peter's dream experiences, still vivid in his memory, anything could be expected from Winston Smith. Anything at all.

A few minutes later Ruth finds Peter in the living room. She looks a little flushed, as if having run a considerable distance. Surprisingly, she also seems at peace with the world. The last words Peter heard her say sounded quite worried. Peter wonders what Winston said to her subsequently to restore her equanimity.

Now, however, as Ruth sits down opposite Peter, a frown returns to her forehead. She seems to be searching for words.

"The children are coming back tomorrow," she says at last.

"Wonderful!" Peter waits. He feels there is more to come.

"Yesterday, there were two reporters hanging around the front lawn."

"Oh? I would have thought they'd buried me by now."

Ruth reaches down and picks up a copy of the *Montreal Gazette* from the floor next to her armchair. She turns to an inside page, folds the sheets and hands the article to Peter. The headline is about a centimetre high. Not the largest, but far from the smallest.

HEALER DISAPPEARS FROM TAVERN

The article that followed was short and to the point.

"Last Sunday, under sinister circumstances, a local hero vanished into oblivion. The ascetic who reputedly possessed formidable healing powers, which he applied freely to all who asked, disappeared in the early hours of Sunday morning. The healer's disappearance is linked to an unfortunate incident, wherein a man whose health he had supposedly restored had used his newly found powers to sate his accumulated carnal hunger. The man is being held on suspicion of rape and murder.

It should be noted that the vanished healer, a Mr. Simon Nomad, had appeared on the scene in St-Henri about the time that a Dr. Peter Thornton FRCP, a noted Specialist, had, in equally mysterious circumstances, disappeared from the Montreal General Hospital. A spokesperson for the MGH praised Dr. Thornton as a physician of quite unparalleled ability. Some extraordinary healing powers have also been linked with his name."

That's it. Short and bitter.

Peter puts down the newspaper. His mind drifts to the inn, the tavern, to the knocks on his minuscule office door. His body appears to shrink further into the soft armchair. He is not ready for this. He expected his holiday to last a little longer. He closes his eyes only to see the face of a woman with dark blotches on the front of her neck. Peter shakes his head.

"I need time," he says at last.

"I am afraid we have no more time."

Peter is only now beginning to understand what Ruth is implying. He has run out of time. He must move, escape. The hounds are at his heels. The holiday really is over.

"I have no money..."

After only a few days in the lap of civilization, Peter seems to be eminently practical.

"You don't need any money, Peter. Winston drove up to Mount Burton yesterday and stored enough food in the fridge and the basement storage to last you a month. I think the headline seekers will give up, once they see that you have not returned here. You should be able to come back in a few weeks, a month at worst."

So the cottage up North has been fixed up for him. Winston thinks of everything. A strange fellow, Winston.

And then a wave of anger swirls in Peter's eyes. Why should I run away? Why should I be treated like a criminal, an outcast, a reprobate? For months I have given all. More than all. I nearly paid with my life.

"Why can't they leave me alone?"

But Peter's anger dissipates as quickly as it came. His face becomes plaintive, his last sentence almost a whimper.

"You will have peace there," Ruth tries hard to console him. "No one knows about you in the village. I doubt that many people even know my name. We had little chance to go there, these last few years."

Peter feels sorry for himself. It is a long time since he indulged in such a luxury.

"I shall be all alone?"

"We shall visit you. Winston and I. But I don't think the children should be told. They might talk inadvertently."

Winston appears at the door.

"The luncheon is served, Madam."

Luncheon at 3:30? That's what comes from eating brunches at eleven.

"I suggest, Madam, Dr. Thornton and I should leave by four o'clock at the latest. His clothes are packed and the car is ready."

Why can't you fly me there on your wings, Peter muses. He stares at the tall butler. Then Peter blinks. He could swear Winston winked at him. The wink had a message, something like: later, my friend, later...

Ruth and Peter eat in silence. The situation is not conducive to a stimulating conversation. At three minutes to four, Winston appears in the hall with Peter's coat. Peter takes Ruth in his arms, or really, the other way round. Peter is still too weak to embrace anyone.

At one minute to four a siren sounds outside. There must be a fire. Nearby. Winston looks through the visor in the front door. Two men loitering at the entrance to the garden are arguing. Then one of them throws up his arms and walks towards the sound of the siren. The other spits angrily on the grass and follows him. He is carrying a professional camera with a telescopic lens.

"If you would, Sir? We must go now." Winston says.

Moments later the Buick is purring up the hill. Within minutes they become part of the *Côte-des-Neiges* traffic. The last time Peter crossed this street, he was a Fellow of the Royal College. A senior staff member of the Montreal General Hospital.

Today he is a displaced person. A man on the run.

A man without a home.

* * *

14

Cathy

The journey takes a little over three hours. They do not talk much. Peter still feels a lot weaker than he lets on. He could hardly walk the few steps between the front door and the garage. In the car, he collapsed against the reclining seat and promptly fell asleep. Winston drives slowly in order not to disturb him. It isn't easy. For the last 45 minutes they have been travelling along a narrow, winding road which must have last seen fresh gravel a good twenty years ago.

They enter Canadian wilderness.

When still motoring along the elegant, three-lane highway, Winston repeatedly steals quick glances at the reclining figure. When he does, his dark, imperturbable eyes seemed to assume a strange warmth. A warmth akin to a deep friendship, perhaps love, rather like that of a caring father towards his favourite son. Or perhaps it is a deep concern, an unconditional compassion for an erring child. Peter is not privy to Winston's feelings, nor to his apparent protector's singular mission. If he were, he would not understand it—not even if his gray cells operated at their best, as they had some long months ago. Now, all Peter needs is sleep. As much sleep as possible. To effect the repairs. While fully awake, Peter is apt to interfere with the functions of his subconscious mind. With its mechanical efficacy. Peter does not know it yet, but he will soon learn that it is a lot easier to heal others than it is to heal himself.

A pothole left over from past thaws shakes Peter out of his slumber.

The sleep has helped to lubricate his veins. He feels much better, restored from the efforts of the first day on his feet. Peter's eyes are wide open now. In the fast-approaching dusk, he strains to discern and absorb the landscape unfolding at each turn of the road, now little more than a meandering track. He is surprised at the still lingering remnants of the jealously possessive winter. He lowers a window. The air is crisp but not icy. Bracing, they used to call it. Real air. The air nature intended for people to breathe.

At last they arrive.

It is too dark to see the details of the cabin. Peter follows behind as Winston opens the door—thick wooden planks held on three oversized, surface-mounted, cast iron hinges. The door gives the appearance of security, of an entrance to a fortress of a bygone era. A gust of warm air carries a promise of comfort within. Winston must have left the heat on since yesterday, Peter muses. He had not visited the cottage in four years. He had no time. He never had any time. Until now. Is this the reason for all this? To slow me down? To give me time? For what? And then Peter stops dead in his tracks.

"I took the liberty to call..."

Although this is the first time since they met that Winston does not complete his sentence, Peter is not apt to notice this historical event.

"You are looking much better." Cathy's voice sounds less certain than her words.

And you are the panacea for all my problems.

Peter's lips move, but no words seem ready to describe his feelings. He was fully prepared, at least during the first few days, to stagger from one chair to another, to crawl on all fours, if need be, to get a drink of water. Even a minute ago, he was not aware of just how weak he was—until he attempted to help Winston with the luggage. His knees buckled under the weight of a single carryall bag. Now, he takes a step back and leans against the frame of the massive door for support.

"Cathy..." He whispers, finally. "Cathy!"

During all his stay in St-Henri, on that one occasion, for that brief moment, she had been his sole link with sanity. With the world he once knew. And deserted.

"Should you not come in, Peter? We are losing all the heat."

Fool! I left the door open. Just then Winston carries in the last bag.

"If you don't mind, Sir, I shall be on my way right away."

"What?" Peter turns his head. Winston. What on earth would I do without his help? I would have become a statistic. Another immortal denied his heritage. "How can I ever thank you?"

Peter reaches out to shake Winston's hand. He and the butler had shaken hands once before. Just once. As Winston accepts Peter's hand, Peter attempts to draw the lanky butler a little closer. For an instant his head is buried in Winston's chest. Then the men step back and Winston bows to Cathy Mondellay.

"Good night, Miss Mondellay. I trust I did not impose too much."

"I would never forgive you if you hadn't!" Cathy's voice is threatening, but her eyes are shining with gratitude. She looks happy.

"Thank you, Madam. Good night, Sir."

The heavy door closes with an age-worn creak. Winston Smith seems to take with him the remnants of the outer world. In a moment Peter hears a quiet purr of the engine. It fades in but a few seconds. He and Cathy are alone.

Only then does Cathy become aware of her rudeness. She feels she ought to run out and wave to Winston, to call him back. Surely he needs a rest after the long drive. Surely... but her feet are firmly anchored to the cabin floor.

Is this what heaven is like?

And then Peter feels close to collapse. How come my blood vessels find it so hard to service my head? Peter looks for the nearest chair. Cathy guesses his need and takes hold of his elbow. Together they make it to the armchair in front of the open fire. The next instant Peter is embarrassed at the incongruous image crossing his mind. Cathy and the fireplace

conjure thoughts of love-making. Of Cathy languid on the rug...
Peter shakes his head. He's too weak to even think about it. He is
too weak to shrug his shoulders.

"I'm sorry. I guess the trip took a bit out of me?"

Cathy stares at him in amazement.

"How on earth did you manage to last that long?" she asks,
her head nodding sideways in disbelief.

Peter smiles. Frankly he has no idea. No idea at all. He
doesn't even know what caused his present condition. He had
worked comparative hours many times in the past. He had also
often missed meals. Many a time. It hadn't been that.

"Perhaps, together, we shall find an answer to that question.
To a number of questions..."

Cathy adds another log to the fire. There was a time when
the cabin could only be used during the more temperate seasons.
In winter it was only for the hardy. Inside and out, the cabin
remained the original building. In the name of old charm, and to
preserve the scanty heritage of the Canadian North, no additional
insulation had been used to add comfort. The rough, hand-hewn
logs, albeit of an imposing diameter, were all that separated the
inner warmth from the bitter cold outside. The Canadian North
rivaled the internment camps of Northern Siberia. Only the
Crazy Canucks came up here for fun. Not as punishment.
Peter's great-grandfather used it as a hunting lodge. In those
days, people also killed animals for fun. Some still do today.

It all changed when Dr. Mondellay succeeded in his
attempts to miniaturize a commercially viable cold-fusion
converter. The scientists had racked their brains about its
viability for close to three generations. Dr. Mondellay made it
work. That day, the North opened up to immigration. With
virtually unlimited energy, it became almost inviting. So were
Siberia, Greenland, Iceland—all the extreme segments of the
globe.

Peter would soon see the beauty of the still unspoiled
nature. Few countries boasted such extensive national parks as
the Canadian Confederation. Most Canadian parks had been
declared Treasures of the World, under the benevolent
sponsorship of the United Nations. No one could build any

structure within the parks' boundaries; but those which were already extant would be preserved, in their original form and expression.

Divergent thoughts flood Peter's mind. He closes his eyes, resting his head against a pillow. He tries hard not to think about Cathy. At least, not for the moment. He feels too weak to cope with the images her presence evokes.

Too weak to think what she means to him.

Gradually, Peter becomes aware of his blood, once more, returning to his starving brain. It must have been the cold air. He hadn't been out for a whole week. Not since the walk in the backyard. A cold shiver runs along Peter's spine. His mind refuses to release the image of the stars crowding the cold sky. All his images seem more persistent lately. It is as if his mind wanted to study them, to scrutinize them for any information which might have slipped by before. Then, the ocean of stars intermingles with the sparks bursting in the fireplace. His mind drifts inexorably towards Cathy. The stars, the sparks and the glitter in his eyes. Why Cathy... Surely she deals in microcosm, not in the infinite realm of the stars. I hardly know her.

Why Cathy?

"Winston called you?" he asks.

"He did the right thing." She dismisses the matter out of hand.

"But why you?"

Peter had seen Cathy exactly twice in his life. Twice in 29 years. Not exactly a long-lasting, well-tested friendship. Anyway, how did Winston know that Cathy is exactly what Peter needs right now?

"Would you rather someone else looked after you?"

"Cathy... I would rather be on a desert island with you than sitting on the top of the world upon a pile of gold with someone else!"

"I would have thought that could be a trifle uncomfortable."

The cracks from the fireplace punctuate the otherwise superb silence. A silence which commands attention, which makes your ears sing with the wind that isn't there.

"I suppose you guessed that I am in love with you?" Peter says, looking at the fire.

"Well, you have a very funny way of showing it!"

Cathy's voice has a dry edge to it. Not the best bedside manner. But she knew. They both knew. Only they had no idea why.

"I had to do it," Peter says simply.

"I know."

She knows. All is forgiven.

The silence stretches. It almost seems a shame to interrupt it. There are no such silent moments in the city. Anywhere. In any place where man has left his indelible mark on nature.

"I sometimes think I am being punished. Of course my mind does not accept such nonsense, but the emotions seem to function independently of one's thinking processes. I suppose it has something to do with conditioning. Brimstone and all that."

Cathy is lost. Later, as Peter tells her about his years at the seminary, she nods her understanding. He tells her about his escape in the nick of time. About the guilt which lingered in his heart for years after.

"...I suppose, I still feel uncomfortable with an excessively solvent bank account. Old habits die hard."

"You mean that poverty is still demanded by the Franciscans?"

"Change is the essence of life. Saint Francis rejoiced in his poverty. Later the Order broke up into three organizations. It appears that organization is necessary for survival, but simultaneously it secularizes spirituality. I was never very good at compromise. When I could not attain to the highest, well, I just gave up altogether."

"And now you feel guilty?"

"Lord, no! I don't feel guilty. I *am* guilty."

"Of what?"

"Of giving up."

Cathy leaves her chair and joins Peter right next to the fire. She curls up on the rug, leans her elbow on the seat of his armchair. She gazes into his eyes.

"After all you've done? Are you being fair to yourself?"

"I've run away from the Seminary. I've run away from medicine. I've run away from faith healing, or whatever you call it. Now I seem to be running away from the media. From humanity."

"Did you expect to stay in St-Henri until your bones shrivelled into a pile of dust?"

"It might have been better than always being on the run." Peter looks away from the fire and tries to direct his eyes to Cathy. He is afraid to look at her. She seems to make his head spin. "You'll find it hard to believe, but for a moment, for a few months, down there, at the inn, I felt... I belonged. I felt I had a home."

Cathy cannot hold his gaze. She turns her head to hide the tears welling up in her eyes. She blinks them away. There is no anger or anguish in Peter's eyes. But there is an unspoken accusation. Not directed at her or anyone in particular. But it is there. His eyes say: Why can't they let me be?

For a moment Cathy recalls what she had once heard or read. She forgets where—it was a long, long time ago. It was something about foxes and birds. Then she remembers: Foxes have holes and the birds have nests, but the son of man has nowhere to lay his head. She has no idea why the phrase came into her head. Peter has Westmount and the cabin. At least his sister-in-law has them. They seem a close-knit family, judging from what little Winston had told her. A strange fellow, that Winston...

"I'll get us something to eat," she says.

Cathy already knows her way around the cabin. She drove up here this morning. She examined the masses of food, which Winston had piled up in the fridge and the downstairs storage. She could feed a small army on the accumulated surplus. From what she remembers, Peter is a scant eater. Well, he will not be a scant eater as long as I cook for him, she mutters to herself, setting the pre-prepared soup on the stove.

For no rational reason, Cathy had been hoping for a drink, a Martini... who knows, perhaps a romantic evening. She knows now that such is not to be. Peter would collapse after one sip; he would disintegrate at the thought of romance.

Peter also was hoping for a Martini, perhaps, he was just hoping...

"How long can you stay up here?" There is no wall between the kitchen counter and the main living space. They can converse while Cathy is in the kitchen.

"For as long as you need me."

"That could be for quite a while..."

Peter's spirits are rising at an alarming rate. If Cathy only knew, her last statement had advanced Peter's recovery by a month. For a moment, he actually felt blood stirring in his veins. Time enough for romantic evenings. Time enough to be a man. A human, an extremely human being.

After an early dinner Peter takes a short nap. Even eating a simple meal taxes his strength. As for his spirits, they have rebounded enormously. Her promise remains at the forefront of his thoughts. As long as you need me, she had said.

How about a lifetime?

They decide against a walk outside, but Peter insists on going out briefly to look at the stars. He misses them. During the last two months, the stars had been his only solace. His friends. Always there, always reliable. Never complaining. Healthy. Sparkling with health. Peter tries not to think about the fenced courtyard. There are no boundaries here. The cabin had been built on an outcropping of solid rock near the top of the hill. A small mountain, really. In two directions, East and West, one could see all the way to the horizon. The far vista is overlooking endless, undulating tops of scraggy, pointed conifers. To the North the hill climbs another three or four hundred feet. To the South, a black line of sentries stands guard. The bushy pines and their cousins, more scraggy firs, intersperse with hemlock and occasional darker, greener during the day, clumps of cedar. They all stand shoulder to shoulder, barring access to any intruder. Only the narrow strip of dirt track, a lighter ribbon against a darker background, cuts into them and then turns sharply so that, on approach, one could see the cabin only when one was already right upon it.

The great-grandfather had chosen well. It is a very secluded spot.

Tonight Peter's eyes do not dwell on the extensive, dark panorama. Instead, as he had done so many times during the early spring, and even on that fateful last day at the tavern, he directs his gaze upwards. He looks up without thinking, yet feeling a great kinship with the countless, ice-cold points of fire. They all are alone. A peculiar, almost painful, thought invades his mind. Even with Cathy at his side, he feels alone. What is this gnawing hunger, this persistent longing, he wonders. His unblinking eyes wander over the vastness, the mesmeric immensity of heaven.

What do you want of me?

They sleep in adjacent rooms on the ground floor. The principal bedrooms are upstairs, but they decide against negotiating the staircase. Not yet. Perhaps in a few days. Before retiring, Peter gives Cathy a gentle kiss on her cheek. It feels artificial. There is so much in abeyance, so much remaining to be shared, so much still unspoken between them.

"I meant what I said," Peter says, letting her go.

Cathy knows he is referring to his earlier confession of love. Of being in love. She only smiles. What could she say to a man she wants with all her heart? To a man too weak to take her in his arms? And did Peter really mean it? He thought he did. A secret part of her heart doubts that she could ever really possess Peter. Maybe his body, but his heart seems to lie elsewhere.

Peter tries hard to impress Cathy. He gets up at seven, washes, shaves, and shuffles to the kitchen to prepare breakfast. Too late. By the time he leaves the bathroom, Cathy is already in the kitchen. She looks vibrant, even younger than last night.

"The birds woke me up," she says. "I don't believe I have ever been awakened by an army of birds!" Cathy is a recalcitrant city dweller.

"They must know you are here. They are just singing for joy."

"Thank you, kind Lord. And how, may I ask, is your Highness today?"

"I'll tell you after I eat a horse. Or a soft-boiled egg.
Whichever you serve me first, Fair Maiden."

Peter sounds a lot better than he looks. But he does seem
firmly committed to his return to the human race. He helps
Cathy with the breakfast, mostly by getting in the way. He seems
to have a need to touch her. Even accidentally. She is healthy.
She doesn't need his healing power. Perhaps he needs hers.

"And what are your plans for the day?" he asks over
coffee.

"To serve you, Master, and to obey."

"I wish you had said that when I resembled a human
being."

"I did."

For the second time in as many days, Peter's cheeks acquire
a healthy hue. He never encountered the slightest problem in
leading platoons of nurses to an assortment of linen
cupboards—but with Cathy? Well, it just wasn't so simple. The
nurses giggled, Cathy looked him in the eye. With nurses it was a
question of releasing tension, with Cathy a hope for a unity of
spirit. A sublime merging. That must be it. The one time they
had made love it started as a physical experience. He was going
to use her, the way he had used other women, albeit willing
subjects. Instead he had been used. Not by Cathy, but by some
power which seemed to have taken over his life. A power he
cannot assign to a god or any supernatural being. At least not a
god of Abraham or Moses or Mohammed or Krishna. Or any
other great Teacher. It was a Power so completely disembodied
that any attempt to incarnate It, to assign to It any human
properties, felt like a travesty of reality. A living lie.

Yet that Power has taken over my life.

After a short walk outside, the hill being too much for Peter,
he and Cathy settle in front of a freshly laid fireplace. There is
nothing like a live fire to warm your spirits, even if electricity
from your own converter is infinitely more efficient. For now,
they are content to while the day away, breathing the country air,
listening to the silence, to the crackling fire. They each read a
book. Cathy, evidently expecting to grow old as Peter's nurse,
had brought a whole suitcase of books. Peter glanced at some of

the titles. There were as many subjects dealing with pure science as with metaphysics.

Now, each with a book in their hands, Peter points to the suitcase.

"Why?" he cannot help asking. "Why all this mumbo-jumbo?"

For a moment Cathy seems slightly miffed by his offensive choice of words. Then she relaxes the vertical line on her straight, high forehead.

"We have to find out what makes you tick, remember?"

"And you think we shall find it in books?"

Cathy puts her book down. "Do you have any better ideas?"

Peter shrugs. He has already read all one can read on the subject of healing.

"Tell me about your vision of the world," Peter asks instead.

"I live in two worlds," Cathy says, after gathering her thoughts for a moment. "I live in worlds which seem at odds with each other. The two are characterized by seemingly diverse traits. One is a continuous world, a world of fields which span the universe with an all-reaching, all-encompassing presence, and the other is a discontinuous world. A world of particles, of bits and pieces, of fragments of reality rather than a whole."

"The electromagnetic and gravitational fields. The other world you describe sounds like one built on quantum physics."

"You went to school then?" Actually Cathy is quite impressed. Most people would not have recognized her description. Peter is very different from most people.

"Yes, teacher. A million years ago."

"Well, in fact, the worlds..."

"Hey, hold it. Whatever happened to matter and energy? Is that not the accepted duality of the universe?"

"Not anymore. There is no difference between matter and energy except in density. Energy is no more than very rarefied matter. Surely you know that, Peter?"

"I know what your voice sounds like, but I still like to hear you talk."

"Oh, be serious..."

"I am all ears."

"Not anymore," Cathy snaps at him for his interruptions. "Your new hair covers them rather nicely," she adds in a softer voice.

Peter never reverted to his old crewcut. He smiles, then his face becomes serious. "Please tell me more," he asks gently.

"Well, my two universes seem to overlap in a manner which we cannot quite understand yet." Cathy leans forward. She is back to her favourite subject. "It seems that a field can also qualify as matter, under certain circumstances. It would be like calling matter spirit and spirit matter."

"You have lost me there," Peter admits.

"We live in a world of duality. Without duality our world would fall apart. Polarity between opposites is the very stepping stone to our understanding of the universe. Yet look what is happening. First we had energy and matter. We lost that. The two are interchangeable. Now we have the fields of relativity and quantum physics. But these seem no more than convenient semantics to describe certain phenomena. Certain laws controlling probabilities."

"Cathy, please make it easier for me." Again she had reached over his head.

"Sorry. Suffice to say that we have two realities. Our duality now consists of field and matter. But—and this is the problem—we seem to be on the verge of modifying our field laws in such a manner that the laws won't break down when the energy is enormously concentrated. In other words, when energy is matter."

"But why would that upset you?"

Cathy stares at Peter with two glowing embers of jade. What incredible eyes, Peter marvels.

"Peter! A true unified field theory would eliminate duality in the physical world. Don't you see that?"

"And is that so bad?"

"What is your definition of God?" Cathy whispers, transfixing Peter with her eyes.

"Spinoza said that to define God is to deny Him."

"Spinoza is dead. How do you define God?"

This is not at all the direction which Peter thought the discussion would take. Actually, Spinoza had taught that there is only one substance with two aspects: thought and extension. But Peter wanted to learn more about Cathy, not metaphysics. He wanted to learn what makes her the enchanting woman she is. Not to go back to something he had left behind the doors of the Seminary.

"Peter," she won't let go. "God is what the opposites have in common."

"The single Source of all... Yes, I'll accept that." Unwittingly Peter feels drawn into Cathy's concepts.

"But don't you see? If we eliminate duality, we come face to face with a single..."

"...with a single Cause."

The silence lasts until Cathy gets up to get a glass of water. Peter asks for one also. They sip the pure spring water like a precious nectar. There is only so much one can say about God without sounding ridiculous.

"You don't propose to define God in one of your equations, do you?"

"I don't propose anything, Peter. You asked me to tell you about my world. I am merely stating the direction which science is taking. It seems that physics and metaphysics are beginning to rub shoulders. I can only imagine where it is going to lead."

"Rub shoulders with God..."

"With the definition of God."

Ye are gods...

The fire is no more than an ashy glow. Peter leans forward and lifts a log to put it on the fire. He had no idea how heavy a log can be. Cathy helps him. He touches her body again. He wonders if their magnetic fields are in some kind of synch—if they vibrate in harmony. Surely, they must, if Winston knows what he's talking about.

Peter wonders what Cathy would say about Winston's theories on healing. They should fit into her philosophy. For himself, Peter feels more down to earth. He gets up from the armchair and moves to a settee. Cathy leaves her own chair and joins him without a word. She places her hands in his palms. Her head lowers onto Peter's shoulder. Neither says anything. Peter's head is swimming, and it is not from exhaustion. Her touch is electrifying.

To hell with duality. This is more than good enough for him.

* * *

15

A Day in Town

Peter is very excited. It is fifteen days since he and Cathy joined forces on the mountain. The mountain with the most enchanting views Cathy had ever seen. She is prepared to stay here for the next ten years. Longer, if need be. But she had promised. She had said that if Peter would extend his walks on the mountain by, say, ten minutes daily, she would eventually drive him to the City. The moment he reaches two continuous hours on the slopes, that is. Without sitting down.

Peter took on the challenge. He started with ten minutes up and five minutes down. He was not up to adding ten more minutes every day. But he tried hard. Today, little more than two weeks later, they have just returned from a two-hour walk. They had admired a panoramic view from the top of the mountain.

"I made it!" Peter feels proud of himself.

As well he should.

Peter not only maintained a good pace both up and down the slope but, during the last two weeks, he has managed to put a few pounds on his skeletal frame. He would no longer scare people by his appearance alone. Not that anyone is likely to recognize his face either. Not even those he had 'treated' in St-Henri. Peter is, or at least appears to be, a very different man. His still sallow cheeks, his whole face, his neck, arms, hands have turned brown with the spring sunshine.

And Cathy? Cathy looked great before. Always. Cathy is not an aggregate of features. She is a whole, a goddess in her own right. She can look and do and say anything she wants. In defiance of the duality of the world, Cathy is perfect.

"What time shall we leave tomorrow?" Peter is already getting ready for the trip.

"You really sure you want to do it?"

"Yes."

So that's that. Some time ago Peter had decided to expunge the skeletons from his personal cupboard. Not that he has any desire to pray, in the normal understanding of the word, but he wants to visit some churches. He wants to do so without feeling guilty. He needs to recapture the elusive sense of freedom that continues to take on new facets during each unfolding season. Mind strives after a new challenge. He feels he must master his body, his emotions, his mind. And now—his memories. The skeletal memories lurking in the hallowed shadows of the long-neglected churches. Skeletal memories of a skeletal man.

It has been many years.

"If the weather is nice, we could leave early. Say about eight?" Peter's thoughts return to the present. He feels alive, almost anxious. He needs action.

"What if it rains? The dirt track might get pretty soggy. It's still only March, you know."

"I wish we had a TV to listen to the weather forecast."

"There is a radio upstairs. Want me to bring it down?" Cathy is still trying to conserve Peter's strength. He hardly needs it, but does not admit as much for fear of Cathy's leaving.

The forecast is great: sunny with intermittent cloudy periods. If it were to rain, this time of the year they would probably get out all right, but coming back up the hill they might well get stuck in the mud. In two or three weeks the access road would settle down. Harden. Right now they have to be careful.

Peter is delighted at finding the radio. He spends the rest of the afternoon fiddling with the news programs. At last some contact with the world. Even before the fateful events of the last few months, he had had little time for the vast world, out there, outside the confines of the General Hospital. Even the iniquities of local affairs had not intruded into his busy schedule. He was a doctor. First and foremost.

Now, to his own surprise, he recognizes within himself a strange stirring, an unfolding process of awakening. To what end? What purpose? This still remains a mystery.

Apparently he and Cathy have missed the 10th anniversary of Quebec rejoining the Canadian Confederation. There had been some minor celebrations in Montreal, but nothing too auspicious or official. The government did not wish to offend the sacred cow: The 32% minority of Francophones—a name people assumed for the French-speaking minority. After all, they contribute to the uniqueness of Quebec *vis à vis* other provinces. In welcoming Quebec again to the fold, the Francophones are guaranteed equal opportunity in all the governmental agencies. What with 27% citizens of Chinese origin and the Allophones commanding a small majority of some 40%, the French ingredient adds spice to the Quebec stew. In fact, they hold the balance of power. Pretty smart for a minority which survived in spite of enormous pressures from the rest of the North American continent.

Later, towards evening, the gyrating dials bring Peter to a program about Solidarity International. Although he had always been conspicuously apolitical, the principles espoused by the SI hold a strange fascination for him.

"You know, Peter, in Western civilizations, the concept of democracy has already been defining the social and moral truths. And now, absurd though it may seem, Solidarity takes this axiom or convention one step further. By an extensive use of pooling, they sound the public opinion and proclaim it as the new code of ethics! They equate the will of the masses with the moral and social paradigm. As the truth of the ages."

The idea of the world masses deciding on the moral rights and wrongs of the democratic system seems too ludicrous for words. Yet this is precisely what is happening. Cathy is not at all impressed with Solidarity's antics.

"Rather clever, I thought?" Peter slips in.

"Don't be flippant, Peter. Very soon ethics will consist of the effluent of the lowest elements of humanity. There was a time when the greatest minds gathered together to put forward the guidelines for the masses to follow. The Declaration of Independence of the US, the various European Constitutions, The Napoleonic Code, the various Bills of Human Rights, the Constitution of the United Nations, there are many examples. And now?" Cathy throws her hands up in the air.

"Now illiterates capable of no more than pressing a blue or red or yellow button on their TV sets will define the Code of Morality." Peter either fails or pretends not to see the inherent danger. He is smiling.

"Well, I do not find it funny." Cathy is really annoyed. "Oh, they will eradicate minor annoyances, abuses by the few against the many, but ultimately they will…"

"….forgive me, but aren't you taking the whole affair a little too seriously? After all, we still have governments, the UN, and a number of para-governmental organizations which will stabilize the situation before it can go overboard."

"This is precisely what Chamberlain said about Hitler, all Western leaders about Stalin, Mondrake about Chou Ming Po. They were all wrong. It is true that the masses have no power, but those who control those masses are gods!"

Peter is a little surprised. He had never seen Cathy so adamant about anything. Not even about her beloved relativity or quanta.

"You feel that the checks and balances imbedded in the structure of our society are insufficient to…"

"Exactly! Furthermore, I believe that the European movement will take on a world scale. I believe they will take over all the long established means of control. I believe they will override the various Charters of Individual Rights. I believe they will…"

"I believe you are gorgeous when you're angry."

"Peter! You are impossible!"

"Thank you, dear. I love you, too."

"As I was saying... You what?"

"I love you, too."

Even as a sudden subtropical storm comes and passes in a twinkling of an eye, Cathy's anger bubbles, spatters and evaporates. Yet her face remains serious.

"That's what I thought you said."

"I shall be happy to repeat it."

"Are you strong enough?"

"Shall we find out?"

Earlier that day, Peter had taken care to check that the master bedroom upstairs had fresh sheets and pillows neatly arranged for an itinerant occupant. He had been surprised to find fresh spring flowers on the bedside table. The room was swept and waiting. For some reason he can neither explain to himself nor put into words, he finds it difficult to approach the subject.

For the first time since his original bout in the linen closet at the General, Peter feels definitely, inarguably... shy.

And now, to his even greater consternation, a strange change seems to beset Cathy's relaxed, easy-going nature. Seemingly under their own weight, her heavy eyelids descend over her eyes, her head bows studiously as though to examine her shoes. What happened, Peter wonders? Where is the poise, the almost aggressive stance, the sophisticated self-assurance? Cathy remains sitting; one of her legs, previously drawn up into a comfortable position, now slides down to the floor, her knees press together as if seeking comfort or self-assurance.

"Is something wrong?" Peter asks very gently.

"Oh, no. It's just... Well, I didn't know you then."

"And now...?"

"Now it's different. I think I may be in love with you." Her voice is no more than a whisper.

"Is that so bad?"

"I do not feel that I can keep you."

"Cathy, what are you talking about?"

"I feel that when you are ready, you will get up and go."

"Why can't we go together?"

"I don't know. I just feel that you... Oh, I don't know, Peter. I only know that I miss you already."

They missed supper that night.

A large breakfast makes up for it with a vengeance. Peter ravishes his food like a lion kept too long on a leash in preventive seclusion. Cathy's blues of yesterday disappear with the first morning sunshine. By 7:30 they are ready to go.

Cathy's car takes them down the winding dirt track in relative comfort. Although Peter knows that he must visit the echoes of his past, he hates leaving his self-imposed exile. Up there, on the mountain, he lived, acted, like a normal human being. He read a lot, he made notes, with Cathy's help he learned more than he did during the last few years. He learned about life. Not about pathological conditions of people who abuse their bodies, but about the art of living. About the living, breathing world around him. Now, even as Cathy concentrates on the road, Peter lowers his seat into a semi-reclining position, closes his eyes and tries to make up for his last night's exertions. Pure pleasure can be tiring at times. He drifts into a languid state of semi-awareness.

His thoughts take him back to the particular evening he and Cathy had spent on the porch, gazing at the stars.

Actually, on two occasions the evenings had been warm enough to sit outdoors. Here, up North, as the City dwellers call it, the sky is totally different from the same sky over Montreal or Westmount. The intense darkness is peppered with a thousand times as many stars. The stars seem both closer to each other and closer to you, yet, paradoxically, farther away. There had been moments when Peter felt he could touch them, literally—yet as he reached out with his emotive arms, the minute giants congealed, froze, seemed to shrink, recede, become even more inaccessible.

Peter recalls reading about such mysteries. Now, he could write about them. All who visit the wilds, the pure air of the Canadian North, experience the same paradoxes, the same wanton, beguiling, befuddling impressions. Both time and distance exist only in our minds, he recalls thinking.

They took the deckchairs out, put them side by side, and covered themselves with blankets. Cathy had told Peter about her father, about the strange way that discoveries happen in science.

"Quite often someone spreads a rumour. Twenty years later, hey presto, the rumour becomes a reality. Makes you wonder if the universe we observe is real, or if it is in the process of becoming."

"You make strange magic with your words, Dr. Mondellay."

Peter had joked but in fact, then and now, he loves nothing more than listening to Cathy unfolding the many layers of her complex, ever-surprising mind.

"Well, Peter, I can safely assume that, in his own time, Euclid was right. So were Aristotle, Galileo, Newton and all the subsequent proponents of Classical Physics. Later so were Einstein, Bohr, De Broglie, Schrödinger, Heisenberg, Dirac, and Born. So was my father. Perhaps we are observing a different universe than they did. After all, we know that the universe continues to expand. Perhaps our observations affect the universe. Not our radio telescopes or other mechanical paraphernalia, but our minds. Ultimately, our minds decide the universe's shape, laws and its future."

"Until proven otherwise?"

"Until proven otherwise." There had been both excitement and sadness in the tone of her voice.

Peter remembers glancing into Cathy's eyes. They shone with a holy fire, a hunger for knowledge, for the secret of life, which burns in so many and is quenched in so few. The called and the chosen. We seem no more than paupers or donkeys carrying the spirits that guide us towards revelations of which we become worthy. 'I am no more than a student,' Winston had said. Or had it been a dream? During the week following Peter's return from the tavern in St-Henri, reality and dreamworld had been destined to remain permanently entangled. All Peter is sure of is that Winston had played a part in his destiny which, for the present, is yet to remain a mystery.

For the present.

The next evening they picked up from where they had left off. This time it was Peter who started the conversation.

"I think you were right, last night. The universe is in the process of becoming. However, it's where *we* fit into the order of things that fascinates me." Peter remembers submitting to Cathy's argument only to find her questioning his own rationale.

"Are you sure? Are you certain that what truly fuels your interest is not a need for the... permanent, for that which does *not* change, that which you might call your true home?"

"But change is the essence of life." Peter found himself on the defensive.

"At absolute zero life ceases," Cathy insisted.

"What ceases is molecular motion. Spirit goes on."

"Spirit cannot *go* on. Spirit is omnipresent, it is already there. And here. Like the gravitational field. It may be more or less powerful in segments of our universe, but it is there, everywhere, all the time."

"Is there an equation in your mind even for the Spirit?"

"Would that be a sacrilege?" Cathy's smile assumed a dreamy quality.

"I don't know. I left Spirit behind heavy metal doors many years ago."

"I don't know, either. But as I observe the universe, amid the chaos and the entropy, somewhere, between the two extremes of destruction, I detect beauty, enchantment and intelligence. To me—these are the qualities of Spirit. Of a living, omnipresent energy..."

"...is rose not a rose that smells the same?"

"What?"

"Nothing. It seems to me, though, that you are talking of life other than biological."

"And of universes other than those we can see and feel."

"What of tangible reality?"

"It's like talking about corpses. It is the field condensing into energy which condenses still further into matter that you are describing. But even so. What do you think is the most common element in the universe?"

"I'm ready to be instructed." Peter remembers Cathy's excitement.

"It is plasma. An ionized stew of electrons and positive ions. You can neither touch it nor see it. But it is there! And do you know how we control it? We control it with magnetic fields. The omnipresent fields!" Cathy pointed upwards, drawing great circles with her outstretched hands. "It is there, Peter. I can almost feel it!"

"I wish I had your vision," Peter recalls whispering as he looked down at the stars shining in her eyes, her lips parted in awe of the universe she loves so. To Cathy the universe seemed a living, breathing entity.

"You envy me? You who are touched by the spirit itself?"

She didn't have to say the word 'gift'. Peter knew it, he felt it. Albeit to Cathy the word spirit possibly carried different connotations. The universe itself, or something in it, was imbued with inherent intelligence. But sitting there that night with Cathy, Peter had learned something new. Something completely unexpected. He suddenly felt certain that his 'gift', for whatever reason, was no more than a tiny step towards a purpose of which he knew nothing as yet.

A pothole brings Peter to objective reality. He dozes off two more times, but only for a few minutes. Cathy insists that he rest as much as possible. She has to remind him that since coming up North, he had spent at most two continuous hours on his feet, and then only once. She chooses not to mention any other reason why she feels he is deserving of a good repose.

Finally they reach Montreal.

Peter follows the streetscape with considerable interest. He had not realized how very engrossing had been his profession. His previous profession. He does not recall having driven through the streets of the metropolis since he had started his internship. During the last four years he had always walked. Or very nearly always. From Upper Westmount to the Montreal General. Down to the Victoria Hospital, on some rare occasions, and back to his beloved Westmount. How strange, how foreign it all sounds now. It all feels like part of a life he had lived ages ago. Perhaps Winston was right. Perhaps we all reincarnate time after time, aeon after aeon. Always learning, always searching. Always walking in circles. The moment we grasp some meaning—the universe changes. It retreats into the ever-farther boundaries of infinity, leaving behind a fragment, a few photons of infrared light. It all happened so many ages ago. But the streets are still here, still busy, still filled with people in their spiral dance of eternal becoming.

Are we not immortal? Surely, under the circumstances, we must be...

When Winston was driving him to the cabin, Peter had been in no condition to absorb any impressions of the humdrum of the city. Now he looks at the cars, at the hordes rushing to and fro, whatever their compulsion, always in a hurry, always late for whatever they were meant to be doing. Keep still and do something, he remembers someone once saying. Or was it: Be still and know that I am God!

A beehive. An anthill. A City.

Originally it was Peter's intention to visit a few churches, at random, to see if anything would stir in his heart at the proximity of God. A religious, personal God. A God unto the image and likeness of man. Not the God whose minute and gigantic fragments Cathy discovered daily in her work. Her Deity only made Itself known to those who searched with the stubbornness of an ocean pounding at the apathetic beaches.

"Are you nervous?" Cathy asks as they approach Dorchester Boulevard that houses the seminary which Peter had once attended.

"Of course I am not nervous." His stomach feels pinched. "I must have had too much for breakfast."

"You're nervous." Cathy asserts with authority.

They don't talk until Cathy pulls off the street and parks on a small lot next to the church. Peter remains in the car. He knows the church well. Gray limestone, neo-gothic, simple yet with sufficient decoration to gladden the eye. Neither bland nor too severe.

Not Franciscan enough.

It had been built in the early part of the last century. Originally it stood in the middle of a field, just south of the Priests' Farm, an immense property of the Sulpicians extending down to Dorchester Boulevard and out west, all the way to his beloved Westmount. The Franciscans had been but poor neighbours. The Sulpicians had proven not only more successful in training candidates for the priesthood, but vastly superior in acquiring and controlling huge tracts of land; presumably an insurance in case the other kingdom was not all it was cut out to be. Both orders had settled well away from the hustle and bustle of the horse-drawn carriages of the City, the *Ville de Montréal*. Of course, the City then had consisted of a few hundred stone buildings east of the Bonaventure Expressway, along the rough banks of the Saint Lawrence river. A major port even in those days.

Another time. Another reality.

The City had been French then. At least it had been the French who held on to the people's hearts. English held on to their money. The church did its best to hold on to both. In basic terms, all had succeeded.

For a while.

By the time Peter entered the Seminary, the Church of Saint Francis of Assisi had grown mostly empty. Even on Sundays. People had spent their hard-earned rest at their country cottages, away from religious obligations. There was little money to maintain the stone which the last century's pollution managed to eat away with incestuous profligacy. In those days, the industry had donated little money to repair the stone gnawed by chemical pollution, which the very same industry had helped to create.

In Peter's time, the gothic arches, the curvilinear windows, the flying buttresses had all been cleaned and sprayed with a transparent plastic coating which the manufacturers guaranteed would last till the next century. It was questionable if the manufacturers would. A transparent coating for transparent parishioners. Only their names, mostly of French origin, remained carved on the empty pews waiting in vain for the sound of human footsteps. Except for the priests and deacons. The acolytes had made little sound. They did not wear leather soles. Their sandals had been made of rough cloth. There had been no money for leather.

Saint Francis would have liked that.

"You might as well do it." Cathy breaks into Peter's reminiscences.

"I'm going." Peter still doesn't move. Cathy doesn't realize that the acceptance of memories is part of the healing process. "I'm going. Will you wait for me?"

Cathy is not a catholic. Even less so than Peter. She had once told him that her parents used to practice the teachings of Lao Tzu, whose works had reformed the ancient writings called Tao Te Ching. Lao Tzu's teachings led to mysticism—they showed the way towards the ultimate reality. Dr. Mondellay and his wife had spent many years in the Orient. Peter believes that Cathy's view of the world, no matter how scientific, will always be tainted by her early upbringing. It is easier to cure the mind of a scientific theory than to cure the heart of a latent mystic of her hunger for God.

"I shall wait for you here."

Peter takes a deep breath. This should not be too difficult.

Many years have passed, many a riptide has rocked his ship on the ever-turbulent waters. Peter is not afraid of a challenge. He is afraid of weakness. If he does not feel free in the darkness of the nave, then darkness has remained in his heart. If he cannot face the cross at the altar, the cross with the symbol of love nailed to it, then he has wasted the last ten years of his life. If he does not feel free of guilt, any guilt, then he should have stayed behind these gray, metal portals he had walked out of ten years ago.

"I'll be right out," Peter assures Cathy.

The main portals are closed. He expected that. He doesn't even know if the church is open today. There are two old, decrepit cars parked in the main yard, but they could belong to almost anybody. Peter doesn't even know if the Franciscans are still running a seminary from here.

The side door is open.

Peter blinks at the eternal darkness. Then the cloud must have passed on and a few rays of sunlight cut sharp lines halfway up the columns, up there, high above the floor of the empty chancel. Peter walks deeper into the engulfing dimness. It is cold here. Had it been as cold then, in his time? Does time move here, among the hallowed—or is it hollow—echoes?

Cathy might like it here. There is peace. A peace of silence. Almost as great as under the great wondrous sky they left behind in the middle of nowhere. Only here there are old ghosts treading the cold stone paving.

A red light announces that the church is not empty. A mystic symbol. A living flame of a living Presence. A tiny, red, flickering light.

How ephemeral...

Saint Francis had spent his life travelling. He did not have time to worship symbols. He lived the life of transcendent happiness. One cannot find happiness away from the world. The world is out there, no matter how dangerous the currents threatening to overpower your tiller. The light out there is much, so much greater. The sun itself, the stars, the universe are the symbols of God's love for man. Not a tiny candle imprisoned within a red stained glass, but the light of a blazing nova.

Saint Francis had known that. There had been a time when the friars had lived in harmony with the world outside. They had lived in the world. Out in the open. Then they built walls between the world and the people. And now the people have left them. An empty nave. A void. Nothing unto nothing. A symbol of a time of passing.

Only the tiny red light is still burning.

Peter turns around. He is about to leave the church when a young cleric picks up a prayer book from the first pew, genuflects in the middle of the nave, then approaches the communion rail and kneels down at the altar. For a while he prays in silence. Then he opens the book and recites aloud. He must think he is alone in the church. As always.

"The wind bloweth where it listeth, and thou hearest the sound thereof, but canst not tell whence it cometh and whither it goeth: so is every one that is born of the Spirit."

Peter walks on his toes so as not to disturb the traveller on his esoteric journey. He opens the side door and is instantly flooded by an intense sunlight. There is life here. Thank you, Saint Francis. I knew you would not let me down.

"You sure you're all right?" Cathy asks when Peter sits next to her without saying a word. He looks pensive.

"Yes, Cathy. I should have done it years ago. Or, perhaps, I wasn't ready then. But... I am glad that we came. I think I understand a little more."

In his ears he still hears the monotone of the young cleric's voice: *"The wind bloweth and it listeth, and thou hearst the sound thereof..."* And you have no idea which way the wind will push your sails. You have no idea where you are going. But you must be ready to go. On a moment's notice.

"...but canst not tell whence it cometh and whither it goeth," Peter mutters under his breath.

"What did you say, dear?"

"I said let's go home."

Until the next wind bloweth.

* * *

16

$E = mc^2$

B ut they did not go straight home. Cathy had wanted to drop in at the Institute to borrow another book. Apparently, quite accidentally, she had bumped into the Director of Theoretical Physics, Dr. Princeton Twan. And now she is furious.

"I simply cannot believe that anyone can be so stupid!" she tells Peter as she climbs back into the driver's seat, slamming the door.

Judiciously, Peter waits until Cathy calms down. He is surprised. The Orientals have a reputation for sporting the best poker-face expressions in the world. Peter had assumed that Cathy's mother had supplied the requisite genetic ingredients to support a stoic disposition in her daughter. Far from it.

"Imbeciles! Myopic morons! I just couldn't believe my ears!"

Nor can Peter.

Cathy takes off with a wheel-spin worthy of a *Le Mans* race driver. Peter feels pushed hard into, almost through, the back of the bucket-seat where apparently he is destined to remain until Cathy calms down. Finally the needle settles at around 20 kilometers over the prescribed speed limit.

Peter takes a deep breath.

"Had a nice visit?" he asks innocently.

"Very funny."

Tart but no exclamation mark. There is hope.

"Serious?" he tries again.

"Oh, I don't know. It's just that people are so weak."

That's it. People are weak. So what else is new?

"I went there to say hello. To ask if I can help with any work I can take with me. To be nice." The tone of her voice is almost relaxed.

The next instant Cathy puts her foot down on the accelerator and veers on two wheels to avoid a large truck from cutting her off the ramp leading to the autoroute. She makes it by the skin of her teeth.

"*Bâtard!*" There is nothing wrong with Cathy's French.

"Are we still on the road?" Peter asks, his eyelids firmly pressed together.

He hears a deep sigh. At last.

"I'm sorry."

Normal. Her voice is normal. Pheeew!

"So what happened?"

"The SOB wanted to cut..."

"No, Cathy. At the Institute."

The Mondellay Institute is her father's baby. Her father *is* the Institute. Surely nothing much could have happened to have upset the brightest daughter of the brightest father in Canada.

"The administrators are morons."

"I thought we had already established that."

"You will not believe what a few years spent in an administrative function can do to a decent brain."

Probably it's like power. It corrupts. But Peter prefers to withhold his counsel. Anyway, there is not much he can say. His own administrator, Dr. Brent, was obviously an exception. A hell of an exception! I wonder what happened to him? And Lucy...?

"They wanted me to sign in to have a subcutaneous implant installed in my forehead." Cathy manages a whole sentence without smashing into any oversized trailers. "The bloody impudence! The fatuous presumption!"

"Whoah... An implant of what?"

"An implant to give me access to the World Bank."

"What, some kind of scanning device?"

"Rather a device that can be scanned. Essentially, it is your personalized serial number. It cannot be removed or altered without destroying the device. Like tattoos used to be. For life!"

"Does it leave a bump on your forehead?"

"Who the devil cares?!" The foot comes down harder on the accelerator. "Anyway, it's done under the hairline."

"Doesn't do much for bald man."

"Peter! *Who the devil cares.* I wouldn't have it done if they gave me year-round access to the Taj Mahal. I have no desire to be serialized."

"Then why did they ask you to have it done?"

"They want me to attend a congress in Europe. Apparently out there it's a lot easier to get by with the implant. You can buy goods at a great many stores, pay your hotel bills—in fact, you don't need any money. You live on credit."

"So it's a credit card?"

"No, Peter. It's a life membership in Solidarity International!"

"Oh..."

"Oh, yourself. It doesn't affect you. But I have a lot of work ahead of me. I have years of study, of research. I have a career, a future..."

Cathy stops in the middle of her sentence. The car slows down, she changes lanes to the middle one. She is biting her lip.

"It's all right, Cathy. You are quite right."

"I am sorry, Peter. I am very sorry. I didn't mean to..."

"I know. It doesn't matter. It really doesn't matter at all. Not any more."

Suddenly the career seems less important. What matters is Peter. This is what mattered all along. Peter. Just Peter.

"I am sorry..." she repeats again. After all, what else can she say?

In twenty minutes they are on the periphery of the sprawling suburbia. Then the land gets greener by the mile, the hills appear on the horizon. A bluish cloud hovers over the nearest mountain and, even as they both look at it, it dissolves. The sky is blue again.

"It was very thoughtless of me." Cathy murmurs almost to herself. She still feels guilty.

"Would you rather I took over the wheel so that you can curl up and feel sorry for yourself?"

"I'm sorry." Then she smiles for the first time since getting into the car. "I mean no. I don't want to curl up and feel sorry for myself. I am still much too angry for that."

"That's better. Now tell me more about this Solidarity business."

"Not much to tell. My Director, Dr. Twan, had his head already fixed. He can travel throughout Europe leaving his wallet at home. I must admit it is convenient."

"Tell me, how does it work?"

"I'm not that sure that I know. But as I understand it, the implant is like a fingerprint or a retina scan, only it emits a radiation which triggers a response in a scanning device. Your serial number, or imprint, tells the man operating the scanner what your credit rating is and enables you to buy any service or goods without the use of a credit card or money."

"Throughout Europe?"

"And in some places outside. But only at the Solidarity International outlets, of course. In Europe this already means close to 70% of small business. By small I mean everything short of an international consortium. It is a sort of 'people against the world'."

"And you think that's bad..."

"I think any monopoly is bad."

"But if it is the people..."

"Oh, Peter, grow up. People are led. Machiavelli would give his right hand for this idea. It's... it is Svengalian!"

Peter is almost amused. He finds it incredible how very far he has strayed from the pulse of the world of today. Wherever he had been, whatever he had ever worked on, it invariably sheltered him from the wiles of the present-day civilization. Or else he had left, or been taken away from, the approaching main current the moment it threatened to sweep him up, or come in close contact with him. It seems that, whatever course his life is destined to take, this course has been protected by powers or influences beyond his comprehension. He was like a cork: buoyant, apparently safe, but having little or no influence on the direction the currents were sweeping him. Why me, he wondered lately? Who am I to stay away from the...

"Peter? Peter!"

"Yes, Cathy?"

"You haven't heard a word I said, have you?"

"The last I heard was a competition between Svengali and Machiavelli. Who won?"

"I have been saying that you are lucky to be sheltered from the wiles of this day and age."

"I couldn't have put it better myself," Peter says.

He also smiles. It happened a few times lately that Cathy and he shared their thoughts. Like a couple married for many years. Or deeply in love.

The *autoroute* takes them out of the outskirts. The Americans have expressways, turnpikes and speedways, the British their motorways. In Quebec there are *autoroutes*. We all have buildings alongside them which never stop, which continue for mile after mile, until one wonders if there is such a thing as nature unfettered by a human presence. The houses will continue for another two hours, but Peter can already look over their rooftops towards the distant hills, the blue-green mountains awakening from their winter slumber. Peter is beginning to wonder how on earth he survived for so long away from the wonders of nature.

Space. Green open space. Canada.

Once the North was opened, eighty or ninety million people are hardly more than a drop in the bucket. A wondrous bucket full of lakes and forests, and rolling hills and plains and mountains...

During his whole life Peter had rubbed shoulders with masses of people. Nurses, interns, residents, patients; before that, cowled acolytes; later the derelicts of St-Henri. And the open spaces had always been there, waiting, undemanding. Just being.

The wind bloweth...

Maybe he had been lucky. All he had had to do was his best, and the rest had always taken care of itself. Provided he did not question the results. It had not been his to mete out justice. Sometimes he wondered, like Job, if the Almighty had, on occasion, perverted justice. Like Job, he pleaded ignorance. He was an instrument. An implement, a utensil. Of whom or what, he knew not. But he was learning fast that there was little point in offering much resistance. It just delayed the inevitable a little longer.

"What do you think will happen with the Solidarity movement?"

Peter returns to the previous subject. There seems to be less hurry, out here in the countryside, to find solutions. Nature tends to slow things down. Or at the very least, it does whatever has to be done at its own pace.

"Your guess is as good as mine. It's a question of Solidarity versus the UN. The UN is backed up, of course, by the politicians who in turn are supported by the international conglomerates. It is like the oceans versus the mountains of the world. Perhaps they can coexist. Somehow I doubt it. Anyway, ask your sister-in-law. She should know more than any of us. But as far as I can gather, Solidarity, one way or another, controls the economy of Europe, and its influence in the rest of the world is growing. My Institute is a good example. Six months ago the initials SI had not even been mentioned. Not once. Now they seem to appear in the middle of a conversation."

"It sounds like an insidious disease..." Peter muses aloud.

"By now it is more like an epidemic. Western Europe comprises well over a half-billion people. That's a powerful trading block right there. But this is not how they work. They don't really hurt you in any way. They make life easier for you. They tend to distribute the world's goods in a fairer way. They are... good to people. Kind. They help you. Make your life easier..."

"And you hate them."

"I do not hate them. I hate being brought down to a common denominator."

Pride? Self assurance? Peter does not as yet formulate an opinion on Solidarity. Whatever its merits or faults, neither have any direct bearing on his life. Except indirectly. Through Cathy.

"I spoke to a fellow once." Peter starts, then stops. He cannot make himself tell Cathy that the source of his information was his sister-in-law's butler.

"Did you enjoy it?" Cathy is still angry. She is very seldom facetious.

"Well, this guy said that there is such a thing as a physical soul. Or something like that. He said that the electromagnetic field is a sort of mechanical spirit. I don't quite know how to put it."

"Are you talking about Kirlian photography?"

"Well, I wasn't actually. But I have been thinking that if a human being does emanate this physical soul, and if the earth also appears to have a magnetic field, then..."

"Peter, get to the point!"

"What I want to know is what would happen if the Solidarity International covered the whole globe with their network of computers. I mean millions upon millions of them all interconnected with innumerable cellular cables, in addition to the three-dimensional effect provided by the satellites. Like a single brain, an amoeba, covering the globe. I understand they are well on the way to doing just that."

"Well, what of it?" Cathy's tone did not encourage him to continue. The subject of Solidarity did not dispose her towards good conversation.

"What I am asking is, would not such a network create a global magnetic field?"

"It would be extremely weak."

"But it would be there?"

"No energy ever dissipates completely."

"I thought so."

"You thought what?"

"I think that Solidarity International is in the process of building a new, superior earth soul," Peter concludes triumphantly.

"And that is what all this was about?" Cathy gives him a dirty look before returning her eyes to the road ahead.

"You think I am talking nonsense?"

"I think you are obsessed with the concept of soul."

Within half an hour they would be taking the dirt road. Peter feels surprisingly relaxed. He expected to be more tired.

Apparently last night contributed to his recovery in some unexpected ways.

Cathy seems lost in her own thoughts. She tries hard to concentrate on baryons and mesons and quirkish quarks, to take her mind off the subcutaneous implant. It scared her, and she doesn't like being scared. She tries to adapt her thinking closer to Peter's train of thought. Provided he does not bring up the SI again. Peter appears to sense that.

"Tell me about the velocity of light."

Cathy smiles. She loves Peter's directness. She doesn't remember that this very same trait had endeared her to him when they had first met.

"What do you want to know?" This is her favourite field of ignorance.

"Well, I heard that all sorts of things happen when you reach the velocity of light."

"They would if you could."

"I couldn't?"

"Only if you had infinite power at your disposal." She smiles again. Cathy vaguely remembers her own first encounter with the almighty photon.

"Right. I remember the bit about the immovable object and the irresistible force."

"Something like that. You see, if a photon had mass, then in a vacuum its mass would expand to infinity."

"I thought photons do have mass."

"Hypothetical only. Theoretically mass is a characteristic of quanta rather than a wave. But I think you'll find that a little too complex."

"OK. Let's talk about an electron if it's easier. An electron is bigger. How big?

"Its mass is about two thousand times smaller than the mass of a hydrogen atom."

"And the hydrogen atom?" Peter keeps probing.

"Imagine twenty three zeros after a decimal point and then 17. The number represents the fraction of a gram that a hydrogen atom weighs."

Peter takes a piece of paper from his pocket and writes down the figure: 0.000 000 000 000 000 000 000 0017 grams.

He then looks at the figure for some time. He scratches his head. Things do not add up. "Now this is its weight, right?" He asks, after a while.

"Right." She is beginning to wonder if all this is leading to anything in particular.

"And this electron is two thousand times smaller?"

"Approximately. And not this electron, only an average electron. We do not deal with individuals here, only with statistical probabilities."

"And if I were to accelerate the electron's mass to the velocity of light, its mass would become infinite?" Peter sticks to his individual electron.

"So they tell me."

More silence. Things don't add up.

"Also its dimension relative to the direction it travels would become infinitely small," Cathy adds, after a little while. She keeps her eyes on the road.

"So I would have an infinitely thin slice of nothing that would weigh an arm and a leg," Peter says slowly.

No answer. He continues to regard the piece of paper with the number indicating the approximate weight of a hydrogen atom. Then he shrugs. He decides there and then that theoretical physics are not for him.

"You know, Cathy? This is worse than metaphysics."

"This is metaphysics."

She may be right at that. Peter closes his eyes and leans deeper into his reclining seat. Soon the road will be too rough for free association of ideas. Then he presses a lever and the seat rises up again.

"Bear with me. If I could accelerate the vibrations of my body (the old prophets called it quickening the spirit) to the velocity of light, then I would become omnipresent. Since, I also understand that there is also such a thing as the dilation of time, I would become eternal. Isn't it a shame that I would have to become paper thin?"

"You already are. You should eat more."

"Imagine, omnipresent and eternal..."

"We forgot to stop for lunch."

"Something is wrong with your physics," Peter insists.

"Oh? How come?"

"I didn't feel hungry until you mentioned it."

At that moment Cathy turns off the paved road and hits the first pothole. She slows down, but only after Peter's head goes practically through the roof.

"Now I am flat in two directions."

"I shall feed you in 30 minutes." Cathy grimaces. "Damn!"

"What have I done now?"

"Nothing. I forgot the book I went to the Institute to borrow."

"I love you," Peter says with conviction. He loves women to be human.

"Later. After the meal."

But after the meal Peter lies down on the settee and falls into a deep sleep. He sleeps for three hours. Like a log. Cathy reads, makes notes and does some thinking. She wonders if Peter is still obsessed with the concept of soul. She wonders what happened at the church of St. Francis of Assisi. She knows little of the Christian faith, but she has read the bible. All of it. After she read it, she discovered that most Christians don't bother. They miss an awful lot of great poetry. Particularly the Psalms. She remembers one verse particularly. Be still and know that I am God. This inherent passivity feels close to the writings of Tao Te Ching. Only, in the teaching she picked up on her mother's knee, the word God would be spelled with a small 'g', and it would refer to the divinity residing in the heart of every being. Lao Tzu taught that a soul is not an independent fragment but an inseparable element of Absolute Reality. In her own way, she has been searching for that Reality ever since.

She wonders if Peter knows that. He seems to regard his soul as something independent, something lost in the vastness of the universes. It is hard to live that way. The universe is too vast for one to become lost in it. One might not find one's way back.

She wonders who are the true teachers of today. Lao Tzu did not provide for any successor. And surely, there must be, right now, people as advanced as he had been. So many years ago. And Jesus. What would he say if he had today's consciousness to deal with? Would he still use those pretty parables? Or would he tell people more about the way towards a higher consciousness in a manner which a modern man could more easily absorb?

She underlines some notes for later discussion.

But does our consciousness expand? Are we sure that we are advancing? What of our consciousness? Surely it is already beyond the limitations of time and space. Peter had asked about the velocity of light, but what of our thoughts? Faster than light but slower than consciousness. Consciousness is a state of being. It is already there. And here. Consciousness is. What is reality then? Certainly it reaches beyond that which we can measure or touch, beyond that whose effects we can observe. You cannot measure love, but would anyone who experienced it ever deny its existence?

I must talk to Peter.

"I dreamt again."

Talk of the devil. We are all little devils. Horny devils extracting all the living we can from the playground of mother earth. It is just that some of us are better at it than others.

"Welcome back."

"I was falling into a black hole. I had been travelling through an intense darkness, so much so that I forgot that all light was trapped inside it. That's right, isn't it?"

"The visible light is, Peter. The long-wave spectrum."

"Right. So I couldn't see it. Or anything. Don't mind telling you it was scary. I couldn't escape. The tunnel sucks you in. Nothing can pull you out. God, it's dark in there! But it was worth it. Eventually I emerged on the other side. Of the tunnel, I mean. I'm telling you the tunnel can feel very long when it's pitch dark. Some might get lost. It seems to have branches leading off at odd angles."

"It sounds like a nightmare."

Cathy gets up, walks up to Peter and sits on the edge of the settee. She strokes his hair. It is too long again. It has gotten a lot lighter in colour. It is almost yellow. It must be the sun.

"Only then a funny thing happened. I got through the tunnel and there, playing around without a care in the world, were Jonathan and Moira. I wonder if they had to go through the tunnel to get there."

"What, two kids in the middle of... wherever they were?"

"Oh no! Winston was there, looking after them!"

"Quite a strange fellow, this Winston of yours."

"He's not mine. He's Ruth's."

"Oh? Does Ruth dream about Winston also?"

"I have no idea."

Strange fellow, this Winston. Whoever he belongs to. As a matter of fact, Peter is quite sure that Winston does not belong to anybody. If anything, it might well be the other way round.

"We should go for a walk."

"It's a pity to waste a perfectly good settee. Later." Peter reaches out for Cathy. She moves away.

"No. The settee later. You must regain your strength first."

"But if I regain my strength, I might be too tired!"

"Your logic is impeccable."

"So are you."

A deep sigh of resignation. "Oh, all right. But only for a short while. Promise?"

"Promise."

She sits down again. She shouldn't have. Since they came up North, Peter has become quite a proficient liar.

* * *

17

As Above So Below

They should have picked up more paper. Ordinary stationery paper. For lack of it, Peter has begun writing on the reverse side of the pages he had already filled with minute characters. Notes, anecdotes, views, intuitive thoughts. Not in any particular order, but they helped him to organize his own mind—to find out where he stood on any particular issue. Peter agonized over not having brought over his computer. He never realized how difficult it was to write without one. He found he had to think before he wrote anything, rather than jotting down fragments of thoughts on a forgiving screen and then, later, arranging them into a semblance of English language. A taxing proposition. Before the advent of computers, he mused, people must have either thought very slowly or written very fast. Perhaps both.

Peter reviewed his notes yesterday. Some peculiar results.

Winston had brought him up North some six weeks ago. Now, in the middle of May, Peter finds that since his arrival he has already diametrically changed some of his original concepts. The initial notes he had scribbled in a hand not used to writing had been little more than emotional outbursts, the desperate howling of a wounded animal, at best cries of a man lost in the wilderness. His lament was occasionally interspersed with tentative fragments of hope. Fragments. Straws cast upon turbulent waters.

By the beginning of May, Peter's notes showed signs of impending order. Not as yet resulting in any profound dissertations, but manifesting a more rational view of the world. Perhaps a touch too sentimental, a view of someone standing still too close to the events to afford an impartial judgment. Nevertheless, the voluminous scribbles evidenced that the intellect had won the battle over the emotions.

"Mind is a magnificent instrument," he wrote in one of his cryptic comments, "but deadly if subjected to an emotional constraint."

Many of Peter's notes were a direct result of his discussions with Cathy. Some were taken down almost verbatim. The phenomenal memory, which had once served him so well in his chosen profession, seemed to have adapted itself to matters which comprised aspects of his everyday life. His interests had changed diametrically. Then, finally, so had his point of view.

During the last few days, Peter had been recording his thoughts rather like a bystander, regarding the events, the new insights, with an emotional detachment. He was watching himself, as though he were a stranger to his own ego, to his own personality—a caring stranger, but a stranger nevertheless. His interest in one called Peter Thornton, *alias* Simon Nomad, *alias* whatever he, or the mind and heart and body which now hosted his inner self, had become—continued to grow. Only...

Only who am I? Whatever is my true self?

One other thing had occurred which had a great effect on his writing.

Peter discovered that he could lie down, close his eyes, and enter into a sort of conversation with Winston. Why Winston? He has no idea. Peter does not pretend to hear Winston's voice in the manner of a ghost addressing him in a haunted house. He merely asks questions and the answers sound as though they had been supplied by Winston. They have Winston's finality, an immutability that precludes doubt. The answers invariably ring true. At least as true as Peter, at his present level of understanding, can convert them into words.

And he is beginning to find words inadequate.

On other occasions Peter was no more than a listener, one of many.

One afternoon, after a long walk with Cathy along the narrow track winding through the dense forest, Peter lay back on the settee, only to find himself in a large covered arena with semicircular steps or seats, arranged after a Greek odeum. Only instead of musicians and poets, a man, way down in front of a large audience, was giving a lecture. Peter sat towards the back, feeling relaxed and inconspicuous in a toga-like robe. He was glad that he was not attracting the attention of other listeners who wore clothes similar to himself. The front seats had been reserved for children. That's right. Jo and Mo sat right in the middle of the front row.

Surely, no dream could be as real, as precise as Peter's vision. Or could it?

Peter had the strangest impression that he had been there, in the vast odeum, for some time, but only now was he becoming aware of being there as... well, as Peter Thornton. (It was a most eerie feeling, particularly since with a portion or peripheral awareness he could feel the softness of the settee behind his back.)

The tall man at the front edge of the small proscenium talked in a deep, well-modulated voice. The lecture he delivered was on the subject of NOMAD. A man, or woman, without a home. A wanderer. When Peter heard the word Nomad he thought that he, himself, had been addressed. He almost raised his arm in an affirmation of his presence.

He stopped just in time.

Without asking anyone he suddenly knew, with utter conviction, that all present had been Nomads. That he was not alone. That the homeless had all shared a home. At this realization, Peter felt a succession of warm waves of pleasure wash over him like the rays of a tropical sun emerging from the tattered edge of a thick cloud. But it was more than just pleasure. Peter felt he had found his home. His true home. Like never before in his life, he had, there and then, experienced a profound sense of belonging. He wanted to stand up, to jump up and down, to wave his arms, to shout at the top of his lungs. He knew he shouldn't, but he couldn't resist it. He got up and shouted for joy!

"What is it, Peter, another nightmare?" Cathy was at his side instantly.

Peter needed a few moments to adjust himself to the new reality. To the cabin in the middle of nowhere.

"Peter! What is it?" she sounded worried.

"Why... what happened?"

"You shouted. Are you in pain?"

"Good Lord, no. I feel just great!"

"As a matter of fact, I am inclined to believe that. Your scream sounded more like a shout of joy. Intense joy." Cathy regarded him with raised eyebrows.

Peter sat up and told Cathy about his dream.

"I suppose I shouldn't really call it a dream. It was more like a vision. Only I do not have visions. Except once or twice, some time ago, after I had too much wine!"

"Who was giving the lecture?"

"Why, I have no idea..." His voice had not been convincing.

"It was Winston, wasn't it?"

"I was sitting almost at the back of the theatre. The place was very large."

"It was Winston, wasn't it?" Cathy repeated.

"As a matter of fact, the man had Winston's voice. And looked about the right height..."

The last such vision or dream, or hallucination, had only occurred two days ago.

They took a long walk, today. Peter was becoming ambitious. He insisted. He said he needed to recover his strength quickly, though he refused to say exactly why. They had climbed to the top of the mountain, then down the other side to the brook for a drink of fresh water. At the brook, Doctor Catherine Mondellay, Ph.D., *etc.*, *etc.*, was being rather playful. She had decided that Peter was well enough to take a swim. Fully clothed. They made it back to the cabin in half the time. They had to. Peter was soaking wet.

Dr. Mondellay giggled all the way up and down the hill.

Doctor Peter Thornton, FRCP (also *etc.*, *etc.*), got even with the vixen under the shower. When she passed him a towel, at his request, she was not given time to remove her clothing, either. Not to start with. The stripping process was long and arduous. They both discovered that wet clothing is a lot harder to remove, although Cathy insisted that Peter was stripping her slowly on purpose, just to get even! (Later she admitted the wait had been worth it.) She may well have been right but, then again, she did little to help him. With the stripping.

They almost ran out of hot water.

Some time later the area around the fireplace looked like Canada Day, or the Fourth of July to our southern neighbours. Multihued flags, strangely reminiscent of various articles of male and female underwear, hung everywhere. The outer clothing was carefully disposed on various branches of a friendly birch a few steps west of the cabin. (Peter made a mental note to tell Ruth to get a dryer. At least, if she ever intended to invite Cathy to the cabin.) They were both tired, but Cathy remarked that it had done them both good.

"The walk, darling?" He had to dodge a left hook to his midriff. For her size, Cathy was a very strong girl. Woman, except when with Peter.

Now, they are enjoying a well-earned rest. They relax as they bid farewell to yet another glorious spring day. In spite of the roaring fireplace, the cabin windows are wide open. Their backs against the sofa, their feet up on the window sill.

There is a serene calm in the air. A peace of the just, of the sated. An air of a day well spent.

Yet, all too soon, Peter's thoughts stray, at odds with the dreamy tranquillity. For some time now, he has been finding it progressively more difficult to admit to himself that his sister-in-law's butler was having a profound influence on his life. Perhaps not as great as on Jonathan and Moira, but great nevertheless. If Winston is some kind of a mystic, then why had he not said so? Surely he was not embarrassed by it? Peter strongly believes that a situation that could embarrass Winston has not as yet been invented.

He shares his nagging discontent with Cathy.

"Who do you think he really is?" Cathy asks, her eyes squinting against the low red rays of the western sun. The horizon, framed by the narrow window, seems so close she can reach out and frame it with her own hands.

Peter has no answer to Cathy's question.

"I was hoping you might have an answer to this enigma..."

"Did you ever ask him?"

"I think I did. But even then, as far as I can remember, I asked him in a dream."

"A vision?"

"Well, no. It was a *bona fide* dream. At least I think so."

"And? What happened?" Cathy sounds hopeful.

"I woke up."

Cathy's reaction is halfway between a laugh and a giggle. Peter finds it less amusing.

Outside, the evening is becoming even more spectacular.

The sun has hidden half its diameter behind a cloud just waiting out there to embrace it. A strange sight if you care to risk ruining your eyes by staring at it. The cloud is dark blue, with a gold lining along its upper edge and a dark, blood red just above the horizon. The forest under its lower edge may well be on fire. The view is stunning.

The next moment the sun lowers its massive head and sinks behind the cloud. The rays seem to bend out and upwards, hover a moment or two, and go out without any more warning. The break in the cloud above the horizon closes, the forest fire dies out. It would be night soon. They would sit outside and look at the stars. Cathy's eyes wander over the darkening mysteries, Peter closes his eyes. They wait in silence.

Peter has just had another of his visions. As always, he tells her about it.

"Cathy... What is going on with me? Am I going mad?"

Cathy smiles, nodding her head from side to side. She stands up, stretches, then sits next to Peter and rests her head against his still meagre chest. She is amazed how much power

Peter has already regained. Upstairs, in the shower. He told her that it's like riding a bicycle. It is all a question of balance, he said. Her smile broadens at the lingering memory. It is not easy to keep your balance under the shower... Her dark flowing hair cascades down to Peter's lap. It is almost dry.

Peter's dreams are often very short. Perhaps outside the confines of time. And space.

"When I lived in China, I visited Tibet and Northern India. Your recent ventures into the unconscious would be regarded as the first signs of an approaching sanity."

"Would they be regarded as mystical experiences?"

"I am no authority on mysticism. But a lot of seekers would give half their life to have been out there, with you."

They prepare supper together. It is such fun doing things together. Anything. People are too alone, altogether. They should share more. Anything with anyone. Mostly themselves. Share themselves. Cathy and Peter prepare food, eat and clean up the old-fashioned way. Peter washes up, Cathy dries with a cotton cloth. Ruth could have had a dishwasher installed here long ago, but she wanted Mo and Jo to experience the way things were done yesteryear. She thinks it part of their heritage. Part of sharing with their ancestors. Even if the children had been adopted. Like living a memory.

Peter is much stronger now. He takes the chairs out by himself. They do not leave them outside unless the forecast is for very dry weather. Even then, the forecasters are not always right. Like last night. After a prediction of a clear night, Peter had to run out to bring the chairs in, in the nick of time.

"Some things never change," Cathy affirmed, "the meteorologists were wrong in China, in Europe and in North America. They have a great deal in common."

But tonight it is clear.

The moon is no more than a thin crescent. The air is warm, but dry enough not to obscure the retreating infinity. Neither of them seems to tire of this view. With such great numbers of people on the Federal Assistance Program, Peter and Cathy wonder how those people can live in towns, cities, glued to their televisions or raising tankards at the local taverns, when they could be sitting outside looking at the history of the universe.

Fifty years ago it would have been impossible. Anyone that far north would have been eaten alive by the squadrons of mosquitoes and black flies. Now, a simple ultrasonic device keeps them at length. Only peace remains. Peace and a myriad of stars.

They sit side by side, their hands touching, their minds growing together.

"There is an old occult saying: 'As above so below'. I wonder if the opposite also holds true." Cathy's voice is as dreamy as the firmament above them. There is so much above them. So much beauty.

"As below so above?"

"It should apply. The sages insist that whatever happens at higher levels of consciousness must irrevocably become manifest at the physical level. Provided that all conditions are met, of course." Cathy's voice is relaxed. She sounds happy.

"What conditions?"

"The creative process follows an old established rule. The spirit inspires, the mind provides the analytical and the synthesizing faculties, and finally the emotions furnish the fuel, which makes the whole process viable. After that, the physical manifestation of the original idea, the inspiration, is a foregone conclusion."

"You sure it's that easy?" Peter asks. Actually, under this sky, whatever Cathy cares to say, Peter is well disposed to believe it. You do not argue with a goddess drawing inspiration from her stars.

"I never said it was easy. Each step requires discipline. To hear an idea you must stop talking. To stop talking means to suspend listening to the turmoil going on in your own head. The noise of your thoughts."

"I always thought that the thoughts were the initiators of the reasoning process."

"Reasoning, yes. But you must first find something to apply your reason to."

Peter wonders why it had been Cathy who sat next to him at the Ritz-Xentung. Had the esoteric powers even then singled them out, together, to join forces on their nomadic journey?

"Point well taken. So you are saying that there is a function higher than thought?"

"It's not my idea. But I believe that our horizons expand both outwardly and inwardly. Otherwise, there would be little point to existence."

"I could exist for quite a while right here, with you."

"And I with you. But we both know that..." she cannot quite say it.

Cathy believes that life on earth is transient. So are all things connected with life. She knows that Peter has placed himself at odds with this tenet. She thinks Peter is wrong. All she knows is that she loves him. She does not even know why. She resents being subject to influences over which she has absolutely no control. Her intellect rebels against such a state of mind. She once imagined that love was either a reasoning or an emotional process, with perhaps some biochemical overtones. She now knows that her theory was totally wrong. Attraction is physical, being in love—emotional, but love? Whatever love is, it is fuelled by forces beyond the scope of one's mind or emotions.

"Not all things are transient, you know..." Peter says softly.

"Name one!" she shrugs almost in anger.

"Our love. I believe it is not transient. I know nothing of eternity, but if such exists, and I firmly believe that it does, then our love will prevail. I am quite sure of this."

For a brief moment Peter feels himself talking with an assurance he once held in matters pertaining only to medicine. Or the confidence of Winston describing... almost anything. Anything at all.

A point of light expands, grows brighter, then, as suddenly, it shrinks and disappears over the horizon, among the celestial family of stars. Its brothers and sisters seem quite unaware of its passing. Whatever it was, whatever it once had been, perhaps for thousands, millions of years, is no more. It took another giant step on the scale of evolution. Or just died.

Cathy strokes Peter's hand.

"In my book," she says, her eyes fixed to the spot where the falling star had flashed in a brief moment of glory, "eternity is a condition prevailing at the velocity of light. Time stops, all is one. Do you know, Peter, that the iron in your hemoglobin was born in the heart of a Supernova? We are all interdependent for our existence. In a way we really are all one."

"And what is the linking factor?"

"Gluons! Theoretical particles which keep us all from falling apart." Cathy smiles. She is not serious at all.

"Consciousness," Peter says as though he hadn't heard her. "Consciousness is what keeps the universe what it is. Keeps it or subjects it to a change."

Cathy draws her feet under her on the armchair. It is good to be here.

"Let us structure a heaven." Peter embraces the vast expanse from horizon to horizon with a sweep of his arms. "The occult law states, 'as above so below'. See if we can invert this proposition. I mean, if we are onto image and likeness, then what is the original like? What are Its qualities, Its aspects? The manifested and the unmanifested. And didn't it ever strike you that the universe may be expanding in a direct ratio to our expanding consciousness? That it might be we who are responsible for its expansion?"

"I think the universe has been expanding long before we came on the scene." Cathy's heart hovers among the stars, but her mind holds on to mother earth.

"In our present form. But do you really believe that we are the most advanced beings in the universe?"

"Of course not. That would be stupid, presumptuous and anthropomorphic. I try to reach out beyond all three!" She sounds almost hurt.

"Precisely. It seems to me that thought or, according to you, spirit, precedes all matter. If that is so, an Idea had to exist before any physical manifestation. And what is necessary for the formulation of an idea?"

"A brain?"

"We already established that the universe was around before a few neurons had been slapped together into a few pounds of gray putty. No. The first prerequisite is a state of Consciousness."

"Go on?"

"Regardless of what happened in your vast universes, or here on earth, we must retreat even further back. On the one hand laws, not destiny, rule us. On the other, destiny seems capable of overriding the laws. A paradox. It seems that man occupies that precarious middle ground where the two opposites meet. It is this middle ground that makes us into the image and likeness. Nothing else."

"Like light in the physical universe. Its behaviour incorporates both the continuous and the discontinuous properties. The waves and the quanta. By this hypothesis, light would be at the meeting ground of matter and spirit..."

"Laws are the restrictive and destiny the liberating."

"And the black holes would be one extreme and the worlds of pure spirit the other."

"What?"

"Ah... you were saying?"

They both laugh. The world seems big enough for the two of them. Even if they start at different rudiments on their eternal journey.

"I love you, Peter."

"That is a continuous property," he affirms gravely.

"As is spirit? But I love even your crummy, dilapidated, skinny body..."

"Then we have to convert it to light, and our problems will be over."

"Not unless you take me with you."

Peter falls silent. He almost said: I don't know that I can. But please, please come. I can't take you because I don't know where it is that I am going. All I know is that the kingdom of Nomad is beautiful and warm and inviting and I have no idea how to get there. But if I can find it, then so can you, darling, so can you, my love...

"We shall be there together. One day. That I promise," he says instead.

"One day is such a long time."

"We are immortal."

"Yes, I know. You told me."

There is no wind at all. A delicate silence stretches for a while. Gossamer silence—like the delicate patterns on the black cloth above them. Under such a sky there is no need to talk. Not all the time. Just recharging one's batteries is enough, at times. And being together. While we can. But Peter feels inspired tonight.

"This earth is not ruled by some imaginary gods or esoteric clique from an inaccessible Olympus. They don't rule this world."

"Who does then?" Cathy wonders aloud.

"Not who. What. The Laws. The Laws rule the material behaviour of everything we can see or smell or detect with any of our senses."

"And the rest?" There must be the 'rest'. There must.

"The rest is covered by a state of consciousness."

"So we are back to duality again?"

"We never left it. But duality can start and end in the heart of man. This is what makes us gods!"

"Immortal?"

"I suppose..."

"You sound no longer sure."

"Oh, I am sure all right. It's just that I may have to adjust my method of achieving this immortality. So far I contented myself with my mind. Now, it no longer seems enough."

"Consciousness?"

"Right."

"You know, I made some notes about this yesterday. We just about covered it already, earlier..."

"Go on?" Cathy's eyes leave the stars to regard Peter's face.

"To recap: one—when matter becomes excessively dense, this state denotes extreme scarcity of spirit, or a condition wherein the consciousness is extremely dormant. And the second is its opposite, a complete absence of matter, when consciousness roams free."

"It begins to sound like a parallel evolution."

"You put your finger on it. This is precisely what it is. The first is controlled by the Law, the second by Ultimate Consciousness. For as long as the universe exists, the duality is maintained."

"And where do the laws come from?" Cathy's world must be orderly.

"The Consciousness, of course. The alpha and the omega. Consciousness precedes all and ultimately absorbs all. The phenomenal world is little more than a venture in search of self-awareness. A transient though recurrent condition. There may be a way to retain one's awareness of the process while being part of it. I don't know yet."

"Buddhists say all is absorbed." Cathy had learned a lot when she lived in the Orient.

"I cannot really argue. But it seems to me that even when you do not regard light as a bunch of photons, we may still think of each stream of light vibrating at a specific rate. Diversity seems infinite in nature. Like continuity. Why not in states of consciousness? I can visualize each ray of light retaining its individuality."

The stars wink their approval.

"Tell me about the states of consciousness."

"As far as I can see, there are four stages to the evolution of physical consciousness. The first pertains to matter. It resides in stone, in rock, in all elementary matter. When man's consciousness descends to this level, it is concerned with things. With objects such as money. The condition, or the state of consciousness, is characterized by greed, it is sated only and temporarily by success."

"It sounds pretty selfish," Cathy wonders aloud.

"It is. But make no mistake about it. Man is quite prepared to risk, even sacrifice, his life in its name. Many a man died in pursuit of money and power."

"It is hard to believe..."

"Nevertheless, history is replete with examples."

"And the second stage?"

"In its second stage, the consciousness will sacrifice everything for lust. It concerns itself with both, the vegetable and the animal kingdom. The absurd profligacy of nature is evident all around us. The seed of a single tree, if it were to fall on fertile ground, would cover half a continent. A male produces sperm with absurd abandon. It is all an expression of lust. But mark, a man will also risk and forfeit his life in pursuit of lust."

"So would a woman. A little later?"

"Be serious."

"Yes, master."

"The third is human love. From the previous incontinent abundance blossoms a marvellous, equally insatiable desire. It is manifested in a mother going hungry to feed her children, in a man offering his life for his brother. It is a love that translates all that is physical into a first rise above its inherent limitations. A family is the school nature arranged for its development. Both men and animals take part in the studies."

"There is more? Is love not the highest of qualities?"

"Oh, yes. It is by far the highest. But even love can mature in its form. During the fourth and last stage, man's development, or the development of physical consciousness, concerns itself with ideas. Also with ideals, concepts, with the things of the spirit. Of absolute freedom. I am talking about Unconditional Love. This state of consciousness dismisses all that is trite and transient. It reaches out to the highest potential of which man is capable. It offers everything, including physical life, for an ideal. It gives all to a total stranger. Even to an enemy. Why? Because at this stage of evolution man has no enemies. He only recognizes the immortal in every man, woman and child. The glowing embers which, in time, will grow into conflagrations to rival your supernovas. At this stage man becomes an immortal!"

"Like you?"

"Oh, Cathy, don't be silly. I am only attempting…"

"I know, dear. I know. And you may well be right. There seems to be no real freedom as long as we have desires that attach us to this earthly plane. I guess I am still at the halfway stage. Between the second and the third."

"I have learned more from you…"

"You live what you preach. I only aspire."

"I didn't mean to preach at you."

"You didn't. I only used the word as a figure of speech."

Peter sits back. His eyes cannot resist rising again to the stars. Perhaps those shimmering icicles are units of consciousness at an early stage of development. Perhaps one day they will become men. Human beings with all our imperfections. Suddenly, for the second time this evening, a single glowing ember detaches itself from the shimmering beehive and draws a lazy arc across the western sky. Just before touching the rim of the horizon, it goes out in a momentary brilliant glow. Another falling star.

"Is it hard to sacrifice so much, Peter?"

"I don't believe I ever sacrificed anything of any value. I only learned more and more..." And then Peter smiles. His voice softens even more as his eyes reflect the twinkle of the nearest star. "There is no such thing as sacrifice in the Spiritual Consciousness. It is complete. All inclusive. And yes, It is immortal."

"Like love?"

"Yes, darling. Just like you."

"Did you make a wish?"

"Yes, and it came true. You are still here."

* * *

18

Lazarus

T he man driving the coupe only slightly resembles the
gaunt derelict that once escaped with remnants of his life
from a decrepit tavern in Lower St-Henri. Of course, there
is no such thing as Upper St-Henri, but if there were, the man
who once called himself Simon Nomad would not qualify to
return there, either.

Regardless of gifts he might have to offer.

Peter, or Petrus Latter, (the new name indicative of the latter
of the two, thus of the last change of surname necessary to
protect his privacy), is a man of glowing health, of fine muscle
tone, of a man capable of climbing mountains while keeping a
multitude of insects away by an act of his will.

"But, darling, I would not recognize you myself!" Cathy
insisted.

She thought Peter could very well return to civilization as
Thornton. Perhaps just dropping the medical credentials.

"That's because you think of me only as an object of your
desire," Peter replied, "while I think that there is little point in
giving the opposition any advantage if we can avoid it." He
completed the second part of the sentence only after proving his
new-found agility by dodging a kick directed at his shin.

Cathy well understood that Peter had to set about finding and building his new life. From scratch. A process of re-integration into today's society. In spite of their many discussions, she had no idea how Peter intended to set about it. Possibly because Peter had no idea, either.

"We shall see," he assured her. "There is a purpose to everything. We must simply learn to allow it to happen."

Right now, she regarded Peter with admiration and... a smidgen of pride. After all, it had been her cooking, her stringent demands that he partake in long walks out there, in the open, perhaps even her acquiescence if not encouragement that his manhood be reawakened after some four months of self-imposed restraint. For his part, Peter had not found his past celibacy a trial. He simply had not thought about it. Frankly, neither had Cathy, until she found herself, thanks to Winston, in Peter's immediate proximity. They both lived intensely in the present.

On one occasion, Peter remarked on an apparent contradiction between Cathy's joyful attitude toward sex and her predisposition to mysticism.

"I know that Nature tends to rebel when deprived of its most fundamental expression of creativity, and one's sex drive cannot be regarded as any less. I also know that what you and I refer to as Nature is the Law. Yet, with all your talk of Lao Tzu and his profound mysticism..."

"Peter," she replied, her voice dogmatic with self-confidence, "Lao Tzu was a man. A real man of body and soul. I would wager my life that he knew that one does not achieve spirituality by opposing the Laws of Nature. *Au contraire*. You raise your consciousness by fulfilling the Law, not by denying It!"

They never discussed the subject again. They enjoyed it instead.

And yes! She did regard Peter with pride. The new, renewed Peter.

If a man of 'gift'—or, better still, of preponderant spirituality—is to be equated with a gaunt body, neglected beard and unprepossessing facial pallor, from which sunken eyes regard the world with fatigue and resignation, then Peter's deep suntan and humorous spark denies any semblance of spirit in his soul, mind or body. The hounds of media could not recognize Peter. Not because he looks different but because he is a different man. Not only from the man who once snapped at innocuous interns and residents, but equally as different from the derelict who was willing to give his life so that others might not have a chance to learn by their own mistakes.

The abuse of power always carries a penalty. The abuse of great power is liable to kill the abuser. Peter had learned his lesson.

He had spent the last weeks arranging his notes into a manuscript that had some order and erudition. He checked his references from the books Cathy had brought with her. Other data he correlated by lying on the sofa and reaching back into his memory, all the way back to his days at the seminary. His recall, provided he withdrew from the distracting influence of his surroundings, had become even more phenomenal. Peter found he could recall events, segments of the past, not as a series of symbols or even selective sensual fragments, but as the events themselves. His memory attested equally to all his senses which initially participated in filing the information in his memory. The smells, tastes, the textures, the tonal value carried equal importance to his visual images.

And all this had transpired since the end of March, since Lazarus rose from his grave of an emotional stalemate. Peter was dead. He is alive again.

Another change of name, another chance. Another life?

Perhaps. *The wind bloweth and it listeth...* Only time will tell, he told Cathy.

Peter realizes fully that the notes he jotted down are little more than ideas to be worked on, questioned, edited, massaged, before they coalesced, hopefully, into a semblance of a philosophy of life. Philosophy of Immortality. Yet he thought that the questions had been, are, as important as the forthcoming answers. Perhaps the questions were universal, the answers individual, personal, different for each one of us. For reasons he could hardly justify, Peter had assumed that eventually Winston

Smith would help him sort out his notes and extract those notions which would be of interest to other people. One day. At present his manuscript suffered from the same weakness from which all first drafts suffer: his notes were strong on intuition, weak on intellectual digestion.

Or, as Cathy had said, that was their strength. *The wind bloweth...*

The day after the discussion with Cathy on the subject of Consciousness, Peter wrote in his diary:

May 29. Discussion C/P. Parallel Evolution (Consciousness)

N.B.: Consciousness is spelled with capital 'C' in order to distinguish It from e.g.: an awakened as opposed to the dormant state of one's awareness.

I put it to you that reality manifests dual evolution. The evolution of the body and the evolution of the soul. This first is phenomenal, i.e.: limited to material or physical manifestation. Quite independent of it is the evolution of our Consciousness which, while preceding the phenomenal evolution, can and does, on occasion, interject its presence into the phenomenal or gross matter. It must be stressed that at a certain stage, the two can, under particular circumstances, become one.

An example of the merging can be observed in the mutation which matter undergoes at the fringe of the velocity of light. In such an environment, one can no longer regard light as a phenomenal occurrence, but, in order to experience light, one would become light. Ultimately the perceiver and the perceived are, must become, one.

The velocity of light, however, should only be regarded as a horizon line; not limiting but ever receding in front of our unfolding journey.

Another example of this event is illustrated by circumstances wherein the phenomenal effect is a direct result of a cause based solely in Consciousness. This principle postulates the feasibility of ultimately full control over one's material surroundings. To achieve this result, we must come into accord with the Consciousness residing in the phenomenal manifestation of that which one wishes to affect. The Consciousness residing in all gross matter below that of man, may become subservient to man's will. It must be stressed, however, that if rather than reaching concordance with the Consciousness residing in any object, plant or animal, one uses the power of one's mind to affect control, the Law demands that the perpetrator of such a crime against the other less developed Consciousness, is extracted in full.

It appears that the Velocity of Light is indicative of an elusive horizon, below which the Single, Static Condition splits into two evolutionary trends, namely matter (including all forms of energy) and Consciousness. Since no phenomenal existence is possible above this horizon line, once we rise above it, we enter into the realm of Pure Consciousness, or what some more advanced religions of the world refer to as Spirit.

I would suggest that the horizon line, as defined above, being indicative of both evolutionary conditions, is not a fixed, but rather a flexible phenomenon.

In the worlds of duality, the phenomenal world undergoes a further split into matter and energy, while the Consciousness is likewise subjected to a dilution, principally referred to as pure Consciousness, that which is not affected by any phenomenal events, and the fields, such as electromagnetic and gravitational fields, which retain the characteristics of Discontinuity (Vide §17: Relativity and Pure Consciousness) as well as manifesting observable behaviour of quantifiable, i.e.: of Discontinuity.

(The Laws of Continuity always characterize all aspects of Consciousness. ibid.)

I must also stress the inherent interdependence of the two channels of evolution. Pure (Free) Consciousness cannot affect the phenomenal realm without the participation, and in the cases of more advanced animals such as man, without a degree of acquiescence. It may be argued that Pure Consciousness and the animal soul as expressed through its magnetic field, must cooperate to achieve phenomenal results. Ultimately the Consciousness, which initially identified Itself with the animal soul, frees Itself of the association. Paradoxically, It achieves this end not by negating or destroying, but by integrating the phenomenal entity, (i.e.: human physical, mental and emotional nature) into Itself. Thereafter, the process becomes reversible, though after the integration, the phenomenal manifestation is a construct of Its will (a conscious creation).

Consciousness is always the Cause, the Initiator, the Enlivener.

All biological functions are part of the phenomenal evolution.

Life can only be defined as the presence of a state of Consciousness within a phenomenal manifestation, never as the biological construct itself. Pure Consciousness is, of course, capable of independent existence, but as such it cannot affect directly the phenomenal universe.

Peter had jotted down over 300 pages of such notes, all written in his minute handwriting, all meticulously cross-referenced. The prolific author would be the first to admit that he would be the last man to understand all that he had written. He regards himself as no more than the means through which the information became translated into symbols decipherable by man.

By men a lot smarter than he. In time.

Peter and Cathy stand a long time, just looking; their arms interlocked, a solitary tear itching at the corner of Cathy's eye. They are saying good-bye to the ancient log cabin. Neither thinks that they are ever likely to spend any appreciable time here again. Their lives seem disposed to consist of fragments of intense living, of intense pleasure, of intense sharing. The pain is forgotten. There is neither anger nor anguish in their shared farewells. Just a detached acceptance of the inevitable. And a handful of those joyful fragments which would remain theirs in the mosaic of eternity. At least Cathy hoped so.

Cathy thought in the past tense. Peter in the present.

"Oh, I do hope you're right, Peter...." She was not yet quite as strong as Peter.

"About what, darling?"

"About us being immortal."

And now Cathy's slick two-seater is taking them back to Peter's beloved Westmount. The once-beloved Westmount. Cathy would have been content to stay up North for another few seasons. At least until the fireplace could be set again. Just once more.

Peter had said no.

"It is time to go, dear," he said only yesterday.

"So soon, Peter, now that summer is coming?"

She loved all seasons. With Peter. She objected. She had put forward superb arguments. The arguments were bristling with logic. With great floods of words flowing straight out of her heart.

"I know, dear. But it's time to go."

"But WHY?" A last desperate cry.

"I don't really know, dear."

He didn't want to go. The wind bloweth..., he told her.

Peter has no idea if he will find Westmount as enchanting as he had once thought it was. On the other hand, he no longer feels like a Nomad. He is glad for the foxes and for the birds and their nests, but, unlike the Master, he always finds a place to lay his head. Perhaps thanks to the Master. Perhaps he is looked after by a Power that chooses to remain anonymous. Admittedly, he has not a home of his own; but Peter feels, more and more, that wherever he does lay his head, that is his home.

On earth or in realms he had not visited until a few months ago.

The mountains flatten into hills, the hills into rolling fields, then... the short plains surrounding the Island of Montreal. An island with its mountains. Once the City looked clean, exciting. Now, rather dirty. Polluted. Crowded. Impersonal. Why must people live in a beehive? Then the discomfort passes; a smile of acceptance takes its place. There is absolutely no point in fighting. *Que sera, sera.* Doesn't it always?

"Shall I see you in town?" Somehow Cathy sounds distant.

"I am sure you could stay with us. Jo and Mo could well do with a beautiful auntie. Winston would appreciate you."

"Be serious, Peter."

She drops it. Peter had already admitted he has no idea why they are, right now, on their way back. Only he is adamant. Quite immutable. Strange. Most of the time he is so flexible. Almost malleable, like well-worked clay. Bending with the wind.

Then she remembers. The wind bloweth... She is not quite sure what he means by it. Normally... Peter is not normal. There is nothing normal about him.

It is a long drive, and they are not coming back this time.

"I love you." She has nothing else to say.

"What, dear?"

Peter does not own a car. It has been many months since he sat behind a steering wheel. He must concentrate on the road.

"I said, ah, h-how are you? Do you feel confident driving?" Cathy stammers. She hates lying.

"Not as confident as I would like to be."

"Do you want me to take over?"

"What, and miss all the fun of the city traffic?"

Peter has three close shaves with egomaniac drivers before reaching Westmount. Three, though he made no attempts to cut off monstrous trailers from gaining on him. By the time he pulls up in the front drive, he feels quite confident. Cathy a little less so. Peter's confidence is augmented by the conspicuous absence of any strangers on or around his sister-in-law's property.

"Come, darling. You must meet Ruth and Winston. Not to mention Jonathan and Moira. They will all love you, or I'll eat..."

Peter never wears a hat. He is looking around for something suitable to eat.

"You sure it would be all right?"

Even as Peter switches off the engine, the front door opens. It is blocked solidly by Winston, on the vertical axis, and by Jo and Mo on the lateral projection. In the background they can hear a hurried voice calling.

"I'm coming!"

Peter only just manages to get out of the car before the children charge at him in a reckless if not *kamikaze* attack. He catches them one in each arm and brings them back into the house. Winston opens the car door for Cathy and picks up the baggage.

"You sure that I should?" she asks Winston. Heretofore Cathy has been confidence personified.

"Your room is already made up, Dr. Mondellay. I don't think we should leave Master Peter alone until he becomes readjusted to civilization." Winston manages to imbue the title 'Master' he conferred on Peter with the English meaning: the way one refers to a lad not quite old enough to be addressed as a Mister.

"Oh." Cathy is instantly satisfied. "Of course." She precedes Winston to the front door with mounting self-assurance. She just experienced the first whiff of the Winston magic. The next moment she falls into Ruth's arms.

"Dear Cathy. How shall I ever repay you?"

Ruth embraces Cathy and refused to let go. Jo and Mo stand to one side, watching without a comment. Five minutes later, after many more hugs and expressions of mutual admiration, Jo clears his juvenile throat. Mo echoes her brother with an even higher soprano.

"Oh dear. And what have we here?"

Cathy has absolutely no experience with children. Not only is she herself an only child, but she had spent her life in a bunker lined with books and experimental equipment. Mostly underground. Next to a tunnel called a cyclotron. Now she looks stiff, uncomfortable, having no idea what to do. Jo helps her out.

"Allow me to introduce myself, Miss Mondellay. My name is Jonathan Thornton. While Uncle Peter is away, I am the master of the house." With that he reaches out his right hand and shakes Cathy's limp hand with vigour.

"And I am Moira. I am Jo's sister!" She would not be denied.

To Jo it must seem that the world is unfair. The moment he stopped shaking the hand of the newly arrived lady, the lady in question bends down and scoops his sister up in her arms. There his sister is cuddled, kissed and generally made a fuss of. Not that the master of the house would indulge in such frivolity, certainly not in front of everybody, but, well, it would be nice to be given a chance to refuse. Of course, with Uncle Peter it's different. Among men one can do all sorts of things which women wouldn't understand. With Uncle Peter, Mo only copies whatever he does. Like a little girl that she is. And that's as it should be. Isn't it? Jonathan steals a glance at Winston. He receives a wink from a great height.

Finally Mo is reinstated to her own feet.

Nothing much happens until after supper. The children are allowed to stay up a little longer, but finally Winston appears at the door. The two rise, distribute kisses to each and all (Cathy comes in for her share) and follow the tall shape upstairs.

Ruth, Cathy and Peter all try to say too much, all at once, and as a result no one says anything of importance. No great or famous men or women had died in Peter's or Cathy's absence. No wars had been started, no great scandals rocked the foundations of society. At least not greater than usual. Ruth is about to say something about Solidarity, but Peter waves her down. At that Ruth tells Peter, for at least the tenth time that he is looking just marvellous.

"But it is not just that. You don't just look different. You are different. Cathy, do you not agree?"

Cathy agrees. Peter offers an explanation.

"We can only assume that Lazarus was a very different man before and after his regeneration. After all, the latter man had the benefit of partaking in Pure Consciousness, not hampered by the body which weighs us all down."

"What happened to our immortality?" Cathy interjects.

"Oh, it's still there, only it adapts with the times!"

Peter is in a great mood. He is a true Lazarus. In body and in spirit. He seems as unconcerned about tomorrow as a man who has just won millions in a lottery. Ruth, on the other hand, feels almost out of place. Peter and Cathy have developed a language of their own. They use words like 'pure consciousness' as if they both knew what such an expression means. Ruth tries to steer the conversation to a more mundane level.

"Do you have any plans, Peter?"

"Oh yes. Lots. Only I am not quite sure, as yet, what they are."

Ruth looks to Cathy for help.

"Oh, it's all right, Ruth." The women had instantly switched to first-name terms. "Don't worry about it. In a few minutes he'll descend to our level. When he does, he'll actually make some sense. Occasionally."

"I have to get a job," Peter asserts, ignoring Cathy's sarcasm.

"Not necessarily. I opened your mail. I hope you don't mind, but I didn't know what to do. It could have been important, and..."

"It's all right, Ruth. Thank you. I'm glad you did."

"Well, the Montreal General has sent you a check in lieu of a six-month notice, at a Senior Teaching Staff pay. I think you have enough money to last you a couple of years."

"What?! B-b-but I've been a senior staff member for less than a day!"

"Don't fight with me, Peter. I only report... Anyway, considering the hours you've worked for as long as I've known you, I would have thought you earned the money many times over." Ruth's tone is almost indignant.

"Bah! All the same, life will never cease to amaze me. I bet John Brent had something to do with it. I suppose he is honouring my appointment."

"Actually, he called a few times. He always spoke with affection about you. He is really concerned."

"Thank you. I shall see him." Then he mutters, as though speaking to himself. "So what else is written for me in the stars?"

Just then Winston materializes on the landing at the top of the stairs. Cathy is not used to Winston's sudden and silent manifestations. To her he is looming down over them like a dark, lofty apparition, while to Ruth Winston's appearance is but a well-established signal. The children are ready to be kissed and tucked in. At Winston's nod Ruth gets up. A moment later Peter joins her on the way up the stairs.

"Can I come, too?" Cathy feels left out. Peter waves her on.

Ten minutes later all are back, including Winston.

"Where were we?" Peter asks no one in particular.

"You had been inquiring into the ineptitude of the astrological prognostications, Sir." Winston supplies the answer with his usual precision.

"Was I?" Peter is no longer used to Winston's vernacular. At least not when delivered from the astronomical height of the lanky butler's physical body. Then Peter remembers. "Ah, the stars?"

"Yes, Sir."

"Would you care to enlighten us, Winston? May I call you Winston? I would really appreciate it." Cathy had heard more than a thing or two about Winston from Peter. Evidently she is curious if Peter's stories have any basis in fact.

"Yes, Miss Mondellay—on both counts."

Again Peter has to sort out the answer. Winston has a much easier delivery in his non-physical body. Or whatever body he had used in his chimerical appearances over the last few months.

"Astrology, Madam, is a lost science." Winston addresses Cathy from the archway leading into the hall. "But even in distant antiquity, it had been no more than a study of the electromagnetic fields surrounding the giant celestial objects, such as planets, and the manner in which such sources generate influence on other magnetic fields, such as those emanating from our bodies."

Cathy leans over to Peter and whispers into his ear: "Does he always talk that way?" Peter ignores her.

"It must be clearly understood that astrology has always been a science of probabilities. Its statistical laws apply to vast magnetic aggregations, not to the individual fields, such as a single human being. There is no known law governing a single field. If I may, Madam, I would think of them as a probability wave in quantum physics."

"Good Lord! He talks about quantum physics as he would about yesterday's pudding," Cathy whispers again into Peter's ear. A strange comparison indeed, but the best Cathy can come up with on the spur of the moment.

"The giant magnetic fields affect both the formation and the later development of our own, ah, emanations." (Winston seldom searched for the right word. Perhaps there isn't one, Peter wonders.) "Thus, theoretically, the date of birth as well as the later chronological relationships between the macro and the micro fields are of some consequence."

"Are you a scientist, Winston?" Cathy's open mouth suggests surprise and a bit of amazement. Cathy is not often openmouthed.

"What is wrong with the science, if I may continue, Madam, is that it takes into account certain phenomena without paying adequate attention to their causes. Regrettably, we can safely assume that this weakness is inherent in all the Western sciences, as I dare say you can well confirm, Madam."

"I dare say that I might well do so, Winston. Though we do attempt to guess at the causes by observing the results."

Cathy continues to regard Winston with a mixture of disbelief and bafflement. Her mouth no longer impersonates a flytrap, but her head is cocked to one side, her eyes riveted to the butler's own smouldering embers.

"Thank you, Madam. Studying the results of events which took place millions of years ago is generally referred to as astronomy, thus not far divorced from astrology as it had once been. The study of the same effects but originating a handful of billions of years earlier we now call astrophysics. The first few nonillions of a second in the life of our universe preoccupies the minds of the scientists limiting themselves to the exigencies of particles so small that in most cases they must invent them in order to give their theories a *raison d'être*."

"How do you know all this, Winston?" Cathy feels she must interrupt.

"It is all common knowledge, Madam. All we are doing is observing. And since observing is all that we seem to be doing, then we must ask ourselves, who is the observer?"

"I do not follow—who is the observer of what?"

"Precisely, Madam. Since we are part of the effect, then who is the observer?"

"You mean that we are indulging ourselves in staring at our cumulative navels?"

Winston bows and withdraws into the penumbra of the entrance hall. His departure is followed by a silence punctured by frequent sighs, deep inhalations and significant head shaking.

"How the devil did we start all this...?" Cathy falls back against the pillows of the settee. "Ruth, you never told me you live with a living, breathing enigma!"

"Only if you can understand what he is talking about." Ruth tries to calm Cathy down.

"You sure that you didn't miss the whole point?" Peter asks, a dry smile hovering on his lips.

"You sure there was a point to all this?" Ruth does not sound willing to pursue the matter any further. She knows that Winston is perfectly capable of talking plain English when he chooses to do so.

"Yes, dear. There is. Cathy, think about it..." Peter urges her on.

Cathy is too excited to apply her excellent brain to the poser. She is simply swept off her feet by the inimitable butler.

"You asked about astrology, remember?" Peter prods encouragingly.

"Yes, I did. But..."

"The point which Winston was making is that the field is not the result of a mass, but that it precedes matter. It is the..."

"How in the world do you figure that out?"

"Winston gave you all the elements of the puzzle. You have to piece it together."

"But he did say that the celestial bodies generate magnetic fields..."

"No, he did not. He said that magnetic fields surround the celestial bodies, and use such to generate influence on the formation and development of our own magnetic fields. That is a very different way of looking at the field. Rightly or wrongly, Winston postulates that the fields precede the formation of the celestial bodies, and thus are the cause and not the result of vast configurations of matter. You work in theoretical physics. Doesn't that have something to do with the Big Bang? And don't you guys assume the Big Bang to be the prime cause? Winston is suggesting that the Big Bang is a result. Think about it. If you dare!"

Cathy's eyes indicate growing understanding. If Winston is right, then science would have to start again on a completely new tack. Although who on earth would listen to a gaunt butler speaking with a ridiculous English accent in the middle of North America?

I did! She answers her own doubts.

No. It doesn't make sense. It can't.

Only, it sounds so right... and I don't even know why!

* * *

Summer

When his branch is yet tender,
And putteth forth leaves,
Ye know that summer is nigh. . .

Matthew 24:32

19

The Present

To live at the Summit Circle on the top of Westmount is to know everybody who is Anybody. Summit Circle is as high above the Thornton Residence as the Thornton Residence is above Lower Westmount. And many people would give ten years of their lives to live in Lower Westmount. Even for a while. One could make contacts to last a lifetime.

The Mondellays, however, live at the Summit Circle. The top of the top. Cathy told Daddy that she needed a publisher. Next morning two women and one man representing major publishing houses called. Long distance. They asked if Cathy would like to send them her manuscript or would she rather that they presented themselves at her doorstep with the requisite contracts.

Perhaps it wasn't just the Summit Circle.

The name Mondellay still packed a considerable punch. Only the manuscript was not signed by a Mondellay. It had been signed by a man called Petrus Latter. But it did not seem to matter. Anything which father and daughter Mondellay deemed erudite and cared to recommend was perfectly acceptable to all three publishers.

"It is your duty to have it published, Peter. Your absolute duty!" Cathy had insisted only a few days ago. She had read his notes. All of them.

"But these things are essentially private, personal." Peter did his best to oppose.

"You have no right to keep your insights to yourself. If people do not want to read them, they won't. Let them decide. You must respect their judgment."

That did it. There is a word Peter is still afraid of. Judgment. He had had to make too many judgments in his time. Perhaps had used up his quota. He had made judgments, daily, during his four years at the General. Judgments affecting the life and death of many men and women. Later Simon Nomad had abdicated practically all responsibility and acted like an indifferent channel through which power flowed onto the just and the unjust. An error in judgment? He might never know. Virtually all his visitors, patients, had recovered from their mental or physical abrasions, from the loss of their wholeness. Like the *petit* Henri, the first beacon to point to a new course in Dr. Thornton's life. Virtually all had benefited... Had some abused the fruit of his gift? What of the state of their Consciousness? Had they advanced a single rung through their experience?

"Are not my insights as much a gift as the other I misused so badly?" Peter asked Cathy the day following their argument. His mind kept returning to his manuscript. He repeatedly tried to dissuade Cathy from publishing his work. Yet, he had no precise idea why.

"Ultimately, I shall abide by your judgment, Peter..." she replied.

"Why am I so afraid to share my deliberations with others? What possible consequences could result from people reading my notes? Assuming anyone would ever want to..." he wondered aloud.

Physically, Peter had recovered fully from the four months in St-Henri but, within the deeper recesses of his heart, some scars still festered. Peter had lost the courage necessary to pass judgment. He would not admit it, even to himself, but he was afraid. Afraid to heal people. Afraid to influence their minds. Afraid to make decisions.

"Let others be the judges. Let the just liberate the just—even as the dead must bury the dead..." he told her. There was a plea in his voice.

Cathy was as sure of Peter's manuscript as she had ever been of anything in her life. She searched her mind to find an argument to convince Peter. She understood that he was afraid. She even knew why. Indirectly, he had told her.

"I've made too many mistakes already, and 'raised' myself. Or have been 'raised'. How many times do you think I'll be so lucky?"

And then Cathy found her answer. During the last three weeks at the cabin, in order to get closer to Peter, to understand him better, she had reread the Bible. The Old and the New Testaments. She also knew of Peter's preoccupation with justice, particularly since he had accepted the responsibilities inherent in the concept of karma and reincarnation.

"...*a just man falleth seven times, and riseth up again,*" she quoted a Proverb from memory. "Relax, Peter. By my count you have a few falls to go!"

Peter was stunned. Rather than argue, he burst out laughing.

"How dare you quote the Bible to me? Your expertise ends with the Tao Te Ching!"

But he knew he had lost. It was not easy to win an argument against Cathy's keen intellect. At least he had tried. To protect himself. As best he could. He did not apologize.

"Is not the instinct for self-preservation a Primal Law of nature?" he asked later.

"Indeed, though one ought to be very sure what it is that one is preserving."

That day Peter gave Cathy the manuscript. There was another brief discussion about the prospective title, but it settled quickly. The manuscript had been named THE *DIALOGUES*. The title was fitting. Most of Peter's notes had been the result of conversations with Cathy or with more esoteric interlocutors. They both liked the title. During the next few days Cathy set about having the manuscript transferred to an electronic diskette, while Peter made some marginal editing comments which were immediately incorporated into the *corpus delicti*.

"You do realize that the body of the manuscript is a damning evidence of my crimes?" For the final time he expressed his reticence.

But it was too late. A copy of the diskette went on to one of the publishers whom Cathy had selected as the one professing the best attitude towards the subject matter contained therein. That was yesterday.

Today, they have very different problems.

Ruth lost her job. Resigned, really.

The family now consisting of Ruth, Cathy, Peter, Mo and Jo (and Winston flowing in and out of the woodwork) all gathered together in the living room to hear the news.

"Mommy shall be with you a lot more from now on," Ruth tells all as Jo and Mo jump up and down in perfect unison and in evident approval of the announcement.

"I can jump higher!" Mo makes her own announcement.

"No, you can't!"

Etc., etc.

"Can we now go to our playroom, please, Mommy?" Jo asks, when nothing but jumping appears suitable to commemorate the occasion of Mommy coming home to stay.

"Yes, you may. Only please go quietly?"

The children are gone before Ruth completes her sentence. Thanks to the carpet, almost quietly.

"So much for the tears of joy at my homecoming!" she says, shedding crocodile tears herself. "Ah, for the joys of motherhood..."

"So what happened?" Peter asks.

"Actually, it's quite a long story. You know that I am not a particular advocate of the Solidarity movement. I believe that here, in Canada, we are probably better off having people make decisions in a less electronically controlled way. But let's face it. In Europe, since its inception, the Solidarity International has already achieved results which the cradle of European culture and civilization had failed to achieve in over two thousand years."

"A good game of baseball?" Cathy asks, looking at the ceiling.

"No, Cathy," says Ruth. "They succeeded where the European Congress, the EEC and other attempts at unification had failed. The Solidarity has created a decent distribution of wealth throughout Europe and a goodly part of Russia and North Africa, to boot!"

"But..." Peter stops Cathy from presumably making another inane remark.

"Whatever we personally think of the Solidarity, we must give credit where credit is due."

"I don't want their credit. Not when it is inserted subcutaneously into my head!" Cathy insists.

"But Cathy, you are looking at details of implementation, not at the results. And the results are quite stunning. There is no hunger, no restrictions on medical treatment, no exploitation of the many by the few. It is almost a utopia." Ruth tries to explain.

"And I suppose Walensa represents the Second Coming of Christ?" exclaims Cathy.

"That is uncalled for. First of all, Walensa is a woman. Her first name is Lena, and although she is a granddaughter of Lech, she is not of the house of David. She is, however, extremely well educated, modest, lives on a meagre 3X average income. She has been elected by more millions of people than any man or woman wielding power in the history of mankind. And she seems to be in the process of creating a paradise on earth. At least, over there, in Europe."

Cathy is tired of being the only one to oppose her hostess with what she realizes would be futile arguments. Ruth has made up her mind, and she is not about to change it. At least, not very quickly, if at all.

"That is as it may be, Ruth, but what does all this have to do with you losing your job?" Peter steps between the two women.

"I have refused to work against Walensa. I happen to have met her, and judge her to be a perfectly reasonable, honest and highly principled woman."

"Aha..." Peter lets the air out of his lungs. And so is my dear sister-in-law, he nods at his thoughts.

From the corner of his eye Peter sees Winston studiously polishing the dining room table. He is well within earshot. Peter wonders if Winston will have his say on the subject of Solidarity.

If not, then it will be the only subject on which he would not have an established, well-balanced if surprising position.

Ruth apparently needs to further justify her decision.

"Do you know that Walensa's income is a lot less than many of her delegates'? They still allow up to a 5X factor. And she has been personally instrumental in making abortion virtually illegal!"

"You like that, do you, sister?" Cathy almost sneers. Like Peter, Ruth had been brought up a Catholic. Not that Catholics hold a monopoly on telling women what to do with their bodies.

"Well, she did not make it illegal, but quite unnecessary. Every baby automatically receives life access to the World Bank, provided they are members of the SI, of course."

"Of course! And instead of circumcision they receive subcutaneous insertion? Lose a little, add a little." Cathy is still catty. "At least it's fair on the girls."

Ruth takes her remark in good faith. "Everything is fair over there. Everything. I know, I've been there!"

"A paradise on earth?" Cathy is scornful. "All made to measure. You behave yourself and Big Brother will look after you, right?"

"Cathy, there is no Big Brother. Everything is done on a volunteer basis. I have met a number of people. You are free to be what you want to be, to act the way you want to act. There is absolutely no compulsion for you to do anything you don't want to do. Really."

"As long as you behave yourself," Cathy insists.

"No! The Europeans have more freedom than we do if you take into account the dos and the don'ts imposed by our many levels of governments, our conglomerates and the trade unions. Anyway, Lena told me that ultimately it was your father who made the Solidarity International possible. Until energy was made economically viable to everyone, and particularly available to an independent small businessman..."

"Please, Ruth, have the goodness of heart not to bring my father's name into this."

Cathy can no longer contain herself. She stands up and starts walking the length of the room. Peter follows her with his eyes, then, apparently satisfied, turns to Ruth.

"And what happens to people who do not wish to join Solidarity International?"

"I don't understand. Why would anyone not want to benefit..." Ruth begins.

"Just bear with me. Are you telling me that everybody in Europe is a member of the Solidarity?" Peter presses his point.

"Well, I really don't know... I suppose it is only a matter of time..."

"So there are people who are not members. Tell me, Ruth, what is their *modus vivendi* right now?"

For the first time since Ruth came in with her announcement, there ensues a protracted silence. Cathy stops pacing; even Winston, apparently satisfied with the deep shine of the rosewood table, disappears from the dining room. Seconds later he looms again, this time through the hall archway.

"Would Madam care for some refreshments?"

Ruth's sigh is louder than either Cathy's or Peter's. Winston has again performed his magic, though in quite a different manner. It is evident that he is capable not only of saying the right things at the right time but also of making his presence felt at the most appropriate moments.

"Yes, thank you, Winston. Very much. Perhaps some coffee would be nice. Cathy? Peter? Any preferences?"

"A fruit juice, please, Winston?" Peter asks.

"Me, too," says Cathy.

"Make that three, if you would, Winston." Ruth coordinates, then holds up her hand. "How are the children?"

This was Ruth's first day home. It would take her a while to be able to answer this question herself.

"They are at present visiting the Shrine of the Sages, in Northern India, Madam. I shall tell them that you have inquired." Winston withdraws into the pantry.

Peter wonders. Mo and Jo are studying the computerized atlas which can zero in on any part of the world and, at a push of a finger, provide details of the selected spot on the globe, or...?

Or Winston has given a cryptic answer on purpose. Peter has had occasion to see the children attend all sorts of lectures, which had not been easily accessible through a computer. Peter is sure that Winston is basically incapable of lying. He is, however, extremely able to present the truth in a manner so veiled as to be ambiguous beyond recognition.

By the time Winston serves the cool orange juice, the discussion has resumed—happily, as equally cool reason takes precedence over the more volatile emotions. The problem of Solidarity is indeed unique in the history of mankind. The organization—Movement, as Ruth still calls it—appears to wield virtually unlimited power, yet it accomplishes its purpose without actual coercion. It is not a question of a carrot or a whip. It is a question of a carrot or nothing at all. Or, almost nothing.

Even Cathy manages to detach herself from the anger stimulated by her recent experience with the 'movement'. She tells Ruth about them. Ruth listens without an interruption, then smiles her understanding.

"I happen to have resigned for the same reason you refused to undergo the implant installation," she comments finally.

"Yes, I can see that now. We both seem to sit on our high horses. Only, for a while there, the heads of our nags appeared to be pointed in opposite directions," Cathy admits.

Peter does his best to remain impartial. Now, however, that the women are not only friendly again (which condition they found it necessary to seal with another hug), but apparently willing to pursue the review of the relative merits of the Solidarity movement, he tries to balance the issue.

"It seems that the system could be successful in the elimination of the drug problems, of excessive indulgence in alcohol, perhaps in the elimination of crime itself?" He formulates the statement in the form of a question.

"If you not only empower the majority of people but simultaneously eliminate the *raison d'être* for hard cash, or any currency for that matter, yet provide sufficient funds to assure that everyone has sufficient goods and services to maintain a comfortable living, well, no wonder..." Ruth is quite calm now.

Her last job had trained her to take part in long diplomatic arguments.

"Yes, but at what price!" Cathy still feels strongly about her loss of freedom.

"Yes, Cathy, but imagine a society in which there is no crime," Ruth counters.

"There is none on a desert island. Nor is there an army contingent nor a concentration camp. Nor is there a choice. Nor progress." Cathy feels she is sinking.

"I think what Cathy is saying," Peter interjects, "is that if you remove people's opportunity to choose, you can selectively remove a number of negative trends in a society. What you give up is an opportunity to learn. To say: I have negative tendencies, but today I shall not steal, nor take drugs, nor practice whatever my weakness. Today I shall overcome."

"By an act of my will!" Cathy adds unnecessarily.

"Perhaps..." Ruth is not disposed to battle. She had resigned not because she is a member of the Solidarity International, but because the UN had wanted her to make battle against her own will. "I suppose that Solidarity is creating conditions in which a juxtaposition of the UN and the like Seats of Power is inevitable."

"I would suggest to you," Peter says, "that the conditions have already been created by the UN and by the conglomerates and, as you call them, the Seats of Power, by which I gather you mean essentially the various strata of governments. Particularly the latter had been exploiting the masses with insidious taxation for countless centuries. Isn't it time to balance the scales?"

"Yes, Peter," Cathy says, "but the Solidarity is going to the other extreme. Two evils do not make a right!" Belying her genes, she is still the most emotional among them.

"I put it to you that if the conditions had not been ripe, Solidarity would not have succeeded. Or... it will not succeed," Peter says. "We might care to examine our own conscience and see what we have done to assure that Solidarity will not fall on fertile ground. I for one have been much too busy staring at my own navel."

"You are not being fair to yourself." Cathy jumps in to
protect him.

"Yes, I am. Had you spent a few months in St-Henri, you
would agree with me. We who live on Olympus have rejected all
responsibility for those who are less gifted. Live and let die.
Provided we remain at the top of Westmount."

"What could we have done?" Ruth and Cathy seem to have
shared this question.

"I would say we should have removed our blinders and
cared a little more. When I needed help, all of you came to my
aid. There are thousands, millions, who have no one to aid
them." Peter's smile manages to express both gratitude and
sadness.

There is little more anyone can say after this. Anyway,
Winston again appears at the archway to announce that lunch is
served.

After the meal, Peter calls Dr. Brent. The doctor is out and
Peter does not wish to leave a message. There is no point in
attracting unnecessary attention. Within half an hour Dr. Brent
calls back, anyway. His secretary had recognized Peter's voice
immediately. Strange, Peter thinks, I could not have spoken to
her more than a couple of times on the telephone. They arrange
to meet that evening at Dr. Brent's home. Around nine. For a
nightcap.

During the afternoon Cathy drives Peter up to the top of
Mount Royal and insists that they walk for at least an hour. She
wants Peter to be a normal human being. At some level of
perception, she knows that she is fighting a losing battle. She is
not sure why but, well, call it intuition. A vague cloud on the
horizon. It may have gilt edges, but its shadow casts a painful
spectre over her future. In fact, she cannot see her future.
Whatever her relationship with Peter, no matter how deep their
love for each other, she cannot find in her heart to believe that
what they share can be permanent. Other than the love itself.
That is all she is sure of. Love. And nothing else.

Sometimes it just isn't enough.

After an hour's walk they settle on the grass overlooking
Beaver Lake. Only there are no beavers. Just a few kids playing

with total disregard for the problems of Solidarity or the UN or the world at large. They live in the moment. The Present.

Late June is the most glorious part of the year. All the green is greener. The verdant shades are still delicate, still imbued with the joy of spring yet already sure of themselves. They already show individuality of maturity and are not reduced to the common denominator of the all-equalizing summer. The Autumn may wear Canada's rich crown of gold and rubies, but June is the epitome of the marvels of green. The colour of life. Of vitality.

And the kids are just playing.

They seem oblivious even to the beauty of nature all around them. Perhaps they cannot see it because they are standing and running and jumping too close. Perhaps they *are* nature.

"We must bring Mo and Jo with us—the next time we come here," Peter says.

"Do you know, that's exactly what I was just thinking?"

They both smile. Perhaps they, too, are a part of nature. Just a little. Still...

They get up and walk to a paved area overlooking the vast sprawling metropolis. Here and there, a strategically placed monocular offers a peek at some distant hills, the hills they had left only yesterday. At least it seems that way.

"Sometimes I wish we could accelerate the vibrations of our bodies to the velocity of light, so that time would stop, and we would remain together forever," Cathy says, ignoring the view and looking at Peter.

"Oh, but we are together forever. Trust me," Peter says, his arm around Cathy's slim waist.

Peter sounds as though he means it. His voice seems to gather authority every day. A little like Winston's only without the thespian accent. And a lot less enigmatic. Cathy would so like to believe him. She wants to. So very much.

Peter looks down at the enormous panorama spread before them.

"All this I shall give to thee, if thou wilt fall down and worship me."

"Were you talking to me?"

"No, darling. I have not been talking to you," he assures her. "But it is quite a view, isn't it?"

"You were quoting the Bible, weren't you?" Cathy glances at the view and again turns her back on it to face Peter. "I said something when I was angry at Ruth, but frankly, I don't really understand the sentiment involved."

"You spoke in anger?"

"Well, let us say in the heat of the moment. Anyway, what is all this talk about the Second Coming of Christ? I thought the Catholic Church rejects the concept of reincarnation? Am I wrong?"

"Not the last time I discussed the issue with my superiors at the Saint Francis."

"Then how it is possible?"

"He is to come in clouds of glory, at the end of the world."

"You mean in a few million or billion years?"

"Well, no. In fact a great many sects believed that the beginning of the present millennium had presented an opportune moment."

"Then what are they talking about?"

"Frankly, my dear, you would have to ask them."

"You mean you don't believe in such..."

"I believe in a different explanation. It's a long, to me personally almost tragic story. It was perhaps the single most important factor contributing to my leaving the seminary before being accepted into the priesthood. You sure you want to hear about it?"

"I want to hear if you sneeze in the middle of a desert." Cathy is dead serious.

"Well, I discovered that a great many years ago, within the church, the Symbol had become more important than the Substance. It was like with Carroll's Cheshire cat—only the smile remained. Only in this case it was the Symbol. I felt that symbols were extremely necessary to express certain intangibles, a certain untenable Truth, but they could never take the place of the Substance. It seemed to me, at the time, that most people had retained the Symbol, though they had forgotten what it stood for. Perhaps I was wrong..."

Even today Peter does not find it easy to talk about the subject which he recognizes as his first and perhaps foremost failure. The just may raise themselves seven times, but there seems little point in dwelling on their failures. It has nothing to do with any feelings of guilt or regret, only of a possible error. An error in judgment.

"Please go on?" Cathy pleads when the silence stretches. She desperately wants to know this man; this unusual man, who finds it so difficult to criticize anything. Even the church he had left so many years ago.

"There is not that much more to say. Jesus had once been a man. He had attained the Christ Consciousness. A state beyond limitations. He became the Cause. To achieve that, we must live a conscious life and not be propelled by the conditioning imprinted on our subconscious mind. To most of us it is more than we even dare to aspire. This state of Consciousness is surely His greatest legacy. That and the message of love. He had once quoted an old psalm that proclaimed that: 'Ye are Gods.' Well, show me a man who thinks so. Most Christians would consider such talk blasphemy."

"Do you?"

"I don't think it matters what I think. I try to think less, to listen more. To the voice within. But it seems to me that Jesus had come once as a historical man. His Second Coming takes place in a cloud of glory within our hearts. Not as a dictator to end all dictators. Jesus became the Christ. Now it is our turn."

On their way back to Beaver Lake, Cathy again watches the children. A state of consciousness, Peter had said. The children continue to play. They are happy, carefree, as though in a different universe altogether. Perhaps it will be their turn.

Perhaps it already is.

* * *

20

The Prophet

"I t's going to be a hot summer," Peter says, looking out into the front garden. Then he steps back, quickly, drawing a curtain between himself and the people outside.

The air-conditioner is working overtime. Day and night. The heat itself might be bearable if it weren't for the humidity. It feels as though a thunderstorm could strike any second—only it doesn't. The sky remains a dirty blue; at night the stars look as if their light were being filtered through a glass dome someone forgot to wash for a long time.

Summer in Montreal.

The people in the front garden do not seem to mind. Mostly women, they are content to shed most of their clothing, to stand, lie or sit cross-legged, like unfinished statues waiting for the sculptor to come and wipe the excess water from the outer layers of clay.

They had first come almost three weeks ago. Little more than a week after Peter's, or rather Petrus Latter's, book hit the bookshops. They drifted here one by one, seemingly meeting by accident, like indolent moths drawn to the one place where they hoped the light might be disseminated. They all shared patient, wide-open, distant yet expectant eyes. No one seems to know how they had traced their way to the Thornton residence. Peter had given no press releases, no interviews, no autographing sessions. The women and a few men just came, sauntered up the hill, to wait in silent, hopeful resignation. Hardly a whisper gave advance notice of their presence. They stood on Holy Ground. They communed with each other in silence.

It was nobody's fault. Really.

To say that *The Dialogues* had been published ahead of schedule would be a flagrant understatement. When Cathy was little, her mother tried to have a novel published under a pen name. She had tried for seven years. Cathy vaguely recalls the story.

Her mother's manuscript had found its way to a literary agent, where it gathered dust for an indefinite period of time.

"It always does," Mrs. Mondellay had recalled later. There was no more bitterness in her voice—just an acceptance of the inevitable. "It gathers dust for a period inversely proportional to the agent's degree of financial success. If the agent managed to have a few titles accepted by the almighty publishers, then the manuscripts might well lie around their dusty, messy desks until they matured into their own obsolescence. If the agent was hungry, then the author might be lucky enough to benefit from the inadvertent critic's experience in the matter of style, arrangement, story lines and what-have-you within as little as six to twelve months."

"But don't they make their living from selling manuscripts?" Cathy remembers asking.

Her mother had smiled. "Ah, you see, my dear. In addition to their literary expertise, the agents are the self-proclaimed experts in the matter of surviving on a negligible income, all being sacrificed in the name of literature."

As the memories came back to her, Cathy became quite nervous about subjecting Peter to her mother's experiences.

"Finally," Mrs. Mondellay had continued, "after a requisite number of idiosyncratic changes aimed at satisfying the literary frustrations of the self-appointed, 'informal' or 'unofficial' literary critics, the manuscript commences its multiple journeys to the publishing houses. After another year or two, if the author is lucky, the second cycle of editing begins. This time in earnest. The Editors—this new bunch is spelled with a capital E—insist on leaving their personal imprint on the submission."

"But the manuscript had already been accepted..." Cathy recalls raising an objection on behalf of her mother and all frustrated writers.

"...in its original form. That's of absolutely no consequence. The Editors will have their way with it; rather like a man, frustrated after being shipwrecked on a desert island, will have his way with almost any woman. Given a chance."

"Mother!" Cathy had called out. In those days, mother was full of surprises.

But mother was caught up in her memories. "After the rewriting process is complete, only a miracle can protect the manuscript from reminding one of the willing one who, out of the goodness of her heart, agrees to sate the stranded reprobate's hunger. The man may emerge from this experience sensually satisfied, but the willing one's lot is seldom improved by more than a 'wham-bam-thank-you-ma'am' attitude."

"Mother!!!" Cathy had led a sheltered life. She recalls being profoundly shocked by her mother's expressions of dubious literary merit. Later she couldn't help smiling at the memory.

"Nor is the author's," Mrs. Mondellay had gone on. "She'll get ten, if lucky fifteen, percent of the publisher's profit. After expenses, of course. Expenses amounting to a great deal more than the author's annual income."

Dear mother... At that time, Cathy had no idea how deeply her mother felt about her brief flirtation with Erato.

"But the deed is done. *Littera scripta manet.* Loosely: the written word lives on."

To the victor the spoils. No money. Just the spoils. Fame or infamy. (Cathy's mother did not need the money.)

Or—the privilege of being branded a Prophet.

The latter is Peter's particular spoil. Unwanted, unwarranted and, as far as Peter is concerned, most emphatically undeserved. His, nevertheless, to experience. And the illustrious publisher did not even have the decency to go through the usual process of the manuscript 'improvement'. At least the due process would have delayed the inevitable. Alas! Two days after Cathy transferred the contents of the diskette by a cellular modem to Birngham & Birngham, the publisher's principal Editor (the one with a capital E), a Mr. James Bernhardt Fitzpatrick, a soft-spoken man of a politic disposition, telephoned Cathy to say that they were willing to advance Mr. Petrus Latter $100,000 and forego the usual editorial process. The legal documents would be sent for review directly to the Mondellay lawyers.

"That will be just fine, Mister James Bernhardt Fitzpatrick," said Cathy, who had absolutely no idea what a privilege had been bestowed upon her, not to mention upon a Mr. Petrus Latter, who apparently preferred to remain in the background.

"We would appreciate if you or your father would care to jot down perhaps a short preface to the hardcover edition," Mr. J.B.F. added. "Can we count on such a small favour?" His voice was liquid honey.

"That would be just fine," repeated Cathy, who would have agreed to dance in the nude in the middle of Mount Royal to have Peter's insights shared with all who cared to take advantage of them. "I shall get on it immediately."

She did. That evening a few bursts of electrons left Cathy's modem and passed on her glowing appraisal of *The Dialogues* c/o Mr. James Bernhardt, *etc.,etc.*

Money had never influenced any of Cathy's decisions. When one lives on the Summit Circle, even if temporarily abiding at a slightly lower stratum, one does not discuss money with people from Toronto. Not unless one deals with millions, and Cathy never had. There are the fiscal advisers, consultants, wizards of the fickle world of finance, of the collateral, contingent and confusing capital, who deal with such matters. Cathy is a scientist. She would always get excited about the probabilities inherent in the behaviour of any of the up or down or top or bottom quarks—or any subatomic particles. She could not become excited by the behaviour of even the most charming of Editors.

A month to a day after Cathy met her part of the bargain, the book hit the stores. It hit them with an impact. The house of Birngham & Birngham was sure to make a killing. Not on the book, of course, but on the preface by Dr. Mondellay. On the cover they carefully forgot to include the initials of the Mondellay in question. Surely, these were but details. The first edition sold out in three days. The second reached the stores a week later. Birngham & Birngham are professionals. They know how to handle success.

By the time the second edition sold out, the book had developed a following. The name Mondellay may have started the snowball, but Petrus Latter was responsible for the avalanche. A week later, Peter was declared a prophet. Petrus Latter of the Latter-day Prophets.

Peter was mildly disgusted.

The success, however, soon proved to be yet another failure.

After a few days of weaving his way through the growing throng of followers bent on touching, ever so gently, the hem of Peter's trousers, Cathy and Peter decided on the menu of their last supper with Ruth and the children. After dinner Winston said something which they all thought very significant. Not that Winston ever ran short of significant statements.

"You will note, Sir, that, contrary to popular belief, there is a growing hunger for that which cannot be supplied by the Solidarity International."

Winston did not elaborate, but all fell silent examining the repercussions of his insight. Solidarity did sate man's hunger for material well-being, but perhaps that wasn't enough. At least, not on this side of the Atlantic. People may well have enough to eat now, but the hunger remained. A different kind of hunger.

"It is time to go, darling."

The dinner is over. *The wind bloweth...* It is time to go.

Peter has to cheer Ruth a little. "We shall stay in touch this time. It won't be like before." He has no idea how it will be this time. Might as well ask the wind.

Six weeks in the comfort of Upper Westmount. Six weeks of frantic scanning through Peter's inexhaustible computerized data, of the vast libraries, all accessible by his modem. Six weeks of access to information that the books Cathy had taken up North could not have provided. Peter scanned the screen at a rate that would make most men wince in disbelief. He covered the equivalent of fifteen books in a twenty-four-hour cycle. He would have done more but for Cathy, who insisted he take his daily walks on the top of Mount Royal and sleep at least four hours a day. The walks had stopped almost a week ago. Peter could not stand the adulation in the front garden.

All that is now over. To everything there is a season...

It has gotten quite dark now. Peter and Cathy draw the heavy curtains.

There is a time to stay and a time to go. Now is the time for tearful farewells. Peter wanted to leave on his own, but Cathy would not have it. You have no right to kill me before my time, she had said. She might well die without him. It was her turn to have lost some weight, to take on the duties of maintaining Peter's body and soul together. Not by feeding him, but by supplying the life force from which Peter drank like a man near starvation. Her smile, her serenity, her total acceptance of the inevitable had become Peter's elixir of life.

Cathy had taken on one other self-imposed duty. Like Elsie before her, she prepared baskets of cold snacks and distilled, cool water for the people in the garden. She took the hampers out and put them on the grass in the evening. By morning they were all empty.

"Someone has to do it." She was almost on the defensive.

And Cathy still carried the burden of being instrumental in Peter's agreeing to have *The Dialogues* published.

"I'm truly sorry, darling. How could I have known?" Cathy looked crestfallen.

"It is not your fault, Cathy. And anyway, from what I can see, and in light of what Winston has said, you were right. *The Dialogues* had to be published. Regardless of the consequences to either of us. Welcome to a new life, Mrs. Nomad."

"I'll never stop loving you, Peter."

"I know. You told me. If you did, living with me would drive you crazy within twenty-four hours."

"I would rather be crazy with you than sane without you."

"You might live to regret that sentiment," Peter said, but he doubted it. Cathy had been growing at a most incredible rate.

Later on that evening, each carrying two large baskets filled to overflowing, Peter and Cathy wind their way between the tired hopefuls. They all regard Peter with eyes begging for he knows not what... For a touch, a look, a kind word? What good would it do to tell them that they each are the Way—a sacred, inimitable individualization of the Infinite? Each single one of them. They must have read *The Dialogues*. Why can't they understand? Only today Peter doesn't care. He humours them. Why not? It is the very last night.

Isn't it?

Later still, in a third-class motel, where Peter felt certain no one would recognize either of them, Cathy undergoes her very first dream *experience*. Obviously not her first dream, but a first-ever dream experience. She and Peter had met and attended together one of Winston's lectures. The next morning Cathy is flabbergasted. She simply cannot believe that they both shared the same memories.

"But how is this possible?" She returns again and again to the subject.

"Why shouldn't it be? What makes you think that the awakened state is any more real than that experienced in your dream?"

Peter no longer draws such a strong distinction between any of his states of awareness. Consciousness is one. His job is to explore it. The less he feels shackled by his physical awareness, the better. Peter practices his convictions to the letter.

"Did you create this dream, Peter? Did you impose it on me? Was it some form of trance transference which is yet another gift of yours?" Cathy asks.

"My sole gift is my life, Cathy. And, as I have always said, we are immortal. It is my search for immortality that has resulted in this misinterpreted gift for healing. I have inadvertently programmed my subconscious to accept the concept of immortality and thus act as though it were an indisputable fact. Most people are not quite sure what they want, what to believe in. In my case, my aura, or the magnetic field surrounding my body, due to my absolute conviction, easily influenced the configuration or the vibration of the auras of my so-called patients."

"You mean you have not been curing them consciously?" Cathy interrupts again.

"Good Lord, no. I am far from that level yet. To cure someone 'consciously', you must be able to control your magnetic field at will. To do that takes a spiritual Master. A man who is fully conscious of the totality of his potential. A man who has what has once been called 'Christ Consciousness'. I know of no one who has reached this level."

"You mean it is an act of faith?"

"We believe in things we cannot understand. Once we understand them, we no longer need faith. We just know."

"But... but how do we know?" In spite of her background in Lao Tzu's mysticism, Cathy's scientific mind rebels against the untenable.

"Cathy, do you believe in the gravitational field of a distant galaxy which bends light from a source still farther away from you?"

"I don't believe in it. I know it's there."

"How? Can you touch it, or smell it, or feel its presence?" Peter asks.

"I see what you mean. I need an act of faith to initiate an experiment, but once I see the effect of something, the effect is sufficient to convert my faith into knowledge."

"So it is with a state of consciousness. People are afraid to allow a new knowledge to enter into their subconscious. They are afraid of whatever might upset their little stabilization. The little world they live in. Their tiny terms of reference. What they call sanity. Yet there are few people who have not experienced sufficient evidence, first hand, to accept fully that their consciousness is their *only* reality."

"Whatever you believe in, that is what you are..."

"That depends on your definition of the word 'believe'. I would rather say, whatever you believe in your heart, that is what you are. In other words, whatever you *know* to be, *that* you really are."

"I am that which I am," Cathy says, her eyes showing growing understanding.

"Never more and never less. You always are the state of consciousness which you manifest at the particular moment on your journey."

"And you are immortal?"

Peter smiles. "I, too, am that which I am. For better or worse. I am a student. I want to be fair to myself. I don't want to shortchange myself, I want to be..."

"....a just man," says Cathy.

"One just man among many."

"Diogenes couldn't find one with a lantern in broad daylight." Cathy sighs.

"Diogenes was a cynic. We both saw them yesterday in the park."

"The children... When do we lose the spontaneity, the joy?"

"When we stop believing the evidence of our senses."

For a while neither says anything. There are things to be done, decisions to be made. Why is Peter so relaxed? Surely a man like him cannot go through life in hiding? Cathy tries to review what Peter has said. It all seems so simple. Why is it so difficult?

"What is a saint?" she asks after a few minutes of silence.

"A saint is a man who is considerably underweight, whose eyes are sunken deep into his sockets, and who goes around healing people. You know? You met one some time ago."

"Be serious for a moment."

"Me, serious? Don't be silly, darling. The last time I was serious I had to make a run for it!" Peter puts on a very serious face, then starts laughing. It doesn't work.

Peter watches Cathy's face. She is becoming too sombre lately. Much too reflective. Then he shrugs. What a pity, he thinks. We lose the joys of childhood before we are ready to face the world as grown-ups. And yet the world hasn't changed; only we have. Peter takes her in his arms and kisses her full lips. She relaxes instantly. Whatever he may have lost himself, the healing gift remains. Only now he seems to be able to impart peace and trust, not just mend bones or lungs besmirched with tobacco.

"Oh, I don't know, Cathy. I would guess a saint is a woman or man whose heart is permanently filled with joy. Who is acutely conscious of the blessings surrounding him or her. Who spends his or her time on earth in awe of beauty and wonder. Like children..."

"Is this possible?"

"Saint Francis did it."

"But don't you ever worry about tomorrow?" She is not satisfied.

"Of course I do. Sometimes. But there again, I have absolutely no delusions about my status on the scale of evolution. Saints are giants. Their consciousness is developed beyond our wildest dreams."

"Like children's?"

"Well, yes. In some ways. But don't get me wrong. Not all adults are degenerates, and not all children are saints. I'm only saying that unless our attitude towards the phenomenal world is closer to that of the children, then our chances of expanding our consciousness are vastly reduced. It's all up to us."

"But the way you talked the other day, it sounded as if we don't really have any free will, as if our destiny had been predetermined." Cathy sounds very confused.

"Both statements are true. It simply depends whether you identify yourself with your body or with your consciousness. You see, the spirit is constantly experimenting. Be it with plants or flowers, trees, insects, birds, fish or mammals. Humans, too. If we imagine that in the long run we are the masters of our destiny, then we are more stupid than a simple animal which submits to the dictates of the spirit with total abandon. If the spirit so chooses, it can lift us up from a pit of vipers, whisk us up and place us gently on soft ground from a burning airplane, raise us out of a speeding train about to smash into another. Read books. Study documented reports. Believe the evidence. Act like a scientist... But remember, the spirit can also let us be... and absorb with total detachment our innocuous, insipid, puerile attempts at mastery of our environment."

"But surely, we ought to master our environment, shouldn't we?"

"We can, but it is such a short-term measure. Isn't it better to master ourselves and leave the environment alone?"

"But your bible says that you should master nature..."

"The Bible addresses our soul. Do you identify with it? The Bible says that our consciousness should become master over the phenomenal world, the body. This is what our soul is doing all the time. It is learning mastery over its sensory devices, its bodies. Over the instruments it has created, through which it is gaining experience."

"It all sounds so futile."

"It depends. Our consciousness can withdraw at any moment, forever, permitting our bodies, our emotions, our minds to rot, dissipate in ether, be absorbed into the elementary matrix of the universe, into the electromagnetic fields, a biological plasma from which one day it may choose to build once more another toy for its amusement, another experiment in its endless search for wholeness. In a way you are right. It is a futile endeavour, since our worlds, or universes, are bound by the laws of polarity, laws of contrast, where any deviation from the norm must, sooner or later, be balanced by an equal and opposite reaction. But the principle of duality enables the soul to learn. To experiment with its own self-awareness."

"So what is our way out?"

"I would suggest that we change our point of view."

"You mean think of ourselves as soul?"

"Can you think of a better method?"

"Not in your universe..."

More silence. These concepts are not new to Cathy. It is just that, for the last ten years, she had been observing and judging the physical universe by its effects and, at some point, began confusing the effects with the cause. She knows that we all do that. Particularly the scientists. Peter still does, sometimes. It is his medical background.

"But, Peter, what is our soul...."

Peter smiles. An eternal question of an eternal traveller. How many days, nights had he spent searching his consciousness to find that which had done the searching. You cannot use mind to know mind. A vicious circle. The old adage states that the perceiver is not the perceived. That's true. But only up to the moment when the perceiver gives up. Submits to that which he is searching. It can be confusing.

"Our physical body, our emotions, mind, memory, are all but external accoutrements of our soul. That's all they are. I, too, have been confused. Then it became apparent that soul, in order to gain direct experience, must become the object of its interest. It becomes 'us'. No wonder we become confused and think of the accoutrements as the essence of our existence. Yet, whenever you spell the first person singular pronoun with a capital letter, you attest to your inherent divinity."

"But what is it?"

"It is the seat of your Consciousness. It is the individualization of the Infinite. In your language, it is that which is continuous as against the accoutrements which are discontinuous. At this particular moment, It is you, Cathy."

"How do you know?"

Peter cannot answer. A loud bang shatters the near silence of their room. The sudden noise is followed by muffled murmurs of discussion or argument. Peter opens the door. Two men are blocking a number of women from going up the stairs leading to his bedroom. One of the men had slipped, fallen half a flight of stairs, and apparently twisted or broken his ankle. When Peter opened the door, the man looked up, a smouldering fire burning in his eyes.

"Don't worry, Sir, we shall keep them away. You go and get a good night's sleep." The man winces as he raises his considerable bulk from the floor. As he gets to his feet, he seems to waver and then, in a grotesquely slow motion, lowers himself back onto the worn terrazzo. The man's ankle is bent at an unnatural angle.

"Let me look at that leg," Peter says.

A sudden hush envelops the corridor. There are no more than a dozen people present there, but they all seem to hold their collective breath. Peter comes down to the first landing, carefully takes the man's ankle in both his hands, holds it for a moment or two, adjusts the angle of the joint and straightens it out.

"There now. You will be all right in a little while," he says.

The man grins with tears swirling in his eyes. Even as Peter turns to return to his room, the man raises himself to his feet. He gingerly tries to put his weight on his injured foot, then steps firmly on it and bounces up and down.

"Glory be to the Master!" he says in an ear-shattering whisper.

Peter closes the door and leans heavily against it. Cathy is still sitting on the bed.

"What did he say?" she asks, her eyes wide.

"He said 'thank you, Mister', I think." But Peter's voice does not ring true. He wonders how the men, women, have found him. Him and Cathy. They didn't look like people who read books prefaced by Dr. Mondellay.

"It's started, hasn't it?"

"Yes, Cathy. It has begun."

Neither of them dares to elaborate on the innocent words. They both seem to know what the words mean, only their minds refuse to even think about the consequences.

* * *

21

The Mountain

"The rest of the night should be peaceful," Peter assures Cathy. Of course, he has no way of knowing.

Peter is fairly baffled. The people outside had taken what must have been an inordinate amount of trouble to discover his whereabouts; and now they seem content to just stay there, as if his proximity were all they craved, all they searched for. They do not place any demands on him; no requests for cures, physical or otherwise. They just share adjacent space. Breathe the same air. If anything, they seem willing to help or protect him rather than call on him to use his gifts, if any. A sort of silent, volunteer bodyguard contingent.

Where did they come from? What need brought them to his vicinity?

Why to *me? What am I doing here?*

It must be the book. *The Dialogues.* Peter actually saw one woman, sitting on the lower steps, clutching a book to her breast. Up North he had listened to a radio program about the advancing illiteracy. Apparently, more people can still read than the government statisticians had imagined. Television had not yet destroyed the minds of all people. Not even in the districts of third-class motels.

"What shall we do?" Cathy's voice does not reflect Peter's confidence.

She cannot sleep. She had slept badly these last few days. By now, Peter has enough strength for the two of them. It is his turn. He takes her in his arms, holds her close and repairs her body. Her mind, her emotions—her aura. Gradually she is learning acceptance. Not resignation. Acceptance. The latter calls for active participation. There seems a silent battle raging between her inner knowingness and her outer, the pre-programmed desires. The new and the old. The realm of intuitive freedom versus the preconditioned. It is like being two in one. A dichotomy. To Peter, each Cathy is as beautiful. To him, they are both one. Immortal and beautiful.

"I don't know. Relax, Cathy," he says gently.

"But... but... it is not easy to relax when you have no idea at all what will happen tomorrow."

"That's all right. I shall know when the time comes."

"Shall we be alive?"

"We are immortal."

"Peter, how can you say that?!"

"Trust me."

"Oh, Peter, I do trust you!"

"I know. I know, darling."

She calms down.

This last week Cathy, the heretofore self-assured, proudly confident Cathy, has been behaving, well... a little like a child. At a certain moment she sensed that Peter had come of age. He, who had been so terribly lost after his trial in St-Henri, had become quietly confident. Independent. Yet it had been she who had nursed him back to life in that forlorn cabin. He had been so weak. So weak... Had it not been he, then, who looked and felt and acted like a lost child? So lost...

And now? And now he is a Tower of Strength. Enough for the both of them. She has done her job. Yet, though she would never admit it even to herself, she would give the rest of her life for another three months up there, in the middle of nowhere. Just the two of them. Alone. She would cook, and work. Do all the work... If only they could go back. Back in time. Peter had needed her then. So much. Even as she needs him now.

Cathy even looks like a child. She forgot her makeup in Westmount. Her body was always petite—now it seems fragile. Even her eyes are trusting like a child's eyes. Her smile, like a child's smile. Only she cannot trust quite enough yet. But it's coming.

"Sometimes it takes time, darling. Do not rush it. You have all the time in the world," he had told her when they first came here. "All the time in eternity."

"And where will you be?"

"I shall always be with you. Always. It cannot be otherwise."

She did not understand yet what he meant by it. When he said something, it always sounded so simple; and then, when he looked the other way, it was not simple anymore.

"It will come..." he repeated frequently. "It comes to all who..."

It's all right for you to talk. You have a gift...

Only she could not say it out loud.

But Cathy is learning. It is always darkest just before the dawn.

Last night she had dreamt again about Winston. He was so tall. He looked down at her from so high, he seemed to fill half the sky. But she wasn't afraid. He had such kind eyes. She had never seen eyes filled with so much kindness. He said he would explain it all to her in her own words. In her own language.

"In the language of astrophysics?" She almost giggled. Actually, with Winston she did feel a little like a child. He even let her sit up front, with the other youngsters.

"Think of Relativity. The universe is like a field," he said. "This field is broken into segments. Each segment tends towards gelling. A very dense field is matter. First energy, then matter. So you see, all things are made of spirit."

To many this would sound like a jump from physics to metaphysics without rhyme or reason. To Cathy it made perfect sense. Spirit, Field, Energy, Matter. Simple. A natural progression. Cathy liked to hear things explained this way. It made sense when one used words one could understand.

"When the gravitational field is very concentrated, matter collapses upon itself. The effect is called a Black Hole. All matter eventually collapses into innumerable Black Holes, which in turn collapse into each other, and ultimately upon themselves. And then what is left? A Field of Consciousness, or Spirit, amid nothing. All matter originates in Consciousness, all matter is, ultimately, absorbed into Consciousness. No matter, no energy, not even thought. No time, no space. Infinite mass converted into infinite consciousness. Some of you have been taught to call this the Night of Brahma."

Cathy remembers. She had read about it in some Vedic stanzas.

"Thus Consciousness has its existence beyond the boundaries of the space/time continuum. Beyond the visible or detectable matrix of the universe. It is independent of the field of matter even as soul is independent of the biological construct known as man. Individualized soul, or unit of consciousness, can be regarded as a light wave of a particular frequency within the Field of Consciousness which, at raised vibrations, loses its quantitative properties and becomes an indivisible field. Conversely, should the vibrations slow down, the individual frequencies begin to resonate at their own characteristic level."

The next morning, Cathy recounts most of what she had dreamt to Peter. He listens without interruption, then smiles and shakes his head.

"We all have to find our own terms of reference. There are as many ways of raising one's consciousness, of achieving an understanding of reality, as there are people in the world. What makes sense to one might not much help another. Anything which is reduced to symbols, or words, becomes no more than a means, at best a probability..."

"But, Peter..." Cathy sounds ready to battle.

"...rather like when dealing with your electrons. You can describe or predict a probability of behaviour of your quarks or electrons, but you cannot construct laws to control the individual quanta any more than create laws to control an individualized soul. Winston does no more than... than whet your appetite. The rest is up to you," Peter insists.

"All the same, Winston has made it all so simple, and they are not *my* electrons. A child could see that the velocity of light is the middle ground. The vibrations can slow down all the way to a Black Hole and beyond. For instance, enormous densities, a mass of a billion stars, would inhibit high frequencies. Any frequencies. Imagine a photon at rest! Conversely, the Spiritual Consciousness starts when the frequency of vibrations reaches the velocity of light. You might notice that in physics, a capital C stands for the velocity of light. A strange coincidence that it also could stand for Consciousness!"

"Or for Coincidence..." Peter mutters.

"Be serious! Once the vibration rises above C, time stops. All is one. Soul can affect the past as well as the future with equal facility. It is beyond time. Don't you see? It is all so simple!"

Peter starts laughing. Cathy's eyes are shining with the joy of understanding. To each her own, he muses.

"And you got all this from just one lecture?"

"Well, I've also done some thinking on my own."

"Ah...."

"Peter, are you laughing at me?"

"At myself rather. I have been thinking of my physical consciousness as a donkey that carries the real me. Now I see that I might well collapse into a Black Hole if I do not watch out for myself. One can never be too careful."

"You *are* laughing at me!"

For a moment Cathy looks hurt, annoyed and angry. But only for a moment. She cannot sustain such a complex expression on her face. The edges of her mouth twitch, then wiggle, then her eyes become narrower. Then she gives up and starts laughing.

"Well, it's all Winston's fault, anyway. I had nothing to do with it!"

"Poor Winston. But someone has to take the blame," Peter agrees.

"I wonder if he knows..." Cathy's smile wavers, then she becomes serious again. "Do you think he knows?"

"About what? About us attending his lectures in never-never land?"

"Well, yes, sort of."

"I doubt it." Now Peter's face assumes a slightly more serious expression. "I think it has something to do with points of view."

"As in soul versus body?"

"In a way. I believe you once told me that if you were to propel a starship towards some distant star, and the starship were to accelerate to, say, 90% of the velocity of light, then an observer from outside this ship would see it foreshortened to say 50% of its length, and the time seen on the shipboard clock, through a port hole, would slow down to a crawl. But to the astronauts inside the ship all would appear normal. Am I right?"

"You surprise me, Peter. You have just described some of the mainstays of the Theory of Relativity. Anyway, you are right, the postulates have been questioned but never disproved. How come you remember all this?"

"I had a good teacher, and I've done some reading myself, recently." Peter dismisses the question. "This is not the point I am attempting to make. I was merely recapping from memory. I am drawing a parallel between the different points of view. When we regard a Being imbued with a highly spiritualized consciousness, or as you would say, a Consciousness at very high frequency of vibrations, then it depends from which point of view you are regarding It. What I am trying to say is that a soul body regarded from the standpoint of physical consciousness is infinite. From our point of view, all the spiritual giants who have risen to such levels are one; but among each other, they..."

"...they are as the astronauts within the spaceship. All appears normal."

"Well, yes. I believe this is what happens. The Theory of Relativity is a reflection of the world above. As above so below, remember?"

"And vice versa. Sometimes."

"Peter?" Cathy's brow furrows again. "Why did you use the term 'soul body'?"

"I was trying to use your analogue. In your language, a spiritualized consciousness would correspond to a soul body, which would consist of pure light. Am I right?"

"I can buy that." Cathy sounds happy. "So where does Winston come in?"

"I believe that Winston draws a very definite line between his physical and spiritual consciousness. And anyway, I'm not sure that one can enjoy a split consciousness to such a degree. It might give you a headache."

"You are joking, of course?"

"Well, a sort of spiritual headache. A spiritual dichotomy. Though it might well be possible for very advanced states of consciousness."

"And you don't think that Winston is one?"

"I don't know. Ask him."

"Seriously, why do you think a man of his incredible potential works as a butler for a widow in a well-to-do Westmount environment?" Cathy wonders.

"We all have specific functions to fulfill while occupying a physical body. From our myopic points of view, the actual function may or may not seem important. Winston's physical purpose may have something to do with Mo and Jo. Or it could be that the job of a butler is sufficiently innocuous to allow him lots of time, sort of spiritual freedom, for teaching within the inner states."

"But why inner, why not...?" Suddenly Cathy has a million questions.

"Because people are a lot more relaxed and therefore receptive in the dream state. You can select and instruct far greater numbers while they are asleep than while they are busy abusing their bodies or minds or even emotions by inordinate attention to matters of no consequence."

"Do you know your function?"

"No. But it is very close."

"How do you know?"

"I cannot answer that. But I can tell you that every single thing which happened in my life up to this very moment has been targeted specifically for this purpose." Then Peter looks hard into Cathy's eyes. "In fact, for a number of lives."

Suddenly Cathy stops asking questions. Something is looming which she does not want to hear. Oh, please, not yet. *Not yet?*

"I am afraid so, Cathy," he answers the question she has refused to ask.

"But why so soon?" The fire in her eyes oscillates between jade and pure emerald. Neither colour has ever looked more appealing.

"Ruth needs you. And you can also learn a lot more from Winston than from me."

Peter kisses her gently on the forehead, then on her trembling mouth. "I'll see you soon. And, in a way, I am always with you. Remember that."

He takes her down the stairs and calls a taxi. They had come here by bus, but there is no reason for Cathy to risk the asperities of this district after dark. As Peter and Cathy come down, the quiet group of people huddling on the still-warm pavement outside step aside. The two burly guards have disappeared. There seems to be no need for them. People appear to have an incredible respect for Peter's privacy. They only want to be close. Just in case.

In case of what?

There were signs of tension on their faces when Peter hailed a taxi. First sadness, then tension. Now the faces are relaxed. The girl is gone, their eyes seem to say: Petrus or Peter is staying.

Peter returns to the motel, walks up a few steps of the open staircase and then stops. He turns and glances at the upturned faces, hesitates, then sits down on a worn tread.

What am I doing here?

Only now he really looks at the gathering. There are about forty or fifty people. Some sit on the ground, others lean against the brick walls of adjacent buildings, some squat on staircases leading to other upstairs rooms such as his own. Simple, ordinary people. There seems to be nothing special or particular about them at all. There is no talk, no discussion. Just waiting. For a while he and the upturned faces stare at each other. Quite blandly, Peter attempts to catch the eye of any individual: a woman's or a man's. Or a child's eye squinting against the security light on the top of the staircase. There are three pairs of them. Three children. Peter wonders why the young ones have come. Surely he has nothing to offer to the young ones?

There is a strange silence. A silence of expectation. He smiles.

"Why did you come here?" Peter asks at long last. *Why did I come here?*

A head moves here and there, the lips part, but the silence is interrupted only by a few halting sighs. Then there is more silence.

"Is there anything I can do for you?"

Some of them transfer their weight from one leg to another, look at the person next to them, look again at Peter, and then, once again, lower their eyes to their feet. Why did they come here? Did any of them associate Petrus Latter with Peter Thornton, the once physician, once healer, once relic of a man? Did they all come for a word of cheer? What drives people to leave the comfort of their homes and travel by bus or metro to the outskirts of town, to stand or squat outside a motel? A third-rate motel in the middle of a sea of other motels, normally frequented only by transient salesmen or people who change jobs, usually from a bad to an even worse one?

"Did anyone read my book?" Peter tries again.

Three hands go up holding a book, about ten more hands are empty but attesting to their knowledge. After a little while the hands go down, almost shyly, as though embarrassed at having called attention to their owner. And then, quite suddenly, a boy steps forward from behind a fat woman. He looks like an overfed street urchin, confident that his weight will command attention from his juvenile gang. He is a tall boy, perhaps overgrown, but judging by his face, he can't be more than twelve or thirteen.

"Mother said not to ask you anything after what happened to you in St-Henri."

So they know.

"And what do they say I did in St-Henri?" Peter probes.

"You nearly done yourself in. You did." The boy repeats his assertion after the woman behind him tries to pull him back. The boy pulls away, and now he is standing all alone in front of the small crowd. In the meantime some more people gather—they seem to appear from nowhere—and watch this interchange. The single bright light behind his head keeps Peter's face in shadow but casts a halo around his blond hair. The boy's face is fully illuminated.

"Well, we shan't worry about what happened to me in St-Henri. Is there anything I can do for you?"

The boy glances at the woman behind him, perhaps a mother or a relative, but she no longer interferes. Yet the boy seems hesitant. Suddenly he looks embarrassed.

"I don't want to be fat no more," he almost whispers. All his confidence seems to have evaporated. Perhaps he is prepared to give up the following he commands by his size alone, just to be more normal. To be accepted as one of the boys.

"Did you try eating less?" Peter asks gently.

"Yussir," the boy mumbles, pouting, "but it done me no good."

"Aha. Well, we shall have to do something about it. I'll tell you what. You promise me to eat less, and I promise you that it will work. Is that a deal?"

"Yes, Sir."

"Then come here."

The boy looks a lot shorter with his head hanging on his plumpish chest that looks concave by contrast with his stomach. Peter raises the boy to stand two steps higher than himself and embraces him. Then Peter whispers something in the boy's ear. The boy listens attentively, then starts laughing. On his way back to the obese woman his head is held high. He feels as though he has lost twenty pounds. His mind is slim already; his body and his eating habits would follow.

The moment the lad gets back to the woman, a little girl steps forward.

"Please, Sir, can we get all we pray for?" she asks without any preambles.

"If you ask for the right things, then you get them. It applies to everything."

The girl is older, could be as old as sixteen. That is a lot for a girl from below the tracks. They mature a lot quicker there. In spite of this, she is no taller than the overfed boy who stood his ground before her.

"And why are you asking?"

"Because mother said if I prayed for a boyfriend I was bound to get one," she says, looking straight at Peter. If she is blushing at this declaration, the bright reflector over Peter's head doesn't show it.

"Well, you see, it's not so simple. The world is, sort of, set on automatic. You know, like a washing cycle. Once you switch it on, you can stop it but you cannot change it. You've got to start from scratch."

"You mean like dying and being born again?" she asks.

What a strange comparison, Peter muses.

"Yes. Only in a way, you can be born again without actually dying. It's just that you have to start completely from scratch. Do you understand me?"

"My mother says that the Good Book says, that if we pray hard enough, then we can get whatever we want!" The girl is not about to give her ground, either.

"Your mother is right, but not completely. The Good Book, as you call it, says, that if you ask 'in my name', then it will be given to you. Do you understand what it means to ask 'in my name'?"

"No, Sir. I don't know nobody by that name."

A few people giggle. Peter also cannot help laughing.

"When I say the word 'lion', what do you imagine?"

"A big cat with long teeth and great big fangs like nails. It's 'orrible, Sir."

"And a kitten?"

"It is soft and cuddly and... it's so cute, Sir?" The girl evidently has come in contact with kittens.

"Then you see that the *name* lion or kitten describes the nature of the animal or the thing you describe, right?" The girl nods. "By the same token, when you pray *in-my-name*, this means that you pray in accordance with *my nature*. The book refers to the nature of Jesus Christ."

"But what does this mean, Sir?" The girl is evidently willing to learn.

"It means that you have to study the *nature* of Jesus Christ, and then ask for things which will make you similar in nature to the Lord."

"But, Sir, what is the point if the world is set on automatic?" She has been paying attention. You can't get away with anything when you talk to children on the subject they have selected.

"The world is, but you... well, you will discover that you are of this world and sort of not of this world. Part of you is, and part isn't. It is a little like doing your laundry. Some of it you put in the dryer, on automatic, and part you leave free to dry out in the open. Is this not what you do?"

"Yes, Sir. We hung out the better things free in the sun."

"Good. Now you must find out the part of you that is free. Free to roam in the sun. The better part of you."

"Will this help me to get a boyfriend?"

More giggles, more laughter. People are becoming bolder. The Master sounds human. Not the holy Prophet they talked about up there with the toffs, in Westmount.

"It might, but let's play safe. Come here."

The girl comes closer. Peter makes her sit down on the step next to him and puts one of his arms around her thin shoulders. For a moment he holds her close to his side. Again he whispers into her ear. A few moments later the girl smiles, kisses Peter on the cheek and runs down the steps. She feels she is the prettiest girl in the world. She can get any boyfriend she wants. Anyone in the whole world.

Peter takes a deep breath. He turns to the whole gathering.

"Perhaps we should all start by praying to find out what we really are."

All the heads look up, all the eyes shine with a hunger for what has been missing in their lives for so long.

"Be vigilant. Be patient. It is worth it. The rewards are great."

There is absolute silence. Even the cars heretofore speeding along the nearby highway tone down their swishing noise temporarily. There is no real darkness. The highway is as bright as in daylight. The harsh spotlights over the staircases add to the heavy, pervasive grayness. The humid air spread over Montreal reflects the light back to the warm pavement, denying people access to the infinite universe. It seems such a pity.

"Pray that you might fulfill your destiny. Do not prejudge. All destinies are equally as important. Pray that you become what you really are. Your real self. He that reaches his true nature shall live forever. He who enters his true consciousness, though he were dead, shall live again. He who fails, shall be given another chance. You are immortal."

There. A sermon. All of thirty seconds. *Why do I feel like a fool? I know so little myself.*

For a brief moment the silence is almost overpowering. Then the sounds of the city at night return, first slowly, then with an almost vengeful fury. The transient, phenomenal world is fighting back.

"Anyone else would like to have a boyfriend?" Peter asks, but people only smile.

They heard what they had come to hear. They were hungry and they were given food. The food they needed most. Peter smiles back and returns to his room. Within a few minutes the gathering disperses. For now. By the morning light, new people will come.

They will have heard.

It has already started.

A mountain atop the mountains atop the world.

The white crests extend beyond the white horizon. Peak after peak, crags, reaching forever upwards, searching, silent, cold, seemingly eternal. Yet so ephemeral. But a few million years ago the Himalayas had been under an ocean. Washed over by the eternal sea. Only the sea also had its temporal beginning.

Here the stars are at their purest. Each a hard, solid diamond in an ocean of impenetrable blackness, each shimmering with a vivid life of its own. An ocean of souls waiting to start on their eternal journey. The first step of individualization. Though not always. For some it is the last. There are no rules controlling the spirit. Freedom rules supreme.

Winston is talking.

"Think of spirit as a protoplasm of which all things are built. Think of soul as consciousness that builds a nucleus of this protoplasm and endows it with individual properties resulting from individual experiences. At the human level, a soul, to have an awareness of self, must have a body. It must incarnate itself. Even as a physical body is incumbent to a physical soul—the magnetic aura—so an individualized soul acts as a nucleus through which the spirit acts, flows—through which all things are created. All that is phenomenal comes into being at higher levels as an innate state of consciousness. On earth, your consciousness enters states already created at those higher levels. There is a feedback. An evolution. Then the lower states gel, set, coalesce into physical forms. But that is all. The phenomenal universe is no more than a dream. A result. Your true reality is here, in your higher consciousness. In soul."

Part of Peter's attention drifts to another area of the monastery. Here, there are even more people listening to a lecture than in his own theatre. Peter smiles when he sees Cathy, her face radiant, her brows knit together, absorbing her own understanding.

"Think of soul as vibrating at the velocity of light. You do not go anywhere, you accelerate your vibration. It is another way of saying you spiritualize your consciousness. At the velocity of light your mass is infinite, thus you are omnipresent. Your properties are those of spirit. Your fabric is that of the primary building blocks of the universe. They are not atoms, but more like photons. Particles of light, though invisible. Light is like RNA in biology. It is the source of all knowledge."

Peter turns his attention to his own lecture theatre.

"A human entity can only manifest a part of the spiritual energy of the soul through its physical body. A more evolved unit of consciousness, sometimes called a spiritual master, can create a body himself, by an act of his will. Such a construct can maintain a much greater flow of spirit..."

Peter wakes up. He hasn't been anywhere. Jo and Mo look up.

"We really enjoyed the lecture, Uncle Peter!" And they rush off to play in the back garden. They must have just returned from school. Peter returns their carefree smile.

A dream within a dream? An extra. No charge.

The rewards are great.

Now Peter leans back against the pillows and becomes Petrus Latter. He closes his eyes and attempts to recreate his own body. From protoplasm. From spirit. It is not easy. He will have to try again.

He knows that Winston will help him. And then Peter's face breaks into a wide grin. He reaches back to the mountain atop the mountains of the world. He remembers that in Cathy's lecture theatre the speaker looked very familiar. He just remembered who it was.

It was also Winston.

* * *

22

The Note

P eople come daily. Not large congregations; not masses expecting healing or salvation. There is no pomp accompanying Peter's presence. No glaring TV lights, no pushy reporters, no massive demonstrations. Judging by their reserved stance and almost shy demeanour, most people do not appear sure why they came. Peter senses, rather than observes, that something vague, undefined, something dormant for a long, long time was stirring within them; it made them stop in their tracks, get on a bus or into a car and drive or be driven to where? To wherever Peter talked, or chatted, or joked—mostly with children. The adults listened, seldom interrupting. Seldom saying a word.

But often laughing.

Peter wouldn't dream of giving lectures. Now and again, he would share a thought or two, when he sensed that people were ready, or particularly receptive. Otherwise there was no point. There is no point in reaching into people's hearts until the gates are open.

Eight times Peter changed the motel. Not for any profound reason, but it seemed unfair to make some people travel for two hours when others had the opportunity to meet him practically next door. He never announced his forthcoming location. He has no idea how people find out. They just do.

There are still a great many things Peter does not understand. Not so much about his own inner consciousness, but about people. There was a time when he thought of people as a series of groups. He categorized them by their sicknesses, by their pathological condition, by the degree to which they had deviated from the norm. From the standard, statistical model. From the crowd. Now, Peter lives in constant awe of their incredible individuality. They all dwell in sometimes tiny but still intensely private universes of their own creation.

"Ye are all gods!" He wants to scream at them.

He doesn't. They are not yet ready.

They also might misunderstand him. They might think that Peter was comparing them to the Almighty, to the Prime Cause. The Eternal. The Immutable. The Nameless. Yet they all were, are, so much more than they ever imagined. So much more. They are like gods. Immortals, he calls them.

"Live your dreams. Whatever you truly desire, it is your soul talking. Give up all and follow the voice that calls you. You have so little to lose, so much to gain!"

Some understood, some scratched their heads. One man did more.

"How can I walk out on the wife and children?" he asked.

"Do you truly want to do this?" Peter asked gently.

"Well, not on the kids, like, but my missus, well, she drives me bit crazy-like."

"When did you last tell her you love her?"

"What, my missus? That fat co... You couldn't have seen her, Sir!" The man doubled with laughter over his protruding belly.

Peter told the man to approach closer. He thought that if the man took the trouble to come to see him, then he must have left the door to his heart ajar. Peter held out his hand to the man, then embraced him. Unwittingly, the man remembered the day he first met his wife. He had been madly in love with her. Then. Suddenly time seemed to disappear. An instant later, in his heart, the aging man saw his wife at the altar. All in white. When Peter let him go, the man couldn't get home fast enough. He bought a big bunch of flowers on the way.

Peter never saw him again.

The gatherings are never big, but they change all the time. People come and go. Some find what they had been searching for, some leave with their heads down, unable to leave the habits of the ages. Only a few ever come back for a second try. Those who do, invariably succeed. Most come as dwarfs, they leave as giants.

As immortals.

Once it had rained. Poured, really. Peter thought that the moment the people would start dispersing, he would go, too. He had hoped they would go. He had only one shirt, which he washed, daily, in the motel room sink and hung out to dry overnight. Sometimes it didn't quite. He could have bought another one; he had enough money on him, but there was no time. No time away from the people.

The rain had poured down steadily for two hours. No one moved. They had all come even closer to hear better. They formed a sort of outdoor theatre—all arranged in an orderly semicircle. It all turned out fine. Peter didn't have to wash his shirt that night. Nor his underwear. He was soaked through as was everyone. Nobody seemed to mind.

On another occasion, two men had brought another man on a makeshift stretcher. The man they carried had been run over by a truck. The casualty looked pretty horrible. Peter asked him if he would allow him to ease his pain. The man nodded. A moment later the man could talk, haltingly.

"Do you want me to try and help you?" Peter asked.

"N-no, S-sir. I just w-want to hear you t-talk," the man said.

The man listened for about two hours, then he said good-bye and thank you and died. He was smiling throughout the two hours. He is probably smiling even now.

Perhaps the man knew. Peter could have told him that if he were rushed to a hospital, he would probably live. Minus two legs. The truck was a heavy-duty carrier. The man's legs had been squashed to pulp. Later that day Peter helped the driver of the truck. The driver had not been speeding. The brakes had failed. It was just one of those things. The driver had no external injuries, but he needed more help than the victim. He now follows Peter wherever Peter goes. For now he doesn't drive a truck. He's on holidays. He just sits there and smiles.

Just one of those things.

So many stories. Some tears, mostly smiles.

On Monday of the sixth week, Peter says good-bye to the people. He tells them that he may or may not be back. That he has to go and do something. They understand. They all shake hands, some embrace him, also each other, and leave. Each in his or her own direction.

Peter takes a taxi. He had awakened this morning with the knowledge that he is to go home. He suspects that Winston had called him. He knows he must go to see Ruth in person.

On the way home Peter has a strange realization. He had practically not eaten these last few weeks. He had drunk water and eaten a few apples and other fruit people had brought him. Yet he did not lose any weight. At least he doesn't feel or look any thinner or weaker. Not like in St-Henri. Not a bit like then. Perhaps he had learned to build his own body. From first principles. From the essence of life Itself. But the funny thing is, he is looking forward to a good meal!

Ruth meets him at the door. She looks drawn, tired. They go inside.

Ruth kisses Peter's cheek and hands him an envelope, without a word. Right there, in the hall. The envelope had already been opened. The note is written on official Solidarity office paper. The logo at the top of the single sheet has been borrowed from a noble ancestor. It says:

Of the People—For the People—By the People

The motto is printed in elaborate gold italics just under the letterhead SOLIDARITY INTERNATIONAL embossed in bold Roman characters. The note says:

Dear Mrs. Thornton.

We are writing this note to assure you that we shall make every effort to assure a safe return of your children in the shortest possible time. The full resources of the Solidarity International are at your disposal.

The note had been signed by the Secretary General of Solidarity International, Canada.

Peter reads the note twice before addressing Ruth. "Have they called since?"

Ruth looks surprised.

"Yes. Just ten minutes ago. Mr. Pennington said that the children had been sighted at Mirabel airport. They had been seen boarding a jet to Europe. Mr. Pennington said that the Solidarity jet is fuelled and ready for take-off if we care to take advantage of the service." Ruth talks quickly as if time were of the essence.

"We?" Peter gazes into Ruth's eyes.

"Actually, I said that. I didn't know whom to call..."

"You called me?"

"Peter, I left you a message less than an hour ago...?"

Peter does not say anything. What is the point? She left a message where? He had moved to a new motel only yesterday, and hadn't called Ruth since. Anyway, he left the motel long after... Whatever precipitated this affair, it is evident that Ruth wants him to come with her. To Europe. Other than that, Ruth is not making much sense at the moment.

"How did you know that the children had been kidnapped?" Peter asks.

"They did not get to the Social Integration class by 9:30. They called to ask what happened. Ten minutes later there was a phone call. A woman said not to call the police. That I shall be given instructions later. That's all."

They telephoned at 9:40 a.m.. Peter had known that he had to return before seven o'clock in the morning. Things are moving fast, he muses.

"How did Mr. Pennington know that the children were missing?"

Again Ruth looks surprised. "I really don't know, Peter. Does it matter? Isn't it enough that they are willing to help?" And now Ruth breaks down completely. Her head drops down to her chest, convulsive spasms rock her whole body. Peter steps forward and embraces her. She calms down almost at once.

"Thank you, Peter."

Ruth wipes the tears from her eyes. She breathes deeply as if a great weight had been removed from her chest. She almost smiles.

"You will come with me, Peter?"

"Of course, dear. Let me change first?"

Ruth's smile of acquiescence is still a little weak. "I need a minute to fix my face," she says.

Ruth turns and goes to the off-hall powder room while Peter runs upstairs. It is obvious that his self-imposed diet has not robbed him of his strength or agility. As he nears his room, he sees Winston in the upstairs corridor. For an instant their eyes meet. It is for the briefest moment, yet Peter feels he has been imparted some very important information. He feels as though his batteries have been recharged. He feels capable of jumping up to the top of Mount Everest in a single leap. Only it is not really a physical strength he discovers. It only feels like it.

Then the moment is gone. The only evidence is a slight, lingering smell of ozone in the air. A moment later, that, too, is gone.

"It is good to see you back, Sir." Winston bows from the hips.

"If only for a brief moment?"

"There are moments, Sir, when time both is and is not of the essence."

They both smile. For some strange reason this sentence makes perfect sense to Peter. He continues into the bathroom, throws off his clothing and literally vaults into the shower. It's a wonder he doesn't slip on the tiles. Three minutes later, still damp, he crosses the corridor stark naked, whips up clean underwear, shirt and socks from the drawer, gets dressed in under a minute, grabs two extra pairs of socks, one shirt and a change of briefs, throws them into a bag, and meets Ruth downstairs about the time she emerges from the powder room. For some strange reason he is surprised that she's looking so beautiful. Then he knows why.

"Where is Cathy?" he asks.

"She went last night to visit her father. He's alone now."

Her mother had died. Just as well. Her soul needed new experiences.

"I see." He turns to face Winston who, in his inimitable fashion, appeared the instant he was needed.

"Yes, Sir. I shall look after her." This is all Winston says out loud, but Peter hears the butler's thoughts a little longer. "The children are all right," Peter perceives his accented voice saying. "There is nothing to worry about."

"Yes, thank you, Winston."

Winston turns to Ruth.

"I took the liberty to pack this little valise for you, Madam. I thought you might find it useful," he says.

"Good Lord! Winston... My mind must have been elsewhere. I completely forgot... Thank you, Winston. I don't know what I would..." Ruth is prattling.

"I believe it is time for you and Dr. Thornton to leave now. I shall drive you to the airport myself." Winston announces.

For an instant Peter feels lost. Dr. Thornton? Then he smiles, waving his head from side to side. He hasn't heard his name spoken for quite a while. If Winston has used it, then probably there is a reason for it. Some kind of a reminder.

Winston delivers them to Mirabel in no time at all. There are brief good-byes. Peter is toying with the idea of embracing Winston. Somehow he can't do it. Winston radiates a presence that is almost prohibitive. Yet there is warmth in it. Perhaps so much warmth that one is afraid of being scorched.

"Thank you, Winston," he says instead.

Winston bows stiffly from the hips.

Mr. Pennington had spoken the truth. The red and white Solidarity jet is fuelled and its engines are making the expected deafening noise. So much progress yet the airplanes continue to make an unholy racket. A man with the Solidarity insignia meets them at a runway reserved for private jets, and taxis them to the sleek aircraft. Ruth wants to show him her passport, but the man waves it aside.

"You are on protected territory, Madam. The documents will not be necessary."

Peter wonders what is a protected territory on Canadian soil. He prefers not to ask.

The jet had been converted to transport a maximum of ten people in extreme comfort, just short of luxury, across a considerable distance. Ruth had flown it once before, when she had met Lena Walensa, but that was only from Montreal to New York. That was six months ago, while Peter and Cathy were up North. It took place just in time for Ruth to develop an attitude of friendship and admiration towards Lena. She still holds onto it today.

Ruth and Peter are given seats facing each other, which soon swivel automatically to face the engine as the jet taxis along the runway for take-off. Once the man who had brought them on board shut the door to the outside, he smartly saluted and disappeared in the flight cabin up front.

There is no one else in the main cabin.

Almost at once the usual signs warn them to put out their smoking materials and fasten their seat belts. Peter and Ruth do the latter as the jet gathers speed. It takes off at a very steep angle. Peter's back is pressed so hard into the back of the seat that he wonders about the necessity of the seat belt. Should he have wanted to get up, he would not have been able to do so. After the jet levels off, Ruth's seat swivels again to face Peter. If it weren't for the purpose of this flight, the adventure would give them both a lot of pleasure. Ruth loves travelling, and now, due to her resignation from the UN, she remains mostly at home. Like a housewife. "A housewife with kidnapped children..." Her dark thoughts preclude any pleasure, "what would Andrew have said?"

"The children are all right," Peter says, as they unclasp their seat-belts.

Ruth slowly turns her head away from the window. She looks at Peter as though she had not heard him. Then his words reach her awareness.

"You don't have to say that just to humour me, Peter. But thank you all the same."

"You don't understand, Ruth. The children are all right. They are safe. Probably already in Westmount."

The expression on Ruth's face can only be described as ambivalent. Hope seems tempered with anger at Peter's apparently misplaced sense of humour.

"Why are you saying this, Peter?"

"Because I don't want you to worry."

"But how do you know?" Her voice lowers to a whisper. Now hope distinctly overrides the annoyance.

"Winston told me."

"Ah..." Ruth leans her head against the reclining seat. Her body seems to relax. The answer appears to satisfy her completely. She takes a few slow, deep breaths before looking up again.

"Then... why...?"

"I don't know. But I'd hazard a guess that your friends want you or me, or both of us, out of the country. Or in another country. We shall soon find out."

"And they would resort to such... such..."

"We shall see. Perhaps they had a good reason. From what you told me about them, they will come up with the best!"

Peter is perfectly calm. He knows that in some strange fashion Winston is in on all this. Whatever 'all this' is, or will be.

Close to an hour later the captain's door opens and a man of medium height joins them. Peter notices that the man's uniform is well cut, but a little too tight-fitting. As though it had been made to measure, and then the man ate a little too much, a little too often. The officer salutes, smiles, then takes off his hat and places it under his left arm. His gray hair is combed straight back in the style of protagonists of yesterday's diplomatic corps. His insignia indicate that he is a captain.

"I trust you are comfortable?" he asks in a well-modulated voice. "Captain Sawicki, at your service."

Ruth smiles her appreciation, but her eyebrows arch, posing a question. She finds the man's face familiar though she doesn't recall having heard his voice.

"As you were advised, Madam, the resources of Solidarity International had been mobilized the moment it came to our notice that your children had been abducted."

"And you are happy to tell us that they are now safe in Montreal?"

"Why, yes Sir! How clever of you to guess that?"

The captain tries hard to express surprise. Simultaneously, his eyes wander over Peter's face, evidently studying him with a penetrating interest.

"Mrs. Thornton and I met on the way to New York some months ago, but I haven't had the pleasure of making your acquaintance, Sir. Dr. Thornton, I presume?"

The captain is a good actor but not good enough. And his eyes are too steady, too calculating to be able to express surprise or even pleasure. The captain is a very cold fish.

Peter smiles indulgently. He could play the game and pretend that the man had made a mistake. That his name is, for instance, Petrus Latter, or even Dr. Livingstone. But he couldn't be bothered. This farce is farcical enough already.

"Why have you brought us here?" he asks instead.

Captain Sawicki's smile broadens. If it hadn't been for the steel in his eyes, one could describe his smile as disarming. The captain spreads his arms.

"May I offer you a drink, perhaps a coffee? It is a little early for lunch." He glances at his watch.

Neither Peter nor Ruth says anything. Ruth trusts Peter implicitly. Almost as much as Winston. In a tacit agreement they decide to wait and see. They do not have to wait long. The captain swivels an armchair across the aisle to face them and sits down.

"We didn't have any choice," he starts. When neither Ruth nor Peter makes any comment, he sighs dramatically and continues. "You must realize that the Solidarity International is by far the most far-reaching organization the world has ever known. But at this delicate stage of its development, any dramatic event affecting its roots might well upset the lives of countless millions of people. Hundreds of millions, you understand?"

Again, neither Peter nor Ruth bothers to even nod, although Ruth's features indicate a certain oncoming sadness.

"We, who have dedicated our lives to the welfare of the people, are sworn to do what we can to preserve and protect the interests of those countless, nameless millions. We serve with our lives, if necessary." The captain's chest expands a good inch in support of his claim. "With our lives. And any understanding, any respect we expect springs from our total commitment to the service of our people. No sacrifice is too great or too small to us who serve."

Now where have I heard that before, Peter wonders? He closes his eyes. He remembers. *A Master is a servant of his pupil. Those who demand respect seldom deserve it. Those who truly deserve it, never ask for it and reject it if thrust upon them.* Well, perhaps not quite the same sentiment after all.

"Do you know," Captain Sawicki's voice rises as he becomes inspired by his own rhetoric, "that the Solidarity International only commenced its activities some thirty years ago? We have the heritage of Lena's grandfather, of course, who virtually single-handedly mobilized his country, Poland, to stand united against the greatest oppressor the world has ever known. Yes, Sir! An enormous heritage. But that was many years ago. And that was a national movement. An inspiration. We have quite different plans..."

The good captain lets the different plans hang precariously in the air. He also fails to elucidate to Ruth and Peter who the mysterious 'we' are.

"Why have you brought us here?" Peter repeats very quietly, hardly above a whisper. The Captain seems taken aback. His face says: Haven't you been listening???

"But Sir, Madam, this is exactly what I am attempting to explain. In the shortest way I know how."

The captain's head is thrown back, open palms raised in resignation, a look of surprise painted on his diplomatic features. The captain does his best to look hurt, even offended.

Peter looks through the window. Way down a deep blue reflecting a lighter blue above. Straight up the blue is even deeper than that below. The weather looks perfect. Of course at

13,000 meters, it always is. But even way down, hardly a cloud casts its shadow over the ocean. At Mach 3, they must be well past the middle of the Atlantic. Past the point of no return. Is this why the Captain is taking so much of their time?

"If you allow me, Sir, the point I am bound to make is that under the circumstances, we have heritage but no tradition. And tradition, to an organization as powerful yet as new as ours, is of vital importance. It is a question of survival of the whole Movement. A matter of life and death." The Captain is back in his swing.

"Why have you brought us here?" Ruth echoes Peter's question.

"Because, Madam, we believe that Dr. Thornton is the only man alive who can save Solidarity International."

So it's out of the bag.

"And just how am I supposed to accomplish this feat?" Peter asks innocently.

"You see, Sir, our only link with the past, our only roots, if you will, the only hope of an inspiring tradition, is our Lena Walensa. Without her, we cannot hope to maintain the work we are doing, without serious setbacks. We need her as a drowning man..."

"What is wrong with Lena Walensa?" Unexpectedly Ruth interrupts the never-ending monologue. "Has she been hurt?"

"She is being kept incommunicado on a life-support system. She is in a condition referred to as coma." The Captain has made it to the end of his story.

"Idiot! If she is in a coma, she can hardly *not* be incommunicado," Peter mutters under his breath. No one seems to have heard him.

There is a short silence in which the near silent hum of the jets seems to grow until it fills the whole cabin. The airplane is descending at a good clip. They are braking speed for the forthcoming landing. Mach 3 is a lot faster than I thought, Peter muses. He hasn't flown much in his life. In fact, he belongs to that rare breed of eccentrics who, as adults, had never flown at all.

"But why was it necessary to fake the kidnapping of my children?" Ruth is flabbergasted. "Surely you know that my brother and I would have come if you had asked?"

"We deeply regret this subterfuge, Madam. But..."

"They couldn't take the risk, Ruth. They want a physician with my expertise, but essentially they are counting on my so-called healing powers. A sort of two-in-one trick." Peter explains. Then he turns to the Captain. "But why didn't you ask me directly?"

"For the reason you already explained, Sir. We had to make sure we would get you on board the airplane. We needed at least a chance to explain." The good captain looks down at his empty palms reposing on his lap. "And frankly, Sir, we couldn't find your whereabouts."

"I haven't been in hiding, you could have..." Peter does not finish.

"So we understand, Sir. But... we could not make any public announcements. As I have already explained, the confidentiality is absolutely essential." For the first time, the Captain actually looks a little embarrassed.

Only then Peter understands. How did all those hundreds—over the period of six weeks thousands—of people find him amid the large, sprawling periphery of a metropolis of over 6,000,000 people? He had wondered about it before but never really understood. Apparently only those could find him who needed something for themselves. It was a one-on-one contact. A sort of mano-a-mano. At least that was part of it.

"So you kidnapped two little children," Peter says in a dark tone.

"We took them for an ice cream and soda, Sir."

Captain looks eminently uncomfortable. Peter has a distinct impression that Captain Sawicki's discomfort is not induced by a willful act of kidnapping but rather by the almighty Solidarity International's failure to find the one man they wanted. A man who stayed out in the open for the whole world to see.

The good Captain rises to return to his cabin.

"Please fasten your seatbelts. We are coming in for landing in Rebiechowo. That's just outside Gdansk, Sir, Madam." The Captain salutes and moves quickly towards the flight cabin.

The last expression on the captain's face is that of relief. His job is nearly finished. He's done it as well as he could. For the Solidarity.

For the glory of the people.

* * *

23

Gdansk

To reduce the velocity of an airplane from Mach 3 to one suitable for a safe landing takes time. The passenger seats swivel to face away from the engine and adjust for the inclination of the approach. Just as well. Neither Peter nor Ruth feels like talking. There had been altogether too much talking on this trip. Too much had been said which should not have been said at all. The preconceived images had been disturbed, shaken. At least Ruth's images. She feels disappointed. Disturbed by Captain Sawicki's reasoning. She needs time to think, perhaps, to forgive.

At least the children are safe.

Compared to the storm raging in her heart, the mounting hum of the engines is strangely soothing. Monotonous and soothing. Ruth had had such great hopes, only yesterday. She had refused to work against Solidarity. Are not all innocent until proven guilty? And now? Now, the altars she has erected, especially those since she met Lena, are trembling—on the verge of collapse. Ruth refuses to let them fall for one reason only. Lena is in a coma. She alone could not have been responsible. But Ruth's thoughts are not easy.

Peter closes his eyes.

The droning of a thousand bees fills his ears, seems to detach his awareness from the immediate surroundings. He wonders what opinion Winston would form about all that has transpired during the last few hours. He wonders...

It is really quite immaterial what you do, what opinion you hold. In a world of duality, each idea must be balanced by its opposite. This is the Law. Irrefutable Law. To be free of this world you must hold no opinions—just feel the overpowering unity with all. This realization of Oneness is not an emotion but a state of consciousness. It is sometimes referred to as love. In a way it is. Because the awareness of Oneness must be as powerful as only unconditional love can become in moments of great realization. Oneness is timeless, static, eternal. And Love is the dynamic of Oneness...

More squadrons of bees join them, as the hum of the engines becomes deeper. They must be already cruising at a subsonic speed.

...even as phenomenal development is the dynamic of becoming. There are facets to human nature which rival the spiritual Consciousness. The function of breathing, the rhythm of our heart, the facility our cells possess to grow, mature and divide... We need to expend no conscious effort to partake in such functions. Within all that are dormant, such traits are relegated to their subconscious. For countless millennia we are little more than robots set to function in a pre-programmed fashion. We must all wait, and learn, even as a butterfly must bide its time, must wait patiently before leaving its protective cocoon. To everything there is a season. Ultimately, we can all reach beyond the stage of tacit automation. Eventually, we must benefit from all the autonomous traits by the use of direct perception. By the employment of our higher faculties, we can alter, take charge of our programming. But this step is an aspect of the evolution of our Consciousness alone.

A gust of wind rocks the jet. Peter opens his eyes, glances through the window and closes them again.

An ancient Greek promulgated two basic tenets: 'Know thyself' and 'Nothing in excess'. A modern Greek does neither. Ask yourself: are we evolving? Are you? You have interpreted everything you had learned as evidence that man is, or should be, physically immortal. While you accepted Cathy's concepts of entropy for other constructs of the phenomenal universe, such as radiation or the half-life of all the elements, you decided that the regeneration of cells, etc., all backed up your belief. Your concepts have been strengthened by your Catholic upbringing, which conditioned you to believe that you were created in the image of God. They forgot to stress that the reference had been intended to describe your soul or, to be more precise, the potential of your spiritual Consciousness. Not your physical body. You, however, have added the two concepts together and hey, presto, man is, must be, immortal!

"You mean I am not right? What about all my cures...?"

All your cures are temporary. You have extended the period during which the consciousness shall reside in a particular physical environment. But consciousness already is immortal, the body never will be.

"But I can reprogram the subconscious sufficiently to improve and extend the quality of life..."

Of course, but ask yourself why. You have the power to interfere with the Law. Make sure there is an excellent reason. The Law deals with justice. Some refer to it as karma. Be a just man. Make sure that you are acting from the Highest Consciousness.

"What gave me my powers?"

You started with a reasonably clean state. A late child, parents dying early, not many people had an opportunity to subdue your inquisitive spirit. Most of us start with an equally fair beginning, but soon we are conditioned, programmed, by the do-nots. The 'thou shalt nots'. From the day we are born, we are conditioned by the restrictions imposed by our parents, who wish to protect our physical bodies at the expense of our immortal consciousness. Later we are conditioned by our teachers, who wish to force our minds into their personal molds, irrespective of our uniqueness. Then we are hampered by the politicians, who wish to impose on us law and order. Their law and their order, ignoring the freedom of soul. Yet the purpose of all three is to maintain the status quo, until we have ripened, matured. Until we are ready. From the standpoint of higher consciousness, we, as humans, are taught how to give in, how to give up. We are taught now to die—slowly. How to die a protracted death. Not how to live forever.

As for how you 'cured' those people, you already know the answer.

The roar of the engines is now deafening. Finally, after a few hardly noticeable bumps, the engines roar in reverse, then slowly reduce the decibels to a tolerable volume. The landing is as smooth as was the flight. The seats rotate to their last chosen orientation.

Gdansk is a historical city in the very North of Poland, bordering on the Zatoka Gdanska, the shallow bay of the Baltic Sea. There had been a time when the terrain was contested by various national interests. Most lands in Europe were. Since Europe became united, first, theoretically, by the Treaty of Rome, then practically by the progressive dynamics of Solidarity International, for the first time in recorded history Europe is apt to have achieved lasting peace. How lasting is still to be discovered.

Solidarity had chosen this particular site for its Headquarters in order to draw strength from its history; even though the present city belongs to a new era. Towards the end of World War II, Gdansk had been razed to the ground both by the retreating German army and particularly by the advancing liberators, the Soviet Union.

But a longing for history had simmered here long before the Solidarity movement.

Long before even the progenitor of the present Solidarity had grown surreptitiously into power, the Poles had painstakingly rebuilt their city. Brick by cherished brick, stone by stone had been raised, often with bare hands, to retrieve the remnants of history which still remained of their ravished country.

A tough location to live in, Peter smiles a little sadly.

Even as the SI helicopter cuts the shortest route to their destination, Peter's eyes record the images of the tall, elegant houses, the slim façades of brick and stone of the Stare Miasto, the old city. It is quite remarkable. The images he sees remind him more of some ancient Dutch hamlet he had seen on some tourist posters than of a city which had only been reborn in the late forties of the last century. A true labour of love.

Or of need. Need of roots, of history.

The helicopter roars blindly over the steep roofs and deposits them directly at the SI Headquarters. An impressive, state-of-the-art complex, which rose hardly fifteen years ago on the Ostrow Island, an isle formed by the Martwa Vistula and the Kaszubski Canal. Literally, the whole island had been designed as a single building––even more so, as a single computer––capable of functioning as precisely and automatically as the body of a new-born babe.

The SI had chosen the location for their Headquarters carefully. The Ostrow Island is across the water from, and directly opposite, the Nadbrzeze Stoczniowe, the now-famous docks, the cradle of the original Solidarity movement.

"They are all hungry for the past," Ruth shouts over the deafening noise as they touch down on the roof heliport.

"Hungry to make the earth a permanent habitat for the human race," Peter mutters. He makes no attempt to be heard over the roar of the rotors.

Heretofore, Ruth and Peter were treated like high-ranking illegal immigrants. They had been whisked into a jet at Mirabel airport, kept virtually incommunicado during the flight, transferred to a helicopter (which looked more like an army machine than an airborne taxi) by four uniformed men, and whisked again to the rooftop upon which they are now standing.

Before either of them can so much as thank the pilot for such an ingratiating flight path, which allowed them to see the old Gdansk from the air for at least ten minutes, the hollering machine takes off again, and simultaneously the floor under their feet begins its descent at a rapid rate. Seconds later, more uniformed men offer them a perfunctory salute and lead them to a cart, which apparently travels on a single rail attached to the wall of a corridor. Two in front, Ruth and Peter, two in back. The men look armed.

"I don't believe we are illegal immigrants anymore. Now, I think, we are their prisoners," Peter comments dryly.

This is Peter's first time in Europe. He now wishes he had had time to travel. During a weak moment, just before landing in Rebiechowo—which Peter had been told was a restricted airport—(restricted by and for whom had not been made clear), Peter had actually hoped to use the opportunity to see as much of Gdansk, Poland, indeed Europe, as would prove possible. So far he has had a brief look at the moraine hills, reminiscent of southern Vermont, a glance at the steep roofs of the Stare Miasto, and the inside of a high-security corridor.

"They say that travel broadens the mind..." he mutters to Ruth.

"It's nice when it's free." Ruth gets into the mood of their circumstances.

But not for long. The moment they arrive at their first destination, a landing area where the corridor that brought them here splits into three branches, Ruth is politely offered a lunch. Ruth shrugs in resignation. Since the time is 12:30, she agrees. But when Peter steps forward to join her, a man about twice his size blocks his way.

"If you would kindly step this way, Dr. Thornton?"

The man's size discourages arguments. Peter waves to Ruth and steps... this way.

He is led towards one of the three corridors and assisted onto another monorail. Peter is now whizzing along with only two oversized guards. Presumably he is not regarded as dangerous when detached from the apron strings of his sister-in-law.

This time the ride is a lot shorter.

As the monorail reduces its speed to a crawl, Peter's guards, gently but firmly, assist him off the glorified conveyor belt. Two more stern-faced individuals, who evidently discarded their military uniforms in preference for white tunics, greet them. All the sentries, whatever their garb, have three things in common. They do not waste words, they are studiously if grimly polite, and they are consistently over two meters tall. Like products of genetic engineering. Perhaps they are—for the greater glory of Solidarity International. Whatever their genes, Peter feels dwarfed. His nose detects something familiar. The white-coated contingent of wardens contributes a new, though well-remembered distinguishing trait.

They smell of a sterilizing solution.

All five enter a room where the uniformed leviathans remain, while the two white whales escort Peter onward. The next room is impressive. The arched ceiling is high enough to dwarf even Peter's oversized escorts. Somehow, this fact alone makes him feel better. Here, all that enter must immediately feel like pygmies, forsaken, in a monstrous, subterranean cavern. At its centre, the chamber houses a table long and wide enough to seat a hundred men with elbowroom to spare. For some unknown reason, on this occasion, only about twenty men and women are gathered at the far end of the table. Perhaps twenty is deemed a sufficient number as Peter's reception committee. They are all wearing white coveralls; some are sporting stethoscopes flung loosely over their necks and shoulders, a sight with which Peter is well familiar. He, too, had once displayed this dangling badge of office.

He has evidently arrived in the main briefing room of a major medical centre.

As the white behemoths gently propel Peter towards the oversized table, a few men seated at the far end rise to their feet. Most others follow. A man at the very end, probably the head of the table, introduces himself without leaving his high-backed chair.

"My name is Doctor Werner. Doctor Gerhard Werner." Dr. Werner gives Peter a vague nod. "These are my colleagues..." Dr. Werner waves his hand carelessly to his left and right. His gesture serves to introduce his colleagues and dismiss them, all in one motion. "You may meet zem in due course. If you like," he adds, after a momentary pause.

It is apparent to Peter that Dr. Werner can think of no reason why anyone would want to meet his colleagues when they have his presence to look up to.

"Petrus Latter," Peter replies.

A few heads only now spin towards him. There is a look of surprise or consternation on the otherwise bland faces.

"Ah, yes, you will have your leettle joke, Dr. Thornton. Ha, ha! Ha, ha." Both ha-has are devoid of any mirth whatsoever.

"It is good of you to allow me," Peter counters.

At the back of his mind, Peter is trying hard to put his finger on something out of synch. Something which does not tally. Then he has it. From the moment he had landed, Peter had not met anyone who did not speak English without an accent. That in itself wasn't peculiar considering he was in a foreign country. Yet other than for slightly British overtones, their English had been perfect. Until now. Dr. Werner exhibits traces of something guttural. Perhaps Scandinavian or German.

Then Peter remembers.

At the last International Symposium on Stress Induced Mental Disorders, which he had attended in Montreal, Dr. G. Werner had presented a paper on the brain wave activities accompanying extreme comatose conditions. Dr. Gerhard Werner is the world authority on deep trances, particularly those induced by non-physiological stimuli. The doctor is a highly specialized psychiatrist leaning heavily on the technological advances in the electronic sciences. It was said that he had microchips inserted into his brain. (A medical joke, only slightly ahead of its time.) Dr. Werner had worked with computers more so than with patients. Five years ago Peter had found this approach inspiring. Since then, the famous man had put on some weight, but his dome-like forehead remained unmistakable. And at least he does not look much taller than Peter. Although a lot heavier.

"You have been briefed why you are here?" Dr. Werner asks.

"Yes. I have been abducted under false pretenses," Peter answers.

"Ah, so. Security precautions. Very commendable." The doctor is impressed.

Peter says nothing. The gathering of physicians who had risen at Peter's arrival lower themselves into their chairs. Peter remains standing.

"You tell me why I am here, Dr. Werner," he says quietly.

"Why, to help us, of course!" he looks surprised.

"To help who do what?" Peter decides to plead ignorance.

"I have been told that Captain..." Doctor Werner waves his hands in a gesture of no consequence, "that you have been told about our Leader's condition."

"Your... leader?"

"Madame Lena Walensa. The Nominal Leader of Solidarity International." The men and women half rise at the mention of Lena's name.

Oh, my God! Did we not go through all this Leader business a century ago, Peter wonders?

"I have been told that Lena Walensa is in a coma."

"Zat is right!" The doctor is showing signs of slight annoyance. "And you are here to help us!" He half rises in his chair himself.

"And you can kiss my..." *a Master is a servant of his pupil. Those who demand respect seldom deserve it.* "...credentials good-bye. I stopped practising medicine some time ago," Peter says with a straight face.

"We know. Please sit down, Dr. Thornton. We would all like to hear your views regarding our dilemma." The same wave of the hands accompanies the pronoun 'all'.

Peter has already made up his mind.

"If you want me to see Miss Lena Walensa, then I shall see her now."

"But, doctor..."

"Now." The second 'now' is almost a whisper.

The silence stretches. Dr. Werner opens his mouth a few times but says nothing. The other mouths never even get to the starting gate. Finally Dr. Werner rises again to his feet. Now that he straightens out, he is a tall man. Tall and obese. Intellectuals often are. The latter, at least. They spend too much time in front of their computers.

"Please come with me."

Dr. Gerhard Werner does not look at Peter but turns on his heel and walks to the door at the far end of the room. Peter follows him. There are two guards just behind the door who fall in behind them. The doctor and the men walk in step. Peter alternates his, just for fun. They walk for about two minutes. The corridor is dead straight without any particular features. Just doors with numbers and electronic locks. Peter has no idea where the light is coming from. There are no light fixtures that he can see. The dust on the surfaces must be phototropic. Or luminescent. Whatever.

I wonder what Lena looks like? Peter feels excited in spite of himself.

There are two more men guarding the far door at the end of the corridor. They open it for them when Doctor Werner is within ten steps. Dr. Werner must be a big wheel around here. The sentries salute as he passes.

"May I go in weez you?" The doctor asks. Suddenly his voice loses all the previous nonchalance. The doctor is humble. Almost servile. "Please?"

"I am sorry. I must go in alone," Peter says. He well understands Dr. Werner's anxiety. So would he have been, some months ago. Peter smiles his understanding but stands his ground.

"I see." The doctor's powerful chest heaves with a deep sigh. "It eez zee third door on zee right." Werner's accent thickens in direct ratio to the apparent depletion of his ego.

The room they entered has six doors leading to six cubicles. This is an intensive care unit with a difference. Here, the physicians can keep dead people physiologically alive for indefinite periods of time. At the far end of the room there are six nurses monitoring a series of computer screens. The life support system is set on automatic, but the sole patient in just one cubicle is something else altogether. Within her breast beats the heart of Solidarity International.

The door opens as Peter enters the cubicle. Before it closes, he hears Dr. Werner's uneasy voice behind him. "How long will it take you before you know, Dr. Thornton?"

Know what? Whether she will live or die?

"I don't know. As long as it takes. I don't want to be interrupted."

"Yes, doctor." There is total submission in Dr. Werner's tone.

It is not a question of time. Not the way the doctor understood it. Peter has no idea if he can restore Lena to her, according to Ruth, intelligent, vivacious state. The question is whether he, Peter Thornton, should try to restore her. A question that had not left Peter's mind from the moment he began to suspect what the whole game was about. From the moment the jet rose to 13,000 meters over the Atlantic.

Now, the moment of truth.

The woman on the raised bed looks as innocent as a child on her way to her First Communion. A face not ravaged by age or stress. A mass of golden hair is swept back from her high forehead. The girl, woman, is covered by a light blanket. The contours give an impression of a body maintained in good condition—compact and supple. This is no dictator lying in front of Peter. Neither is it a brave Joan of Arc. It is a girl who might well be twenty-five or thirty, yet whose natural beauty remained unaffected by a single dishonest act.

Raphael or Murillo looking for a model to pose as an angel would have to look no further.

What should I do?

People regard life as a linear path. It is not. Even as a planet revolves around its sun, and a sun around the centre of its galaxy, so a human consciousness moves through time around its soul. It cannot be otherwise. You start and finish in the same place. You return to whence you came.

I wonder if the innocence would still be there if she were to be awakened?

You enter your physical body to help you realize your potential. To come closer to the One being the Many. To arrive at the point where the individual and the infinite coexist in perfect balance, perfect harmony. Then you become your true Self, the two become One, the One is expressed in Its individualized Self Awareness.

If I awaken her, will she continue to provide the heart to an organization which would otherwise be guided by mind alone?

You are right, Peter. You are an immortal. But not exactly in the manner you originally imagined.

Is that you, Winston?

All is One and all emanates from Oneness. Nothing can be destroyed since Oneness is all-inclusive. Oneness emanates from within Itself, searching for Its Self Awareness. You are part of All, thus you are indestructible in all your attributes, as long as your consciousness is in harmony with the One. In a state of Balance.

Please tell me, Winston, should I awaken her?

A child must handle a child's problems. An adult those of an adult. Giants impose their will upon giants, and bear the consequences.

She is that which breathes heart into an automaton.

You have come of age, Peter. Welcome to the fold.

Winston, please help me.

Winston?

WINSTON!!!

Are you coming of age, Peter? I am a fool. I am a student. I have infinity before me! I know only how little I know. How can you cast me alone upon the waters?

The innocence of countenance is a mere reflection of the innocence in her eyes. She lies still without moving, staring into Peter's eyes. Whatever distant dream invaded her being, Lena's inner, chimerical consciousness is slow to desert her. She drinks life from Peter's eyes even as a child drinks life from her mother's gaze.

"Who are you?" Even her voice is that of a child. Trusting, undemanding. Just curious.

"I am Peter. I have come to awaken you."

"Have I been sleeping?"

"You were in a coma. In a very deep sleep."

"Why?" Children often ask this very question.

"To learn that which you will need in the future."

"In my dreams? But I remember nothing..."

"You will remember when you need to. There is the right time for everything. Do not worry."

"Should I worry about something?" And then she sits up. "How long have I been in a coma?"

In a single instant Lena's voice changes to that of an erudite adult. She becomes aware of her surroundings. She takes Peter's hand and looks at his watch. Her eyes stare in disbelief. She must have been looking at the digital date.

"I have been away for eleven days?" Her voice refuses to accept the evidence of her eyes.

"Perhaps—it does not matter. Does it?"

"There is so much to do." She attempts to rise but falls back against the pillows. Her arms are both strapped and connected to intravenous tubes. There are also wires attached to her chest, her head and the insteps of her feet. All her functions are being monitored on the computers.

There is a knock on the door. Peter smiles reassurance and places both his palms against Lena's cheeks.

"I hope you will forgive me for bringing you back," he whispers.

"What, I forgive you? I thank you. I thank you deeply." A sudden light seems to flash in Lena's eyes. "You are Ruth's brother."

"Brother-in-law."

"Have I been so dead?"

"You have been far away."

The silence that follows is again interrupted by another knock on the door. The computers have reported their findings. The nurses and the good Dr. Werner are well aware that Lena Walensa, their Fearless Leader, their Link-to-the-Past, the Personification of their Heritage—is alive. Alive and talking. Mustn't let anyone pollute her precious mind.

"Shall we let them come in?" Lena asks with a surreptitious smile.

Suddenly Peter realizes that it is not his request that is being honoured. Since Lena is awake, it is her privacy that is being respected. He nods his acquiescence.

"Come!" Lena's voice has none of the innocence of some moments ago. She commands her subordinates.

Dr. Gerhard Werner opens the door and puts his head in with apparent misgivings.

"Come in, Dr. Werner. Please have the goodness to have your staff remove these instruments of bondage." She points her head at the straps on her arms and legs.

Dr. Werner is followed by four nurses who get busy unstrapping and de-wiring the various portions of Lena's anatomy. Peter remains through all this to one side. Lena more or less ignores what is being done to her and continues to study Peter in silence. By the time the nurses finish, she nods her head as though arriving at some conclusion.

"I know that Ruth is a Catholic, as indeed am I. I assume that you may have also inherited some aspects of Catholic tradition. Would you agree to accompany me to Rome? A sort of pilgrimage of gratitude for my being restored to life."

So the European trip would not be a total write-off.

"Ruth is here with me," Peter says, smiling. He suspects that Lena has other business in Rome, perhaps delayed by her extended comatose condition.

"I have been deeply impressed with your sister. She will accompany us, of course." This young lady is used to making decisions. Then Lena looks up as though angry with herself for having forgotten something. "Forgive me, but there might be someone else you would like to have come with us? I believe Ruth has children?"

The children are a lot better off with Winston. Even if he left me high and dry, dangling on my own.

"I would enjoy the company of Dr. Catherine Mondellay." Peter says, without qualifying his answer.

Lena Walensa looks at Dr. Werner, who nods and leaves the room.

Lena sits up and swings her legs to one side over the edge of the bed. She is wearing only a short tunic. Peter smiles at the dim memory of his past. Lena Walensa is endowed with excellent legs.

A nurse pushes in a wheel chair, which Lena dismisses with a wave of her hand. Instead she takes hold of Peter's arm and proceeds to leave the room.

"If you give me five minutes, I shall slip into something a little less comfortable, Dr. Thornton." Her smile is quite coquettish. It would be more so if it weren't for the sharp intelligence in her eyes. Somehow the two seem at odds with each other. That is what had been wrong with Cathy when he first met her.

Lena Walensa is true to her word. In five minutes she steps out from behind the door of the nurses' quarters wearing a very simple black dress which seems to be clinging, though not excessively, to her near perfect figure. For what once had been Peter's taste in women, the Fearless Leader is a little too well endowed in the upper pectoral region, her hips carry a little too much of Slavic heritage. Lena is a delightful personification of Mother Earth. The youthful version.

"And now let us go to the chapel," she announces unexpectedly.

Ruth has already been notified. They all arrive at the doors to the chapel simultaneously. The women embrace like old friends. Ruth is relaxed. She had already spoken to Winston and to each of her children in turn. The children sounded not only healthy but none the worse for wear. It is apparent that the ice-cream and soda left no permanent scars.

Just before they enter the chapel, Peter takes Ruth to one side.

"You have been right again, sister. Lena did not know anything about the actions of her cohorts," he says.

"I've known it all along." Ruth smiles confidently. "But what, dear brother, convinced you?"

"Oh, I just know such things," Peter says. grinning mischievously.

There is absolutely no reason why he should tell Ruth that Lena Walensa has been out, stone cold, kaput, for over eleven days.

Is there?

* * *

24

Rome

The same jet, or an executive plane exactly like the one in which Ruth and Peter had been abducted, is airborne again. This time, the seats are arranged into an elongated oval. Four men and six women (in addition to Ruth and Peter) sit facing each other. Lena presides at the head of the table which, once everyone was seated, had lowered itself from the ceiling.

"A useful gadget for a busy executive, but when does she take a rest?" Peter murmurs over the steady, almost delicate purr of the engines—as though the powerful jets were idling at hardly a fraction of their power.

But there are other surprises in store.

Without warning, a series of flaps open in the smooth surface and a meal setting appears miraculously in front of everyone sitting at the table. The meal is simple and tasty. Efficient. Next, Lena proceeds to receive reports from her ten lieutenants. She listens with hardly a question or comment. Simultaneously, the fingers of her right hand move smoothly over a built-in keyboard. Peter is impressed. Since Lena does not take her eyes off any particular interlocutor, her dancing fingers appear to have a life of their own.

"The woman is a marvel, isn't she?" Peter whispers into Ruth's ear, nudging her with his elbow.

Frankly, Peter is fascinated. Ruth, on the other hand, smiles as though she herself were responsible for Lena Walensa's abilities. Lena does leave an indelible impression on the people she meets. At no time did Ruth hold Lena responsible for her subordinates' behaviour. It is evident that the means the SI had employed to get her and Peter to Gdansk were in direct contradiction to everything Lena appears to hold dear.

Peter reserves his judgment, but he continues to admire Lena's unfolding attributes. He is in awe at the economy of her words, actions or even facial expressions. At 34, Lena Walensa is a consummate leader. She is in total command of the proceedings. Ruth and Peter are allowed to sit in as a matter of course. There are no confidential matters requiring secrecy or security.

Lena Walensa believes in absolute freedom of the press. She said so.

She is also extremely resilient. She shows no signs of any aftereffects ensuing from her last eleven days. Only later does Ruth tell Peter that, apparently, Lena's vital signs had shown a dramatic drop on the morning the children were abducted. Early that morning, about the time Peter had felt the sudden need to return home. It became evident that Pennington's decision was an act of unpremeditated despair. Within hours of her revival, Lena had learned about the measures her subordinates had employed to save her life. She refused to condone their behaviour. Mr. Pennington had been fired as the head of Solidarity International for Canada. Lena would not have people in charge sink below the Charter of Individual Rights, which she herself helped to define. It was only at Ruth's intercession that Mr. Pennington was allowed to remain a member of Solidarity. His implant was not removed, but his 4x rating was reduced to the bottom rung.

Ruth was so happy, so relieved, she felt a need to be generous.

And now they are on their way to Rome!

This trip is a very different experience. Not only on her nerves, but the flight itself. Lena refuses to fly at supersonic speeds when travelling within the European territory.

"The population is too dense, and I have no desire to break their favourite china with my sonic booms," she told Ruth.

Peter wishes the Canadian Air Force showed the same consideration.

"And frankly, the ETA is of little consequence. I can contact almost anyone, world-wide, right from here. So why rush?" she says as they relax after the conference.

The table is up. Lena, Ruth, Peter and Mr. Frank Norman, a charming elderly gentleman whom Lena had introduced as her mentor (which title he immediately relegated to that of a private secretary) are at the front of the cabin, their chairs swivelled to form an intimate 'square circle'. There is, however, little time for pleasantries. Within ten minutes they would be landing in the City of the Seven Hills.

It is hard to believe that only yesterday the extremely feminine leader of the world's most powerful organization seemed destined to take a one-way trip into oblivion. Peter makes a comment to this effect.

"Or to heaven, as we Catholics prefer to call it!" Lena quips as she again thanks Peter for his part in restoring her to full consciousness.

"Think nothing of it, Lena. I'm sure you'd do no less for me."

Peter remains in awe of Lena's versatility. A moment ago she was a hard-driving chairman, and now, seconds later, she is the most charming, time-is-of-no-consequence hostess.

"I wonder if one ought to...?" For the first time since they met, Lena's voice is hesitant.

"...take liberties with the natural life span of a human being." Peter completes the sentence for her.

"I do not mean to be ungrateful, but yes. The thought had crossed my mind." Then Lena Walensa looks directly into Peter's eyes. "But I am sure you have dwelled on the question a lot longer than I have, Peter."

Peter does not comment at once. There is a pensive tension while the implied question hangs in the air. Peter remembers well the last moments in the ICU. The innocence of her face. He also remembers being left alone. Deserted.

"Believe me, my dear Lena, if it hadn't been meant for you to survive, you would not be here right now. No matter what some vain prognosticators or long-bearded gurus might tell you."

Lena seems satisfied with Peter's answer. She leans forward in her chair and puts her carefully manicured hand on Peter's arm. Her lips smile, though her eyes remain very serious.

"I want you to know, Peter, that I shall do my utmost to do justice to your decision," she says so quietly that only Peter can hear her whispered commitment.

"Thank you, Lena. No one can ever promise more than that."

"If only time could be slowed down..." Lena murmurs, almost as though she suddenly found herself quite alone, "There is still so very much to do. So much..."

As if to confirm the scarcity of time, a buzzer announces that the jet is coming in for a landing. Peter even forgot to peek through the window. A pity. He shrugs. Perhaps this is not meant to be a sightseeing trip, he muses? At least, not for me. Then he smiles. He knows very well why he is here. It had been obvious to him from the moment he brought Lena out of the coma.

A limousine with SI insignia takes the foursome to the SI hotel. There, an elevator with the SI monogram sandblasted on its glass walls, lifts them in respectful silence to the suite reserved for the SI VIPs.

"I'll wager that you and I are the only non-members of the Solidarity who ever put their foot inside this building, let alone this suite," Peter comments when, for the first time in three days, they find themselves alone.

Ruth and Peter are given a three-room apartment with a western exposure. If the view is not intentional, then, particularly in Peter's eyes, it is prophetic. The hotel soars twenty stories over the east bank of the Tiber, at the corner of Via di Monte Brianzo and just off Lungo Tevere Manzo. There is one aspect that makes this location unique in all of Rome—thus, unique in the world. It is the only site which, looking West, points directly over the Piazza Pia and along the full length of the Via della Conciliazione.

"The Road to Reconciliation," Peter whispers as they both admire the view.

Via della Conciliazione leads directly and irrevocably to the Piazza San Pietro and thus to the Basilica itself. The hub of the Citta del Vaticano.

The heart of the Vatican.

"Do you realize, Peter, that, over the last two thousand years, countless millions of people have walked the Via della Conciliazione in the hope of finding a spot on St. Peter's Square close enough to the Basilica to see the Pope?" Ruth's voice is filled with emotion.

Il Papa. The successor of Saint Peter himself.

The successor of the Master.

Peter smiles a little sadly. Not all is what it seems, he muses. It had only been through the insatiable greed and personal ambition that S. Pietro is where and what it is. Ambitious for the Catholic Church, but even more ambitious for himself, Pope Julius II had razed to the ground one of the most ancient and most venerated places of worship in the Western hemisphere. He ordered the destruction of the church, which marked the place where St. Peter had been martyred. Pope Julius II brought together the genius of Bramante, Michelangelo and Raphael. He cajoled, coaxed and bullied them to produce the greatest theatrical extravaganza the world had known up to that time. The Basilica was not completed until a hundred years after Pope Julius II died, but the ties with history had been torn there and then, in the early 1500s. The ties with ancient thought, with the prose of Cicero—the link with the civilization of early Greece and Rome—had been severed forever.

The new Humanism in the Catholic Church never looked back.

There had been feeble attempts to remind Rome, or rather the Vatican, of its roots. The last such, in the middle of the 19th century, Pope Pius IX issued a Syllabus of Errors, in which he denounced, *inter alia*, materialism, free thought and nationalism. But it was too little, too late. People no longer believed him. Five years later, to add weight to the Word of God, and certainly to the *dicta* of the Church, to gain power, Pope Pius convened the Vatican Council, later known as Vatican I. In it he declared the dogma of Papal *ex cathedra* Infallibility. But the Papal pronouncement was not taken seriously. Spain, France, even Italy denounced it.

The Church had lost another battle.

A hundred years later, John XXIII, tried hard to reverse the course of history. He opened wide his loving peasant arms... He tried to reconcile the irreconcilable. He did his best to advocate compassion and *discussion* instead of harshness and the imposition of power. He died before Vatican II was over. His successor preferred... a more conservative approach.

It was too late by then. Much, much too late.

"Yes, dear. Perhaps people were looking for reconciliation. I wonder what they found," Peter says after a while. "I wonder if they found what they came looking for."

The people were not ready. Their consciousness would have remained dormant, had the Popes succeeded in reversing the tide of history. Not yet.

"Lena told me that our audience is scheduled for 11:30. It is only for ten minutes. The Pope is very weak, she tells me."

The Pope is very weak indeed. The College of Cardinals had met over two weeks ago in expectation that the Pope might not last another night. They were ready to do their duty. The king is dead, they were ready to declare. God save the king!

But surely, my kingdom is not of this world?

It is late. Ruth decides to order a snack from room service, and retire early. The worry over the children, the two flights only a day apart, jet lag, the overall nervous tension during the last few days have left her on the brink of collapse. Peter refrains from helping her unless she asks. She doesn't. Ruth has ambitions of being independent.

An hour later Peter is left alone. He sits back in a chair, in the salon, facing the window. He looks at the eternal city, at the volumes of history at his feet. So much history. So much human strife and endeavour. So much pain, anguish...

Have I been right? He asks himself for the tenth time. Have I done the right thing? His sigh empties his lungs. I give up, he whispers. I give in. I submit to Your will...

That's what I have been waiting for.

Peter closes his eyes. "Who are you?"

I am you.

"Where are you?"

I am within you. And without you. I am also everywhere and nowhere.

Peter remains silent.

I am a state of Consciousness. Your soul. Your salvation. Your immortality. Your Lord. Your Master. I am also your friend, your mate, your benefactor. I am that which you are, which you always wanted to be. I am Alpha and Omega, the beginning and the end—yet I have no beginning and I have no end.

"And who am I?"

You are nothing, an illusion. You are a journey, a vehicle, a way, Tao. You are a means of self-realization. You are that which enables me to be that which I am. You and I are one.

"I do not understand."

I know. Nor can you, ever. Trust me.

I am to trust that which is everywhere and nowhere, which says that I am nothing.

"Do you increase the vibrations of the atoms in my body to the velocity of light?"

Not exactly. I quicken your spirit. You can think of it as increasing the vibrations of your field of consciousness. Your atoms will follow, so to speak. You see, whatever happens to your consciousness, the rest of reality must follow. This is the Law. It cannot be otherwise. Can you imagine anything within the physical universe which has not been initiated in a state of consciousness? Be it in full awareness or at an unconscious level? I am a state of consciousness. My body is light. My consciousness is my life, my existence. My assurance of immortality.

"Cathy said: 'That which exists not for itself is immortal.' She said this is Tao."

This is why you and I are one. I cannot take over until you give in.

"Was it I who cured all those people?"

Yes and no. You reprogrammed their subconscious, then they cured themselves.

"Explain?"

I am your consciousness. I am he who pushes the keys on the keyboard of your computer. But there is little I can do if the computer is filled to the brim with both memory and software which is set as irrevocable.

"But..."

Let me explain. I, your consciousness, cannot experience anything in the phenomenal reality without an instrument through which such an experience is made possible. It is rather like a photon. The vibrations in the gross, physical universe are very slow. A photon cannot exist in such a reality. It cannot travel slowly, let alone be at rest.

You have convinced yourself, which means that you have programmed your subconscious, that the physical body is immortal. Well, no reality can deny the rules of a particular plane of perception, but as long as the basic rules are not broken, those same rules permit a great deal of latitude.

Therefore, when you laid your hands on the people requesting your assistance, your physical soul—i.e.: your magnetic field—affected the patients' magnetic field sufficiently to, at least temporarily, reprogram their own subconscious. Once done, it is their own subconscious which does the rest. Remember the ancient saying: 'Thy faith has made thee whole'? This is exactly what happens. You have altered their subconscious belief. It is not easy to do. It took you over ten years of medical studies before your own subconscious, the belief within your own heart, had changed sufficiently to begin manifesting in the physical reality.

"I already knew that."

Then why did you ask? I know. You needed to hear it again. You still lack confidence. It will come. Trust me.

"And now?"

Now you've given up—within your heart. This act of submission, this 'let it be thy will' but spoken with equal conviction to that which it took to give you healing powers, this submission-resignation-humility, empowers me to enter your consciousness. Your body, as all human, animal and plant bodies, is no more than a temporary construct of clay for my experiments. I, too, have to learn. For eternity. Even as the Source of Spirit is infinite, so I who embody a fragment of the Infinite Consciousness shall learn for infinity.

"But why must you embody in the phenomenal reality at all?"

Expediency. Cathy once told you that at the velocity of light time stops. I am here to learn. In the phenomenal reality I learn faster. I see the effects of my experiments faster. I faster become more useful to the Whole.

"Not to mention the advantages of duality," Peter contributes all by himself.

There is a silence filled with a gentle humming. Serene musical frequencies which, although sensed, cannot be defined as being heard. It is a melody of peace abiding outside space and time.

"Yet, don't you live in an eternal now?"

Don't you?

"I think, I am beginning to. I no longer desire anything in particular..."

...to desire nothing for yourself is the beginning of immortality.

"The particular versus the universal?"

The two in one. A concordance. There is no paradox. Looking at me through physical eyes, I am eternal, omnipresent, all powerful. I am whatever anyone wants me to be. Looking through my own eyes, so to speak, I am no more than a spark of consciousness floating in an endless Ocean of Love. Remember what you discussed with Cathy about the inside and outside observer?

"You really know about Cathy?"

From your point of view I am all knowing.

"Are you?"

Yes. From your point of view. I know all that a human mind can know, and more. But in my own environment, I know next to nothing. Though I am eternal, this instant marks the first fragment of the eternity ever receding in front of me. Perhaps it is wiser to say that I am not so much eternal as that I am infinite. Direct perception, remember?

"Peter!"

"Yes, dear, what is it?" Too late. The telephone has stopped ringing. Almost immediately it rings again. "Sorry..."

"It's for you. I am going back to sleep." Ruth's voice is very sleepy.

"Good night, Ruth, and I am sorry." Where is the stupid telephone?   "Hello?"

"Peter, it is I."

"Cathy, where are you!?"

"Downstairs. They will not let me come up without your permission. You're some kind of VIP around here!"

Peter speaks to the men at the desk, and two minutes later Cathy walks through the suite's door. The door hardly closes when Peter crushes her in his arms. They stay that way for a long while, both hungry for the touch of each other's body. Or perhaps it is a merging of their respective auras, though Peter doesn't think so. It is Cathy's pliant body he loves as much as any part of her being. Peter breaks away first.

"It's nice to be human," he says to himself.

I know.

Peter ignores that.

They talk for an hour, then retire to Peter's bedroom. Then follows a night Peter has not tasted of for quite some time. No wonder people get reincarnated again and again. Being human is very nice indeed.

All three join Lena at breakfast at 8:00 a.m. Lena has already given two briefings. The woman is incredible. So seem to be most people around her. If anyone can put a stop to the conditions that precipitate most of the negative traits in the human character, she can.

Only... it cannot be done, Peter sighs. Not in a world of duality.

Ruth wonders about the children. Peter momentarily closes his eyes.

"They are playing billiards with Winston."

"Billiards?"

"Yes, he is explaining to them the Newtonian physics."

"You are joking, of course!"

"Of course," Peter says with a straight face. He is quite a good liar. But strangely enough, Ruth is no longer worried about her children. She doesn't even insist on telephoning them.

At 9:00 a.m. Peter takes Ruth and Cathy for a whirlwind tour of Rome. They intend to stay a few days as guests of the SI, but Cathy and Ruth cannot resist the call of the Eternal City. The call of the Seven Hills. However, two hills later it is time to direct their steps towards the Vatican.

The Pope is half sitting, half reclining on an ancient settee. He looks a little how Peter had looked when Winston picked him up at the tavern in St-Henri. Only the Pope's eyes smoulder with a dark, stubborn fire. Lena is the first to be directed to the Pontiff's side. She genuflects and kisses the Papal ring. The Pope leans forward and holds both her hands for a moment or two.

"May God bless you in all your endeavours, my child," the Pontiff says softly. His voice is an echo of his emaciated body.

"Thank you, Your Holiness," Lena says and rises to her feet. She has had audiences before. "I came to the Vatican to thank God for restoring me to health."

"God is everywhere, my child, but I am sure Our Lord appreciates your effort and good intentions. And We thank you for all you have done for His Church." The Pontiff makes a large cross with his right hand in the air.

The Solidarity has been very generous in maintaining some heretofore-crumbling churches in a good state of repair.

The crimson Cardinal at the Pope's side raises his hand. It is a sign that Lena's audience is over. The Pope is in no hurry, but his body refuses to stay awake for longer than a few hours at a time. And there are so many people. So many souls...

Ruth approaches and follows Lena's example. She, too, receives a Papal blessing. She looks happy but on the verge of tears. Not specifically because of the blessing just bestowed upon her, but at the sight of the old man at the very edge of his life, still working, still giving. This sight is more than she can tolerate with inbred detachment.

Next comes Cathy. She is not a Catholic, but it does not seem to matter. She, too, might benefit from the sage's blessing.

Finally, it is Peter's turn.

He, too, genuflects. As he touches the Pope's hand to kiss the ring, the Pope stops him. He tries to pull Peter closer to his face. Peter complies. Their eyes meet.

"Leave us alone, please." The Pope's voice is little more than a whisper. The Pontiff continues to hold Peter's head in his long, bony fingers.

Lena and Ruth bow and move towards the door. The Pontiff raises one arm and waves at the Cardinal.

"You, too, my friend. I am sorry." There is real regret in his voice.

"*Santissimo Papa...*" the Cardinal starts, but the Pontiff again waves his thin hand.

"*Vai, vai.*" He dismisses his adviser in Italian.

The Pope and Peter are alone.

This is not the usual hall in which audiences are held. It is smaller, more intimate, but still abounding in the splendour of the ages. Great masters adorn the walls; even the ceiling is a work of art unequalled by other buildings of the world.

The Pontiff leans back and breathes deeply, yet his chest hardly moves.

"Can I help you, Holy Father?" Peter asks.

"I don't need help, my son. But all this..." For the third time the old man waves his hand, but this time at the space around him. "This needs your help."

Peter asks the Pontiff again.

"Will you not let me help you?"

"To restore my life to me? This is not help. I have lived for ninety-four years. I deserve to die. I've earned it. Only..." Apparently, with an enormous effort, this shadow of a man clad in white vestments of innocence raises himself to a sitting position. His human shell is almost empty, but the eyes are still burning with a strange determination. "I dreamt of you last night. I am not sure if it was a dream, a blessing, or a nightmare. I am too old to think very well. But I trust in my Saviour. Do what you must do, my boy." The Pope speaks slowly, haltingly, towards the end, taking quick breaths between the words.

Peter studies the tired, worn features of this tired, worn man. He did all he could. We each have our function to fulfill.

Peter gets up and stands very still. The old man leans back again and closes his eyes. Gradually a great peace relaxes the features of his dried-out face. He seems at peace with the world. At peace with the whole universe. Peter sits on the edge of the settee and bends over the limp body. He remains in this position for a short time.

"I am the Light and the Resurrection. He who believeth in me shall never die." Peter whispers into the Pontiff's ear. But it's too late. The Pontiff has already joined the ranks of the immortals.

Now let me take over. You've done all you can.

Peter doesn't move, but he is a little afraid. The instinct of self-preservation is a powerful one.

Trust me. There are few limits for me on earth if we are in agreement.

But in both of us? Both bodies?

I am omnipresent. By earth standards—omnipotent. Why should it be any more difficult for me to manifest my consciousness in two bodies instead of one?

Let your will be done.

Thank you. Henceforth it is our will.

There is a knock on the great portals. Peter stands up and moves to open them. The Cardinal's face looks worried. He comes in and quickly walks to the Pontiff's side. The Pope appears to be sleeping. His breathing seems deeper and more regular. As the Cardinal approaches, the old man opens his eyes, winks at Peter and pulls himself to his feet.

"I think it is time for lunch, don't you agree, Giuseppe?" The Holy Father reaches out for the Cardinal's hand. His grip is unexpectedly firm.

Ruth and Cathy stand in the open doorway, eyes wide open with curiosity. Like children, Peter muses.

"Go in peace, my children. I shall always be with you." The Pontiff sends them all away with another blessing.

Peter grins, nodding and shaking his head from side to side. "It's all right for you to talk," he mutters under his breath, "you're omnipresent."

"You're right, darling," Cathy agrees as they walk away among the countless marvels of the Vatican's treasures. "Your book has made thousands. I do owe you a present."

L ena leaves Rome the next morning. Ruth and Cathy and Peter stay on for another three days, then return to Canada on the SI jet. The return trip is more noisy. They all have thousands of impressions to share from the ancient city. The City of the Seven Hills.

Two weeks following their return to Westmount, a late news program is scheduled to report on what became known as The Vatican III Consensus. Ruth calls them to the TV the moment the screen displays views of Rome.

A moment later, Ruth looks flabbergasted.

Briefly, the report states that the Pope (who seemed to have found a miraculous new lease on life) has declared, *ex cathedra*, that all the worldly domains of the Church are to be disposed off. The Pope also said, also *ex cathedra*, that all the clergy will henceforth earn their living without resorting to alms; that there are to be no more charitable donations received by or collected under the auspices of the Church; that the Vatican III Council will be the last Council ever to be held; that those who wish to preach, to act as the servants of God, of the Lord Jesus Christ, will emulate the Master or be freed of their clerical bonds; that...

The list is long, and apparently all of it was delivered *ex cathedra*. Pope John XXIII's intuition, at the Vatican II, had not been in vain after all. Just a little early.

"But what of tradition...? My goodness, who will tell us what to do now?" Ruth seems to be in shock.

S he is better now. She is about to begin the long search. Within her. Yet, just when she thinks that things would get back to normal, a gentle knock on her door announces Winston. He is in a habit of knocking even when the doors are wide open.

The tall man bows, walks up to Ruth and, without a word, gravely hands her a sealed envelope.

"I shall no longer be needed, Madam," he declares stiffly, bows again, and without another word withdraws through the hall doorway. A moment later, the front door closes softly behind him. Ruth sees his gaunt shadow passing the window. For some reason it makes her nervous.

With tense fingers she opens the envelope. It is a neatly typed letter of resignation. There are also expressions of gratitude, best wishes and the letter ends with the customary:

Your obedient servant,
Winston Smith

"How quaint," she whispers to herself, "how very British..." Then her eyes fall on the date of the letter. It is the day on which Peter met the Pope.

She is holding back her tears. What shall I do with my little darlings? How shall I cope? Why did he have to leave now?

At this very moment, Jonathan and Moira run into the room. "Walk, don't run..." she's about to say, but reaches out for them and hugs them instead. "My little darlings..." she murmurs, and this time cannot hold back her tears.

Two weeks later Jonathan tells her that he and Moira meet with Winston regularly.

"He was teaching us how to make do without him for about two months, mother. And he still teaches us..."

"He's gone, darling, He's gone..."

"But we see him, mother, we really do!"

And that is all she can get out of them. They would not ex-plain any further. Yet, unbeknownst to all three of them, these enigmatic trysts would go on for years to come. But at the time Ruth noticed only one thing. Jonathan had called her mother, not mom, as he did usually.

Three months after the Vatican III Council, Solidarity International begins to make plans to move their Headquarters to Rome. In fact, to the Vatican. A Godsend opportunity. The Solidarity is the only organization, worldwide, with sufficient resources to 'buy' and maintain the enormous human heritage left behind by the Church. And what will the Church do with all that money? Well, it does not really matter. Solidarity does not actually use money, as such, to buy the treasures.

It just offered to maintain them.

And what of the other Holy Sees, the Bishoprics? A number of them had broken away from Rome. The new, spiritualized Rome. The unparalleled, uncompromising break with the money, with acquired rights, with the attendant prestige, with simple creature comforts... had been too sudden. After all, they said, spreading their arms clad in generous, flowing robes, the Church has the duty to maintain tradition... Even if most advocates of this sentiment could not quite specify—the tradition of what?

There had also sprung up a few brand-new popes. The position appeared vacant, even though the Pontiff was reported seen in many different places, sometimes at the same time. It was a bit confusing to start with, but people tend to accept most realities if the realities are repeated a sufficient number of times.

"As you know, Cathy, it is all a question of balance. Superb materialism balanced by the return to a spiritual awareness. Yet none of this could have happened without the Solidarity International."

"And the Solidarity would not have survived without a certain Peter I know."

"Oh, it would have. Only it would have taken a little longer. There is never really any hurry, you know."

Ruth has a different perspective on the events.

"You know, Peter," she once said, "it is as though the Master had returned, but not as one man, not as a mighty king ready to rule the world..."

"...you're right. Solidarity already does that," Peter put in.

"Yes. What I mean... it's as though the Master had entered the hearts of a thousand people, some who had been, and in a way still are, I suppose, priests of the Roman Church, and others, strangely enough, who never seem to have had any religious training. And would you believe, many of those are women!"

Indeed they were.

Ruth was referring to the shy, insignificant individuals who had appeared from nowhere in some out-of-town motels, around whom little gatherings had formed, here and there. Those timid men shun publicity. They seem to linger for a little while, then they go on their way.

And very strange beings, these men appear to be. Strangely, to date, there are no women among them.

They seldom affect any cures or miracles, although all seem to possess powers previously quite unheard of. They use them seldom, as though at great discretion. It is as though the spirit which for two millennia had been spread so very, very thin now gelled, concentrated in those few who were ready and willing to accept it. There are some strange stories milling around the world. And yes, some still claim that they have seen the Pope. In the most unheard-of places. They say the Pontiff looks old and emaciated and, paradoxically, full of life and vigour. People like hearing such stories. The stories give them hope. Some swear that they are true. Who can tell? We all create our own realities.

Don't we?

The world has not changed at all. Yet, it is a very different world.

In this world, Lena Walensa sits on the throne of the Vatican. Actually, she seldom sits anywhere. She's too busy. She works around the clock to better the human condition. The physical condition. But she fills the throne well.

She is much prettier than most if not all the Popes who have ever graced it. And she does more for the good of her people than any emperor or empress in history. She will continue to do so for as long as Peter will keep balanced her phenomenal universe with Soul. Lena and Peter have become good friends.

So much so that, sometimes, Cathy seems a little jealous. But only a little.

Both Lena and Peter have achieved great results. The Empress and One Just Man.

"Only Empires fall, as do Empresses," Peter still muses with just a hint of sadness. "Whereas I? I, until proven otherwise.... Until proven otherwise, I still feel that I am immortal."

Perhaps he is.

* * * * *

The Story continues in

ELOHIM
Masters and Minions

Acknowledgments

My thanks to Madeleine Witthoeft for her diligent editing, and to my many friends for their careful proofreading. The Second Edition benefited additionally from the meticulous scrutiny and literary expertise of Kate Jones. My thanks to all of them.

As always my gratitude to my wife, Bozena Happach, who put up with being a grass widow for weeks on end, and then offered me her inspired insights.

Sincerely,

Stan J.S. Law

ELOHIM – Masters and Minions
sequel to
ONE JUST MAN
coming soon.
To preorder contact info@inhousepress.ca

INHOUSEPRESS, MONTREAL, CANADA
http://inhousepress.ca
email: info@inhousepress.ca

107718